IT'S

Dreamy-eyed Washington, D.C. bachelor Taylor Worth is down on American women. He has experienced everything they have to offer—and been left wanting . . . wanting the thrill of the chase, the trip to the moon on gossamer wings, and the love.

Leave it to his friend Ned to come up with the solution—the ultimate fantasy bet. All Taylor has to do to win Ned's prized Mercedes is seduce Erin and Eleanor and Veronica, propose marriage, and tape-record their acceptance.

Taylor is sure it's a sure thing . . . until all three women learn of his wager and highroll him—in one of the wildest, wackiest, sexiest three-card-monte games of love and consequences ever to end up right on the money. . . .

WORTH WINNING

(0451)

LIGHTS! CAMERA! SIGNET!

☐ **COOKIE by Todd Strasser.** Based on the hit movie! Cookie was a punk princess with a Godfather for a dad, and everyone wanted her. Even the bad guys, who wanted her to help set up her dad for a fall. But this time the bad guys were in trouble, because this was one tough Cookie. Join her on her thrilling, but wacky, adventures through Greenwich Village. (159918—$3.95)

☐ **MISSISSIPPI BURNING by Kirk Mitchell.** Based on the compelling movie of the most savage civil rights showdown of the sixties. Three young civil rights workers—two whites and a black—were missing. The F.B.I. wanted justice, but it wasn't going to be easy for the law to beat the odds in a seething southern town where old ways died hard and hate killed savagely.... (160495—$3.95)

☐ **AMADEUS by Peter Shaffer.** The exclusive movie edition of the great long-running broadway play—with a new introduction by the author, and 8 pages of photos from the magnificent motion picture directed by Milos Forman. "Triumphant... we leave the theatre possessed."—*The New York Times* (158946—$3.95)

☐ **ON GOLDEN POND by Ernest Thompson.** Here is the delightful, heartwarming film that starred Katharine Hepburn, Henry Fonda, and Jane Fonda—together for the first time! With 16 pages of unforgettable film scenes, and a special introduction by Richard L. Coe describing the filming of *On Golden Pond*. (161602—$3.95)*

☐ **THE GRADUATE by Charles Webb.** The zany misadventures of a well-heeled young man who gets a thorough postgraduate education from a worldly woman... "Makes you want to laugh... makes you want to cry."—*Cleveland Plain Dealer* (155262—$3.95)

☐ **THE GODFATHER by Mario Puzo.** The all-time bestselling novel in publishing history, this is the sweeping saga of a family and of its leader, a benevolent despot who stops at nothing to gain and hold power. He is a friendly man, a "reasonable" man, a just man—and the deadliest gang leader in the Cosa Nostra. (157362—$4.95)*

*Prices slightly higher in Canada

Buy them at your local bookstore or use this convenient coupon for ordering.

NEW AMERICAN LIBRARY
P.O. Box 999, Bergenfield, New Jersey 07621

Please send me the books I have checked above. I am enclosing $_____
(please add $1.00 to this order to cover postage and handling). Send check or money order—no cash or C.O.D.'s. Prices and numbers are subject to change without notice.

Name_____
Address_____
City _____ State _____ Zip Code _____

Allow 4-6 weeks for delivery.
This offer is subject to withdrawal without notice.

WORTH WINNING

DAN LEWANDOWSKI

AN ONYX BOOK
NEW AMERICAN LIBRARY

NAL BOOKS ARE AVAILABLE AT QUANTITY DISCOUNTS WHEN USED TO PROMOTE PRODUCTS OR SERVICES. FOR INFORMATION PLEASE WRITE TO PREMIUM MARKETING DIVISION, NEW AMERICAN LIBRARY, 1633 BROADWAY, NEW YORK, NEW YORK 10019.

PUBLISHER'S NOTE

This book is a work of fiction. Names, characters, places, and incidents either are the product of the author's imagination or are used fictitiously, and any resemblance to actual persons, living or dead, events, or locales is entirely coincidental.

Copyright © 1985 by Dan Lewandowski

Grateful acknowledgment is given for permission to reprint lyrics from the following songs:

FOR EVERYMAN by Jackson Browne © 1973 WB Music Corp. ALL RIGHTS RESERVED USED BY PERMISSION

SISTER GOLDEN HAIR by Gerry Beckley © 1975 WB Music Corp. ALL RIGHTS RESERVED USED BY PERMISSION

CAROLINA IN MY MIND by James Taylor © 1969, 1971 BLACKWOOD MUSIC INC., and COUNTRY ROAD MUSIC INC. All rights administered by BLACKWOOD MUSIC INC. International Copyright Secured   All Rights Reserved

THESE TIMES YOU'VE COME by Jackson Browne © 1970 ATLANTIC MUSIC CORP., and OPEN WINDOW MUSIC

All rights reserved. No part of this book may be reproduced or utilized in any form or by any means, electronic or mechanical, including photocopying, recording or by any information storage and retrieval system, without permission in writing from the Publisher. Inquiries should be addressed to Permissions Department, William Morrow and Company, Inc., 105 Madison Ave., New York, N.Y. 10016.

This is an authorized reprint of a hardcover edition published by William Morrow and Company.

ONYX TRADEMARK REG. U.S. PAT. OFF. AND FOREIGN COUNTRIES
REGISTERED TRADEMARK—MARCA REGISTRADA
HECHO EN DRESDEN, TN, U.S.A.

SIGNET, SIGNET CLASSIC, MENTOR, ONYX, PLUME, MERIDIAN AND NAL BOOKS are published by New American Library, a division of Penguin Books USA Inc., 1633 Broadway, New York, New York 10019

First Onyx Printing, October, 1986

3 4 5 6 7 8 9 10 11

PRINTED IN THE UNITED STATES OF AMERICA

*For Lynn Whitener,
with love*

PROLOGUE
THANKSGIVING

"I've talked to Earl already, Ma. Yes. Stan, too. I believe I've said hello to everybody and I'd better . . . Uh-huh. I wish I were there too, Ma . . . That's right. I'm having dinner with friends. That's why I'd better . . ."

Taylor Worth, interrupted again, pulled the phone away from his ear and held it at arm's length. His mother's voice became a thin, tinny song, similar to others being sung all across the country, a tune of long-distance wishes and wistful contrition, a holiday hymn of the technological age.

"I miss you too, Ma," he said. "I said I miss you too." In his mind's eye he saw the ruins of Thanksgiving dinner still on his mother's table, the gaggle of uncles and cousins gathered around the television set watching the football game, his father in his favorite chair, dozing despite the noise. "I love you too, Ma . . . Yeah. Maybe next year . . . I've got to go now, pick up my date, and . . . Her name? Her name is Anne . . . Of course she's pretty, Ma . . . I'll tell her you said hello. Right. Love you. 'Bye."

Taylor sighed like a deflating dirigible as he hung up

the designer phone. Its brass, horn-shaped mouthpiece reflected the color of the decorative spittoon next to the overlarge rolltop desk and stylistically complemented the blue and green Tiffany lamp illuminating the dark room Taylor called his den. The phone was a gift but not from Anne. In fact, he didn't know any women named Anne. The ship's clock above the desk chimed. Taylor slid his hand under his robe and scratched his chest. Two o'clock in the afternoon and he hadn't even taken a shower. Things have come to a sorry pass, he told himself, when you feel compelled to lie to your mother about something as insignificant as a date for Thanksgiving dinner.

Taylor shuffled into the bedroom on worn-out slippers, past the unmade, king-sized bed littered with yesterday's clothes and open sections of *The Washington Post*, into the larger of his two bathrooms. He sat on the edge of the tub and turned the tap. Perhaps a nice bath, he thought, a nice, long, leisurely soak in the capacious oval tub. Taylor watched the water run for a minute before turning it off.

He wandered into the living room, whose decor women never failed to compliment. Large, south-facing windows admitted cheery, natural light in which the colors of the Persian rug and Taylor's only legitimate art object, a framed De Kooning print, shone prominently. Except for the den, with its massive furniture, classically masculine dark oak stain, brass, and leather—a style he was less inclined to favor than to affect simply because a man should have a man's room—he had chosen his furnishings with women's sensibilities in mind. He had similarly chosen his car, and whenever he bought new clothes, he appraised them with as much regard to how women might perceive him as to his own comfort.

Taylor flopped onto the sofa and watched ten minutes of the football game. He went to the bookshelf and ran his hand over the spines of at least a hundred hardcover volumes, but no title leaped out to grab his imagination. The quiet, like an encircling army, advanced on him.

In his mind he heard the festivities of the holiday: toasts offered, familial laughter, proclamations of thanks in song and prayer. He saw men giving flowers and women giving hugs. He saw hands being squeezed and loving smiles exchanged. In a mirror above the bookshelf, he saw his own unshaven face and uncombed hair. A lump of grief formed in his belly and rose slowly to his throat. Taylor wanted to know why. Not so much why he didn't have a date—he could have found a date if he'd wanted one—but why he continued to be without a woman to love. In his fantasies he had a girl to joke with and walk hand in hand with; who enjoyed him and whom he enjoyed; a woman who wanted more than anything else—more than money, more than beauty—to be happy.

"Is that so difficult?" he asked the face in the mirror. "Is that impossible?"

CHAPTER ONE

"I knew that one for eight months," Taylor said. "Can you believe it? Eight months. We slept together, practically lived together, and I never saw her without eye makeup. She'd go into the bathroom and lock the door to wash off the old and put on the new. She absolutely forbade me to see her without that gunk on her eyelids."

Ned Brody nodded. He hadn't listened carefully enough to absorb the specifics of Taylor's soliloquy, but he recognized the whine in his friend's voice. "You don't say," he grunted, staring up at the tote board on which race results were displayed. He glanced down at his tip sheet. Ned didn't adore off-track betting, especially since it wasn't legal in the District, but until springtime and the opening of Pimlico in Baltimore, it was the only game in town.

"I actually believed she might be a good one," Taylor continued. "She was intelligent, witty, and had a good job but she was obsessed with cosmetics." He shook his head. "When am I going to learn, Ned? When's it finally going to dawn on me that all women are . . ."

"That's what nixed her for you, eh?" Ned interrupted, brushing a speck of dust from his otherwise immaculate wool suit. "The cosmetics, right? She liked cosmetics and that disqualified her." Ned didn't want to discuss it again, to hear again what his friend had to say on this most ancient, most worn subject. Ned acknowledged that one of his functions as a friend was to listen to complaining, but Taylor's monologues—previously entertaining and insightful, deriving, as they once did, from practical knowledge and clever observation—had begun to sound like rehearsed speeches, no longer racy and suffused with funny anecdotes or softened with recollections of the odd pleasurable moment. Ned had enjoyed the old routines when Taylor was still collecting experiences like mossrocks for a fireplace or a decorative fence, sorting them, arranging them, matching them for color and effect, but those times were gone. Now Taylor was cementing them in, laying the mortar between them, regrettably without special regard to aesthetic effect. The entire philosophical construction, from Ned's viewpoint, looked like too many others he'd seen—prosaic, unimaginative, suburban—unworthy of his creative, vital friend.

"All women aren't anything," Ned said. "Any more than all men are."

"I beg your pardon?"

"I interrupted when you said, 'All women are.' It doesn't matter what you were going to say next, Taylor. Whatever you would have said would have been wrong, untrue, erroneous, incorrect, false." Ned knew he was entering dangerous territory, but he also knew two men as willful as he and Taylor Worth, longtime friends, in broad agreement on so many other subjects—politics, religion, economics—could not for too many more years continue to disagree on this basic issue, a practical matter, a provable point, before one or the other made the classic masculine demand: Put up or shut up. Ned wasn't positive this dreary February afternoon at his bookmaker's was precisely the best time and place, but on the other hand, Taylor was becoming a bore, something Ned could not tolerate in a friend. He drew a deep breath. "Has it ever occurred to you, Taylor, that the trouble is not with them, the harlots, the harpies, and the whores you love to hate, but with you?"

As he spoke, he felt the words taking on a life of their own. They seemed to march from his mouth like military columns, fully armed and outfitted, prepared for war. Unsure of what to expect from Taylor, Ned looked directly into the younger man's handsome face. First he saw astonishment and then, deep in Taylor's normally cool gray eyes, something seething, something hot. Ned ventured one more sentence. "It might be, Taylor, that you are unloved not because women are wimps or saints, sirens or angels, but because you are unlovable." There. Done. Said. The moving hand having written and all that. Ned sat back, unburdened.

Taylor, utterly astounded, opened his mouth and shut it again resolutely, realizing he could speak with only one voice while the number clamoring for expression was, like the names of Satan, legion. Completely without warning, Ned had demolished a venerable and respected treaty under which, in the interest of the maintenance of a friendship, certain subjects had been sacrosanct.

One of the voices was vengeance. Taylor knew precisely how to retaliate. He knew Ned as well as Ned knew him. They'd cried on each other's shoulders for years, and although Taylor respected Ned as a comprehensive human being, valued him as an essentially good man, considered him his mentor, and in many ways a role model, he was well acquainted with Ned's vulnerabilities. If the older man wanted to match flaw against flaw, Taylor was ready.

Another of the voices was outrage. As far as Taylor was concerned, no one, neither mentor nor master nor one's most trusted soulmate, had the right to attack one's tenderest sensibilities peremptorily and offhandedly. One minute it was conversation as usual between them, and the next minute it was the Japanese at Pearl Harbor.

Another voice, however, was caution. Taylor reminded himself that this was Ned, a man whose judgment he honored, whose opinions he often sought, and not some bimbo with injured pride intent on making a scene in a public place. Taylor collected his wits somewhat and, speaking in a whisper, said, "Before I shred your logic, would you like to elaborate?"

Remaining outwardly implacable, as unruffled as a houseplant in a terrarium, Ned absorbed wave after wave of Taylor's silent fury and weighed his choices. He could retreat unilaterally from the confrontation by faking a laugh, slapping Taylor on the shoulder, accusing him of having lost his sense of humor, and directing attention toward the feature race at Hialeah, or he could speak the truth and provoke Taylor further. Ned turned away from the heat of his friend's gaze and consulted the racing form. Both alternatives seemed correct. Taylor needed shaking up. His misogyny was turning him into a hermit. He needed a new point of view and Ned knew of no one better qualified to provide it than he, Taylor's closest friend. On the other hand, disapproval from said closest friend might force Taylor into total isolation. He would ossify and the loss would be Ned's.

"Taylor," he said finally, "the problem as I see it is

you've been out of circulation too long. You had that sour experience with Sylvia and then you had a long run of bad luck. You made a whole string of bad bets. Some extremely bad ones, in fact. I thought Chris Whatsername was especially, uh, well, sorry, and so I can understand your bitterness but everybody has a losing streak now and then. Your luck will change but you can't meet a good woman unless you meet women. You haven't had a date in . . ."

"How do you know? What are you talking about? I can get a date anytime I want. Women are after me all the time, in their pathetically backhanded way."

Ned recoiled, surprised. A queasy feeling overcame him. He thought he'd started gently by citing the obvious. Ned knew for certain his friend wasn't dating, not only from Taylor's behavior but from conversation. He always talked about his women, either to brag or complain, and in the bragging category at least, he'd been unnaturally quiet lately. Ned turned his face away. Watching Taylor's automatic defensive response was like watching a husband and wife quarrel at a dinner party. Despite Ned's affection for Taylor, he was neither prepared for nor interested in a slow-motion, closeup view of what Ned was afraid might be a gruesome private illness. Alarms went off in his brain, but rapprochement was impossible. Ned realized too late he could not have done worse. He had impugned Taylor's charm, his *savoir-faire*, his status as a man irresistible to women.

"Do you know anyone who's dated more beautiful women?" Taylor demanded, shimmering with anger. He practically levitated. "What do you know about my private life? And who are you to talk? You're the only man I ever knew who pursued middle age as if it were a goal. How many women have you slept with? Three?

Four? How many women do you know? Maybe a dozen total, including your precious Clara, your two kids, your mother, and your secretary. What you know about women wouldn't stuff an olive."

Ned watched irrationality overtake his friend, and although he knew Taylor's ranting issued from fear, he bristled at the reference to Clara and the girls. Ned's marriage was his rod and his staff. It was true he had not bedded many women. He had married young and, against all odds, remained faithful, but in the same way no man can challenge any woman's pronouncements with regard to pregnancy, Ned believed Taylor was enjoined from assailing his matrimonial bastion. In marriage, Ned was privy to something of which Taylor was ignorant. More than once, the invocation of this experiential difference had put an end to discussions. It was an argument-stopper on the order of "If you're so smart, why ain't you rich?" or the tongue-out proscriptive "sour grapes." Also, and more significantly, Ned knew his trusting, gentle relationship with Clara was precisely what Taylor envied and admired most about him. Women were still, after all these years and all his girl friends, a mystery to Taylor, who was intrigued and fascinated that Ned with apparent effortlessness had lived so well for so long with the same woman. Although intellectually Ned understood the futility of challenging unreasonable anger, he needed to let Taylor know he was out of line. "Don't belittle what I have simply because it's something you want and can't have."

Having been wounded, Taylor responded like one of Hemingway's bulls. "You're pretty smug inside your little marital security blanket . . ." Taylor meant to say snug, but in his rage he was liable to lose a labial or two. " . . . hiding in there like a horny old nun under her vow of chastity. While honest men and women are repudiating traditional sex roles, revealing them to be simple indentured servitude, you and Clara wrap yourselves in a moldy platitude and snuggle in. How much time do you spend here and at the track when it's open, and at the dog races? How many trips do you take to Atlantic City or Vegas every year? How much time and money do you piss away in sleazy back rooms in illegal poker games? Huh? I didn't think happily married men wanted to be away from their families that much. Marital harmony. What a joke. It's only harmonious because as a duet with limited talents, you and Clara agree to sing simple songs. How about the big band sound, Ned? How about some orchestration? Pardon me if I call you a phony but your gambling is just your particular brand of infidelity. You'd probably be better off if you fucked around some, but I don't think you could take it. Your secure little deal with Clara makes everything convenient. You don't have to wonder about how—or even if—you could handle a modern woman who'd knock off a piece of your ass just to see the size of your dick and laugh when she does it. And you never will either, not because of your commitment to holy matrimony, but simply because you don't have the balls. Get off your ass and deal with modern women, and then maybe you'll have something to talk about."

Ned's brain responded to Taylor's evocative images with images of its own, of Ned's own modern women: Clara, smart, independent enough to run her own business, and still good-looking at forty; Jessica, the sixteen-year-old who looked twenty and who was enough of a modern woman for Clara to trust with the running of the shop; and Betty, a year older than *Ms.* magazine and just as opinionated. Ned's first impulse was to toss all this in Taylor's face, but he held back. Taylor knew all about the family. At issue here was Taylor's life, not his own; and as sorry as Ned felt for his demented friend, he couldn't resist a rebuttal. "You forget, Taylor, I've watched you operate for years. I've seen your women—the tall ones, the short ones, the good ones you let get away, and the mistakes. I know the way you deal with women and it's ludicrous, getting worse every day. You say you hate women's pettiness, yet you analyze their every gesture. You say you despise calculating women, yet every move you make is planned. A woman who doesn't fall all over your handsome ass is an iceberg, but let the same girl get intimate and she's trying to crowd you. You require physical beauty in a woman and at the same time you resent it, resent her for having it and the exceptional privileges it accords her as a result of your worshiping it in the first place. What's your problem, Taylor? A death wish? A self-fulfilling prophecy? I'm sure there's some good pedagogical term for the condition, but it comes down to this: You pick the very women who are most likely to substantiate your prejudices. You contend every woman is a type, then you go out and find the type to prove you're right. I'm no Phil Donahue, buddy, no champion of feminism, but you don't give a girl a chance. As soon as you impress her or seduce her and she shows the tiniest interest in you, you start disqualifying her. She does this or she doesn't do that. She has too much of this or not enough of that. A female to you is a symbol. She's not just a woman, small 'w,' flesh and blood, different from you but still human. Instead, she's a specimen of Woman, capital 'W,' against whom, for reasons legitimate or otherwise, you are viciously predisposed. To you, all women are gold diggers or shameless takers except the ones who want to give and they're neurotic altruists, martyrs, suffering from motherhood complexes. No, Taylor. You're without a woman not because you haven't met a good one but because no good one will have you."

Although Ned was talking, Taylor heard Clara lecturing her daughters about him: Pay attention, girls. This is the kind of male you must avoid. She hadn't let up for a minute since an unfortunate summer night a few years back when, in a moment of candor, Taylor had disavowed his reputation as a confirmed bachelor and admitted his yearning for a lifetime partner. Before his confession he represented mystery, a kind of romantic indomitability, even to old, married Clara, but as soon as he acknowledged his wishes, she reclassified him as a man with an unfulfilled desire—in other words, a failure. "Poor Ned," Taylor said in a pitying tone. "How can you be so wrong so consistently? If my lack of success with women is as obvious as you say, why do so many women want to marry me?"

"Do they?"

"Well, of course. You may not realize it, old man, but I'm something of a prize. Good job, good credit, no former wives, no diseases. I'm what they're all looking for."

"Can you prove it?"

"That women want marriage?"

"That they want to marry you. Ever asked one?"

"Wash your mouth out with soap. In some of my, uh, relationships, the unasked question has grown so large, I've had to make reservations for three for dinner."

"Do you know the ratio of proposals to acceptances nowadays?"

"I don't read *Redbook*. Pray, tell me."

"It's from *Cosmopolitan*. One acceptance per three proposals."

"Typical Helen Gurley Brown research," sneered Taylor, shooting his cuffs, straightening his tie. "She undoubtedly counted every post-last-call proposition ever made: 'Hey honey, I love you. Let's go someplace and get married.' Ned, my friend, there's not a girl in this city—providing of course she'd accept a date with me—who I couldn't persuade to marry me if I took the time and expended a minimum effort. It'd be ten out of ten for me. Perfect record."

Ned took a deep breath. Having had his say, he felt purged of anger, faintly embarrassed, and terribly uncomfortable. He could not remember ever having exchanged so many angry words with Taylor Worth and it seemed unnatural. Ned was convinced all Taylor needed to be sprung from his destructive funk was to get back into the world and begin again to engage women on a one-to-one basis, and as he listened to his friend's hollow boasts, he formed a plan. When Taylor finally shut up, Ned said, "I know for a fact you haven't had more than three dates with any one girl in the last year and you expect me to believe all those women are sitting home right now, withering on the vine, just waiting for your call."

"You don't test a gun by shooting yourself in the foot, Ned. Line up a dozen women. You pick 'em. I'll plug 'em into my formula, turn the crank, and out will pop a procession of blushing brides-to-be."

Ned smiled. As a gambler, he loved to see overconfidence in an adversary. It was the stuff of which sure things were made. "You might get four," he conceded. "One out of three women are probably desperate."

Taylor Worth, full to the brim of himself, replied, "That's where you're mistaken. You presume their decisions would have something to do with their current life situations, which in actuality wouldn't matter at all. With a little money and a little time, the Taylor Worth method is foolproof, extraneous circumstances like career goals or vows of independence notwithstanding."

Ned figured the odds: of getting his friend back into circulation—excellent; of snapping him out of his funk—excellent; of teaching him a little humility—excellent; of having a bit of sporting fun in the bleak, late-winter season—excellent. He set his confidence squarely against his friend's pomposity. "Are you interested in a wager?" he asked.

Taylor's dogs of war snarled in their cages.

After the terms of the bet were set, Taylor went straight to the spa, intending to use exercise to dispel his anger, diminish further his few misgivings, and delay the inevitable case of bettor's remorse until after he had developed his strategy. Ned, he knew, would go home exultant until reality reclaimed him and forced him to realize he might have to tell Clara he'd lost Grandma's Mercedes in a bet. Not that she cared about the car per se. To her, it was just another extravagance inherited from Ned's side of the family, but undoubtedly she perceived it as joint property if not already as part of the children's legacy. Taylor enjoyed the image of Ned supine in his recliner, eating his liver, because for Taylor Worth not the slimmest glimmer of doubt existed regarding the eventual outcome of the bet. It would take time, money, and precise concentration, but in the end it would be a piece of cake. He would have met an interesting challenge, enjoyed himself, and won a Mercedes-Benz besides.

Taylor slid onto the vinyl cushion of the exercise machine and heaved the weights through five repetitions. Already he was savoring the moment when he'd ride with Ned in the classic car to the fishing cabin on the river. They'd walk down to the water and step to the end of the pier, where he'd clap his friend on the shoulder and say, "Just think, Ned, all this could have been yours." Ned's jowls would droop a little further and Taylor would gloat, having succeeded by wit rather than hard work in gaining the last of the material objects he had promised himself he would own by his fortieth birthday: his own place in the city, a house on the water somewhere, and a Mercedes-Benz. And all with five years to spare.

He charged through the first two exercises in his hour-long routine, but his adrenaline began to wane and he struggled through the remainder, grunting, sweating, expelling poisons with every repetition. At the end he stood before the mirror and made an inspection. Hah. Excellent. Thirty-five years old and still in shape, no beer belly and plenty of hair on his chest and head. His might not qualify as the best of male bodies, but it still fit into the hunky-attractive range with ease. He wiped sweat off his mouth and grinned. Choose carefully, Ned old boy, he thought, and bring 'em on.

On the way home, after a sauna and shower and a light dinner in the spa bar, he recounted the terms of the bet. He and Ned had agreed on the number of women to be wooed: three. Ned wanted four, but he compromised when Taylor agreed to a three-month time limit. Ned was to choose the women (no uglies allowed). They were to be courted simultaneously, and the women's acceptances of Taylor's proposals were required to be on tape by the last day of the bet, which was to be exactly three months to the day after the last woman agreed to her first date with him. The most difficult point in the negotiation concerned expenses, but the two men worked out an elaborate system that seemed equitable. Taylor expected trouble on this point but he wasn't too concerned. He considered the expenses an investment in the Mercedes, and he knew it would be cheap no matter how much he spent on flowers, champagne, lingerie, and other bribes. It was agreed Taylor would not take the girls out of the country, nor would he incur outrageous expenses like trips to San Francisco for Sunday brunch. The stakes were the car against the fishing cottage Taylor owned on the Pamlico River in North Carolina. All very neat and eminently acceptable. Taylor was pleased. Home now, he told himself, and steady.

Years before, following high-school graduation, acting on the advice and example of his mother, Taylor compiled in writing his goals for his college years. Encouraged by her to explore his deeper feelings, he produced a manifesto that included his thoughts on morality and fairness, on the difference between wisdom and cleverness, on the nature of reality, and so on. He still had the manifesto among his important papers along with a similar although longer treatise written at the time of college graduation and another, shorter one compiled six years ago when finally he concluded his apprenticeships and embarked wholeheartedly on his career. Not only did these writings represent his philosophical development, they also represented his game plan, his life outline, a set of precepts to which he could refer when things became confusing.

For some time, at least five years, since he had become suspicious of bachelorhood, he had considered writing another paper to explore his thoughts and attitudes about women because Ned was right, he had become grievously cynical and his liaisons with women decreasingly satisfactory. Although he believed his opinions were correct and justifiable, based on sound theory and thorough experimentation, they remained disorganized, a condition which because of the bet he could no longer afford.

Taylor welcomed the challenge. The wager would force him to organize his thoughts about the only remaining chaotic aspect of his life; it would inject adventure, perhaps even pleasure, into this bleak season, and at the same time bring him a coveted material reward. He unlocked the door to his town house (purchased in 1978 at nine percent), hung his overcoat (Cardin) in the closet off the foyer, dumped his spa bag (Adidas) on top of the washing machine in the utility room, fetched a leather notepad (Gucci) the size of a ledger book, took his pen (Mont Blanc) from his pocket, switched on the Tiffany lamp, and sat down at his antique desk, intent on unraveling the complexities of "God's *second* mistake" (Nietzsche).

CHAPTER TWO

"Number one. Veronica Bristow," said Ned, tossing a three-by-five card across the desk at Taylor. "I met her only once, at an Equal Rights Amendment panel discussion Clara dragged me and the kids to. She was one of the participants." He smiled like a speed-trap sheriff. "You might as well sign that deed over right now, boy. Try your Cary Grant routine on her and she'll grind your nuts to peanut butter. There were a couple of lawyers on the other side of the panel. Tough guys. They brought out the heavy verbal artillery and fired away but the shells bounced off. This broad is armor plated."

"Dyke?"

"How would I know? She sells pharmaceuticals."

"Is she good-looking?"

Ned shrugged. "She's not unpretty."

"What the hell does that mean?"

Ned shrugged again. "Well, she's sort of—what can I say?—unremarkable except for her hair, which is a deep red color. It's not long but it's not short, either. She's just average, you know, not overweight but not skinny.

When you look at her, top to bottom, full in the face, she's attractive, I guess. Pleasantly built. She's OK. Not beautiful but by no means ugly."

Taylor knew the type. He'd spent as much time thinking about the kinds of women Ned would pick for him as Ned had spent doing the picking, and the choice of a feminist, or quasi-feminist, or whatever this Ms. Bristow considered herself, was inevitable. Taylor stared at the name on the card. He believed, as it is reassuring for gentler personalities to believe that honest politicians and fair-minded businessmen exist, that somewhere in the nation women genuinely intended to express a comprehensive philosophy defining feminine values; to advance, for everyone's perusal, a system of thought—not necessarily a political strategy—representing new ideas, new interpretations of old ideas, new perspectives, and new explanations for "the current crisis" based on a feminine viewpoint; but so far, in Taylor's view, feminist rhetoric represented only reactions or rebellions against the masculine viewpoint. "It's not fair," he'd heard feminists say. "What men do to women is not right, not equitable, not Christian, not humane," and Taylor couldn't agree more. To the surprise of many feminists he'd spoken with and about whom Ned knew, he would not begin to argue the point because it was demonstrably true, not only with respect to the past—when women's rights were at best a bad joke—but also with respect to the present. In his profession, the computer business, perhaps the most progressive of Third Wave industries, a woman with his credentials and capabilities today still could not expect the same opportunities or the same salary as he received. So he conceded the point. "No question about it, it's not fair," he'd say, which disarmed the women. His next comment, though, floored them, "So what?"

Men had established a culture that was universally unfair, rooted in inequality and injustice. The clichés heard in boardrooms and locker rooms—It's a dog-eat-dog world; There's no such thing as a free lunch; God helps those who help themselves; etc.—applied to everyone indiscriminately. Whenever Taylor heard a woman lament that she was being taken advantage of or being punished for doing as she was taught, he would laugh. Only women, it seemed, and maladjusted men, took their early training, morality lessons, and so forth, seriously. Rules, as the young male learns long before reaching adulthood, are made to be broken. Even "Thou shalt not kill" is violable in war. The little boy learns this or he does not survive, and if he manages to survive, he most certainly does not succeed.

In discussions with feminists, however, Taylor did not proceed into this predictable, Social Darwinist explanation of the way of the world because Taylor, unusually for a successful man, didn't believe the clichés, didn't believe the world was inherently unfair, that men, struggling, fighting, brokering power, disregarding ethics, were faithfully following the rules of life.

As a youngster, Taylor Worth neither experienced nor exhibited sexual ambivalence. Having received x and y chromosomes in equal proportions, he played rough-and-tumble sports, took apart machines, and chased girls in childhood like any "normal" little boy, but his participation in these healthy male activities, no doubt as a result of some obscure psychological malfunction, was motivated by a simple, honest desire to have fun rather than by a lust for power or a need to prove his superiority over anyone. Perhaps because of his effortless success in school and sports, Taylor was slow to realize the games he enjoyed were intended as one-to-one allegories for real life. Thus he began—later than normal and begrudgingly because it took the fun out of things—the education most feminists envy and covet, which has as its vocabulary the language of war, which emphasizes emotionlessness, single-mindedness, and ruthlessness, and which regards compassion as a quality of weaklings or idiots. Although he tried, Taylor never felt comfortable with the old Vince Lombardi-General Patton-Jay Gould state of mind. He never spoke out in opposition, however, partially because he didn't want to be branded a fairy but primarily because it seemed useless. The cool, dispassionate, aggressive male was society's (men's *and* women's) most respected, most admired, and most rewarded individual. To decry the set of qualities that elevated to social prominence dedicated scoundrels and geniuses alike was to suggest envy, thereby revealing a weakness, the absolutely worst thing a man could do. Taylor kept his own counsel and competed, but he was flawed. Without the killer instinct, he could never achieve those positions of responsibility and power he would always desire and for which he was otherwise suited. Fortunately for him, the computer came along. He dedicated his disciplined, logical mind to this new science and found a comfortable, respectable niche in the manic madhouse of business. Unfortunately, however, from this safe, comparatively detached position, he saw that the same linear, masculine thinking capable of producing the computer, the Mercedes, and other terrific things also produced the nuclear-arms race.

When the modern women's movement began, Taylor was encouraged because as a male who understood the dangerous flaws and contradictions in masculine thinking, he hoped women would offer alternatives. The ancient "survival of the fittest" philosophy, while temporarily effective, had ultimately failed, he believed.

WORTH WINNING

The existence of the equivalent of one hundred pounds of dynamite per human being in the world's nuclear arsenals indicated to Taylor that the philosophy had turned on itself, invalidated itself, become its own caricature, and he figured the time was ripe for a fresh viewpoint, a completely new analysis of "the way of the world" and where better to find it than within the brains of the population's disenfranchised majority, women? Taylor could hardly wait. The timing, the setting, everything was perfect for a nice, quiet thought revolution. The masculine mind with its toolmaking, mathematical proclivities had brought the world simultaneously to the brink of ultimate success and ultimate destruction. Now women, by a simple act of will, by recognizing and utilizing their unexploited powers, could easily direct the next phase of the planet's history. Taylor bought a ticket and took a front-row seat.

And what happened? All women wanted—of course, what else?—was an opportunity to be, or to prove they could be, as competitive and destructive as any head-hunting defensive end. They stood onstage at the performance Taylor had been so eager to see and pointed at him, accused him of being their oppressor, whereas Taylor Worth, all-around nonviolent fellow, wasn't inclined to force anybody into anything. Once again, he had failed with women.

After a couple of months of absorbing vilification at the hands of radical feminists, Taylor went home and reassessed his thinking. He decided women weren't the answer after all. (He had suspected as much but hope springs eternal.) Wasn't it obvious men pulled all sorts of insane stunts just to get women? Wasn't it obvious women revered the traditional masculine role as much as men did? If not, why did they fuck the bad guys all the time? What gangster didn't have his molls? What mogul didn't have his pick of women? To Taylor, the solution to war was simple. All women had to do was refuse to fuck soldiers. But women weren't interested in peace, only in becoming Mrs. General Somebodyorother.

Whenever Taylor made this case to Ned, Ned would tease him, saying something like, "What's the matter, isn't issums getting enough cuddling?" and Taylor would be back to square one. He was getting plenty of cuddling but always for the wrong reasons: for how well he lived up to the masculine ideal in bed or in business. He did not, however, want to switch roles because he knew it was impossible. Not only would his genes prevent it, but his socialization was too comprehensive. Also, he couldn't possibly respect a woman who aspired to the masculine ideal. He was too aware of statistics like the one that proved the male death rate past age fifteen is one hundred percent higher than the female's; like the one that proved a man is forty percent more likely to contract a fatal cancer than a woman; like the one that proved a man is twice as likely to be the victim of a crime than a woman; like the one that proved men live almost eight years less than women. How could he respect a woman who wanted to sign up for that?

Taylor tried to picture Veronica Bristow. She would wear very little makeup and low-heeled shoes, and be suspicious of everything a man said or did. She would have adopted all the worst masculine characteristics—argumentativeness, belligerence, pomposity—without regard to the best—good sportsmanship, graciousness, generosity—and retained all the worst feminine characteristics without regard to the best. She would despise men for their past treatment of women and deride any enlightened contemporary behavior as too little and too late. Ms. Bristow was probably the worst of the new breed of broad who wanted everything at once and wanted it both ways. Taylor swallowed bile and composed his face. He looked up at his cunning, leering friend.

"This kind's easy, Ned," he lied. "As long as she isn't a confirmed lesbian, she's probably ready to confront her femininity along with her feminism. That's the newest trend, you know. These oldtime libbers miss playing dress-up. The thing is, you can't pay too much attention to their rhetoric. I'm not saying there aren't sincere feminists, but the key to a woman is her body. It tells you everything you need to know. Despite politics, Ned, all women want to be beautiful and more of them are beautiful than think they're beautiful. This girl, you say, is attractive but plain. The difference between attractive and plain and attractive and striking is a man's devotion. I'm adorable when I'm adoring." He slipped the card into his jacket pocket. "Next."

"And you're a wahoo when you're cavalier, but I'll give you an A for arrogance." Ned was having a great time. Not only had he enjoyed his weekend of deciding how to nail Taylor's ego to the barn door, but his friend, as predicted, had shed his defensiveness and rediscovered his lovable insolence. Ned considered the venture a success and the fun had hardly begun.

"You might be right about feminists in general, Taylor, but you don't know this Bristow woman. I saw her defeat clever men in will-to-will combat. She's icy, formidable, about as approachable as Annapurna. In fact, I don't believe you'll entrap her into the first date which would exclude her from the competition which would be a shame but because it'd be interesting to watch her use your cock as a razor strop, I think you need the workout. I think you need a good, solid defeat before you forge behind to total humiliation."

"Sounds to me like you're angling for a little side bet. A box of cigars on this one? A case of wine?"

"Cigars."

"Done. Now. Next. Come on. Bring 'em on."

Ned looked like the man who had fixed the fight, drugged the horse, stuffed the ballot box. "Number two," he said serenely, tossing another card onto the desk.

"Wait a minute," said Taylor, reading the card.

Ned smiled, thinking strawberries and cream and Grand Marnier, an afternoon at the lake with nothing to do, clean sheets and a down quilt on a winter night, contentment, satisfaction, afterglow.

Taylor squirmed. "This wasn't in the deal."

"It wasn't not in the deal either."

"But I said . . ."

"You said no uglies."

"But . . ."

"Any woman who would accept a date. That was the agreement." Ned nodded at the card Taylor held like a death announcement. "And I believe Mrs. Larimore will accept a date." He laughed again. This was better than hitting the daily double.

Taylor ransacked his mind for a legitimate objection, replayed the conversation, recalled the terms of the bet, the handshake. How could he have overlooked something so obvious? "You're asking me to break up a marriage," he said in a half-hearted appeal to Ned's sense of familial devotion.

Ned howled. "Not to disparage your talents, Taylor—I've been your biggest fan for years—but the Larimores aren't exactly the Waltons. You couldn't break up that marriage with an ax. You could break up General Motors quicker. It'd be less of a legal hassle. I can't wait to see how you play this one, Taylor old friend. Promise me one thing, though, that you'll take pictures of her. I've wanted to see her naked for five years. I've seen her in bathing suits, tennis skirts, and assorted cocktail dresses and she's built nicely, although a little on the thin side for my tastes. I've even seen her in a towel, but I'd give a lot to see her stripped because she's the kind who looks like she ought to be stripped. Know what I mean? So promise me you'll show me pictures, Taylor, and I'll promise you can come down to my fishing cottage every once in a while."

"Tell me about her," said Taylor.

Ned could have told Taylor a great deal about Eleanor Larimore. He could have told him she was the kind of woman who played come-hither games with every proximate male, who radiated a wanton sexiness, a casual availability tha belied her role as the overattentive mate of Howard Larimore, a business acquaintance of Ned's who'd made a calculated and concerted pass at Clara, and had shown an inordinate interest in Jessica since she began to fill out her bikini. He could have told Taylor about the number of men Ned had known who'd tried and failed to follow Eleanor's scent to its source. He could have told Taylor about the rumors of Eleanor and the lifeguard, Eleanor and the young waiters, Eleanor and any male who couldn't possibly threaten her position as Mrs. Larimore. "You know enough already," he said finally, "and you'll discover the rest presently."

"Any children?"

"One. Howard Junior."

"Where do you know her from?"

"The country club but you don't have to be the tennis instructor to get her attention. All you have to be is willing to take a chance."

Taylor stared at the card. He knew this type, too: a high-gloss, hard-finish Junior Leaguer who appraised you like a prize animal at a pet show; the kind with a diamond as big as a cashew; the kind who took everything but a genuine risk. "A real minx, eh, Ned?"

Ned gave Taylor his bookie's grin.

Taylor slid Eleanor Larimore into his pocket alongside Veronica Bristow. "And who's next?" he asked. "Who's the third lucky girl?"

Ned looked at his wristwatch. "I don't know," he said. "We're going to pick her out right now."

Prowling, Ned called it, although the practice enjoys many names—cruising, honky-tonking, hustling—and until a few years ago, until Taylor gave it up, it had been Ned's primary source of sexual adventure, even though he never made a move on a woman himself, never jeopardized his ability to look Clara straight in the eye by so much as buying a girl a drink. His thrills came from voyeurism and—though he'd never admit it even if he thought about it in those terms—hero worship. In the old days, Ned and Taylor would hit the happy-hour bars. Ned would scout the room, noting the available women, watching them from the safety of his marital commitment, rating them on his one-to-ten scale, and judging their readiness. He was neither a pimp nor a shill. He was a fan, a live-theater buff. He'd report his findings to his handsome friend and watch the subsequent drama, comedy, tragedy, or, as often as not, overture to pornography, while charming, slick, masterful Taylor made his moves. Some men watch sports to experience, albeit vicariously, the excitement of moment-to-moment survival, the primal thrill of imminent danger, the here-and-now-not-later-not-maybe immediacy largely absent from everyday life, but Ned would pass up tickets to the Super Bowl to watch Taylor prowl. At risk was an ego—which in Taylor's case was enormous—and the reward was flesh—fresh, supple, delicious, fragrant, alluring, female flesh. It drove Ned crazy. Even when Taylor didn't score, Ned's proximity to the sebaceous gore of exposed emotions made him as light-headed, as electrified, as vital as if he had been involved in the action.

So one of the great disappointments of Ned's life was when Taylor retired from the field. Now with an opportunity to dictate terms rather than merely to make suggestions, he led his friend to Omar's Bar, where they joined the legions of Washington, D.C.'s cute and trendy young professionals just in time for the weekly TGIF celebration and mating ritual.

Ned perched on a barstool and studied the crowd. His intention was to find a certified looker, a woman who physically at least would satisfy any normal male. He believed the choice of such a woman would accomplish two things: First, it would preclude Taylor's peremptory disqualification of the girl on the most obvious of bases, looks; and second, it would force Taylor to work hard. A beautiful girl would see in him just another handsome, moneyed male, just another suitor, no more, no less, whose own good looks would be merely an application fee, a minimum prerequisite for consideration. Taylor not only would be required to rely on his charm, but also because of the girl's obvious value in the marketplace, he could not contend he was casting his pearls before swine.

"She's in here somewhere, Taylor, the girl of your dreams. What flavor do you prefer: blonde, brunette, or redhead?"

"Find me a punker," Taylor replied. "Something in bright orange with a purple streak on the side. I always wanted a girl with pierced nipples."

"We're in the wrong bar. Seriously, Taylor, do you prefer them short or tall, buxom or slinky? I'm just trying to make it easier for you."

Taylor scoffed. "Sure you are. It's exactly in character for you to try to lose a bet."

Ned smiled as he continued to scan the bar. He couldn't have been more certain of the safety of the bet. All good intentions and the incentive of the Mercedes aside, Taylor could never win, not because he wasn't charming enough to enchant three women simultaneously, nor because of Ned's ingenious choice of women; but because he, Ned, knew that Taylor would have neither the stamina nor the stomach to suppress his personality for the required amount of time. Women needed deference, something Taylor was incapable of giving for very long. Grandma's car was hardly in jeopardy.

Fortunately for everyone then, it was a harmless bet. Ned already owned a chalet in the mountains and a condo at the beach. He needed Taylor's fishing cabin like he needed another foot. He demanded it as Taylor's stake because he knew how much Taylor loved it. Ned's conscious intention was to teach Taylor as many lessons as possible during the course of the wager. After his friend lost and after a judicious period in which he would allow him to meditate on his shortcomings, Ned planned to return the deed as a birthday or Christmas gift or simply as a gracious gesture of friendship. In the meantime, Taylor's process of emotional ossification would have been halted and maybe—Ned searched the room hopefully—maybe he would find what he needed, a little bit of love.

Twenty minutes later, she waltzed past the bar. She was blinding—incredible, tall, and stacked, not long and lean, not high-fashion-model material, but big and built. Not as soft as Loni Anderson and not as hard as

Susan Anton, but that was the body style—voluptuous, abundant. Ned's heart broke like an eggshell. He took a quick swallow from his drink to suppress his amazement. He loved his wife—anyone who knew him would testify to that—but there wasn't a man alive who wouldn't wonder what it would be like to have this woman welcome him to her body. Strutting alongside the bar on spindly high heels, she was dressed in a silky green blouse and a simple, slim black skirt that took her curves like a Ferrari. Ned dragged his eyes up her body, past her fabulous tits, to a face which by itself revealed nothing of the astounding roundness of the rest of her, to cheekbones prominent enough to throw classic shadows toward her jaw, a straight, slender nose that made her face all pleasant planes and angles, and sparkling green-blue eyes. Full, dusky-blond hair topped off the package, feathering away from her glorious face and falling halfway down her back.

"That's the one," Ned whispered to Taylor as the girl brushed past within smelling distance. "Best of luck."

Taylor watched her like everybody else—everybody, that is, men and women, bartenders and waitresses—and he wondered what it was like to live in that body, to be somebody just because of your body, without having to do anything special with it, like teach it to shoot baskets or commit football. He wondered what it was like to command attention—as well as adoration, wonder, awe, and worship—not for what you could say or do, or for what you owned or could control, but just because you were alive and breathing among common mortals. Talk about power. Talk about freedom. Show me a man who can do that, Ms. Veronica Bristow, at that age, without skills or talents beyond sheer physical beauty. With the same intensity Ned felt desire—and as quickly—Taylor felt resentment which, superheated by spontaneous envy, became something akin to rage, the frustrated, uncomprehending fury of a peasant in the presence of a prince. Behold Taylor Worth, intelligent, attractive, productive citizen, reduced to commonality, to inferiority, simply by the appearance of a creature who had only to stand up and walk around to command respect. Taylor despised her—or at least her glorified status—as passionately as Ned wanted to touch her.

"Yup. She's the one," repeated Ned confidently, signaling the bartender, who was himself having trouble recovering from the heavenly visitation.

"Obviously she's not a regular," Ned said when the barman had uncrossed his eyes.

"No, sir. Never saw her before. Now I'll never forget her."

Ned accepted the drinks and handed one to Taylor, who seethed and scowled beside him. In a way Ned almost pitied him. Ned had only to confront the despair associated with a glimpse of the divine, but Taylor had to face the glare full front, naked, most likely. "You asked for it, old boy."

Taylor accepted the drink and shook his head. "She might not have two nights open over the next four months, Ned."

"I've had this pain right here in my side," Ned replied, putting his hand on his rump. "It's a shooting sort of a pain but it comes and goes at the oddest times." He frowned and sipped his drink.

"What I'm saying is," Taylor persisted, "she's probably booked up through the tricentennial."

Ned glanced idly around the bar. "Will the constant February drizzle affect the rutabaga crop, do you think?"

"OK," said Taylor, adjusting his lapels, "if that's the way it is, then stay out of my way." He shot off the stool and out the door of the bar.

Earlier Taylor had noticed the hostess for the restaurant next door sitting at one of the empty tables, arranging freshly cut flowers into vases. He made for her like a honeybee.

"Pardon me," he said, handing her a five-dollar bill. "May I buy one of those daisies? Just one will be fine."

She hesitated but Taylor dropped the bill on the table, grabbed a flower, thanked her, and headed back for the bar just in time to see his prey fending off compliments and wisecracks, soaking up stares and envy, making her way between tables on her return trip.

Automatic blenders such as Osterizers or Cuisinarts go from dead stop to four thousand revolutions per minute instantaneously. Push the button and top speed happens. So it was in Taylor's guts: from dead calm to fulminating nausea in the time it took him to take his first step toward the oncoming beauty. The sensation was, as an old friend described it, like putting your testicles up on a table and giving everybody in the room a hammer. Taylor held the daisy concealed at his side and looked away as he passed her, brushing shoulders, catching a whiff of her perfume. As soon as he was beyond her, he turned around and tapped her on the shoulder. "Excuse me, miss, you dropped something," he said quickly as he touched her.

She stopped and faced him; he saw predictable skepticism in her eyes. She was young. She was gorgeous. He returned her questioning gaze with a twinkle of mischief, a look he had practiced and perfected, containing equal parts good humor, frank appraisal, and gentle condescension. He handed her the flower, struggling to keep his eyes from roaming down that extraordinary body.

"But I didn't . . ." she said, reaching, hesitating.

"I know," he said, smiling, bowing his head respectfully, taking her hand, and placing the daisy in it. "Take it anyway." He nodded again and turned away from her, walking slowly between the tables, concentrating on keeping his rubbery legs from collapsing. He didn't look back until he returned to Ned's side. The blonde had gone away, presumably back to her companions, wherever and whoever they were.

"How was it?" asked Ned. "Did she come?"

Taylor knocked back his drink with a shaky hand and ordered a beer. "According to the Taylor Worth formula," he said when he regained his voice, "two necessary elements for success are romance and mystery."

"I love that kind of talk," Ned said, delighted to see his friend back in action. "What's next?"

"Well, after I go throw up and eat a package of breath mints, I'll . . ."

Ned harrumphed. "You always make these little meetings out to be such a big deal. You did it with ease, with grace. It was as smooth as Glenlivet."

Taylor marveled at the difference between appearance and reality and struggled to keep his hands from around Ned's throat. "When was the last time you tried it?" he demanded. "You're as bad as a woman. You think that's easy? I wish someone using the Kirlian method could take pictures of one of those encounters. That's the photography of auras, you know. Can you imagine how much is going on in the realm of the unseen between two people in that kind of situation—experimentation, inquiry, spiritual touching?"

"Now you're going to make *me* throw up. Auras, spiritual touching, realm of the unseen. Welcome to the Hotel California, astral travelers. Today, for your entertainment we'll be surfing the alpha waves." Ned was disdainful of some of his friend's ideas.

"Neanderthal," Taylor taunted.

"Est-hole," Ned replied.

Taylor swilled about half his glass of beer and reflected momentarily on how bad Ned was for his liver, not to mention his caloric intake; but a warm surge of alcoholic vigor and a thrilling sense of indisputable superiority washed his conscience clean. He checked his watch. "Time," he said calmly and got up and walked away. Just like that. No hesitation.

Ned scrambled after him. He hadn't enjoyed himself or his friend as much in months.

Taylor eased around a partition and casually scanned the second and more luxurious room of the lounge. As he suspected, he had no trouble locating her. She was like the bull's-eye of a target, surrounded by concentric rings of admirers and hangers-on. Fortunately, she faced away from him and even more fortunately, he overheard bits of her conversation. She seemed to be unattached, although eager suitors leaned toward her like trees pointing the wind, and they were teasing her about her name. "Erin-go-bragh," said one. Another said, "She's better braless." The crowd tittered.

Erin was seated where Taylor couldn't get to her without stepping on someone, which was bad; plus she was more or less automatically touching a gigantic man to her right, which was worse; also the quality of her company seemed in no way inferior, which was discouraging. Taylor noticed one favorable sign, however. She wore the daisy in her hair. He slipped around to the other side of the partition.

In physics, work is defined as moving an object through a distance. You perform work every time you walk across a room. Taylor planned his assault on the queen and noted that no work he would ever attempt would be more difficult than his next little stroll. Inhaling deeply, he stepped boldly into his future.

Taylor took the long way around, first heading away from Erin, not looking at her, outside the perimeter of her circle, sending out silent mental signals, hoping she'd look up and see him. He made a big turn and made directly for her, taking his time, excusing himself politely, nodding and joking with the people he disturbed on his trek. He knew he looked attractive if not impressive, dressed for success in his best three-piece gray wool worsted and red tie. Doggedly, he continued toward his goal. With each step, the world seemed to recede from him in every direction. The noises of the bar seemed to fade out like a song nearing its end as his mind filled with a glaring white light within which appeared a single spot of color, the gold of Erin's hair, decorated with a single tiny flower. As he approached her, she sat back in her low chair and regarded him with unconcealed interest.

"Hello, Erin," he said easily and saw she was surprised he knew her name. "Good to see you again." He offered his hand. She leaned forward without saying a word, touched his hand, and leaned back. Taylor felt like a giant, like a naked giant, like a naked giant intruding at court, allowed the luxury of breathing by the precarious whim of the monarch. The courtiers reclined around him, inspecting him, and the two men flanking Erin, threatened by the new arrival, resembled guard dogs, baring fangs, assuming aggressive postures.

"Excuse the interruption," he said, addressing the sentinels, relaxing them, further amusing Erin. "I'm Taylor Worth." He offered his hand to the man on Erin's right, the huge fellow, who shook Taylor's hand while seated. The man on the left, however, was more polite. He stood up as he introduced himself, "I'm James Davenport," and Taylor used the crowded space to his advantage.

"Oops. Pardon me," he said, looking down as if he had stepped on someone's foot and, still holding on to Davenport's hand, he maneuvered him a step to the left, all that he needed. "I have to speak with Erin for just a minute," he continued, squeezing Davenport's hand, staring sincerely into his eyes. "Thank you," he said and took Davenport's seat. One day, he knew he would be decked for a stunt like that but again he forged on, turning as much of his back to Davenport as possible. Erin covered her mouth to hide a laugh but saved him. "Hello, Taylor," she said, defusing the potentially volatile situation. "I wasn't expecting you."

Taylor, relieved she had picked up his name, smiled his first honest smile, revealing another dimension of his good looks. Like that of most successful men, his usual facial expression might have been titled Perspicacity. With a slightly wrinkled forehead and slightly narrowed eyes, he gave the impression of peering raptly into the future. He had the look of a surveyor on the open plains, squinting into the distance, holding a set of plans in his hand. But when Taylor smiled, someone let the sunshine in. All that masculine resoluteness melted away, and a good-natured, gray-eyed, black-haired gentleman appeared.

Erin looked away after seeing this version of the bold man at her side and said, "Jim, will you get me a drink, please? I seem to have finished mine." She squeezed his hand. "Thanks, hon." Turning back to Taylor, she said pleasantly, "You're an interesting one."

Taylor's smile remained, although he disliked the instant classification. He knew he had to move fast. "The florist," he said, nodding toward the daisy, "who incidentally told me yours is the only beauty he knows that rivals flowers', is giving a small dinner next week. I'm certain he'd appreciate your company. Can I tell him you'll come?" Despite his automatic resentment of her, her beauty was hypnotic. He wanted to dive into her aquamarine eyes and splash around.

"Will the dinner be at home or in a restaurant?" Erin asked, crossing her elegant legs.

Their eyes carried on a lengthy conversation. Hers inquired about his manners and his sincerity. His responded with humor and *savoir-faire*.

"At Montaldo's," he answered, naming a favorite and expensive restaurant. Although he believed it was more difficult for a beautiful woman to be honest and unaffected than for a rich man to enter the kingdom of heaven, he felt his heart melting anyway. He wondered if any man anywhere could be indifferent to beauty like Erin's.

She touched the flower in her hair. "Only if it's Thursday night," she said, ignoring the groping hand of the overlarge courtier to her right.

Taylor tried not to look at the hovering fellow whose size dominated the room almost as thoroughly as Erin's loveliness. "Perfect," he said, barely holding his composure and his water. His facade of ultracoolness was crumbling rapidly. "I don't think I have your number," he continued, fumbling for a pen. "I . . ."

"I'll meet you there," she said. "Eight o'clock?"

The heat of Taylor's smile threatened to wilt Erin's daisy. He stood up shakily. His legs worked like Tinker Toys. "Thursday at eight. Montaldo's." He touched her hand. "Till then," he said and they parted with the secret nods of conspirators.

Taylor wobbled out, insides quivering. He grinned at Jim Davenport as he passed him on the way out of the room, met Ned at the partition and propelled him toward the bar.

CHAPTER THREE

Eleanor Larimore cherished the smell of a clean house. It gave her a feeling of duty fulfilled, purpose achieved, and consummation, a feeling which at this stage of her life resembled love and in that sense, love covered the surfaces, piled up in the corners, gathered itself into wispy balls beneath the beds of her house in exactly the way dust did not. Howard Senior brought home the money to provide a sanctuary for himself, his son, and his wife—in that order, Eleanor knew and understood—and her job was to maintain it, a perfectly acceptable arrangement to her because she saw in her role, the one for which she had been trained and to which she had aspired, absolute value. It had become fashionable in this age of two-career households to disparage the homemaker, to consider her deficient in talent or creativity, but Eleanor recognized the trend for what it was, a social movement intended to encourage the lower classes to strive for improvement. Every family unit needed a minimum income to participate actively in American life, and if a husband were incapable of providing that minimum, then it was correct for the wife to seek employment. If it could be proved the wife could outperform her husband with regard to money-making, then she should accept that role; but whatever the financial arrangement, it was imperative that someone take care of home base for the sake of the survival of the nuclear family, the basis of Amerian life. Even armies in the field had mess halls and headquarters. The need for safe, secure shelter was basic, and a comfortable, well-situated retreat was the proper and necessary reward for survival in the mad, modern world. She saw her job as indispensable, not merely supportive, and was pleased that her fastidious nature suited her for it so well.

Eleanor, with her coat on, at the door of her spotless kitchen, surveyed the immaculate counter, the crystal dome enclosing the brightly frosted cake, the copper utensils displayed in precise, glittering rows on the hard-rock maple panel above the inlaid butcher-block work area, and inhaled the curiously complementary pheromones broadcast by lemon wax and fresh chocolate cake that fit into her sense of security like the big key into the front-door lock. This was her domain. Hers. She had designed it and it represented efficiency and more. It represented abundance and excellence and quality. Her cooking tools were the best money could buy, and the furnishings, like those of the rest of the house, spoke eloquently of superb taste. This house, her car, her social position, her titles of mother and wife were to her what her husband's law practice and professional status were to him. She had worked and sacrificed for them, set goals and achieved them, and now that Junior was eleven years old and Howard Senior a full partner in his firm, Eleanor finally felt fulfilled. She was respectable, relatively unencumbered, and agreeably comfortable.

Unfortunately, she was also the slightest bit bored—not with her role, she wouldn't trade it; she had absolutely no interest in getting a job—but with the pace of things. Like the businessman who achieves wealth and power and can foresee only more of the same, Eleanor had become faintly dissatisfied with the potential of her life. She was thirty-two years old, trim, well-kept, and she had done better than any of her friends; but Howard Senior was often abrasive and her son was already beginning to adopt too many of his father's superior attitudes. The family had no plans to leave Washington, or even this neighborhood. They could certainly afford a bigger place, but Howard was opposed, contending prudently that they had no need for a better home or a more upscale location. So Eleanor could look forward realistically only to adjustments in her existence, more exotic vacations, redecorations, different cars, etc., and very little that was indisputably new. This was fine with Howard, who, true to his conservative political philosophy, valued stability and predictability above all.

Eleanor shrugged and fished around in her Aigner bag for her keys. Perhaps her mild displeasure had to do with the season. February qualified as the most devastatingly dull of all months. Thank God it was nearly over. And if she had begun to see the unmistakable sheen of cliché in her life, well, she liked the glint of gold, the patina of fine furniture, the sparkle of genuine crystal. Whose life wasn't a cliché of some type? Whose life didn't fit into some well-recognized pattern? If hers happened to fit the "Prelude" pattern by Orrefors, then what of it? She'd take it any day over barware by Anchor Hocking.

Out reconnoitering on his lunch hour, Taylor spotted Eleanor just as she was leaving her driveway and he followed her to the shopping center, where he waited outside the grocery store, watched her press a tip on the bag boy, who wasn't supposed to accept tips, and tailed her into the mall.

Ned had described her accurately: about five feet five inches tall, although she looked taller because of her high heels and a tailored dress that accentuated her long body lines. She had black hair, softly curled, not teased or sculptured, and was generally attractive in a conventional, correct, cared-for, upper-middle-class sort of way, with hazel eyes, straight nose, thin lips, and not too much makeup. She carried herself well, which was unusual for a woman with small breasts, but her best feature by far was her long, sleek legs.

Remaining inconspicuous, Taylor followed her through the shops, attempting to get some idea of her tastes and predilections from her browsing habits.

Eleanor had no particular reason to be in the mall. She simply had nothing else to do Thursday afternoons after grocery shopping. Mondays, she cleaned house, always an atrocious mess after a weekend of the Howards; Tuesdays, the afternoons were reserved for News and Reviews, her weekly luncheons with old friends Randall and Byron; Wednesdays, she played bridge; Fridays, she spent the day at the spa and the hairdresser. It was a boring winter routine, but it could be counted on to change soon. With the coming of warm weather, she could resume her love affair with the sun at the club pool. In the meantime, she contented herself with fantasy trips into spring via the new fashions already appearing in the stores: shorter skirts, barer swimsuits, skimpier sundresses, sexier evening gowns, and, of course, the new shoe styles.

Shoes, for Eleanor, were as nourishing as food. She had a closet full of them, some she'd worn only once, but her appetite for more never diminished. As a child, her first suspicion that a thing like sexiness existed at all arose one day when she saw her mother in high heels. Frivolous, impractical, mysteriously provocative, inexplicably they turned young Eleanor on, and she'd been a shoe junkie ever since, wearing the whitest sneakers, the flattest flats, the most outrageous platforms fashion allowed. She knew she could never afford to dress like a model—Howard was fairly wealthy but to outfit herself in the best, she would need the indulgence of a multimillionaire—but a hundred dollars, even today, could buy first-quality footwear. She knew she could look down anytime and see as shapely a leg as any man could find anywhere and, at the end of it, as good, as sexy, as stylish a fashion accessory as any worn by any woman, regardless of social status. Eleanor liked that kind of equality. It excited her.

At her third store, trying on her fifth pair of shoes, Eleanor noticed Taylor Worth unabashedly appraising her as she inspected a pair of pumps in front of a mirror, and she felt a sweet, not unfamiliar discomfort in the pit of her stomach as she hiked her skirt up slightly and turned sideways to the mirror, facing him.

"Nice," he said to her, staring downward.

"It is a nice style, isn't it?"

"I meant the legs," he said and his eyes met hers. She blushed. He grinned.

"Oh," she said coyly. "I, uh, well, thank you." She stepped closer to the mirror, took a final look, glanced quickly at Taylor, and returned to her chair, where she slipped off the pumps and reached for her own shoes.

The saleswoman, bored and peevish, asked, "Is there anything else I can show you?"

"I don't think so," Eleanor said. "Thank you."

The saleswoman began gathering boxes.

Taylor, implementing a plan he'd formulated earlier,

selected two of the sexiest styles of high heels from a display and approached Eleanor. His stomach churned but not from fear, as had been the case with Erin, but from pure sexual fervor. He felt like a caveman. Eleanor was no threat; she was a victim. She wasn't wary; she was ready. She wasn't accustomed to advances and therefore prepared to rebuff him; she was flattered and eager to encourage him. This sort of thing just didn't happen to married ladies out shopping of an afternoon, except in dreams or maybe on the soaps.

"Pardon me," said Taylor, suppressing a rush of pure sexual power, holding the shoes by their slim heels—one an extravagant confection of sequins and criss-crossed straps, the other an elegant shoe with one band across the toe and thin laces for wrapping around the ankle. "Please forgive my forwardness of a moment ago. My intention was to be appreciative, not fresh." He gave her the same look he had given Erin, frank, appraising, and faintly condescending. She looked back at him like a girl who'd been asked for her first dance.

"I didn't think you were, uh, that's OK," she said.

The saleswoman stood up with an armload of boxes.

"Before you go," said Taylor, looking at Eleanor steadily, maintaining the connection between them but touching the clerk lightly on the arm, "may I ask a favor of you?"

The clerk sighed and Eleanor smiled and tried to talk, but couldn't quite get her mouth to work. Mentally she was describing him for later reference: about six feet tall, black curly hair, gray eyes, trim, athletic build, and a five o'clock shadow at noon, which meant a hairy chest, hair on his back, furry, luxurious hair everywhere.

"I would like to buy a gift," he continued, "but I can't tell what these would look like unless they're on a

WORTH WINNING

foot." He handed the shoes to Eleanor, who accepted them. "Would you model them for me?"

The clerk glanced at the two styles, frowned, nodded. "I'll be back in a minute," she said and walked away.

Taylor thought of the early books of Carlos Castaneda. He recalled a passage in one in which the sorcerer tells the apprentice about certain centers of power within the human body, one of which is located in the midsection, in the general area of the navel. In one of his trances, the apprentice sees a beam of power emanating from that area of the sorcerer's body, and via that beam the sorcerer is able to transport himself to the tops of the trees or to the bottoms of deep, otherwise inaccessible mountain crevasses. Looking down at Eleanor, Taylor felt the same power in himself, as if a huge engine in his belly were processing something as vital as light into a force that would envelop and absorb the woman. This was confidence, the seductive quality of certainty all women desire in a man, the element of self-assurance all women mistakenly believe all men are born with, just as they are born with external genitalia.

"Did you know," said Taylor, stepping over and perching on the clerk's stool at Eleanor's feet, "high heels have been proven scientifically to be the most potent sexual stimulant known to man?"

Eleanor crossed her legs and felt the slick friction of her nylons between her thighs, which she knew were visible to Taylor. Her own vision was somewhat occluded. Except for Taylor himself, whose wavy hair, dreamy eyes, and broad shoulders were perfectly in focus, the rest of the room appeared gauzy and indistinct. The halo, which she did not consciously apprehend, which she would not remember except as a hazy characteristic of the moment, consisted of auras commingling, hers and his, natural, magical human qualities that Ned would never believe existed—and which Taylor wished he could photograph. She reached down to remove her shoe, but Taylor took her ankle gently in his hand.

"Please, let me," he said, allowing his fingers to glide along the bottom of her foot.

"Certainly," she said, but only the tiniest bit of her voice managed to slide around the lump in her throat.

Taylor spoke and perhaps Eleanor even responded, although she could never recall the exact conversation because of the sexy thrill of having a gorgeous man at her feet, caressing her legs shamelessly, adjusting the straps of the evening slippers. Gradually, the first flush of enchantment subsided and she began to catch her breath, but her glands kept pumping out lubricating fluids despite her first small pang of guilt. She tore her eyes away from her footman and glanced furtively around the store, afraid someone from her neighborhood or from the club might see her, but the jolts of pleasure speeding to her brain up four-lane neural pathways from wherever he touched her, on her leg, her ankle, her toes, were too powerful to ignore. Besides, she hadn't done anything wrong, yet. She was flirting but flirting was healthy. She'd read it in *Cosmo*.

"There," he said, fixing the second shoe, running his hands up her calves quickly before leaning away from her. Surprisingly, Taylor found his voice a little shaky. He had been concentrating on tactile sensations, picking up tiny charges of sexual electricity through his fingertips, feeling the always pleasant slick-smoothness of nylons. That powerful engine inside him had begun forcing blood to his groin, and he had to swallow once to maintain his composure. "Now it's time for the show." He took her hand and brought her to her feet.

Eleanor stepped to the mirror. The heels were at least

WORTH WINNING

four inches high, but her ankles didn't waver at all. She turned sideways to the mirror, saw the radical angle of her foot and the long shadow of her tightened calf muscles. "What do you think?" she asked finally, after finding her voice under bedsheets and pillows.

Taylor had retired to a nearby chair, where he sat back regally with one hand at his chin in a studious pose. "The legs are still the best part."

"Stop that," she said insincerely and turned to face him. "Of course this isn't the right sort of dress for shoes as fancy as these."

"So lift it up out of the way," said Taylor and Eleanor froze, bent over slightly in order to see her feet more clearly.

It was a straightforward invitation to come out and play. Eleanor stood up and faced him squarely with her hands on her hips and a scolding look on her face, but he only smiled, daring her with his eyes.

She glanced around the store once more, and her separate sensations—from her head, from her midsection, from her groin—all connected, interlocked, formed a contiguous internal network of brightly firing sexual impulses. She raised her skirt above her knees and further, several inches up her thighs.

"Mmmm," Taylor purred. He didn't open his mouth for fear the noise of the sexual riot in his brain would echo out into the shoestore, drown out the Muzak, and disrupt the carpeted quiet.

Eleanor turned and showed him her back. Then, because her knees began to shake, she took the chair beside him and tugged down her skirt. She felt drunk, out of control. She wanted him to speak, but more than that, she wanted him to kiss her, to lean forward, grab her, and devour her. He knelt down to strip off her shoes and Eleanor wanted him to continue with the rest of her clothes.

Taylor, fiddling with the tiniest of buckles, interpreted the color of Eleanor's aura and the aroma enveloping both of them correctly as signs she was his to do with as he pleased. He felt like growling. He wanted to sink his teeth into her thigh, and the damnedest thing was, he knew he could. He had seen the phenomenon before—a woman, eager for adventure, cutting loose her inhibitions with a single swipe—but it had always amazed him. He never understood how they could do it. How did she know he wasn't a psychotic? How did she know he wouldn't hurt her? She'd looked at him, talked to him for a minute, and judged him reputable, just like that, no hesitation, trusting instinct or intuition or whatever it was women called their flagrant disrespect for logic. He'd had maybe twenty quickie "zipless fucks" with women who didn't know him from Willie Mays, and every time he'd come away believing they were crazy. So conditioned by their own training to expect and welcome romance, they were willing to discount the man's conditioning, which is to do violence. He enjoyed the fucks all right. As a rule they were fabulously exciting, appealing to the impulsive, outlaw streak existing in every man, but afterward, without exception, he had felt, irrationally perhaps, cheated somehow. Supposedly, complete feminine surrender was the ultimate, the sexual ideal. Weren't power and sex, for the male, related? Wasn't dominance required for spectacular screwing? The manuals said so. The legends were full of words like conquest and triumph. So why did he mistrust that peculiarly feminine quality of unequivocal capitulation? Up to the moment of surrender, Taylor's lust responded equally to the woman's signals and his own cockiness, to the combination of wills, the intermingling of ideas, the simultaneous yet separate approach to a sexual peak. As soon as the woman gave herself up to him, however, he felt like a mountaineer whose climbing partner had collapsed.

Taylor flung aside the sequined sandal and fit Eleanor's foot into the second shoe style, looping the slender leather lacing around her ankle. It was a sexy moment, one which Eleanor would claim as her own because she was present; but was her claim legitimate? Taylor thought not because she hadn't participated, hadn't contributed anything but her body, which was required certainly, but which could have been supplied by any woman with a yen to be seduced, of whom there were millions. He had supplied the impetus, the energy, the will, all the intangible elements necessary for this episode to occur, elements which Eleanor, as a creature trained to react and respond, not act or create, could never acknowledge. He strapped her into the other shoe. He wasn't concerned about the possibility of temporary impotence—something other than his self-respect, a Mercedes, was at stake here—but the need for him, the man, to do all the thinking added something unnecessary to the act of love, made it less valuable, less a serendipitous moment of joy and more an earned reward. Perhaps Taylor was simply one of those men who despised responsibility, but he wished, contrary to legend, he could meet a woman for whom sex remained a shared sensual journey right up to the end, not a battle to be fought and strategically lost or a game in which she was a prize to be won.

Eleanor uncrossed her legs and Taylor heard the soft rustle of her nylons brushing against each another, smelled the musky scent beckoning his nose to the shadowy place between her thighs. He concentrated on her slim ankle, on tying the sexy bow of the extravagant bedroom shoes. He leaned away from her, inspected her legs, and whistled.

Eleanor was over the edge. She walked to the mirror, tall and proud, turned to face Taylor, and in one grand motion, swept her skirt up her legs to the legal limit and posed—front view, side view—until self-consciousness crashed in on her and she hurried back to her chair.

The saleswoman appeared. Taylor pointed to the shoes on Eleanor's feet. "We'll take them," he said, "and she'll wear them." He offered a credit card.

"You wanted to buy a gift," said Eleanor, straining toward him, shimmering with lust.

Taylor signed the credit voucher and chuckled. They walked out of the store together. "All a ploy," he said, "to look up your dress." He took her arm and entwined it in his.

Eleanor, disbelieving the events of the day but jealously holding onto the feelings, savored the slishiness between her thighs as she walked with Taylor, unheeding of their destination.

"You're right about that skirt not being right for that style of shoe," he said, steering her into one of the shops he had seen her browse through earlier and over to a rack of dresses with short skirts and open backs. "What size do you wear?"

"In those? Seven."

Taylor flipped through the skimpy garments until he found one he liked. "Here," he said handing her perhaps one half ounce of black wispiness.

Eleanor blushed and buried her face in his coat, inhaling him, coveting him. "I'd have to strip naked just to try it on," she whispered.

He grinned lasciviously. "You'd better."

Eleanor stepped behind a long partition and entered a changing cubicle. She hung the tiny dress on a hook,

WORTH WINNING

looked at it, hesitated only an instant, and started stripping off clothes. She stopped when she was down to her pantyhose and shoes, but hesitated again only an instant. This dress was for summer nights and one went barelegged on summer nights.

Taylor meanwhile walked away from the changing-room door in order not to call attention to himself. His cock was growing with every frantic beat of his heart, rising like a hydraulic jack. This wasn't just sexy, this was dirty. His brain fed him the same image, over and over, of Eleanor standing in front of that mirror, legs shoulder-width apart, sweeping her skirt up to her crotch. Again and again he saw the same motion, saw her sleek legs and those outrageous shoes and that seductive look on her face, the look that said, touch, now.

"Psst," hissed Eleanor, her head poking around the partition. "I can't come out there like this. I'm practically nude."

Taylor glanced around for suspicious salespeople as he moved toward her. "Got your shoes on?" he asked and she thrust out her leg for him to see. He caught his breath. No stockings. His cock surged again. "Then I'll come in there," he said.

She looked great. The dress was made for her slim, long, almost breastless body. It was a halter style, open down the front to her sternum, with a short, slightly flared skirt brushing the middle of her thighs. Eleanor didn't look quite relaxed in it, but Taylor didn't spend much time looking. He motioned her toward the cubicle, panting like a St. Bernard in August. She turned and he touched her bare shoulders. The dress had no back at all. He ran his fingers down her spine and she shivered.

He closed the door behind him and they assaulted each other. Her mouth, open, wet, soft, and deep, devoured him while his hands tried to touch every square centimeter of her at once. And then the dress was gone and she was standing on one of two low benches and he was slurping between her thighs. Then, pants down, he sat on a bench and she covered his cock with saliva. Then he was shushing her and she was shushing him while they thrashed against the insubstantial partition, his mouth to her nipples, her hands to his testicles. Then they settled on a position, giggling, shushing each other. He sat on one bench and stretched out his legs as best he could. His shirt was undone and his penis stood up like the mast of a schooner. Dressed only in shoes, a necklace, and wedding rings, she poised her cunt above his cock and, with a single downward thrust, absorbed him completely. She groaned from the vicinity of her soul, the place the head of his penis finally stopped, and bucked once and shuddered. Taylor opened his eyes to see a nipple crash into his face, and he came, thinking of his Mercedes-Benz, into seamless, viscous, illicit deliciousness.

CHAPTER FOUR

Veronica Bristow turned ten years old in 1964, the year of the Beatles' first American hit, "I Wanna Hold Your Hand." Economically speaking, that infamous decade might have been the best of times to grow up a lower-middle-class white girl in the USA, but spiritually speaking it might have been the worst of times, because at precisely the moment intelligent, easygoing Veronica began to assimilate the homey lessons of childhood, when she began to meditate on the meaning of truth, heroism, dignity, etc., the critical moment in adolescence when her murky amalgam of ideas and ideals was about to coalesce into conviction, to set up like a freshly poured sidewalk, a gang of blacks and hippies came along and wrote "Burn the Motherfucker Down" in it with their fingers. At the crucial time in Veronica's life when notions of goodness and rightness should have connected with the idea of nationalism, producing a solid concept of "us," the good guys, protectors of freedom, advocates of all those marvelous notions set forth in a pair of her favorite documents of Americana, the Declaration of Independence and the

Preamble to the Constitution, the sounds of the civil rights movement roared through her transistor radio accompanied by riotous rock-and-roll. She heard accounts of the investigation of a murdered President in which the government itself was implicated. She heard the noises of war interspersed with the protesting cries of children not much older than herself. She listened and read and asked questions, but received contradictory information at exactly the time she needed honesty, simple and straightforward. She would probably have matured into an entirely different person had someone taken her aside and told her the "facts of life" then and there, had trusted her intelligence enough to explain that truth and rightness in the "real world" are secondary to expediency, that greed motivates more people than moral rectitude. She could have managed that information—she knew the difference between a dog in a cartoon and her pet in the yard—but nobody bothered to speak to her. Instead, everybody yelled and when that amalgam of ideals finally did coalesce, a couple of dangerous mental gates were cemented in the open position, thereby guaranteeing a steady flow of anger through her hopes and beliefs.

Veronica arrived at college too late for the excitement of mass demonstrations, but she was in a prime position to watch Watergate and she became a junkie. Here it was, this was it, the perfect opportunity for catharsis when all the demons could be exorcised in a single stroke. The Vietnam War with all its lies and tragedies; the deaths of Martin Luther King, the Kennedys, the children at Kent State and Jackson State; and the hippies, the Yippies, the Panthers, and fifteen years of moral frustration could have been dismissed efficiently and expeditiously by discrediting, repudiating, convicting, and jailing one man. That Veronica's hopes were

WORTH WINNING

based on illogic didn't matter. What appealed to her was the simplicity of it all, and she prayed to every god for relief. She didn't want Richard Nixon stoned or tortured or confined cruelly or unusually. She simply wanted him denied the honors due a former President. One day in jail would have been enough, twenty-four hours of incarceration during which time he would have been subjected to the law and order he most fervently espoused and most arrogantly defied. This, for Veronica, would have been justice, grand and splendid and satisfying, and would no doubt have changed her from the bitter citizen she had become, wishing secretly and masochistically for some terrible judgment to befall her hypocritical country, into what she desperately wished she could be—proud of her society, eager to participate in its future, and contribute to its destiny.

Her friends were frightened by her obsession. She ate cheese and crackers in front of the TV while she cheered the good guys and booed the bad guys of Watergate. Her spirits rose and fell with the fortunes of the special prosecutors. She became a slave to the hearings, bound by testimony and tormented by deliberation. The mere mention of the word "lawyer" caused exquisite love-hate vibrations to thrum through her body. Then in 1974, after two full years of cruel teasing, she felt the climax coming on. The tension grew. She held her breath, clenched her teeth, writhed in torturous anticipation, and just before the glorious moment, the *petit mort*, when every molecule of her being strained for fulfillment and release, something happened. Her lover rolled away, lit a cigarette, and stared out the window as if nothing had occurred. The pariah had been pardoned even before he was accused of anything. He left the White House for his California beach house, where he received not only the rights and privileges of his former office but also obscene amounts of money, some of which was Veronica's.

Veronica felt more than scorned. She felt defiled, outraged. "They" had betrayed her by revealing honesty and respect for the law as fool's delusions. "They" had destroyed her faith. "They" had disdained her belief in honor and integrity as childish, unsophisticated, and naïve. Grow up, "they" said. At first she characterized "them" as society, but society was too amorphous an entity to hate effectively. Veronica wanted a target, something specific on which to concentrate her fury, but "the American electorate" was too broad a descriptor and "politicians," too narrow. Finally, she started thinking about who exactly ran the show, who was in charge, who, precisely, established and maintained the system that elevated vermin like Richard Milhous Nixon to the presidency of the nation. In order not to be sidetracked by philosophical considerations, she restricted her inquiry to tangible facts. When she closed her eyes and imagined "them," what did she see?

The image was almost too plain and too simple for her to take seriously, but she couldn't dispel it, and the more she concentrated, the clearer it became. The answer was as obvious as the cargo of a commuter train. "They" were white men in three-piece suits.

Veronica became a feminist.

Over the next several years, Veronica played, at different times and to varying degrees, a series of roles in the local movement: political strategist, social activist, day-care commando, benevolent altruist dedicated to loving the world to enlightenment, and devout demagogue dedicated to mass castration. Eventually, the work exhausted her, and by the time of her withdrawal from active participation, she had learned four things: First, that the struggle for equality would not be won in her lifetime and therefore must be considered a moral crusade rather than a tactical contest; second, that women are as much to blame for current problems as men and are as great an obstacle to change; third, that the antifemale bias is invidious and, therefore, constant vigilance rather than flashy demonstration is needed to resist it; and fourth, that despite overwhelming injustice, she would enjoy her life because too many of her good years had gone up in anger.

She hadn't given up the good fight—she was still available for counseling and the occasional discussion or workshop—but after eight years, she decided she'd had enough, not only because it took up so much of her time and energy, but because since the failure of the ERA and the military victory of Maggie Thatcher, people had forgotten that the initial thrust of feminism was concerned with sexual liberation, not politics. Too many of her sisters had been persuaded to forget their destiny would be determined at boxes entirely inappropriate for ballots. For Veronica, the situation was similar to the youth revolution of the sixties when the hippies, in her view, attacked the wrong institution. Duped into believing politics, not economics, decided the course of the nation, they assaulted Washington, D.C.—where the central issue was patriotism with all its implications for Iowa farmers and Peoria hardhats—instead of Wall Street, where the issue would have been money. Veronica felt the same sort of deflection had occurred, was occurring, in the women's movement. Women, she believed, in their eagerness for battle had abandoned their only stronghold, the bedroom, much too quickly.

Veronica saw the great "they" looking down and laughing at all the little political spats occurring on hundreds of different local and regional fronts. She could hear the head three-piece suiter saying, "If you want to struggle in the legislatures, then step right over this way, ladies, where we have a parliamentary expert who will argue with you till the moon turns blue," while the rest of "them" went about business as usual, exploiting everybody, not just women, because everybody agreed to play—and even fight—by their rules. The rules then, as far as Veronica was concerned, had to change and the only rules she knew were surely in women's control were those governing sex. In bed men were, no pun intended, exposed. They could hide behind neither their wallets nor their reputations nor their business acumen. In the words of Popeye the Sailor Man, they are what they are and that's all that they are, something Veronica had taken a long time to learn.

In high school her first love, a handsome jock, dropped her their senior year for a beautiful cheerleader. Afterward, Veronica decided she needed someone more mature, and during her second year of college, she found him, older than she by seven years, well-to-do, and happy to take her to grown-up places and do grown-up things. Unfortunately, his goal was to secure for himself an acceptable wife so he could get on with his father's business. He proposed. Veronica declined. Next she thought she might like someone a bit more daring, and she tumbled for a campus marijuana dealer who supplied her with plenty of excitement in the form of good concerts, better drugs, kinky sex—including a couple of orgies—gonorrhea, and, finally, paranoia. Once she regained her health, she wished for someone sensitive. He appeared, but turned out to be a wimp who ate all her food and moved in before he was invited. She threw him out. Her next fantasy was for an intellectual. She had been smarter by several quanta than any of her previous partners and she wanted a challenge, and when

WORTH WINNING

this finally came into her life, she thought she had found her man: pleasant-looking, well-read, extremely bright, socially aware, and funny. Veronica fell hard. Unfortunately, within a year he had made her crazy. With him, there was no such thing as a discussion, a sharing of ideas. Everything was an argument, and without agreement or capitulation by one party to the other's thesis, no argument could end. Whenever she lost patience with his carefully controlled games, he would accuse her of being hysterical, which prompted her to hysteria, thereby proving his contention. When she broke free of him, she felt like an escapee from a sane asylum, and it was then she developed her plan.

Realizing no individual male could possibly embody all the masculine qualities she wanted, and realizing with equal conviction she would never settle for anything less, Veronica resolved to seek those qualities in a number of different men, as many men, in fact, as were required. Just slightly ahead of her time, without having heard of either Alvin Toffler's or John Naisbitt's books, as yet unpublished, Veronica decided on her own to employ a Third Wave or Megatrend principle: networking.

Her current network, which she proudly considered an original artwork, consisted of: two intellectuals, a brainy, funny, socially awkward biochemical researcher, and a sharp nontrial lawyer working in the State Department; a beefcake who drove a truck for the Washington Post Company; a soul-mate, an aspiring writer who waited tables in Georgetown; and a businessman, a fast-moving salesman in a rival pharmaceutical company. Sometimes scheduling became a bit confusing, but she didn't see every man every week; and although she never bothered to explain the network to any of her partners, they all recognized her independence and more or less respected it.

Only one category remained unfilled in Veronica's network, the aggressor, the man who courted her because he wanted her specifically. This category she was precluded from filling. Ironically, she faced the same dilemma which had confounded Taylor Worth before he made the bet. Taylor wanted a woman who wanted him. He also wanted an unconventional woman. Therefore, for him to be convinced of a woman's honesty, she would have to seek, then court him. He was precluded from making the first move, which put him in a kind of negative situation. It was exactly the same for Veronica. In establishing her network, she had in most cases made the first move and often the subsequent moves. Because of her aggressive personality and marginal beauty, the passive role was as frustrating and unproductive for her as it was for Taylor, who picked up her trail on a Saturday afternoon.

He had been following her on and off for two weeks. He knew where she lived and the location of the offices of the pharmaceutical company she sold for. He knew she was on the road locally almost constantly, and that she was not exactly sex starved. In the relatively few hours he'd been able to observe her, he'd seen her with two different men who had broadcast, via body language, messages of physical possession.

As with Eleanor, Ned had been accurate in his description of Veronica Bristow. In a room full of average folks, she would not be conspicuous. She stood five three and was solid—not muscular but not fat, either. Her ass was OK but unspectacular. Her breasts, which she accentuated nicely in her choice of clothes, appeared to be in proportion to her height and body type, which, though pleasantly rounded, was altogether unfashionable in this era of the long and the lean and the anorectic. Her face, usually devoid of makeup,

WORTH WINNING 67

lacked classic high cheekbones, but her mouth was full and expressive. Her most exceptional feature undoubtedly was her hair: It was a rich shade of russet, darker than auburn but more iridescent than chestnut, very pretty, waving and curling busily, but not frantically, not quite to her shoulders. In the looks contest with Erin and Eleanor, she definitely came in third.

Taylor reviewed his strategy for the ensnarement of the feminist as he watched Veronica lock her apartment and get into her car: Meet cute and truckle. He planned to wear his chauvinist guilt as prominently as adulteresses once wore their shame. Taylor likened modern feminists to oldtime preachers, more interested in finding penitents than converts. He would beseech her to enlighten him.

Veronica was poring over the meager selection of February fruit in the produce section of a grocery store when Taylor appeared beside her.

"Nice pear," he said, looking unabashedly at her chest.

Veronica, always a sucker for a novel approach, withheld the scorn that popped immediately into her mind and took a moment to look Taylor over. Expecting to find a jerk, she was surprised, and pleased, to see an attractive man in a soft gray sweater that matched his friendly eyes. She decided to play along. "Why, thank you," she drawled in her best Carolina whine, "I'm plum complimented."

Taylor grinned. There's nothing worse in the world than a failed joke and Veronica not only got it, she responded with one of her own. Oh, hooray, he thought, a feminist with a sense of humor. Isn't that a contradiction in terms, like odorless paint? "You deserve it," Taylor replied proudly. "You're berry pretty."

Veronica had had fantasies of meeting a man this

way. Word games were among her favorite pastimes and very few people appreciated them. "I declare," she smiled back, "you're raisin my blood pressure."

Taylor had planned to proceed from the introductory jokes directly into a feminist rap: "Aren't you Veronica Bristow? I heard you speak at a panel discussion. I wanted to talk to you then but . . ." He wasn't prepared for a pun competition. He grabbed a handy melon. "Then kiss me my little canteloupe. Squeeze me honey, do."

Veronica laughed out loud and pushed her cart away from him down the aisle while she tried to come up with a worthy reply. She noticed a package of dried fruit. "Oh pshaw," she said, maintaining her southern drawl, "you're just teasin'. You don't care a fig for me."

Taylor, unaccustomed to intellectual challenge from anyone, especially a woman, groaned out loud and scanned the rows of fruits and vegetables quickly. "Perhaps you'd be convinced of my sincerity," he said when inspiration finally struck, "if I asked you for a date then." Perfect, he thought. She has a nice, graceful exit if she wants to take it.

Veronica was impressed, but she was way ahead of him with puns at hand and puns in reserve. "I don't know," she said. "You look pretty seedy to me."

"There's not a kernel of truth in that," he shot back. "I have firm roots in the community." This was fun, much preferable to "Hi, my name's Taylor Worth. I'm a computer programmer. What kind of work do you do?"

"I wonder how long it'll take me to digest everything that's been said here?" Veronica asked and her eyes twinkled.

Ned had given Taylor the impression Veronica was a harridan, but the only thing he'd been right about was her looks. "I haven't said anything that's gone against the grain, have I?" he asked, tearing a green grape from a bunch and offering it to her.

She ate it and nodded gratefully. "No, but you do have a rye sense of humor."

Taylor shook his head. "You're exceptionally good at this," he said, but he had no intention of giving up. It had become a matter of principle. "Well, I always say rye is better than corny."

Veronica's shoulders sagged. "So are you." Puns are like radioactivity. The damage they do can't be assessed immediately. "I'm frankly a-maize-d," she said carefully.

"Aurggh," he said. It was getting to him, too.

She said, "We must stop soon. It's driving me bananas."

Taylor recoiled involuntarily. "Back to the fruits, eh?" he said, casting about for an answer. "I'm not getting out of lime, am I?"

Veronica smiled but shuddered. The competition was getting brutal. "I have to get to the vegetables," she said, "because you're squashing my self-respect."

Who is this girl? Taylor wondered. Panic seeped into his mind. He had drawn a blank.

Veronica recognized her opponent's hesitation. She smiled triumphantly. "I can see you're exhausted, so may I make a proposal?" She held up two fingers in a gesture popular during the sixties. "Peas," she said, grinning.

Taylor's breath went out of him. He felt as if he'd run and lost a long race. He slumped against a bin of onions, but his brain lit up. "I wish I could believe you but I think you're chiving me."

Veronica's eyes narrowed. "OK, buddy. I gave you your chance but now I'll have no mercy. I want you to know this is nothing personal, that I don't relish what I have to do to you, but I've mustard all my resources and I know I can beet you."

Taylor took the puns like a triple blow to the midsection and slumped to one knee, acknowledging defeat. "Not the condiments," he pleaded. "Please not the condiments. I couldn't compete. Already my resolve is beginning to leek."

Veronica threw back her head and laughed. "I can taste victory. You'll never ketchup now."

"I'm afraid I'm done for," Taylor whimpered. "I feel like I've been maced."

Veronica moved in for the kill, unable to resist one final salvo. "I'll try not to get caraway with this, but my mother gave me some sage advice. She said to keep your kind at bay. Therefore, friend, your thyme is up."

CHAPTER FIVE

"To praise the delicacy of Oriental porcelain is redundant, like praising the fluffiness of clouds or the endurance of the ocean." Byron Busby held a cup from Eleanor's tea set up to the light of the window at arm's length. "It sings its own song. Listen." He pinged it with his fingernail and it rang, but dully.

"Isn't he wonderful when he waxes eloquent?" Randall Danforth asked, carefully placing his own cup in its matching saucer. "Even when he confuses his images. You're thinking of crystal, dear. He used to speak that way about me. I was his inspiration then, when we were young, before this accursed, ubiquitous flour settled into my deepening wrinkles like the dust of ages." He brushed invisible particles from his manicured hand. "Well, isn't someone going to compliment me? Byron? We notice *your* poetic utterances. He'll sulk if we don't. I think it was a delightful image, but mine don't count, is that it? I'm just an old woman, prattling to myself. It's fine if you go on ignoring me. I'll just slash my feeble wrists with this lovely little knife. Vertical lacerations are most effective, aren't they?"

Byron picked absently at his boutonniere. "The wrinkles on your hands are not your only dust-encrusted cracks, love," Byron answered, raising an eyebrow, curling a lip.

"Well, aren't we being intimate today?" Randall protested.

"Now, now," interrupted Eleanor, pouring more tea for Randall. "Another croissant, Byron?" she asked appeasingly.

"I really shouldn't," said Byron, reaching for a pastry with pudgy, elaborately ringed fingers. "But I must decide exactly what's wrong with them. Not that they aren't good. They're very good, aren't they, Randall?"

"Oh, quite, but I do agree," he said, taking another for himself, regarding it critically. "Something is not right." He tasted the crescent-shaped roll and chewed thoughtfully. "You don't think . . ." He let his words trail off.

Byron's eyebrow shot up again as if following the pointed direction of his little finger. "I was thinking the same thing, but no one would dare, would they?"

"Not, and pass them off as genuine croissants!" Randall munched again. "But there's a definite greasiness about them."

Byron nodded definitively. "It's criminal what some bakers will do to cut costs."

"Not everyone is as fastidious as you, Byron."

"If you're not willing to do something properly, then you shouldn't do it at all," Byron said, popping the last bit of crust in his mouth. Randall leaned forward and brushed an errant crumb from Byron's chin.

"But what is it?" asked Eleanor, concerned now. She had purchased the croissants from the best specialty bakery on this side of town. She was always careful to buy the best of everything for her luncheons with her two eccentric friends. These treasured get-togethers were her only real opportunity to indulge in elegance. Her husband, Howard, regarded all domestic refinement as profligate. If he weren't required to give dinner parties at home, Eleanor knew their china would be sold and the money invested in "useful" things, like stocks and bonds. To jeopardize her afternoons with Byron and Randall was therefore unthinkable. She nibbled a croissant. "They're not . . ."—she nearly choked on the word—". . . inferior, are they?"

Randall patted her knee and allowed his hand to remain there to caress the silk of her colorful Japanese pajamas. "Don't worry, dear, there was no way you could have known."

Eleanor fretted.

Byron dabbed his mouth with a linen napkin. "Unclarified butter," he announced triumphantly after a proper interval of silence. "The pastry chef, if he dares to call himself one, used unclarified butter in these croissants. It accounts for the slightly heavy texture."

Eleanor touched her hair. It was bobbed and held in place with a pair of cloisonné barrettes. "I wish *you* would bake specialty items. You could do them so much better than anyone else."

Randall placed his other hand on the sleeve of Byron's wool suit, and allowed it to play there. He took a moment to savor the contrasting sensations reported to his brain through the fingers of his two hands, then he returned to the conversation. "No," he said. "We will not, will never, and for the same reasons this baker should not. A patisserie is too demanding. I'm afraid we'd never have time for anything else. For each other. For you. No. When we began our business we agreed to specialize. Bread it would be and only bread. But the best bread. Isn't that right, Byron?"

For once, Randall's boast was not immodest. The Queen's Bakery, which he and Byron had established eight years previously, after they had become moderately wealthy and monstrously bored with food service—each was a qualified headwaiter, both had worked as *maître d*'s at quality hotels and clubs in the Washington, D.C., area—produced excellent bread for the restaurant trade. It was not incomparable bread, but it benefited from a reputation for exclusivity, which was invaluable in a status-conscious market like the District, but which initially was strictly unintended. They had started small in order to guarantee sufficient quantities of fresh bread to their few customers, but their decision to control growth was misinterpreted. Soon their bread became known as the best simply because it wasn't available to anyone who wanted it. It could not be purchased at retail, and Randall and Byron, by default, acquired the luxury of selecting their clients. To their credit, they still worked five days a week, Randall in the office, keeping a close watch on expenses, and Byron in the plant, keeping a close watch on the recipe.

The first house they bought together, which they still owned and rented but from which they had moved several years before to a better neighborhood where their peculiar life-style would be tolerated or at least benignly neglected, was next door to the Larimores', and Randall and Byron had remained loyal to Eleanor since she befriended them when it seemed as though the rest of the suburbanites, Eleanor's husband included, were ready to lynch them. The friendship flourished because Eleanor never mixed Randall and Byron with Howard Senior socially, and promised always to keep them away from Howard Junior, which was easy because like his father, the boy was away from the house during the day, the only time the bakers could visit.

WORTH WINNING

Their workday began at two or three A.M. and ended at nine or ten A.M., after which they could begin socializing, which consisted of things like Weekly News and Reviews, a combination gossip session and dress-up party with Eleanor. Fresh flowers were always present as well as at least two bottles of wine. Little gifts were frequently exchanged. Their afternoons were chic and genteel, sumptuous and luxurious and deliciously bitchy.

"Well, who should we talk about first?" asked Byron gleefully. He and Randall provided gossip about Washington's rich and famous, which they gathered from their friends at the restaurants; and Eleanor provided gossip about the old neighborhood and Howard's family, a favorite topic, since Byron and Randall in the old days had front-row seats for family gatherings at the Larimore house.

Randall began. He spoke of an aging Washington celebrity who "insisted on wearing these outrageous low-cut gowns, exposing her bony, liver-spotted chest as if she had breasts that would be of interest to anything but a starving goat" and whose hair "had the color and texture of Owens-Corning fiberglass insulation," while Eleanor listened politely, sipped conservatively at her tea, and struggled mightily to contain her secret, which clanged and banged inside her head like an enraged animal.

Since her escapade in the undressing room, she had changed her mind about telling her friends more times than a congressman caught between lobbyists. At first, she resolved to keep it to herself, like a child's treasure; then she decided to tell all, down to the last gooey detail, as much to entertain her two confidants as to relive the experience herself, which never failed to start her juices flowing the way they hadn't since she was a teenager. Then she reconsidered, frightened her infidelity might upset Byron and Randall; then she feared that to conceal the story would constitute another infidelity, perhaps more deceitful than the "affair." After all, she felt closer emotionally to them than to the Howards, and to jeopardize that intimacy might be less honest than a quickie, afternoon fantasy fuck with a handsome stranger that she was sure was a one-time aberration to be replayed in memory only when she wore those particular shoes or caught a chance whiff of that spicy cologne he wore or . . .

"Don't you agree, darling?" Randall asked, snapping her out of her reverie.

"I'm sorry."

"Are you all right, dear?" asked Byron. "You look absolutely radiant but you seem so far away."

"Perhaps we should open the wine," Eleanor said. "I have something especially juicy to tell you but I'm afraid I'm going to have to get a bit juiced before I do."

After some wine, she recounted her adventure, and Randall loved it, but Byron, the more traditional of the two, received it less enthusiastically. "Don't pay any attention to the sour old puss," said Randall, encouraging Eleanor to reveal more details. "He has this archaic thing about motherhood. It doesn't have anything to do with you or Howard or Howard Junior. It has to do with the shining ideal of motherhood. You must close your eyes to appreciate this. Picture her now, the Immortal Mother, resplendent in lacquered hair and gingham apron, clucking nurturantly, scurrying about that great laundry room in the sky, selfless and—and this is critical, darling, absolutely indispensable to an understanding of our dear Byron—utterly sexless. Elvis Presley had a similar problem. He couldn't perform with his wife once she gave birth. She'd become a mother, you see, angelic, inviolable. Harry Houdini was of the same school.

WORTH WINNING

And at least one of our Presidents, the enormously fat one I believe, but none of that matters. Please go on. Tell us more about this daring Lothario. Do you think we'd like him? Would he like us?"

CHAPTER SIX

"Given the same exceptional good looks, not another ounce of brains, and a different set of parents, Erin Dolan might have been a TV star or something else dynamic and marketable instead of merely a highly paid receptionist, but her mother and father, good Catholics, fawningly obsequious, terrified of and insulated against the outside world by a family as tightly knit as a warm sweater, instilled in her a fondness for mediocrity disguised as humility which prevented her not so much from seeking excellence as from recognizing it, or her right to it at all. Discounting a few lapses and allowing for modern social mores and the opportunities for adventure automatically hers by virtue of her beauty, Erin was basically a "good" girl, thus an anomaly, thus universally misunderstood by males because, like Taylor, they assumed she was spoiled beyond redemption, and by females because, out of envy, they distrusted her genial disposition and sincere friendliness. If Erin had appreciated her body, had understood what it symbolized, she might have been able to respond to the expectations of strangers, to fight manipulation with manipulation, bitchiness with bitchiness, to slap a few faces and bust a few balls, but steeped like a tea bag in uncritical, familial love, she not only lacked sophistication, she also resisted sophisticating influences, preferring to rely on a tried and trusted feigned immaturity, an informed ingenuousness like a debutante's, but without the debutante's hard inner shell of world-wisdom. Erin accepted favors and attentions—gifts, dinners, trips to the Super Bowl—not as if they were her due but as if they were every good girl's due, and, as might be expected, she found her share of trouble upon her emergence into the "real" world. She was slapped around once by a man with whom she would not go to bed after the third expensive date; she was raped by a different man on a sultry night in the Bahamas who, before they left for the weekend on his company plane, had promised her a room of her own; she lost two good jobs because of the envy and animosity of other female office workers who suspected her of being the boss's whore, which she wasn't, and so on. Eventually, she learned what to expect and what was expected and settled into her current job with the Washington professional football club. When she accepted the position, she promised herself she would not sleep with anybody associated with the team, and after months of tussling with the boys, resisting passes, tackles, and front-office pressure, suffering all manner of teasing about tight ends and backfields in motion, she established herself as the team virgin, solidly protected by both the defensive and the offensive lines. If someone affiliated with the club honestly needed a date, she would oblige and in this arm-charm capacity, had enjoyed the company and favors of plenty of interesting men, but if anybody threatened to grab her, all she needed to do was cry foul and she would be rescued or at least avenged. When

Taylor met her, therefore, she was once again, or still, cloaked in uncritical love, pampered, protected, and, except with respect to the specifics of her job, undisciplined. That's why, on Thursday, when she was supposed to meet Taylor for dinner, she half-forgot about it, didn't bother to take the date seriously, didn't decide actually to go until eight o'clock, at which time Taylor had already been at Montaldo's for twenty minutes.

He expected her to be late. Fifteen minutes was fashionable. At thirty minutes, he was nervous but hardly discouraged. It was not inconceivable to Taylor that a girl like Erin could keep some men waiting for years, but at forty-five minutes, he began to lose his temper, and when nine o'clock came, he went to his table and ordered dinner. Ned would, no doubt, hold him to the exact provisions of the bet. Erin had accepted—and that was the key word, accepted—a date with him and was therefore officially part of the trio. Taylor tried to swallow his anger with his soup.

The cocktail waitress in the lounge had been exceptionally nice to him. He hated her. A woman at another table, across the restaurant, flirted with him. He hated her. He hated them all, the gaping, voracious cunts who greedily ingested everything men had to offer, not just money and flowers and houses and cars and whatever materially was left after men worked themselves to death to please and satisfy them, but creativity, too, and resourcefulness and wit and cleverness—in other words, the essence of everything good. They were lifesuckers, self-serving and ever-consuming, the original black holes of the universe. Taylor drank wine and seethed. He ate *escargots* and fumed. Here he sat, Taylor Worth, mature, handsome, bright, self-sufficient, prepared not only to pay for the privilege of sitting next to but also to exhaust his reservoir of charm to entertain a female whose absolute right it was to soak it all up without offering anything in return. Here he sat, as docile as a Labrador retriever, eagerly slobbering in anticipation of being jumped through hoops by a bitch who neither noticed nor appreciated the risks he took or the obstacles he overcame to meet her, whose body, whose physical form, a genetic gift, was valued above all else on the planet. Taylor was enraged. Women and children first, said the stewards aboard the *Titanic*. Why? Could anyone tell him why women were more valuable than men? No women are to be allowed in U.S. combat units. How come? Young men are bred to grow up and go to war, to have their bodies shredded and blasted apart, but never women. Oh no. General George Patton said something about ". . . when you put your hand into a pile of goo that a minute before was your best friend's face." Why is it more acceptable if the face once belonged to a male? For Taylor, these were legitimate questions nobody bothered to answer, yet here he sat, wallet open. Here, woman, take, take, take. I'll gladly pay, money and attention, just to look at you for a moment, because your body is so precious.

"Sir?" the waiter said.

Taylor jerked upward. So furious was his concentration, his head had been mere inches from his plate. He had forgotten entirely where he was.

"Are you finished with your appetizer, sir?"

"Yes. Take it away."

Taylor dabbed his forehead with his napkin. He sighed. He had needed that. A little catharsis. Let the old anger out. Call the cunts what they are, recognize them as the enemy. Taylor looked around the room again, attended the low drone of conversation and the bright noise of silver striking china. He took a deep breath and a sip of wine. Now he could think clearly. He would

WORTH WINNING

win that goddam Mercedes and the blond goddess Erin would in part pay for it.

The problem of course was how. How could he get to her? What could he possibly do to impress her? He could take her places and give her things, but a broad like that received gifts and invitations like other people received junk mail. Taylor understood that a woman's fantasies were more important than reality, but what could this girl possibly want? Taylor toyed with his salad. Before she stood him up, he had decided to go the old-fashioned courtship route, to worship her, but now that particular approach was out. She had insulted him and if he played the sycophant, he couldn't expect her to fall for him. She'd undoubtedly seen that type before, and if that was what she wanted, she could find richer men than he to lead by the nose. What universal good thing then could she be lacking? Taylor took out his notepad and pencil and wrote them down. Love: the ultimate objective, not immediate enough. Respect: too vague, could mean anything. Honor: women didn't give a shit about honor. Fame: impossible to bestow. Taylor tapped his nose with a finger. The waiter took away the salad plate. Security: too involved with wealth. Challenge: who was he kidding? Adventure: bold was probably her lipstick color. The waiter delivered the entrée. He put down the pencil and took up his knife and fork. The aroma of the lamb made his mouth water. What else? Taylor caught the eye of the flirting woman again and repressed a desire to splat mint jelly in her eye. He tasted his lamb and chewed appreciatively. Get down to serious matters, he told himself. What would *he* value and welcome more than anything else from a member of the opposite sex, from a member of his own sex for that matter? What is it that everyone can always use more of but is impossible to buy? Taylor knew there had to be something, and it came to him like a revelation. Just before Erin entered the dining room on the *maître d*'s arm, he jotted it down on his notepad: Friendship.

Taylor looked at his wristwatch as he stood and waited for her. She was almost two hours late.

Erin launched a series of apologies like cut-rate fireworks that popped and fizzed ineffectively. Taylor, without humor, returned to his lamb chops. "Would you like a drink?" he asked dispassionately, barely acknowledging her excuses.

"Will the lady be having dinner?" asked the sneering waiter.

"No," said Taylor definitely. "But a drink would be nice. Erin?"

"White wine, please." She allowed the slightest hint of petulance to color her voice. She reached for the breadbasket and selected a roll. "Pass the butter, please."

A Kirlian photograph would have revealed considerable incendiary activity as Taylor's and Erin's auras clashed and rasped against each other. Taylor wanted to backhand her, to watch tears smear her artfully applied mascara. Erin wanted to do no damage, but she wanted the awkwardness to end, and she was certain it would because if he made no accommodating gesture, she would use her most potent weapon in any confrontation, her physical presence, which seemed to be of supreme importance, positively or negatively, to everyone. She would simply absent herself.

Taylor knew it would not do to antagonize her because every beautiful woman he'd ever met had the same defense mechanism as standard equipment: If she were wronged, heaven could wait; there were no accidents, only negligence. But if she did wrong, then let's be reasonable; what's done is done and should be forgotten. He gulped his wine and welcomed the desiccating effect of the Saint-Estèphe. If now his wit could only match the wine's dry subtlety. He finished his last bit of lamb, placed his knife across his plate, dabbed his mouth with his napkin, smiled at Erin while he chewed and swallowed, and sat back comfortably in the booth. "Well, what do you think?" he asked brightly.

"What do you mean?"

The waiter arrived with her drink and cleared the table. "Coffee, sir?" he asked.

"Please, and a glass of port." He addressed Erin again. She looked stunning. Her hair was piled on her head and twin thin tendrils curled down her cheeks. She had chosen a Victorian look for the evening: a long-sleeved blue dress with a high collar, a bit of lace and a cameo brooch at her neck. Her eyes, reflecting the dark color of the cloth, were larger than Taylor remembered and carefully lined and shadowed in shades of blue. He looked away for a moment, to regain perspective and to warn himself to look into, not at, this girl. Everyone else looked *at* her, stopped right there, and reacted with envy or admiration or lust or covetousness. Taylor reminded himself to act, not react, to probe, to continue beyond the startling beauty, to resist the automatic impulse to become self-conscious in the presence of physical flawlessness. He tried to keep the word "friendship" between himself and her. Cynically, he judged as slim the chances any honest humanity remained within that spectacular human form, but he remembered his Mercedes, *his* Mercedes, and peered again into those cerulean, no, make that cobalt, starbursts.

"I mean, what do you think?" he said, as gently as he could.

Erin turned up her nose. "I've already apologized. If you expect me to . . ."

Taylor shook his head and cast down his eyes. He patted her hand patronizingly. He tried to look resigned, even plaintive. "No, Erin, no more of that."

Applying what little he knew of Method acting, Taylor concentrated on how he felt the morning after starting a new exercise program. He willed himself to look old. "May I tell you a story?" initiating a practice that would become routine with Erin. He took his hand away from hers, toyed with his cordial glass, and stared into the candlelight. "There was once a handsome man. And because he was handsome and well suited to deal with the affairs of living, everyone who saw him assumed his life was wonderful. To other men he was a business associate or a golf partner, and to women he was a good date, perhaps even a potential husband, but nobody knew him very well because no one cared to try to know him." Taylor paused, adjusted the studs in his French cuffs. "But this man didn't give up on people because he thought perhaps there were others elsewhere who felt as he did. Therefore, he kept trying to meet people outside his business, outside his circle of acquaintances, and sometimes he was quite clever about it." Taylor glanced at Erin out of the corner of his eye, but she maintained an expression of impatient distraction. "Despite his attempts, though, he continued to eat his dinners alone."

Taylor lifted his glass and drank, then he turned his sorrowful countenance to the blinding radiance beside him. "I'm not angry you were late, Erin. It seems to be the prerogative of exceptional beauty. But I can't deny that I'm disappointed. Not," he added quickly, "in you—please understand that—but in me." He smiled wistfully. "I suppose my hopes are interfering with the proper functioning of my radar. When I saw you, Erin, I saw past your loveliness, at least I thought I did, to

. . . well," he said, breaking the monologue, changing his face, reaching for his coffee, "what could I say that wouldn't sound like a line you've heard hundreds of times before?" He tried a smile. "Let's just finish our drinks, shall we? and call it an evening."

Erin indeed had heard every line in the world, but she was enough of a good Catholic girl to accept a couple extra kilos of guilt when they were offered. Also, this particular rendition of the poor-me routine was similar to one of her own lamentations. Nobody, it seemed, ever wanted to get to know her, either. Erin placed her hand on his. It was a ploy that always worked. Some of the nation's strongest, most forceful men had puddled under her merest touch. "Say what you were going to say."

Taylor jerked his hand away from hers. "I must be getting too old for all this, Erin. Your touch just now, was it an honest gesture or something you knew would soften me up?" He signaled the waiter to bring the check. "Beautiful women don't have to be honest, do they?" He asked abruptly. "Of course they don't. No more than rich men, I suppose." He became more animated. "But doesn't it ever get to you, Erin?" Suddenly he was sincere. This was pure Taylor Worth, shining forth like the beacon of righteousness. "Don't you ever wish for someone who isn't trying to con you into or out of something? Men must wear you like you wear jewelry. 'Look at the gorgeous little bauble dangling here on my arm.' Don't you ever wonder if there's anything other than the old barter system?"

Taylor shut up when the waiter arrived with the check. He flipped a credit card onto the tip tray and refused to look at her. Part of him was afraid he'd gone too far with her, let his anger get the best of him. Another part of him didn't care—what he'd said needed saying—but through it all he knew if she reacted the wrong way, he'd have to backslide for the sake of the bet. Finally, with trepidation, he looked at her and saw that he had gotten to her. Bingo! Score another one for the Taylor Worth method. He thought he might publish when this was all over.

Now Erin wanted a hand to hold but couldn't force herself to reach out. An alien feeling swept through her that couldn't accurately be called self-consciousness because she was always self-conscious. With everyone looking at her all the time, how could she not be acutely aware of her gestures, her postures, the minutiae of her appearance? But this was different, strange, and discomfiting. She felt ugly for one of the few times in her life, as if, if she reached out her hand, it would be a grotesque claw, or if she tried to walk, it would be on clubfeet. Spontaneous tears sprang to her glorious eyes.

Taylor judged that his performance had devastated her. As he gave her the handkerchief from his breast pocket, he was positive he had spun the perfect web, a web within a web in fact, but he was wrong. It was the brief moment of honest inquiry that had tipped her over, not his acting or even the questions he asked. Erin had responded instinctively to what was unusual in her experience, the momentary, human-to-human contact his anger had inadvertently sparked.

He signed the check and gave her a minute to compose herself. "Let's get out of here," he said. "This place is oppressive." He led her from the booth to the door of the restaurant. She still hadn't spoken. "Did you eat at all this evening?" he asked.

"No."

"I bet you're hungry."

Erin nodded.

He smiled. "How about a hamburger?"

She smiled then and it took every bit of Taylor's willpower not to kiss her.

CHAPTER SEVEN

"Done. Finished. Ended." Harriet Ingram burst into Veronica's apartment like the annual Rose Bowl Parade. "I'll never have to see those people again, listen to their bitching, put up with their stupidity. I'm free, Veronica. Free! Do you hear me?"

"As Oscar Wilde said," said Veronica from the kitchen, "I 'overhear' you."

With a single grand sweep through the living room, displaying a talent peculiar to her, Harriet seemed to occupy every corner of every room of the apartment at once, as if she were, all by herself, a wild, mobile party or a matron with a scampering brood of children. With any of her other friends, with anyone else at all for that matter, Veronica, at the stove, her back to her company, would have a general idea where they were, but not Harriet, whose personality emanated outward and bounced off obstructions like a rampant radio wave in the mountains, confounding all proximate receivers. Harriet was a large girl but not fat, as one might expect someone with her special aptitude to be, and she was certainly ebullient—some might say loud—but despite her physical qualities, she was the only individual Veronica had ever known who could be described honestly as ubiquitous.

"Congratulations," Veronica said. "There's no feeling quite like quitting a job."

"A job? I feel as if I quit a religious order, as if, just this morning, I renounced solemn vows." Harriet occupied the kitchen, filled up every unoccupied liter of space with sound and her individuality. "And there were plenty of them, too," she announced, counting them on her fingers. "The vow of gossip, the vow of meanness, the vow of intransigence . . ."

"The vow of adultery," Veronica suggested unsympathetically.

"Oooh. Low blow," Harriet said, nipping an olive from a condiment tray. She had indulged in a brief affair with a married office staffer, and Veronica had never let her forget it. Harriet feigned a genuflection. "I yield to Our Lady of the Immaculate Reputation." She inspected the tray more closely, selected a cube of cheese. "I'm still not sure you're as guiltless as you say you are. How about that guy who was available only on alternate Thursdays, that political type you hung around with for a couple of months? You never came right out and asked him, did you? You wimped, played the old Ignorance Is Bliss game. I'm sure he was married."

Veronica didn't answer.

"And how about your latest acquisition, the guy you were so tickled about the other night? What's his name? No, don't tell me. It sounded like a department store. Lord and Woolworth? Is that it?"

Veronica poured salt into a kettle of water. "His name is Taylor Worth."

"Right. You went to lunch with him. I bet you let him put his hand on your leg."

WORTH WINNING

Veronica munched a marinated carrot from the tray and replied to Harriet's impertinence with a monumental frown.

"While he was fondling your thigh, did you ask him if he was married? Did you?"

"We're still a long way from an afternoon rendezvous at the Hit and Run Motel."

"But you accepted a date with him, didn't you?"

"No."

"Why not?" Harriet demanded. "You made him sound terrific. He asked you, didn't he?"

"Yes, but I'm booked this week."

Harriet threw up her hands and all the appliances seemed to come to attention as if waiting for a command from their conductor. "You and your stable," Harriet scowled. "Who's on the dance card this week? The poet and the iron pumper? Or is this the week for Mr. Wizard?"

"None of your business," said Veronica. "And what's with the third degree?"

Harriet carried the tray to the table. "Your lovers are like these goodies here," she said. "They're all appetizers. You meet a new guy, good-looking, funny, smart, a possible full-course meal and you pass him up for pepper jelly on a cracker."

"You're just jealous," said Veronica, opening the refrigerator.

"Sometimes, when I'm eating leftovers," Harriet answered, "but I don't know about you. You've told me a number of times your stable lacks the kind of guy who's confident with women. You said yourself none of your many current lovers would have had the balls to approach you on his own terms, that you had to encourage them, if not launch an outright assault. So here you find a guy who makes the first move—and a creative, witty, entertaining move at that—and you don't have room for him in your schedule. Excuse me for applying dishpan psychology, but if I were asked for an analysis—which I haven't been but so what?—I'd say we have evidence that Ms. Veronica 'Hard Case' Bristow is a little bit scared of a competent, well-adjusted male."

"I wish you wouldn't beat around the bush like that. If you have an opinion, just say it."

"That's what friends are for. Do you have anything to say in rebuttal or may I assume my analysis is correct?"

Veronica stuck out her tongue at Harriet. "Here." She handed her a plate of grated cheese. "Well, maybe you're right to a degree. I was put off just a tiny bit by his breezy, not to say arrogant, manner but, I don't know, there was something forced about the whole episode. It didn't seem to be exactly spontaneous. He *had* seen me before, you know—I told you that, didn't I?—at a panel discussion. Maybe you're right. Maybe I was slightly intimidated but he seemed so cocky. I got this weird idea he had set himself a goal, like he was going to meet a different woman every day for a month or something and so far his record was perfect. Do you understand what I mean?"

"These pickles are good," Harriet said, licking her finger. "Yeah, I know what you mean. Where any other girl would be flattered by the attention, you're suspicious. It comes with reading too much feminist literature."

Veronica threw a dishtowel at her.

Harriet caught it, folded it, and set it neatly on the counter. "Let's change the subject. Have you decided to quit your job and travel with me?"

"Do you have any other plans for this evening?" asked Veronica.

"Besides dinner here? No. I'm not going to celebrate

my voluntary unemployment by burning down Georgetown if that's what you mean. I'm going home after we eat, take a hot bath, maybe watch the late movie, and go to bed. I'm even going to set my alarm clock so that when it goes off in the morning, I can roll over, turn it off, and go back to sleep."

"Now *I'm* jealous."

"Why do you ask?"

Harriet was answered by the popping of a cork. Veronica came into the dining room with two slender glasses brimming with champagne. "To your career decision," she said. "Cheers."

The champagne was a special touch, but the dinner was an ordinary event. Harriet and Veronica, in an attempt to assure themselves of decent nutrition—neither of them liked to cook for one and usually didn't, opting for snacks or otherwise unwholesome food—had shared dinners regularly, at least twice and as often as four times per week, since Veronica had moved into the building.

Veronica placed her glass on the table and returned to the kitchen. "You certainly picked a strange time to quit. I would have waited a month or so, until spring arrived. I'm not sure I'd want to be idle during the dreariest time of the year. I'm afraid I'd get suicidal."

"I traditionally get these great bursts of energy in the spring and take to jogging and dieting," Harriet said. "I usually lose this surplus fat which drops my body from the 'Abundant' category into the 'Luxurious,' and men start sniffing around and I tend to grab them by the back of the head and direct those curious noses into fleshy folds and orifices."

"You ought to start an obscene phone service."

"Evocative, aren't I?"

"Ready for some pasta?"

"Only three or four hundred pounds, please. So I decided I'd quit when the weather was miserable so I wouldn't have an excuse not to sleep late, watch the soaps all afternoon, and lounge around in my nightie until dinnertime. Oh, Veronica, my fine friend," she exclaimed as she accepted a plate piled high with spaghetti and steaming mushroom sauce. "Well, it's been nice talking to you," she said, taking up her fork. "I'll be indisposed for an hour or so." She dove into her meal.

Veronica filled their glasses with clear, bubbling wine. "You're not going to loaf until you leave for Europe, are you? God, that sounds exciting. 'Leave for Europe.'"

"So c'mon along! What's to hold you back? Take a leave of absence from your job and we'll go together." She slurped an errant noodle and didn't wait for a response. "Actually," she continued, "I prefer to say, 'My departure for the Continent.' It sounds so much more sophisticated. But to answer your questions, no, I'm not going to loaf till I leave. Not that I don't have the disposition for it, mind you, but it would be imprudent, financially I mean, not to work a bit." A splatter of tomato sauce leaped onto her cheek and she dabbed it away with a paper towel. "It'll be easy to pick up a job. Everybody's looking for word-processor operators. I'll sign up with Kelly Girl or Manpower and work when I please. It's wonderful to have such a mobile profession. Now, quit interrupting me," she said and attacked her spaghetti again.

"You realize, in these tight economic times, extravagant vacations aren't exactly in vogue."

"Nonsense, my dear," said Harriet, affecting a lisp, "traveling to the Continent is always fashionable. Besides," she continued, dropping the phony delivery, "I was still in pigtails when the cool people were trekking the world with knapsacks on their backs. But why should I hoard my money? To feed it into the nuclear incinerator? To wait for the imminent international banking collapse to gobble it without so much as a burp? I am one of the billions of the world economy's interchangeable parts. The kind of work I do will get done whether I'm here to do it or not. When I want to do it again, there'll be plenty for me to do." She lifted her glass. "Wow, that was some sentence even if I said it myself." She finished her champagne, picked up the bottle, and refilled her glass. "So how about you? What are you saving your money for? And you must be saving money because you make lots more than I do."

"It's not the money," said Veronica, still working on her meal.

"But you'd like to make the trip, wouldn't you? Drink some stout and look up a few kilts in Scotland; sip some *vin ordinaire* and do some real French kissing in Bordeaux; take a day cruise down the Rhine; maybe take a side trip to Greece and the Aegean islands. Eh? No?"

Veronica ate silently.

"So what's the problem? Do you have your vacation planned?"

"No, I . . ."

"Well, then. Tell 'em you want to take some time without pay and make sure your passport is current."

"I can't just up and go like that. It'd upset the balance of everything. My life is so nicely organized now. I've worked for a long time to get all the elements in place."

"Aha," exclaimed Harriet. "Now we're finally down to it, aren't we?" She pushed away her plate. "OK, Veronica. I'm going to say this once and then I'm going to drop it. I promise. I'll never again try to convince you to go to Europe with me, but I'm going to take advantage of my new sense of freedom and have my final say." She put her elbows on the table and cleared her throat. "Veronica, my friend, I have heard and I sympathize with your ideas regarding women's liberation. I have heard your antimarriage speeches. I have heard your antibaby speeches. Also, I admit, as you have observed, to envying the variety of men you sleep with. However, I have known you for two years and I have seen your system in operation for about eighteen months, and I submit, respectfully, that your—how can I say this?—that your behavior with respect to your affairs is every bit as limiting, as stultifying, as, forgive me, dishonest as the least communicative marriage of convenience." Harriet reached across for Veronica's hand. "Now, believe me, this is the last I'm going to say on the subject, but if the best thing you can say about a situation is that it's nicely balanced, I have to believe you've enclosed yourself in a philosophical ring as tight and restrictive as any wedding band." She released Veronica's hand. "There. I've said it. I think you should open the stable doors, let the studs run free, and come on a long vacation with me, but it's your business and I won't mention another word about it. Period. Are we still friends?"

Veronica sat still and quiet for a full minute. Harriet was right, of course. Lately she'd been feeling less like a daring adventuress and more like a strumpet, a pass-around. And frankly, she was just begging for a case of herpes, or worse, by sleeping with men she knew were sleeping around as much as she was. "I hate being a grown-up," she said finally, apropos of nothing.

"I beg your pardon?"

"I don't mind making decisions. I like making decisions. But I don't like making every decision all the time."

"Ah," said Harriet, not understanding. "So we are still friends?"

"Of course we're still friends."

"Good. I feel like getting drunk. Join me?"

"What are friends for?"

CHAPTER EIGHT

Taylor wheeled his car off the beltway at its easternmost point, and he felt like a spacecraft being spun out of the solar system, away from the energetic sun that was Washington, D.C., into the serene, uninhabited reaches of the countryside. Too bad he wasn't driving his Mercedes. It would be nice to pilot a machine more capable of cornering than his ponderous Monte Carlo. The tires squealed. He let up slightly. Not would be, he told himself, will be. Maybe he'd have it painted. It would be pretty about the same luminous shade of blue as Erin's eyes. But there's a fine line between confidence and arrogance, he cautioned himself, so remain in the present. Pay attention to the here and now.

"You're being too mysterious, Taylor," said Erin, sitting beside him. On his recommendation, she wore jeans but naturally she had added a few high-fashion touches, like woolly leg-warmers over her Calvin Kleins and a pair of classy stacked-heel boots. "Should I be worried that you're kidnapping me?"

Taylor grinned at her. "You're certainly worth kidnapping," he said and meant it. Her splendid hair, in a single long, lazy twist, fell down the front of a black cowl-neck sweater, and she fondled it, played with it, caressed it as if it were a pet. Taylor experienced conflicting impulses, one to leap on her, the other to freeze her in amber to preserve and admire. Reluctantly, he wrenched his eyes back to the road and thought about his route—over the Patuxent River, through Galesville and Churchton to Franklin Manor, north of Herring Bay. Such fine, chowdery words, hearkening back to Colonial days when the Chesapeake River, for which he was headed, still ran blue and clear, replete with healthy fish instead of murky with the sludge of Baltimore and crawling with contaminated crustaceans.

"Where are we going?" she asked, reaching across, poking his ribs. "It had better be special. I don't leave work early just for any old date, you know."

"I'll give you a hint," Taylor answered. "We're on our way to witness a spectacular and colorful cosmic event, as ancient as the earth itself."

"Is it bigger than a breadbox?"

"You can cover it with a pea held at arm's length, but it appears to be huge."

"Hmm," Erin mused, stretching a strand of hair beneath her nose, clutching it with her upper lip to form a long, blond moustache. "I need another clue."

"OK. It happens only twelve times per year and its presence is associated with hysteria."

"Are we going somewhere to celebrate my period?"

Taylor laughed out loud. "I wouldn't have known that, would I?"

"You're not offended, are you?"

"Of course not." Well, score one for Erin, he thought, happy she was beginning to loosen up with him. He had devoted a great deal of what young parents called "quality time" to her—more than to Veronica or Eleanor. Veronica's sharp intellectual edge often cut unexpectedly and Eleanor's frenetic fucking wore him out. His strategy to keep his hands off Erin, to treat her as a gentleman should treat a lady—with flowers, gifts, phone calls, etc.—had served two purposes: First, Erin had begun to trust him and second, the inexorable pressure of sex was, if not off, at least relieved. It was a novel experience for Taylor and surprisingly pleasant. He wasn't required to perform, yet she was happy. Her happiness showed, so his reputation was safe. She was, in a sense, like money. As long as he had Erin, no one, especially Ned, would question anything he did.

"Did you know," she asked, "that the word 'hysteria' comes from the Greek word for uterus?"

"I didn't know that," he said, pleased again. Erudition was not one of Erin's strong points.

"Yup," she said, crossing her knees, tugging at her leg-warmers. "So you see, I have an excuse for being a lunatic. It's tradition. I'm supposed to be crazy." She fondled her hair.

"Aha," said Taylor, swinging the car onto a two-lane road, taking a typical country shortcut that added miles and time to the trip. It was the prettiest route, though, and considering the woman beside him, the time was right for pretty. "You've almost got it."

"Got what?"

"The answer. You've almost guessed where we're going."

"What did I say?"

"You said lunacy, which comes from luna, which means moon. We're going to see the moonrise."

"Oh," she said unenthusiastically. "I don't think anyone's ever taken me to a moonrise before. I've had dates for sunsets and even one for a sunrise but never for a moonrise. You're the first."

Erin Dolan, the classic American beauty, who remembered the events of her life as entries in a datebook, every experience associated with the name of the man who initiated the event, who paid the bill. "It used to come up late at night but it doesn't anymore."

"You're teasing me again."

"No. It's true but it's an old story. The full moon used to come up at midnight, but the sun got jealous and put a stop to it."

"Oh boy," Erin chirped, sliding across the seat, snuggling close to him. "A story. Tell me a story, daddy."

During their long evening of conversation at Burger King following their aborted dinner date, Taylor had learned Erin was not the type of person who asked questions. Like so many other beautiful women he had known, she simply was not inquisitive. Accustomed to being paid attention to, she did not pay attention. Taylor understood the phenomenon. Neither her prosperity nor her survival would ever depend on what she knew, so why should she attempt to learn anything? With respect to courtesy, she never thought to apply the golden rule because she received attention whether she wanted it or not. It was not something she needed to protect or encourage or be thankful for. It simply came to her, like oxygen in the air, so she didn't perceive it as something she should return. But comprehending the phenomenon didn't excuse it or make Taylor any happier to be party to it. Not only did he need to be appreciated himself, he despised being made to play the supplicant. His feelings, however—and as a man, he understood this—were unimportant. Emotional needs were the province of the female. Desires in men, he had known since he was a child, existed only as a mandate for action. As a male, if he wanted something, he could only be assured of getting it if he pursued it, gained it for himself. To hope, then, that Erin would spontaneously express interest in him or his job or his hobbies was absurd. Women were taught to attend to themselves, and later to children, not to men who could take care of themselves. Thus, he needed to do something to capture and keep her interest. Accordingly, he told stories, spun yarns, and made up fables to entertain her as well as himself.

"It's a story of the Druids," Taylor began, "a Celtic race. They built Stonehenge, as you might recall, with Merlin's help but that's another tale. Anyway, this was long before Jesus Christ, when the sun and moon were still gods with personalities and rivalries and free will." Taylor automatically placed his hand on Erin's leg and fingered the edges of her leg-warmers. Why, he wondered, were those ridiculous decorations so sexy? They served no purpose outside the dancer's rehearsal hall and they covered up rather than revealed. More enigmatic womancraft, purely cosmetic, intended to allure, provoke, mystify. The damnedest thing was, they did.

"The Druids, because they were terrific astronomers, were favorites of both the sun and the moon, but the Druids, dedicated night people, preferred the female moon and celebrated her, especially during the one night per month when she was privileged to rise full in all her glory. The moon, delighted with the Druids' devotion, naturally wanted to rise when the world was at its darkest in order to so impress her worshipers that they would forget the sun completely. Eventually, she devised a plan. She decided she would delay her appearance in the heavens by just a few minutes each month until, without the sun's knowledge, she would come up at the darkest hour.

"At first, the sun didn't notice because the moon was sneaky, but one day the sun rose bright and glorious as usual and not a single Druid was awake to show appreciation, and you can imagine how infuriated he became. All morning long, he sailed across the sky getting madder and more jealous, but the Druids slept till noon and when they finally stumbled outside, they shaded their eyes from the glare of daylight.

"Well, the sun knew something devious had happened and naturally suspected his old rival, the moon. The sun asked around then and discovered that the night before, the moon had risen unnaturally late and given a spectacular performance. The sun found out that the moon, after dancing brilliantly all night, was on the other side of the earth, sleeping off a hangover."

"Typical party girl," said Erin.

Taylor smiled. "Obviously, the sun wasn't about to allow the moon to monopolize the affection of his favorite people, so he made plans of his own. The next month, when the moon was ready to dance again, the sun planned to wait in ambush."

"Can we stop and get some popcorn?" asked Erin. "I like popcorn with a story."

"We have better treats than popcorn," said Taylor, patting her hand, "but later.

"So, when the appointed day finally came, the moon primped and made herself pretty, dressed herself carefully in her most beautiful golden gown, and waited for the sun to pass out of the sky as usual, but she was surprised—and so were the Druids—when time for sunset came and the sun still hung above the western horizon.

"Well, the moon of course became terribly worried. She knew she couldn't wait forever or else the oceans would overflow and the land would be flooded and her beloved Druids would drown, so she eased herself toward the rim of the world and when she peeked over, she saw the sun struggling to stay up but acting smug and triumphant."

"I know how the moon felt," Erin interjected. "I've known a few men like that."

Taylor frowned but continued. "On the earth, all the creatures were confused and the Druids were running around like crazy, half of them yelling at the sun to go down, the other half pleading with the moon to come up. The ocean's waves were pounding and rolling and still the sun held onto the sky and still the moon resisted.

"Finally the earth began to rumble and shake, and some of the other planets, afraid their graceful, heavenly dance would be interrupted, intervened. Mars, always in favor of a fight, allied himself with the sun."

"Just like a man."

"But Venus, heaven's only other woman, joined the struggle on the side of the moon."

"Hooray for Venus."

"The oceans pounded. The Druids panicked. The planets and animals prayed. Mars was slow to act because he was putting on his armor, but Venus, clad only in her shimmering nightgown, ran swiftly and threw herself at the sun which lost its grip on the sky and . . ."

"I know this part," recited Erin, " 'sank slowly into the west.' Right?"

"Exactly correct. But the effort was too much for Venus, who was being dragged down with the sun."

"Which she didn't like, of course, because she enjoyed showing herself off at night, too, the little exhibitionist," Erin said.

"Right again," said Taylor. "Have you heard this story before?"

"I'm a girl, remember?"

"That's one thing I couldn't possibly forget."

"Finish the story."

"So. Venus, expending her last ounce of energy, made a tremendous effort, reversed her spin, and called out to the moon, who lifted herself over the world during the last purple moments of twilight and, safe at last, rose golden and glorious to the cheers of the Druids and the relief of the oceans."

Erin clapped hands. "Hooray for the heavenly babes."

"And that's why, to this day, the full moon rises, every month, every season, without fail, just after the sun sets."

"No kidding?" said Erin. "That's neat."

"Uh-huh, but there's a twist to the story," Taylor said, steering the car through the last town before the water. "The sun punished Venus."

"Figures." Erin frowned. "What happened?"

"Because she came to the aid of the moon, Venus was never allowed to regain her natural spin. She could still dance within the solar system, but she would forever have to turn slowly east to west, opposite all the rest of the planets."

Erin wrinkled up her face. "Is that true? Does Venus spin the wrong way?"

"Isn't it like a woman to be contrary?"

Erin hit him on the arm. "Tell me. Is that true?"

"Trust me," winked Taylor. "Here we are," and he stopped the car at a tiny municipal park on the bay. He glanced at the sky. "The timing couldn't be better."

"Looks cold," said Erin, staring at the leafless trees.

"You brought gloves, I hope."

"Yes, daddy," she said sarcastically. "Just like you told me."

They had the park to themselves. Taylor spread the blankets, set out the treats, poured a cup of rum-laced cocoa, and delivered it to Erin, who stood where brown grass gave way to water, hugging her short fur coat to herself for warmth. She looked like a picture from a magazine or a scene from a movie, with her blond hair trailing out from under a funny felt hat onto the soft, honey-colored coat as if it were part of the fur, just textured differently and combed differently. The jacket stopped at her waist to allow a good view of her full, round behind, tightly packed into designer denim. Taylor's eyes blinked like a camera shutter, taking a mental photograph to add to his beautiful women collection. He filed the shot but his gaze lingered. She was incredibly gorgeous, a rare physical treasure, but one accustomed to special treatment. She hadn't offered to set up the picnic and as surely as Taylor knew the moon would rise presently from the waters of the Chesapeake, he knew she wouldn't offer to help break it down.

She took the cup eagerly and sidled up to it as if it were a campfire.

Taylor, perfectly warm in a medium-weight jacket, gestured to the water. "Pretty, isn't it?"

"Mmmm," Erin mumbled, sipping her cocoa. "Chilly though."

Taylor's misogyny, no larger than a mogul on a ski run just ten years earlier, had evolved into an enormous volcano, dominating the landscape of his psyche. It rumbled now, preparing to erupt. She couldn't be cold. The temperature wasn't that low. The wind barely rippled the water. It was difference she objected to. Her body, almost always near a mechanical source of heat or cold as the seasons required, was unaccustomed to change, and it was this, the change, not the temperature, to which she reacted. Taylor tried to put the lid on his frothing, overflowing disdain, but it was like trying to recap champagne. If she would, just for a minute, for the briefest second, suspend her obsession with herself and direct her attention outward. Her beauty was her power and her power was enormous. Taylor wondered how much love Erin could radiate or how much good she could accomplish if she spent as much time lavishing attention on other people or other things as she spent just on her makeup. Instead, he said, "Come over to the blanket. I have a second blanket to wrap you in." He had come prepared. He was not about to miss the moonrise.

Erin sat on a blanket in a blanket, a huge, quilted down one, and interrupted her pout only long enough to sip hot cocoa. Her hat was pulled down over her ears.

"Warm enough?" Taylor asked, scanning the horizon through binoculars for the first sliver of moonlight.

"My bottom's cold," she said.

Taylor put down the binoculars. "Lift up," he said. "I'll tuck the blanket under you. It's pure goose down, guaranteed to keep a nudist warm on Everest." Maybe she wanted him to wipe her ass, too.

She lifted. He tucked. She settled and asked for more cocoa. "I brought two pairs of field glasses," he said. "When the moon shows, you've got to look at it through them. You'll swear you'll be able to put a finger in a crater."

"How long before it comes up?" she asked, staring out to sea.

He looked at his watch. "If the National Observatory knows its business," he said, maintaining a jocularity he didn't feel, "this month's only performance of that timeless hit, that long-running favorite of stargazers everywhere, The Rising Full Moon, will commence in exactly twelve minutes."

"When does the orchestra begin the overture?" Erin asked. She had begun to warm up.

"It's already started," he said. "Listen. The reed section is down there, at the water's edge, and the woodwinds"—he gestured to the bare trees—"are behind us."

"You are clever, Taylor Worth," she said, "and you make good hot chocolate."

They sat without speaking, and Taylor soaked up the gentle sounds of the evening. He closed his eyes and his spirit left him for a moment, dispersing itself like molecules of oxygen, to mingle with the brittle grasses, nourish the already or still green weeds, and swap electrons with the river. Gradually his anger subsided. The night was clear, the moonrise would be worth the hassle of getting here. Don't think about her, he told himself. Just look at her. She's gorgeous. Soak up her beauty.

Erin, not as comfortable with the quiet, asked, "Do you like your job? Working with computers, I mean?"

Taylor's eyes blinked open. It was the first time she had asked about his work. He wondered if this could be the first glimpse of a new Erin. He scored another point for her tentatively, and answered affirmatively and at length. Taylor, more than a computer jock, was an advocate of the information revolution, perceiving in it the seeds of future miracles. He held forth for five minutes.

When he finished, Erin said, "I work with a computer. I have a word processor. I don't use it much because I'm not a good typist. I help the secretaries when they need a hand. It's fun, though. Do you have anything to do with word processors?"

Error. Error. Alarms went off in Taylor's head, and he hated himself for making a mistake he'd made hundreds of times before. Erin wanted his opinion like a zit on her nose. She asked the question, not to hear what he had to say, but to establish an introduction for what Taylor called an "I Story." I did this. I did that. When was he going to understand? He erased her latest point from his mental scoreboard. He wanted to tell her that her word processor was to his machines what a wooden spoon was to a food processor, but instead he concentrated on the horizon.

"Here it comes," he said suddenly. Without taking his eyes from his binoculars, he felt around the blanket for the second pair and handed them to Erin. "Oh, God!" he exclaimed. "Look. It's magnificent."

Erin put down her cup and took up the field glasses, adjusting them to her eyes, playing with the focus. When she finally settled down to concentrate on the image burning through to her brain, she understood Taylor's excitement. The moon, only slightly above the water but climbing fast, seemed to be rising from a shimmering pool, as if God himself, with invisible fingers, were fashioning a stupendous, shiny doubloon from a golden, molten ocean.

"Taylor," she gasped. "It's beautiful."

Taylor offered a silent prayer of thanks. If Erin hadn't responded to this, it would have been torture for him to continue seeing her. "Shelley called the moon 'That orbèd maiden, with white fire laden,' and in another poem, 'Bright wanderer, fair coquette of Heaven.' See. Even the greatest poets failed to find sufficient words."

"You're a charming man, Taylor," Erin said. "Come cuddle me under this blanket."

He slid in beside her and hugged her. As good as she looked, she felt better. His heart rolled over like a panda at play. He didn't know what women experienced when enfolded in a man's arms. He'd always heard it described as safety, shelter, protection. If that were true, he pitied them a sense of wonder they'd never know. A bunker could provide protection, but the sensation of Erin's body against his was joy in palpable form. It was feeling made real, emotion made physical. Taylor didn't believe he was odd or unusual to feel awe, to feel as if he had been awarded Erin's highest compliment, her open arms, the warmth of herself.

They watched the moon angle upward, apparently diminishing in size, gradually losing its golden hue. Their picnic area became bathed in a cold, colorless light, and the water beyond them became onyx in motion, streaked by a perfectly straight vein of silver running directly toward the moon.

"Thank you, Taylor," Erin said quietly, "for bringing me here."

Taylor changed positions slightly and guided her head onto his shoulder. Just as he was about to relax, though, to relieve some of the tension in his back, he noticed his right hand hovering above Erin's breast like a bird about to light. He felt as awkward as a schoolboy in a movie house balcony. He wanted to touch her; in fact, he ached to touch her, but he hesitated. It would be too casual a move. The time still was not right.

Erin smiled up at him, aware of his discomfort. Maintaining his gaze confidently, she placed her hand on his and pressed it to her breast.

Taylor shuddered. Erin's gesture was simple, even sensible, considering their postures, but he knew she couldn't have any idea how terrific it made him feel. As many breasts as he'd touched, furtively or boldly, cleverly or after having ripped open a blouse, the first move always made him feel something of a thief. It was a test of wills: his desire versus the woman's decision to accept or reject the touch. The tension invariably bred excitement in Taylor, but most of the time a bit of resentment as well. Too much responsibility was taken and given on both sides. Erin's tiny gesture, as natural as the moon, precluded the test, the tension, the resentment. Taylor loved her for it.

"It's OK, Taylor," she said. "You may. I trust you. Just be gentle. My period, you know. They're swollen and awfully tender."

"As full as the moon," he burbled. She didn't have the first thing to fear from his hand. Although if someone had cut off that hand at the wrist, it would have been able, all by itself, to tear off Erin's clothes and ravage her; as long as the status remained quo, it was as happy as a hand could be.

Erin reached up and took off her hat. Instinctively, Taylor buried his nose in her hair. A small voice in his mind asked: You had some complaint about this woman; would you restate it, please? He inhaled her scent, basked in her aura. He remembered Ned, practically crippled by the beauty he, Taylor, now held in his arms. He recalled the faces of other men who had seen him with Erin, full of disbelief, of unconcealed envy. The voice continued: Your complaint had something to do with the inaccessibility of beauty. What are you feeling now? Consult your hands. Run a quick check on your overall well-being.

CHAPTER NINE

"Hey, Casanova." Ned waved his racing form. "How's your love life?"

Taylor, threading his way through the gaggle of gamblers at Ned's bookie's posh joint, wondered how they navigated without looking up from their tip sheets. He had already bumped into two people, but he was the only awkward one in the room. Everybody else had a built-in radar system that allowed them to move from the tote board, through counter- and cross-currents of other intent, singleminded racing-form readers, all the way to the betting windows without accident or incident.

"Love life's doing fine," Taylor lied when he finally reached Ned.

"Perhaps we should shorten the time limit."

"Throw in your sailboat?"

Ned chuckled to cover an involuntary wince. The sailboat was in hock. He'd been forced to take a loan on it to cover a cash shortfall. "You look tired," he teased but it wasn't true. Taylor looked great. "Seems like you've lost a bit of weight, too." As far as Ned was concerned, the goal of the bet was accomplished. Taylor had reentered the world of the living.

Taylor smiled wryly. "I'm getting a lot of exercise."

"I'll bet."

"You already have."

Ned nodded but Taylor didn't know the half of it. For years—since his wedding day—he had maintained a special bank account he and Clara called his gambling account. The money in it was held entirely separate from family funds, and Ned's gambling proficiency was such that it often benefited the family, financing vacations and extraordinary purchases like the sailboat; but by agreement, Clara never asked about it nor expected to be told about it. Currently, the gambling account was running low.

"I feel lucky today," Taylor said. "What's the hot tip?"

"There's a good horse at good odds in the third race at Hialeah," Ned said, "but the way my luck's been running lately . . ."

"Ned, boy, I can't believe my ears. You can't win without confidence. You told me that yourself." Taylor was ebullient. "Give me that racing form. We'll pick enough winners for you to replace the Mercedes you're going to lose."

Ned would not allow that thought to enter the realm of consideration and not because the prospect was terrifying—the car was family, not gambling property—but because there's a distinction between legitimate fear and paranoia. Ned was an odds player and he knew as well as he knew his own name that Taylor stood as much chance of winning the car as he had of being struck by lightning. "Speaking of your imminent humiliation," he said, "I saw the Larimores at the club the other day. I didn't notice Eleanor walking bowlegged or anything like that."

WORTH WINNING

Taylor rolled his eyes. "I'm the one who walks bow-legged. She's the original marathon fuck."

"Be careful of that one," Ned said knowingly. "Be extremely careful."

"I will, dad," Taylor mocked, but he silently acknowledged Ned's warning. Eleanor scared him sometimes. She loved to ride him as if he were a bronco in need of breaking. She'd get him up inside her as far as he could go, clamp down on him, and try to wrench him out by the roots. She fucked with a vengeance, as if screwing were a contest she was determined never to lose. She always hung on a little longer than he did. Every time. Without exception. "I know your opinion of Larimore, Ned, but I can't help but pity him just a little. No matter what he does for her or gives to her, our slinky Eleanor will never admit to being satisfied. Let me guess what conversation's like at the country club: lots of sexual innuendo, all of it indicating Howard's insufficiency in the sack."

"Incisive guess," Ned said sarcastically. "She and Howard are famous for their sparring contests, but believe me, they deserve each other. Larimore is such a smug son of a bitch—but that's another story. At any rate, last Saturday at the club, both of them were relatively quiet, and the first thing Clara said to me when we got in the car to go home was 'Eleanor Larimore is having an affair.' "

"What!"

Ned nodded. "Scared me, too, but when I asked who told her, she said, 'It's obvious.' You know how women are about that stuff."

"I'm learning." Taylor chewed his lip. "I don't like that it's already common knowledge on the cocktail circuit."

"Neither do I," Ned said sincerely. He could not

predict what Clara would do if she ever found out about his bet with Taylor. The loss of the actual car would be the least of it. More loathsome to her would be Ned's betrayal of their trust, but even if he could finesse that—he'd never dipped into family money before; she'd probably forgive him one indiscretion in eighteen years—she'd go completely crazy over the specifics of the bet. And his daughters would, too. "Taylor," he said, "we both know this wager is not in the best of taste and if this business with Eleanor Larimore gets too sticky . . ."

"You mean if it gets too close to your house."

"I mean specifically what I'm telling you." Ned bristled. "If this thing with Eleanor—or with any of them—gets out of hand and you think you might be in some kind of danger, then I'd be willing to sit down and talk, to renegotiate . . ."

"Danger? What could be dangerous about . . ."

"Just remember what I said." Ned turned his attention to his racing form.

"I love that word, 'renegotiate.' You've been to too many Republican Club meetings, buddy. You're beginning to love euphemisms."

Ned ignored the implication. "Eleanor's only a third of the action. What about the other two? How about Bristow?"

Taylor had to smile. "She's the only girl I've ever known, or even known about, who has a full-length nude picture of herself in her own house."

"No."

"I swear."

Ned glanced up alertly. The results from Hialeah were coming in. He dug into his pocket and pulled out a handful of ticket stubs. All his attention was directed toward the board.

While Ned, in a betting frenzy, took his fix, Taylor thought about Veronica's picture. She owned and frequently used a quality Nikon outfit, and a section of her spare bedroom was set up as a darkroom. Her own framed work hung on the walls of her apartment alongside samples of Margaret Bourke-White, Olivia Parker, Diane Arbus, and others. The nude hung on the darkroom door, a life-size black-and-white print. Veronica told him she'd taken the picture herself, but had had it enlarged professionally. In the photo her hair was long and she had an ironic, self-mocking expression. Her pose wasn't at all provocative—head cocked, one hand in her hair, one knee bent with the toes of that foot curled under. Taylor loved the picture, not only for the exposed naked body but for the attitude it revealed.

"Oh no," said Ned. "Oh shit." The results were in. Ned let his ticket stubs fall from his hand. His shoulders slumped. "Damn," he whispered.

"You OK?" Taylor asked. Ned rarely showed emotion, whether he was losing or winning.

"Yeah. Fine. Minor setback." But his shaky appearance belied his words. He changed the subject. "What were we talking about? Bristow, wasn't it? How did you say things were going with her?" Desultorily, he glanced at his tip sheet.

Noting Ned's rare temporary imbalance, Taylor decided to press his advantage. "I'm happy to say you had her pegged exactly wrong. She's a feminist all right but she doesn't take her politics all that seriously."

Taylor, however, was giving voice to his wishes. Veronica had plenty of opinions and a mental encyclopedia of facts and figures to support what she thought. He had tried the old groveling-penitent routine, but she didn't buy it and he almost lost her early on because she despised sycophants. Also, he couldn't maintain the role. He would make what he thought was an innocent comment; she'd jump on it as if it were an intentional insult; then he'd lose his temper. They went around and around about the weirdest things. Once he was at her house, the TV was on, and one of the networks was carrying a story about a group of women on the West Coast that was demanding to join the longshoremen's union. The women figured it was their right to work on the docks just because some of the jobs paid up to fifty grand per year. Taylor mentioned it in passing. A little woman about the size of Veronica was on-camera, saying, yes, she believed she could haul hundred-pound bunches of bananas if somebody paid her the kind of money the men received. Taylor thought it was funny, an example of how ludicrous some radicals could get. Veronica went wild.

"Fifty thousand dollars!" she yelled. "For being big and dumb enough to drag a bunch of bananas across the deck of a ship. Fifty grand! Do you think my friend Harriet, who has a skill, who has to use her brain in her job, will ever make fifty grand? Hell, no!" Veronica was wild, frothing at the mouth. "Do you think one of those longshoremen, with their meaty paws, could run a word processor even if they were trained? Never happen. So, just because they have the physiognomy of an orangutan, they deserve to make four times what Harriet makes?"

Taylor of course retaliated in kind, hollering about comparing pears and oranges, claiming there was more in common between fish and basketballs than between office work and dock work, but Veronica wasn't having any of it.

"That's one of the most invidious forms of discrimination against women!" she screamed. "Men make a job ten times more difficult than it has to be, then reward themselves for having the God-given brawn to do it. It's criminal. It's another example of men's worship of size. Bigger is better. See the real man. He can hump a dump truck onto his back. Pay him money, lots of money. 'Big' deals are of 'huge' importance. 'Heavyweight' ideas are good ideas. 'To make it big' is to be successful. Men, it seems to me, have a 'small' problem."

"So you're getting along fine with her, eh?" Ned asked. He had returned almost to normal.

"Oh, yeah. Fabulously. We have some discussions, of course, but they're friendly exchanges. You know, a meeting of minds. That sort of thing."

He remembered other "meetings of minds." She complained about double standards. He complained about double binds. She complained about women being used as property. He asked her what she thought conscription was. She bitched about women being disallowed to enter certain fields of business. He asked her who had given Edison "permission" to make the light bulb. She complained about being seen as a sex object. He complained about being seen as a money object. She complained about never being able to go anywhere in public without being pestered. He complained about never receiving attention. On and on it went every time they dated, but oddly enough, they hadn't begun to hate each other. Their discussions remained just that, discussions, objective considerations of social ills. Taylor had to keep his cool, of course, because of the bet, but she wasn't so fragile he had to keep his opinions in check. Their debates were spirited but not rancorous. On the subject of sex roles, they were honorable opponents, but man to woman they had become . . . What exactly, had they become? They had fun together, treated each other respectfully, enjoyed each other's company, but cautiously, gingerly. He wondered what would happen if they ever got into a legitimate spitting contest. His strategy, whenever tempers began to flare, had been to slide off the subject. He wouldn't back down or surrender; he simply wouldn't play anymore. He'd make a pun or make a pass at her, to defuse the bomb, to bring her into the present, to make sure she continued to see him as Taylor her friend, not as a symbol of nasty mankind. The ploy had been effective, but he could tell Veronica was beginning to lose patience. Soon he knew they'd have a showdown, but so far, so good.

"Have you, uh, have you managed to, uh . . ."

"I didn't know you were so squeamish about these things, Ned. You needn't be shy. People do it all over the world. The answer is yes. I've been to bed with her. I told you before. No woman can resist me for long. My formula is foolproof."

Taylor had gone to bed with Veronica, but on her terms, at her convenience, and at her bidding. It had happened when a hot day fell through a time warp and arrived unexpectedly in Washington. He and Veronica had a date, and he arrived in the evening, on time, but she wasn't ready. Instead, she greeted him with a pair of mint juleps in her hands, wearing nothing but a man's sleeveless undershirt, the kind Marlon Brando wore in *A Streetcar Named Desire*. As he looked back on it, the whole evening had had the ambiance of that play. She'd come home from work early and lain about indolently all afternoon. There was a new *Penthouse* magazine on the already rumpled bed, and Taylor suspected the influence of an unseen vibrator because the room held a funky, musky aroma. She removed his clothes beneath an open window, and as nighttime breezes drifted sulkily through her cavelike bedroom, she used him, gently, not disrespectfully, but thoroughly. Taylor became involved—it was far too sexy a moment not to—but not the way he told Ned. Veronica didn't surrender a thing. She brought all her sexuality to the surface of her skin, mixed it with her sweat, and mingled it with Taylor's. They made steamy, slippery, southern-style love, as deep and sweet as the scent of gardenias, as close and hot and hazardous as a cypress swamp in high summer. When it was over, they stood naked in the kitchen, slick with sweat, savory and satisfied, drinking cold beer right from the cans.

"OK," Ned said, "so you've allegedly overcome her defenses. That's a fer piece from marriage."

"You're right about that," Taylor replied, and this time he told the truth. "I've brought the subject up a couple times in a general way, and each time she sputtered and popped like water in hot oil. She's not opposed to partnership, friendship, or long-term cooperation, but marriage scares her to death."

Taylor hadn't told the worst part. Veronica was opposed to marriage on principle and this would pose a problem, but before he could confront her objections to marriage, he had to get her to like him which, beyond a casual interest, he hadn't been able to do. Somehow, he and Veronica always seemed to miss that instant of intellectual and emotional fusion he knew was indispensable. Their sociological disagreements weren't the problem—not exactly anyway. It was something else, something he couldn't isolate. He and she were intellectually compatible—she'd been teaching him about photography and he'd been teaching her about computers—and they were sexually compatible, if their wild, sweaty session was a valid indication, but something was missing. Veronica, unlike Erin and/or Eleanor, wouldn't tumble for a single, simple trick. Not Veronica. Unfortunately.

"And how about Erin?" Ned asked. "How about the beauty?"

"She's terrific," said Taylor, "but she has the weirdest body."

"Are we talking about the same woman?" Ned asked. "Erin's built better than this month's Playmate."

"You're right about that. She has all the right basic equipment. In spades."

"So what do you mean by 'weird'?"

Taylor looked pensive. "A better word might be 'disgusting.'"

"What? What's disgusting?"

"Well," Taylor said, "she has, let's see . . ."—he counted silently on his fingers—" . . . five, no, six extras."

"Six extra what?" Ned asked warily.

"Nipples, my man. Six supernumerary nipples dotted all over her chest."

"Aw, no," Ned blurted.

"Oh, yeah," said Taylor. "And what's more, each one—they're about this round—has a few hairs, a tiny row of little hairs above it, like eyelashes, and when you look at her from a distance, it seems like a half-dozen big, pink eyes are staring at you."

"Oh, God." Ned looked as though he might be sick.

Taylor fought mightily to keep a straight face. "And that's not all."

"Taylor," Ned warned, beginning to catch on.

"No, that's not all by a long shot," Taylor continued. "You can't tell when she's wearing shoes, but she has webbed feet . . ."

"Taylor, you're disgusting. Do you know that?"

" . . . little stretchy, transparent fans of skin between each toe. It's kind of fascinating and you know what else . . ."

CHAPTER TEN

Erin dabbed at the corners of her eyes with the Kleenex, trying to stop the tears before they did irreparable damage to her makeup. "It was so beautiful," she said. "Thank you for taking me. I hadn't seen it since I was a little girl. I cried then, too, but I was worse if you can believe it." She laughed but it came out as a sob. "It's so heartbreaking. Snow White was punished just for being beautiful and good." Erin sniffed. "I'm sorry, Taylor. I know I'm being horribly silly but I just can't help it. It's such a pretty movie. One minute you're laughing at those cute little dwarfs—Dopey is just the most adorable thing—and the next minute you're crying because it's just not fair. Snow White didn't do anything wrong." The inflection in Erin's voice slid upward like a penny whistle, and a fresh trickle of tears provoked a new round of dabbing.

While she sniffled, heedless of their surroundings—the Potomac River, twinkling with reflected city light, the quiet park, every tree and shrub of which Taylor was defensively aware, the fountain spraying water against the starless sky—Taylor led her along, nodding, cooing sympathy, on the lookout for potential muggers. They passed a pair of sailors who stripped and raped Erin with their eyes. Taylor leered a warning, but he couldn't blame them for their lechery. Erin looked fantastic, even more so than usual because she was dressed for a party at her boss the football team owner's house. She wore black pumps, dark stockings, an elegantly simple blacksilk wrap dress that swirled in the breeze and revealed her legs, and a fur stole of genuine silver fox. Her hair was swept to one side of her head and held with a jeweled clip from which her gathered tresses were allowed to hang freely. Her diamond earrings seemed to manufacture their own prismatic light.

He and Erin had looked extremely out of place at the nine o'clock showing of *Snow White*, but Erin said she didn't care. She'd wanted to see the movie and had found no one but Taylor who would agree to go with her. "Let them stare," she said. And they did, they certainly did. Taylor was positive there wasn't a male in the place who sometime that night wouldn't dream longingly of the incredible blonde who had materialized like an apparition at, of all places, a Disney cartoon.

"In a way, though," said Erin, wiping her perfect nose daintily with Taylor's handkerchief, "it's really a cruel movie. I'm not sure if it's good for kids to see. It gives them false hopes, teaches them things that aren't true. All it does is make disappointments worse."

Since their first sincere kiss by the light of the full moon, and since Taylor had resisted the almost overwhelming temptation to drag her into bed, judiciously maintaining the decorous pace of the courtship, Erin gradually had begun to confide in him. She had told him the story of her life, explained why she had not accepted any of the myriad proposals of marriage she had received, and provided him with numerous though unsolicited reasons why his strategy with her had succeeded. Erin was not what Taylor would call smart, but she was determined and if her dreams were relatively pedestrian—a secure existence, a loving husband, a family—she was not about to abandon them for the glitter of the big time, which, perhaps because of her daily experience with glamorous highrollers, she distrusted almost instinctively. At the moment, however, Taylor was listening with only one ear. His attention was directed primarily toward a seedy type, chewing on the butt of a cigar, who looked more than casually interested in Erin and/or her fur. "I'm sorry," he said, turning back to her when the grubby man was a safe distance behind them. "Say again."

"The happy endings," she said. "According to the movie, if you're pretty and good, then somebody will help you and be nice to you just because you are what you are." She sniffed once more. "It's just not true. Mostly, people just want to use you."

Taylor had to smile. Here she was, poor little Erin, who among all God's creatures had been dealt the best hand—a female body of incomparable loveliness—lamenting the existence of injustice. Taylor understood her beauty created problems as well as opportunities. Erin could never enjoy quiet anonymity, for example; she would always be pursued by men, but in the grand scheme of things, he honestly could not take her complaints seriously.

"The world would be so much nicer if the movie told the truth," she said.

Who could argue with that? "You're right, love. It certainly would. There's a Jackson Browne song about how everybody is looking for somebody to offer 'that strong but gentle father's hand.' It would be a much nicer world if songs and fairy tales were true." He guided her around the fountain toward the parking lot. It occurred to him that so pervasive was her ultrafeminine abdication of responsibility for personal safety that he could walk her into the river and she would go placidly. "Do you think we ought to start making our way to the party?"

"Uh-huh."

As they drove, Taylor thought about Erin's complaint. He, too, wished he had someone to depend on, someone with whom he could let down his guard, relax, rely on to protect and defend him. He remembered childhood and nights sleeping in the backseat of the car on the way home after a hard day of play at the lake, his mother and father in the front, his brother sleeping slouched against the opposite window, the eerie green of the dashboard lights reminding him, whenever he turned or his slumber was interrupted by a bump in the road, that his rapidly moving world was as safe as his bed: peace, comfort, mindless security, the complete suspension of personal responsibility, the priceless possessions of childhood. Yes. He missed them, too. Unfortunately, of the two, he and Erin, only she could hope, however wistfully, to regain them. It would indeed be nice, he nearly said aloud, if there were a creature or a person who could be trusted to provide not merely material things but options, succor, and opportunities. Alas, while for her, at least a symbol remained—the kind uncle, the wise grandfather, the bold leader, the daring adventurer, the handsome prince—for him, not even a symbol existed because the fictitious savior was always masculine. He could legitimately seek mother love, but it was to be found at home, out of the storm, away from the struggle. He could find someone to bathe his head in cool towels and whisper endearments until such time as action again was required, but then what would he see? A woman waving good-bye or, like Erin, in tears. He recalled the classic movie line: "You'll have to think for both of us, Rick."

Erin sat beside him repairing her makeup. She was unquestionably beautiful and eminently worthy of protection, but what she didn't understand—and how he could love her if she did understand—was that the need she expressed was not peculiarly feminine but human, a characteristic of all God's people. Her grief at the absence of a universal hero was not, tragically, for all humankind, but for herself and other good, beautiful women whom no man had carried off into the sunset on a white charger. Where was he, Taylor, a man, to find the inspiration or assurance he also craved? There were always generals, politicians, and other lunatics who would guarantee him earthly happiness, but whereas Erin might be able to believe their cocks provided them with the answers to the mysteries of life, he had one of his own and knew better. Could he turn to her for help? Could he lean on her? On womankind? Men were certainly fallible, even cataclysmically stupid in their insistence on killing each other, but at least men had conceived of and produced the tools to break the earth, to transport people away from disaster, to construct shelter. Wasn't there something significant in the fact that not a single culture in human history had developed a symbol of woman as savior?

Two weeks previously, Taylor's resentment would have expanded like a waistline in middle age, but contact with the gentle Erin had softened him. It was his privilege to despise her for her retention of emotions like hope; his right, if he chose, to revile her for feeling simple melancholy over the loneliness of the human condition, but why should he do so?

Because he was male, he had extinguished in himself

the ability to be sentimental, regarding lamentations of the inevitable as maudlin at best and survival-threatening at worst, but what purpose would it serve to destroy her honest wish that things could be better? It would add to the glut of cynicism already polluting the world more virulently than toxic wastes and it would eradicate much of her charm. A month ago he would have reviled her sentimentality, out of jealousy, out of envy, out of a misplaced sense of justice; but now with her beside him, as fragile and rejuvenating as springtime itself, he didn't have the heart or the inclination.

Erin finished applying her lip gloss and put away her compact. "I've never taken a date to any of these parties before, Taylor. You're the first one."

"Why's that?"

Erin fidgeted. "I'm even a little nervous about taking you, but I think you'll be OK. Promise you'll be OK."

"Will I be in danger? This is at the owner's house, right? It's not some NFL orgy where the defensive tackles gangbang the cheerleaders, is it?"

"Oh no. Everybody will be on good behavior. I mean, boys will be boys, but the gross stuff won't happen here. The party will change locations if it starts getting out of hand."

"So what's the problem?"

"These people are, uh, how can I say it? Intimidating. The players are intimidating because of their size and the other men are intimidating because of their money. I've discovered it can be rough on a man's ego if he isn't very secure with himself."

Taylor rolled his eyeballs. She was kidding, of course. He was the baddest cat in town with three women after his body and a Mercedes in his hip pocket. He was well-to-do and well established. He harrumphed. "How can I be intimidated by anyone when the most gorgeous woman on the eastern seaboard is taking me to the party?"

Erin smiled but without her usual trace of simpering. As they neared her home turf, she changed subtly. Mile by mile she developed a persona more appropriate to her sophisticated costume. Her aura changed.

"Flatterer," she said.

"You only get what you deserve," he answered. Taylor liked this classier version of Erin very much. She appeared older, more womanly. As tantalizing, cute, and innocently sexy as ingenues could be, a beautiful woman, mature in her beauty, was for Taylor, in theory at least, more alluring. He put his hand on her knee, gently separated the folds of the silk dress, and ran his hand up her leg. He did it as much to touch her as to prove to himself that she was in fact real and that he, Taylor Worth, was allowed to touch her.

Erin leaned across the seat and, taking care not to smear her lip gloss again, breathed softly in his ear, "Flattery will get you anywhere."

Under your dress? he wanted to ask. In your pants? Will you be naked for me? Will you spread your legs and let me lose my tongue and my mind in you? The Doris Day–Rock Hudson routine they'd developed mutually was a good idea at the beginning, and his and Erin's sexual abstinence probably helped Taylor maintain virility with the other two women, but the game had evolved. What began as quaint play-acting had become ritual. What began as coyness had become principle. Casual good-night kisses had metamorphosed into frenzied groping sessions. Taylor appreciated the special thrill of anticipation as much as the next guy, but kings had abdicated their thrones and armies had marched to slaughter for beauty like Erin's. What bothered Taylor was not so much that his testicles throbbed at the sight of her, but that his desire for her was becoming absurd, an obsession worse than his adolescent crush on Kim Novak, worse than his desperate and also unrequited need for the woman on his paper route whose blouses were never buttoned all the way up. In a way he couldn't comprehend, the worst was happening. The hallmark of his and Erin's relationship—and perhaps it was impossible to deal with someone as gorgeous as Erin in any other way—was idolatry. He moved his hand toward her crotch. She covered his hand with hers and crossed her legs.

The difference between wealthy and rich is like the difference between a circle and a sphere—dimensional. Taylor Worth, if he developed his full potential and moved strategically within the computer industry, could perhaps with luck someday expect to make a hundred grand per year or its inflated or deflated equivalent. If he ever reached that plateau, he would consider himself wealthy. Erin's boss would make that in a month even if he didn't show up at the office. He was one of those relatively few people for whom money was no longer an end in itself but a means by which to deal in and barter the intangible commodities money was purportedly unable to buy. If Taylor's income were a grape, Erin's boss's would be a vineyard. His estate, where the party was held, was magnificent.

"My word."

"It's just a house, Taylor," Erin said, squeezing his hand. Away in the distance, beyond the greenhouse and formal gardens, were a bath house and tennis courts. "Racquetball and squash courts are in that building over there. It's a fully equipped spa," she said.

A valet accustomed to parking Rolls-Royces frowned as he took Taylor's keys. The place was splendid. Taylor couldn't keep his mouth closed.

WORTH WINNING   133

Erin recognized the look in his eye. His mind had clicked into a state of awe and envy and incomprehension. Some men looked like that when they looked at her. "Snap out of it, Taylor," she said sternly. "It's just a house, only a place to live. What would you do with it if you had it? How many rooms could you stay in at once?" But she knew her words made no impression on him. She sighed. "Tell me, Taylor," she said, "was ever a man born anywhere whose brain was equipped with an 'Enough' switch?"

Brawny men, beautiful women, and servants; genuine leather, solid wood, and crystal; original art, sumptuous furnishings, and excellent champagne: Without truly expecting it, Taylor found himself, an hour out of *Snow White*, in an even more fantastic world. Taylor wasn't exactly a bumpkin—he didn't drool and gawk—but there seemed to be something incongruous about mere people, no matter how elegantly got up, idly hobnobbing, bustling and burbling in the presence of so many objects so patently worthy of attention, if not, Taylor thought (by God, that's an original Monet right there, close enough to touch), reverence.

". . . and this is Mr. So-and-So. And this is Mr. Such-and-Such." Erin droned on, introducing Taylor to the boggle-eyed corporate men who were the first to swoop down on her like merger-mad accountants on an unprotected growth property. Next, they made the rounds of the players and Erin hadn't exaggerated. Their sheer size amazed him. Taylor was smaller than all of them, even the slender cornerbacks and the flashy wide receivers, and if any looked at him at all, it was to size him up, this stranger in their midst, this alien no-name who had succeeded where they all had failed, in capturing Erin's affections. " . . . and this," Erin said finally, with more than a hint of pride in her voice, " . . . is my boss." Taylor shook the hand of the master of the castle, the human money-junction to whom everybody present, except Taylor presumably, owed at least some fealty.

"How do you do, Mr. Worth? Erin has told us a great deal about you. Welcome." The man's power was so encompassing, his use of the imperial "we" wasn't out of place. Lean, handsome, blue-eyed, with impeccable gray hair and a knockout of a wife at least twenty years his junior, he was exactly as Taylor had pictured him: as smooth as his wife's skin and as tough as his middle linebacker. His arm encircled Erin's waist possessively. "Do you mind if I borrow your date for a moment? I assure you I'll return her unmarked."

Erin squeezed Taylor's hand and her eyes searched his meaningfully. "He can be trusted," she said, "in public." The master's wife's smile revealed fangs. The three of them disappeared into the crowd, and Taylor, standing alone, never felt as small.

He ordered a Scotch and water, received it almost before he finished speaking, and wandered over to the Monet, where he was joined by one of the players, an all-pro offensive guard who, except for his awesome size, looked like a college professor: wire-rim glasses, shaggy moustache, benevolent eyes, a pipe. "An enviable possession, eh?" he said, referring to the painting.

Taylor looked up at him. He was four inches taller than Taylor and a foot wider. "Do you think it's appreciated?"

"For its effect on people like you and me, yes," the all-pro answered. "For itself, well, that's hard to say. Our leader and benefactor has predictable tastes but unusual values. The Monet, the team, even myself, mean something to him but in an ephemeral sense only."

"Tycoon as transcendentalist," Taylor said.

"Well put." The lineman stuck out a massive hand, which Taylor accepted. "Call me Truck."

Taylor grinned. "Tell me more about your benefactor, Truck."

"He's a self-made man."

"Is that so?"

"Started with only four million. Made the rest himself."

Taylor laughed.

"He's an interesting study, though. They're all interesting in this freaky business. Look over there."

Taylor looked. Erin's boss was presenting her to a brace of business types as if she were an Academy Award.

"See the short, fat guy, the one who's smiling? He's a minor partner in the team. I've been around here for eight years and I've seen him smile perhaps a dozen times, yet your date waltzes up and he turns into a moon pie." Surrounded by three-piece suits, Erin was herded from the room.

Taylor got the impression Truck was trying to tell him something important. "She has that effect on men."

"Lots of women have that effect on men initially, but your friend Erin . . ."

He was interrupted by the appearance of two of his mammoth teammates. Truck nodded to them. "Have you met Maylord Sessums and Buck Bohan, Taylor? May I present the left side of our estimable defensive line."

Taylor shook hands. He recognized Bohan as the giant who had been guarding Erin the day he met her. Taylor backed away a step in order to speak to them without craning his neck, but they closed the distance immediately. Taylor felt danger.

"We want to know if there's anything to you," Sessums said without preliminary ceremony.

Taylor looked to Truck, who had retreated a few steps, observing professorially.

"We got a bet going," Sessums continued. "Buck and me. I say you never fucked her, am I right?"

Taylor felt every physiological symptom of the onset of blind rage. His mind was full of white noise.

Bohan leaned his enormous face closer to Taylor. "Have you ever seen her naked? What kind of tits does she have? Round ones? Pear shaped?"

Taylor clenched his fists, prepared for a fight he could only lose, but he saw Truck shaking his head, as if he'd read Taylor's mind and vetoed its decision. Taylor glanced back at the leering giant and remembered Erin's "boys will be boys." Revelation came: He was being tested. What was the subject of the test, though, his machismo or his sense of humor? He relaxed his shoulders. "Neither of you two man enough to find out for yourselves?" He had decided there would be no fight. Not here. Not in the master's living room. He saw Truck smile.

"I bet you don't even know if her cunt hair is blond," Bohan said. "You're another one of those wimps who suck up to good-looking women just to sniff their shit, ain't you? Another hotshot in public with a private case of blueballs."

Sessums placed his hands on Taylor's upper arms and lifted him straight off the floor. "Yup. There's nothing to him. I knew that the minute I saw him."

Taylor looked down at his feet dangling in the air, down at Truck, down at the faraway world of puny partygoers looking up at him as they would a colorful, hot-air balloon. "I'm reminded of a joke, Truck," he said loudly. "It's about Jesus on the cross."

Truck grinned.

"Jesus, hanging there helpless, starts moaning that he wants to talk to the Apostle Peter. Eventually he makes such a fuss the soldiers go and find him. Peter, of course, is hesitant because it shows he's a disciple of a public enemy, but finally he approaches his pathetic Lord who's all sweaty and bloody, dangling by nails through his hands. Peter, under the scrutiny of the soldiers, finally makes it to the foot of the cross and says, 'Yes, Lord?' and Jesus raises his head and says, 'Hey, Peter. I can see your house from here.' "

The joke got a laugh from Truck and a few others.

"Let me check him," said Bohan. Sessums let go and Taylor didn't move a centimeter.

"OK, fellas," Taylor said. "I may be easy but I'm no passaround."

Quietly but menacingly, Bohan said, "Neither is Erin, right?"

"Definitely not. I mean, right. Absolutely," Taylor said. "Now do you think we might begin our descent into the capital?" He was set down as gently as a teacup.

"You may be small but you ain't slow," Bohan said. Sessums winked at Taylor, and he and Bohan walked away.

"Excellent response," Truck said. "People that large have only one weakness, their reputations as studs. You went right for it. Well done."

Taylor barely heard him. He finished his drink in a single gulp. His hand shook shamefully. "Sounds like you . . ." Taylor had to clear his throat before he could talk normally. "Sounds like you've studied these folks."

Truck lit his pipe. "I'm working on a Ph.D. in psychology. Sports and sports people are my specialty. It's what I was getting at before the arrival of my colleagues."

Taylor ordered another drink from a roving waiter and the fresh glass was in his hand almost immediately. He swilled half of it and it settled his nerves.

Truck continued. "For example. Look over there."

Taylor looked. Erin had returned. She was surrounded by football players, and she was in the process of scolding one of them who stood sheepishly under the disdainful glare of his friends until she finished. It was like watching an elephant trainer upbraiding one of his animals.

"The one she's admonishing is one of the meanest defensive backs in football, and look at him, playing the puppy that's peed on the carpet."

"What are you getting at?" Taylor asked.

Truck puffed pensively. "Your friend Erin is an interesting case. That man is vicious." He nodded toward the object of Erin's derision. "I don't know ten people in the world he'd take that kind of treatment from. I've seen him punch out a coach on the practice field. He could break her like a potato chip, but look." The other players in the knot around Erin were laughing at him. "It isn't simply because she's a woman," Truck continued, "because I know the way he treats most women. And it isn't simply because she won't put out either because a special kind of contempt is usually reserved for women who won't. The male presumes conceit and judges her deserving of rape."

Taylor watched her. It was as if she were a combination queen and housemother.

"And it isn't the old dumb-blonde routine, either," said Truck, "because although Erin might not be brilliant, she isn't stupid and she is definitely not naïve. She couldn't be, not after all the moves that have been put on her."

Taylor looked at him.

Truck smiled. "Practically everybody in this organization has made a pass at her: our fearless leader, our quarterback, the team trainer . . ."—he paused for effect—". . . our leader's wife."

Taylor's mouth fell open, but Truck put a finger to his own lips and winked. "Big secret. I'm Erin's nominal uncle. Occasionally, she comes to me for advice. Somehow, she's managed to resist all overtures and still avoid a reputation as a ball-buster. That's more rare than a defensive lineman with an unbroken nose."

Taylor looked across the room. She was breathtaking.

"Erin's an enigma," Truck went on. "All these powerful men—powerful in every sense of the word—can't intimidate her, can't dominate her, and can't buy her, and they don't know what else to do. A special section of my thesis is reserved for that girl and her peculiar talent."

Erin had turned her back on her gaggle of admirers and walked over to join Truck and Taylor. Attention followed her like a spotlight. She looked poised, completely at ease, completely at home, completely in control of herself and her situation, and yet she seemed as soft and nonthreatening as a flower. "I might have known the two best men in the crowd would find each other," she said, taking Taylor's arm and hugging it.

Truck winked. "Have you seen my wife, Erin?"

"No, Truck. Not yet."

He nodded. "She's probably shooting pool again. I'd better go find her before she takes everybody's money like she did the last time we were here. Nice talking to you, Taylor."

Taylor watched him shamble off. "Nice fellow," he said.

"He certainly is. A terrific ballplayer, too. If his knees

don't give out, he'll be around for three or four more years."

"He told me you're a legend around here."

"Has he been telling my secrets again?"

"Is it true your boss made a pass at you?"

"Is that all? That's no secret. He makes a different pass at me every week."

"Is it a joke?"

"That man never jokes."

"How do you resist?"

"What do you mean?"

Taylor's gesture encompassed the opulent room, the house. "I mean all this."

Erin frowned. "Taylor," she said impatiently, "it's only money." She looked at him as if she thought he understood. "Now let's go mingle. I want to show you off."

Taylor proudly took her arm. He felt taller than any other man in the room, grander than the Monet, richer than the owner of the Super Bowl champions.

CHAPTER ELEVEN

"*Snow White!?*" Eleanor exclaimed. "We only have a couple of hours together and you're taking me to see *Snow White?*"

Taylor couldn't take her to his apartment because his place reeked of other women.

"I suppose you're going to buy some popcorn, too."

Actually, he wanted some. He'd been too busy that morning to grab anything to eat, and if his liaison with Eleanor turned out to be anything like their other times together, what he ate might be delicious but it wouldn't be nourishing. Taylor, already at the candy counter, looked back at Eleanor who stood, her left leg cocked to one side, backlighted by the glass door of the theater, and he agreed to himself that maybe this wasn't such a good idea. She wore a slim, slit beige skirt through which he could see individual strands of pubic hair—she'd given up wearing underwear and stockings after their second meeting. Her white blouse, soft and shimmery, didn't need backlighting. It was unbuttoned past her breasts and her slightest reaching motion revealed tiny nipples. She looked terrific and seemed to look better every time he saw her. Her weight, as far as Taylor could tell, hadn't changed but apparently had rearranged itself. She used to be angular, now she was sleek. She used to be pale, now she had color. And she always wore high heels, which made Taylor want to shinny up her long legs. Today, she'd chosen simple slides, backless, with macramé across the toes. She radiated the slinky, feline variety of sexiness. Everything about her—her posture, the glint in her eye, the way her tongue played over her lips—communicated a single idea. She could just have worn a sign that read: Slam me up against the wall and fuck me. It's what men wanted to do when they got near her.

"Is this something kinky, Taylor?" Eleanor asked as they walked through the darkness to a seat down front. The theater was practically empty. "You can tell me. What do you have in mind?"

Taylor wished he had something in mind. His original plan for the date was to talk to her for a change. He'd never had a conversation with her about anything other than money, their respective private parts, or her husband, and he thought it was time to try communicating with her. Also, he was running out of ideas for places to go for wild, adventurous sex. His appetite for it was shrinking, too. The film had moved Erin to tears, so he decided to try it on Eleanor. Maybe overdone sentiment would prompt her to open more than her legs to him.

Sexy Eleanor, however, looked about as appropriate in the theater lobby as Erin had. He paid for the popcorn and ransacked his imagination for a reasonable explanation for this absurd escapade.

"It's a childhood fantasy, isn't it?" Eleanor asked. "You've always wanted your cock sucked while you watched a cartoon. Is that it? I can do that," she said as they sat down. "I'll be happy to do that, but you've got to promise you'll fuck me sometime today. I need it." She leaned closer to his ear and filled his head with erotic images. "Maybe you don't understand what you've done to me, Taylor. You've made me an addict. My cunt cries for your cock. Every day. Ten times a day. I sit on my dryer while it runs. I've stuffed every tubular vegetable you can think of up my cunt. I slide down the banister of the staircase and lust for you. I've got to have you. I don't care where we do it. We can do it on the floor of the lobby, on the grass in front of the Washington Monument, it doesn't matter. I must have you inside me." She unzipped his pants.

Taylor tossed popcorn at his mouth, but missed about half the time because he kept swiveling his head to see who might be watching them. The movie started. Eleanor grasped his penis in her long fingers and began to massage it. The dwarfs were up on the screen, marching along the mountain ridge; his cock was flapping in the breeze.

"Has anybody ever told you you have a gorgeous dick?" she asked, sliding farther down in her seat. She took him in her mouth, tongued him, sucked him. Above him, huge cartoon characters were singing "Whistle While You Work," while Eleanor, incapable of whistling, did her best to work him up. Taylor felt ridiculous. After a few minutes, he put his hand in her hair and drew her head up, away from his groin. He caught a glimpse of her face and her mad, wild eyes before her mouth attacked his. He struggled to zip his pants without decapitating his cock while she ate his face. "Anything," she whispered between kisses. "I'll do anything. Anywhere. Anytime."

On the screen, bushy-tailed squirrels perched on Snow White's kitchen window; the cutest little mice helped her with her chores; tiny, happy birds chirped in harmony, and Taylor couldn't cope with the incongruity. "Out," he said, and they exited by a door at the front of the theater. Outside, in the eyeball-piercing light, Eleanor looked like the senior class whore, blouse unbuttoned and hair a mess.

In his car, she slunk down in the seat, yanked her skirt up out of the way, thrust his hand between her legs, and started humping. He had heard women didn't reach their sexual prime until past age thirty, but he'd never seen the principle in action. Eleanor was acting crazy, stuffing his fingers up inside herself. She looked like a porno film, but depraved or not, it was a turn-on to watch. Taylor had helped her open a trapdoor to a cellar she'd kept locked since her adolescence. She descended once, found it unbelievably pleasurable, and now refused to come back up. She put one foot on the dashboard for support and strained against his hand. Her musky-sweet scent filled the car. Taylor thought his hand might melt. With his eyes he followed the line of her leg to her long, trim thigh, and suddenly he wanted to participate.

"Wait," he said, and he brought his wet fingers to his face. Her scent lit up the display screen of his brain like a quarter in a video machine. Animated erotic images flickered and danced. He started the car. Across the street was a shopping mall with a huge, fairly empty parking lot. He selected a place far from the stores and other cars, and stopped. "Let me slide over there," he said.

She started unzipping his pants before he was settled. He fumbled with her buttons, and when he couldn't open them, tore at her shirt. Two buttons flew off. She growled with pleasure and released his cock, took it in her mouth, and sucked it erect.

He pulled her head away and guided her on top of him. One of her shoes slipped off and he heard it bump on the floorboard. It would be obvious to any passersby what they were doing, especially since Taylor's head was inside Eleanor's open blouse but he didn't care. Besides, if anyone saw, it was a sure bet they wouldn't get involved.

Eleanor ground herself onto him, squeezing him, riding him. She slipped up him and down him, around and around him. "It itches there, Taylor. Scratch it. Harder." She thrust her chest against his face. "Bite them. Chew them off," she urged, trying to erase his nose with her breasts.

Out of the corner of his eye, Taylor saw a kid on a bicycle ride by. Why isn't he in school? he thought. Eleanor had left the planet, bound for Mars. Fleetingly, Taylor hoped she wouldn't hurt herself, or worse, him. The kid on the bike came around again.

"Go away, kid," he mumbled. Eleanor didn't even slow down for the red planet. She zoomed onward, toward Jupiter.

The kid slowed his bike and stopped. Couldn't be more than twelve years old, shouldn't be seeing this, Taylor thought irrationally. Eleanor had made three turns around the giant sphere before she slowed herself into stationary orbit above the Great Eye, the enormous, swirling Jovian hurricane. Moaning, she prepared to plunge downward toward it.

The kid, straddling his bike, moved right up to the car. Eleanor's moan became a wail. She fired retro rockets and dove. Taylor, eyes closed, ejaculated. Eleanor screamed. In the middle of a spasm, Taylor's head rocked sideways. He opened his eyes and stared into the kid's nose, pressed against the window not five inches away. Eleanor had become one with the eternal storm, declaring her transcendence mournfully. Taylor smashed the window with the side of his fist and the kid fell backward and disappeared.

A few minutes later, Eleanor, slumped against the passenger-side door with her legs spread, holding Taylor's handkerchief between her legs, asked, "What was that pounding noise I heard?"

"The top of my head coming off." he said.

"Oh," she said. "I'm glad you managed to put it back on." She looked drunk or stoned. "You certainly know how to fuck a girl," she said appreciatively. "A lot of women I know would appreciate your service. You sure you don't want to make some money on the side? No," she said, answering her own question. "I couldn't share you. I want that cock all to myself. When can we do it again?"

"Not right now," he said, looking at his wristwatch. "I have to get back to work."

As Taylor drove back to Eleanor's car, she asked, "Why did you want to go to that movie?"

Taylor lied. "I had a psychology course in college and I remember the teacher—she was a fox, like you—saying all Disney films, particularly the animated features, were full of sexual symbolism. I thought it might be a weird sort of turn-on."

"Symbolism, shmimbolism," Eleanor said, still sounding like a drunk. "I hate all that analysis crap."

What was this? thought Taylor. A whole sentence without the words fuck or cunt or cock in it? "What do you mean?"

"They're just stories and they're just for kids. They're not intended for adults at all. Psychologists would analyze baby shit if you let them. I mean, all that melodramatic garbage about good and evil and right and wrong is strictly to keep kids' little minds occupied until they get out of school. You don't have any kids, do you? You'd understand if you did. They really are inquisitive, you know. Even the dumbest ones, it seems, grapple with the eternal verities." She spoke the words as if there were no such thing. Eleanor took the handkerchief from between her legs and looked down to make sure she wasn't dripping. "Here you go," she said, handing him the cloth. "Something to remember me by."

Taylor put it in his coat pocket. Given the quality of their previous conversations, Taylor had begun to think of Eleanor as wholly a product of her husband, without opinions or attitudes of her own. She could talk interest rates and real estate prices with anybody, but she hadn't given any indication that she even considered social or philosophical matters. Taylor prompted her. "I still don't catch your meaning."

"If you had kids, you'd understand," she said, buttoning the few buttons remaining on her blouse, smoothing her skirt, slipping her feet into her shoes. She giggled. "Smells like a mushroom farm in here. What I mean is, these fables are only for kids. They're something they have to have, like milk, or else they'll never make it to adulthood. Think about it. Disney cartoons teach kids that it's best to be honest. That's bunk and everybody above the age of twelve knows it. If Howard Senior were honest and fair and all that fairy tale stuff, he'd be broke and we wouldn't have our house. But how would you teach that to kids? They'd pop like so many little pimples."

Ah yes, thought Taylor, Howard Senior: insensitive, intolerant, amoral, and belligerent, possessed of all the qualities necessary to succeed as a lobbyist's lawyer in Washington, a man whose entire professional life was dedicated to deflection, delay, and diversion, a self-made man who fought like a ferret in the federal pork barrel for subsidies and special considerations for his clients, but who perceived free food for kids as profligacy if not punishable crime. Veronica would love him, a model of modern American respectability.

Eleanor continued: "Those cutesy cartoons teach kids that good people get rewards. Well, that's purest fantasy. But if you taught kids the truth, then not too many of them—and very few of the girls—would get out of grade school. They'd all end up in jail or dyslectic or anorectic or something like that; you know, drooling into their Ovaltine in some school for exceptional children because their little minds can't absorb the truth. It's like liquor. They can't handle it when they're young, that's all. Fables aren't for sexual symbolism or anything deep like that, no matter what your professors taught you. They're just literary Pablum. Baby food for little heads."

Taylor listened for a hint of disappointment or despair in Eleanor's voice, but discerned none. Hers was a recitation of facts, simple and straightforward. If Erin was a ball of cotton with respect to the subject of lost innocence, Eleanor was a ball bearing—smooth, shiny, and capable of withstanding thousands of pounds of pressure per unit of measure. He shivered.

Once upon a time, he'd perceived singleminded, imperious men like Howard Senior as the engines of society, out there at the front of the great train of the population, chugging away, dragging everyone else behind them. Their wives he saw as cosmetics, like the spiffy paint jobs on the old Santa Fe locomotives, but lately—and Eleanor definitely contributed to the change in his thinking—he'd come up with another metaphor: As oxygen without hydrogen can't be water, Howard without Eleanor, or a woman possessing similar properties, could not wield power. The difference had to do with simultaneity. Previously, thinking linearly, he saw men—or those types of men, the leaders—as separate entities, producing not only goods but also values and ideas. He saw them as creators, as self-contained, concept-generating units shaping society according to their unique vision, while everybody else—the followers, the drudges, the drones, the women—contributed support. With age and maturity, however, he had begun to understand the complementarity of things. Straightline cause-and-effect systems, while convenient, temporarily useful, and certainly appealing to simple minds, were essentially illusions. Howard Senior without Eleanor or a duplicate to complement, substantiate, reinforce, reward, validate, corroborate, and authenticate him, would not, could not be what he was. A market does not exist without a buyer *and* a seller. So much for the idea of woman as crucible of compassion.

He pulled up beside Eleanor's car and she leaned over and kissed his cheek. "Don't forget my name now. I'm Eleanor, the one with the skinny legs," she said, smiling. "Don't forget to call me." She started to get out of the car. "Speaking of that, I bought you something so you wouldn't forget my phone number." She handed him a little package, neatly wrapped with a ribbon around it. " 'Bye," she said, opening the door. "If you ever find those buttons, save 'em for me." She waved and was gone.

The gift was a little black address book. Taylor smiled, figuring she'd put her name and number inside but when he flipped through it, he discovered that every page held a message. On the "A" page, she'd written "Anytime," and her name and number. On the "T" page, she'd written "Terrific lay," and her name and number. He flipped to the "Q" page just to see what she'd come up with and found "Quickie?," and her name and number. The "Z" page read "Zip down my dress and I'll zip down your pants," and her name and number. It was cute but it made him uncomfortable, and for the first time since making the bet with Ned, he felt guilty. Then, for no reason, he remembered the little kid's face at the window of the car and his guilt was replaced by another feeling, more foreign, more unsettling: immodesty.

CHAPTER TWELVE

"There's a movie in town I absolutely must see," said Veronica, hustling Taylor out of her apartment. "I know you won't want to go but it'll be good for you, and I'll buy so you won't have to be embarrassed at the ticket window."

Oh no, he thought.

"I want to head off any of your macho objections at the pass, before your John Wayne voice starts grousing about 'sissy stuff.' All boys dote on definitions, so just think of it as a film classic. You don't have to pay attention to the story or listen to the music. Concentrate on the technique, marvel at the amount of work required to produce it, revel in the detail, and you'll be happy. I promise. Do you want to know the title?"

"I already know," he said dolefully. "You want to see *Snow White*."

"You're such a clever fellow, Taylor," she said. "Now come on or we'll be late."

At the theater, Taylor slunk away from the candy counter as the clerk, the same kid who'd drooled into Eleanor's blouse and ogled Erin, gave him a double take.

"Isn't this a bit sappy for you, Veronica?" he asked when they were seated. "I wouldn't have picked you for a fan of Disney sweetness-and-light epics."

"Research, my friend," she said, handing him the popcorn. "A couple of generations of women remember these flicks as consequential events of their childhood. Cinderella, Sleeping Beauty; this one, as told by Disney, did more to influence the way little girls felt and, I'm afraid, continue to feel about themselves than any other single aspect of our cultural indoctrination."

The lights went down. Veronica settled her huge purse on her lap and fished around inside. "When I count to three," she said, "I want you to cough."

"What?"

"Cough. Loudly. You know, as if you were getting a physical."

"How come?"

"Just do it, OK?"

He coughed and as he did, he heard the unmistakable sound of a pressurized can opening. "Is that beer?"

"Certainly is," she said. "You don't expect me to sit through this mind-blasting propaganda sober, do you? Want one?"

"Sure," he said, watching the dwarfs march happily along their mountain ridge, singing "Whistle While You Work." Beers and blowjobs and *Snow White*, he thought. What were women coming to?

Veronica ate a tub of popcorn, drank four cans of Budweiser, and made a spectacle of herself throughout the movie. Taylor, who knew better than to try to quiet her, kept his peace while she shouted "Drivel!" repeatedly and made vomiting noises during the movie's most touching moments.

By the time the film ended and the lights came on, Veronica had achieved high fury. She spoke *ex cathedra*, to all men and all women, and just about loud enough for all to hear. Taylor guided her out the nearest door and into the parking lot.

"There you are, little girls. It's all there," she proclaimed. "Chapter and verse. The world according to Uncle Walter. Aurgghh. What shit! What refined, authentic, unexpurgated shit!"

Exiting patrons gave them wide berth as they cleared the corner of the building. Taylor set a straight course for the car and didn't raise his eyes from the ground. He was the little steam engine who could, who could get Veronica off the streets before she started a riot. To their right, a line of people waited at the ticket window for the next show, and Veronica had a few things to say to them.

"That's right, little girls and mommies, line up right here. Inside you'll learn how to keep your mouth shut and your legs closed. You'll learn how you can't trust women. You'll learn how to be perfect by being pretty and petty." She shouted over Taylor's shoulder. "You'll learn how to be the eternal pussy!"

Taylor neither looked up nor turned around. He marched steadily, one foot after another.

"I'm not embarrassing you, am I?" Veronica asked him in a somewhat lower voice.

"Who, me?" he said, wondering if he could have parked any farther away. "No. Not at all. Nice night for a walk."

Veronica renewed her diatribe, louder now. "See with your own eyes the wonders of frigidity! Thrill to the famous awakening kiss! See how you, too, can find happiness cleaning toilets for freaks!"

They reached the car. Taylor unlocked the passenger door and held it open. He studied the waning moon, took note of the sequence of flashing lights on the theater marquee.

Veronica pounded the hood. "Praise God and passive women! All hail the invincible prince!" She burst into song. " 'There she is, Miss America. There she is, your ideal . . .'"

The starting, steering, and piloting of a car had never before occupied Taylor's attentions quite as much. Stoned to the bone with college friends, cautious and deliberate in drunkenness, he had never before driven with such concentration and determination. Meanwhile, Veronica blustered and boomed and spit fire.

"Can you believe that shit? I can't believe it. And to think I grew up on that stuff. I still carry vestiges of it with me today. Did you catch all the antiwoman bias? All of it? There were tons, you know. That film is a misogynist's textbook. It's a two-hour litany of s'pozed tos. We're s'pozed to be good little kitchen slaves. Did you see how happy Snow White is cooking and cleaning, honing her quaint homemaking skills while the little twerps go out to do the *real* work? What's that tell you? Even half-men, malformed men, are better than women. We're s'pozed to be passive. You caught that, of course. Litle Snow White keeps her own silent counsel while she's kicked around and abused. A little boy would have been shown to fight to regain his rightful place in the kingdom but the little girl is s'pozed to be good and quiet and sweet and help out in whatever small way she can. And we're s'pozed to mistrust other women because they're all jealous and devious like the crone. And we can't forget sexual abstinence, can we? I mean, Snow White. It's the hit-you-with-a-brick school of metaphor. We're s'pozed to keep our cunts under glass and put them on display but we must remain pure and for pure read virginal and for virginal read frigid

WORTH WINNING

until our handsome prince unlocks our passions. And pretty! The A-One s'pozed to. It's the only valuable attribute the prissy bitch has, isn't it? But watch out, girl. There's danger. It may be the only thing you've got going for you but it isolates you because other women despise you for it. And, kiddies, if your nose was too deep in your popcorn and you missed all the aforementioned s'pozed tos, the one you couldn't possibly miss—note the climactic music, note the shining sky—was the clear message that as women, we're s'pozed to wait for our *man*. If we *do* anything to affect our lives, we become like the crone, waiting, egoless, as stationary as goddam tree stumps, for a male to come along and make us his adjunct. Not only are we useless, we are effectively lifeless until he comes along, plugs his dick into us, and injects us with the stuff of existence. And heaven help us if we're ugly because the only tool available to us to attract this God the father, this savior, this provider of life—let alone life happily ever after—is our looks." Veronica took a deep breath. "It's despicable.

Taylor shook his head, not in reply to her many queries, but in disbelief. He was tired. Veronica was his third woman in forty-eight hours who, like Snow White, waited to be found by him. If it hadn't been for his princelike behavior, Erin wouldn't have a friend, Eleanor wouldn't have a sex object to jump on, and Veronica wouldn't have a sympathetic man to bitch to. Perhaps under different circumstances, he would have said, "Yes, dear" and let it go at that. If he hadn't seen the film two and a half times in two days and thought and talked about it so much, he might simply have looked beyond her vehemence. But Erin had blubbered to him; Eleanor, cheating on her husband, had used him as a living dildo; and here was Veronica—who, like the other two, had been called up and asked for a date, picked up and taken where she wanted to go—complaining that women get the dirty end of the stick. He said as softly as he could, "That's funny. I thought it was a woman's fantasy all the way through. I thought it was the answer to the timeless question: What do women want?"

Veronica said, "What?" twice. The first meant "I'm not sure I heard you correctly," but the second, unmistakably, meant "What the hell are you talking about (you idiot)?" Veronica tried to say more, but too many sentences tried to form on her lips at once.

Taylor took advantage of the lull. "I thought the movie was a paean to the inestimable, incomparable value of . . ."—he almost said, "the cunt," but caught himself in time—" . . . of womanhood. You think the movie says Snow White is enjoined from doing anything. I think it says she doesn't *have* to do anything, that she's so precious that everybody, including the little animals of the forest, will take care of her, provide for her, work, like the dwarfs, to keep her happy and fed and clothed and sheltered. As far as you're concerned, the crone serves as an admonition for women to mistrust other women. As far as I'm concerned, the crone means that in all creation, woman's only enemy is herself and her only flaw is her vanity, her obsession with her priceless gift of beauty, which you perceive as a curse. With respect to your comments regarding her waiting for her *man*, my viewpoint is one hundred eighty degrees different. The way I see it, the *man* is s'pozed to struggle through adversity, fight battles, endanger himself, and make sacrifices in order to prove his worth to the woman, who then rewards him, bestows upon him, at her discretion, the favors of her sex. And the ending, the riding off into the sunset, for me means that as a man, if I want to bask in the holy light of womanhood, I had better be a prince able to give the woman everything she might desire, and not a poor schlepper who works his ass off in a mine all day and who has only a hut in the woods to offer her." Taylor sighed. Showdown time.

Veronica, conscious of her open mouth, shut it. Several battle strategies sprang to her mind; paths of defense and attack appeared; batteries of mental computers assessed her opponent's strengths and weaknesses. She had debated men's libbers before and knew the flaws in their logic. She braced for the fight, prepared for the abrasion of wills; then, as if somebody let the spirit out, she lost her enthusiasm to do battle.

Was this classic feminine capitulation, she wondered? Or was it Taylor, this particular man? She believed she could win a fight but what, she thought, would be her prize? She felt slightly embarrassed. She had been loud, she had shouted from behind the ramparts of Taylor's broad shoulders, and allowed him to carry her away from the scene she created. Or was she just getting old? Her first reaction was to wade into battle, feminist guns ablaze. So why stop? Afraid to lose? No. She couldn't lose. She was simply tired of fighting. Veronica knew she could launch into her argument and she would hear the same words she'd heard hundreds of times before, and they would sound like an Emerson, Lake, and Palmer album, still good music, still valid, but dated. She remembered her former self and her many confrontations over feminist subjects, and she recalled her feelings subsequent to her "victories." She seldom felt the masculine glee of conquest. More often, she felt as if she'd been party to an execution. When somebody won, something always died, something as simple perhaps as competition. How very feminine, she thought, to prefer a living connection to an extinct ideal.

"Hello?" Taylor inquired.

"Still here,' Veronica replied.

"Suddenly silent," he said.

"Just trying to decide whether I should put your specious argument through the shredder."

"No argument to shred," he replied. "Just an interpretation of a fable. I make no claims for accuracy, no judgments right or wrong."

With something like disgust, Veronica realized the only argument under way was in her head. It was she who had become combative, who had leaped to conclusions. Unlike what she would expect from a man, Taylor had not tried to quiet her or restrain her in any way. She found herself playing with her hair, and thrust her hand back into her lap, barely resisting the impulse to slap it. "Are you sliding away from the subject again? Is this more of the Taylor Worth ambush-and-run school of debate?"

Taylor stifled a yawn. His brain felt as if it were wearing a sweater, a nice, cozy, warm, Perry Como-type cardigan. His angry outburst had exhausted him, and he knew he couldn't keep up with the hysterical Veronica tonight if he swallowed a handful of speed. Taylor reached the beltway and faced a decision. Veronica's house was to the left and the tavern to which he had planned to take her was to the right. He suppressed another yawn with difficulty, hesitated only an instant, and bore left. "No, Veronica," he said finally. "Your hackles are up too far for me tonight. You wouldn't be talking to me. You'd be talking to the mythical masculine mind, to the enemy. I'm not opposed to debate, but you're ready to go to war. If it's all the same to you, I'll plead conscientious objection."

As he drove, she fought to control her feelings of shame. She reminded herself she hadn't said anything she didn't believe, that she had as much right to say what she thought, in public, as MacDonald's had to put up billboards on the highway, and that any man who didn't respect that wasn't worth her time. She looked at Taylor, who'd been a perfect gentleman throughout her tirade, and she realized she had a crush on him. She had crossed the fine line between assertive and obnoxious, between forthrightness and bad taste. She'd drunk four beers and gone on a public harangue over a Walt Disney movie, and he hadn't made the slightest move to censor her.

Taylor glanced over at her and winked, but the tension in the car was palpable. Veronica told herself three distinct issues were involved here: (1) her politics, (2) her behavior, and (3) her man. In that order. She wanted to tell him her vehemence could be interpreted as moral conviction and her combativeness as spontaneity, two traits rarely found in women, but she didn't.

At her front door, she said, "Nightcap?"

He said, "Rain check?"

She kissed her finger, placed it on his lips, and said good night. She didn't let her emotions show until the door was firmly shut.

In the car, Taylor felt the relieved exhaustion of the victorious warrior. He'd wished for an easy way to make it an early evening and she had handed it to him gratis. He guided the Monte Carlo through traffic and praised his good fortune. Not only had he been able to exit graciously, he had been able through judicious silence to impress and befuddle the wise Veronica. When he left, her eyes were anxious, full of questions. He congratulated himself on his dignity, his calm, his effortless mastery of a difficult situation.

What a broad, he said to himself, and laughed out loud, remembering the shocked expressions on the faces of the people in line for the next show. "Eternal pussy" indeed. But her outrageousness was no more impressive than his coolness, his impassive magnanimity. He hadn't challenged Veronica, but neither had he offered reinforcement. She didn't have any idea what he thought of her outburst and, like nothing else, that just killed women.

He rolled down the car window, hummed a few bars of "Whistle While You Work," and wondered for a minute about the proper procedure for transferring ownership of an automobile without an exchange of money. He figured he'd probably have to give Ned a dollar or something like that, and pay some kind of tax. He made a mental note to ask somebody in the legal department at work. He smiled. Things were working out splendidly. Erin believed she'd found her prince. Eleanor couldn't function without his cock. And now Veronica—tough, sharp, savvy Veronica—was second-guessing herself.

CHAPTER THIRTEEN

During her brief career as a free-lance secretary, Harriet had worked in some good places and some bad places, but never before had she been asked to interview for a job that would last only three days. Mrs. Grabowski, at the agency, warned her of the strangeness of the clients, but she also said that if Harriet pleased them, they were likely to award a bonus when the assignment was completed. Therefore, when Harriet parked her car in front of the expansive home with the landscaped yard and the manicured lawn presided over by a petulant Pan perched on a fountain, she was prepared for at least eccentricity.

"You must be Harriet," said Randall, holding open the door for her. "Please excuse my robe. I only just this moment stepped out of the bath. We were late getting home from the bakery, but that's why we need help, isn't it? Byron is still in the shower. Please come in. I'm Randall. How do you do?"

Harriet shook the limp hand and fought mightily to stifle a laugh. Robe indeed. It was a voluminous caftan, a lurid shade of green embroidered garishly with pagodas, lotus blossoms, and other Oriental frippery, and from its billowing folds wafted more flowery scents than from the cosmetic counter at Neiman-Marcus. Harriet noted that if Randall had "only that moment" stepped from the bath, he must have been excruciatingly careful not to dampen his hair—what there was of it—because it obviously had been arranged and carefully sprayed into plastic semipermanence. A perfect type, she thought, in a perfect setting.

The floor of the foyer was black marble; the walls were white marble. An ornate chandelier of glittering glass ropes and crystal dewdrops hung low enough from the ten-foot ceiling for it to be reflected in a vast, gilt-framed mirror directly in front of her. Guarding the entrance to the main hall and the red Persian rug was a statue of Mercury, clad only in his pieplate helmet and little heel-wings. Harriet glanced at his runner's buns and plaster penis only a minute, before following Randall a short way down the hall, past the mahogany staircase on the right and a pair of enormous, full-length portraits on the left—one of which depicted Randall in youth, dapper in white suit with cane, hat, and handkerchief in hand—into a sumptuous Victorian sitting room so cluttered with paintings, busts on pedestals, mirrors, wall hangings, statues, settees, ottomans, occasional tables, flounces, throw pillows, and cuspidors sprouting plants that only on her second look around did she notice the fireplace, and only on her third look did she spot the piano.

"Please sit down," said Randall, gesturing to a loveseat and sweeping the train of his gown around his legs in a single gesture. "We'll have tea when Byron arrives." He appraised her critically as she took a seat. "Well, I must say, I'm pleased. Good for Mrs. Grabowski. She's finally learning that we prefer substantial girls. I just knew a Harriet couldn't be a fluffball. I cannot stand those Debbies and Dotties and Deanies, those revolting little coed types with their pink blouses, chartreuse linen skirts, and disgusting espadrilles that make their feet look like amphibious vehicles in primary colors. Can you imagine a pair of those shoes against this carpet? Ugh. Makes me nauseous to think about it. Doesn't it you?"

Substantial girl, eh? thought Harriet. You screaming queer. You flaming faggot. She restrained her tongue, however, because she found Randall rather cute in an Elizabeth Taylorish way. Also, he had directed his bitchiness against a breed of females Harriet herself disliked, so she made her voice sound like a mouse caught in a rusty door hinge and said, "You mean those girls with the neat spots of rouge on their apple cheeks and their perky little ponytails?"

"And we can't forget their add-a-bead necklaces," said Randall.

"Or their alligators."

Randall beamed. "I just knew I could get along with someone named Harriet."

Byron entered, looking elegant in crisp white shirt, sharply creased gray slacks, and shined penny loafers. Like Randall, he was in his fifties, but he definitely comprised the "masculine" half of this pairing. His full head of white hair, combed straight back from his broad forehead, resembled Kirk Douglas's, and his dark eyes sparkled beneath bushy gray eyebrows. Despite the hint of eyeliner and a dusting of powder on his freshly shaved face, he was gorgeous, elegant. Two thoughts came to Harriet. One, a lamentation: What a waste. The other, a question posed on behalf of all womankind: How did we fail you? His perfume was a confusion of aromas, sweet but dusky, tobacco-y but flowery.

He smelled like a funeral in a leather shop. What a pair. What kind of life must they lead?

"I suppose Randall hasn't said a word about the job?" asked Byron.

"Well, no," Harriet replied, "but we've had a nice chat."

"I assume Mrs. Grabowski told you the job would last for three days only."

"Yes."

"But that we would need you for consecutive days."

"Yes."

"Don't be such a Republican, Byron," Randall interrupted. "You can type, can't you, dear?" he asked Harriet.

"Yes, and I'm a fair bookkeeper as well. Mrs. Grabowski said you needed both."

"There," said Randall. "She'll be fine. You can tell by looking at her. She's not a priss and besides, she doesn't have a single designer label showing. Isn't that wonderful?" Randall leaned forward and patted Harriet's knee. "I'm so glad of that. I despise designer labels. Whatever happened to individuality? It must be television. Once upon a time people read quality in the cut or the fabric of an item of clothing. Now all one needs is a miniature billboard on one's behind. It's appalling. If I wanted to advertise for Yves St. Laurent, I'd wear a sandwich board and demand wages. Honestly. Would you give your ass to Gloria Vanderbilt?"

Harriet was wary. This "interview" was either an elaborate con or a legitimate attempt by flagrant eccentrics to find someone with whom they could get along, and as she could discern no reason why they should harass her, she decided to play it straight. If their intention was to locate a kindred spirit, if they were so careful in their associations they wouldn't tolerate even three days of discomfort, then there was something perversely refreshing about them. Besides, Harriet prided herself on her ability to be as catty as the next girl. She decided it might be fun. She reached out and patted Randall's knee in return. "I was just saying the same thing to my friend Veronica the other day."

"Oh, Veronica. I adore that name. Is she stately?"

"Majestic. Positively noble. At any rate, we were discussing this very matter. The world has gone upside down, inside out. Everything is backwards today." She squirmed around on the loveseat, tossing pillows and plumping cushions until she was comfortable. "There. Now, where was I? Oh yes. The upsidedown world. Well, I remember the old days, when merchants were happy to receive a client's patronage. Do you remember those times? I might be showing my age, but today it's all different. Today it's 'Thank you, Paine Webber,' or 'Thanks, Chevy.' Can you imagine? Self-promotion is one thing, but self-aggrandizement is quite another. I can just hear what my mother would say if the butcher expected her to thank him for taking her money. Outrageous!"

"I'll fetch the tea," said Byron, smiling.

"And that's exactly why we need help, Harriet," said Randall. "This is the end of our fiscal year so I'll need some assistance gathering up the figures, but besides that, we take time—actually Byron takes the time—to contact everybody we do business with. We either praise or scold our suppliers, and we thank our customers and solicit suggestions about how we may improve our service to them. You'll be required to type those letters and—don't tell Byron I said this—make sure the grammar is correct. Can you handle those tasks?"

"Certainly."

The phone rang. Randall ignored it. "We work odd

hours but you will not be required to be at the bakery at three A.M. as we are. If you could arrive at seven, that would be fine. Have you ever tasted our bread?"

"On a few special occasions when I've eaten at the finer restaurants, yes. It is as delicious as it is famous."

"Remind me to give you a loaf before you leave."

Byron arrived with the tea. Randall asked, "Who was that on the phone?"

Byron sighed, obviously distressed. "It was Eleanor. She can't make Weekly News and Reviews this week."

Randall clucked. "Again? Byron, Byron, I'm afraid we're losing a friend. Honey or sugar, dear?" he asked Harriet.

"A drop of honey, please."

"I worry about her so," said Byron. "Something is very wrong. Very wrong. I know it."

"I miss her as much as you do, Byron, but I can't help thinking you're just a little bit jealous." He handed Harriet her tea. "A good friend of ours," he explained, "a married woman with an eleven-year-old son, has found what she thinks is the perfect man. It began as a fling but now we're both concerned she might leave her husband for her lover."

Byron sat down across from Randall. "I admit to some jealousy, of course, but I don't believe this fellow is playing fair. He's a bachelor—or so he tells her—and well-off, and here he is, skulking around to arrange this torrid affair with Eleanor. I mean, Eleanor is attractive, in a bony, Anne Bancroft kind of way, but why would this eligible bachelor, this prize catch, court Eleanor, a—let's be honest, Randall—a thirtyish, average-looking housemouse?"

"Byron!" Randall exclaimed. "Shame on you."

"Well, isn't it true? She's nice and we love her, but she's not what you would call exceptional, is she? And her paramour is supposed to be handsome and unmarried and educated. And here in the District! Where women outnumber men two to one! Why would the ideal man slink around for afternoon quickies with Eleanor?"

"You're so suspicious, Byron." Randall turned to Harriet. "I think he's just upset because Eleanor's become such a bore about this man. He's all she can talk about. He's so handsome and so thoughtful and so outrageously sexy. Do you know what she told us? He became so excited after they saw a movie—and not even a pornographic movie—that he attacked her in the car in a parking lot in the middle of the day. Can you imagine? She said he simply would not be denied. He had to have her immediately. It's sort of tacky, but at the same time it's awfully romantic, isn't it?"

Harriet put her teacup in its saucer. "Romantic men are breaking out all over, like some kind of epidemic. Why can't I catch it? My friend Veronica has met one, too. He's pulled some incredibly exciting stunts. He invited her to a picnic once, and when she arrived she found him sitting under a tree—all alone, no blanket, no nothing—and in ten minutes a catering truck arrived and out popped a crew of waiters dressed in tuxedos. They had a linen ground cloth, candelabra fixed with inextinguishable candles, pâté, champagne, even a flaming dessert. On a Tuesday!"

Randall clucked. "How terribly sexy."

"How did your friend react?" asked Byron. "Are they married yet?"

"No! You'd have to know my friend Veronica to understand. It was too flashy for her, too extravagant."

"Foolish girl."

"She doesn't trust him, claims he's too slick."

"Is she playing hard to get?"

"She's playing impossible to get. She says he's all flash and no substance, but I know the real problem. She's extremely political. Staunchly feminist."

"No. Are those kind still about?"

"Oh yes. And Veronica's Don Juan won't play."

"What do you mean?"

"She can't pin him down. Sometimes he'll argue with her, but more often than not, he slides away from the subject with some clever pun or debonair gesture. She told me about one time they were walking downtown and she was holding forth about something or another and he raced out into traffic and came back with an armload of flowers for her. Not just a couple of stems but an enormous bouquet. He bought a street vendor's entire stock!"

"That's charming."

"Dashing. You don't see that sort of thing very much anymore, even in the movies."

Harriet shrugged. "If it would only happen to me. But tell me more about this sexy fiend who's courting your friend. You're right, Randall. It sounds tacky but awfully exciting. He assaulted her in a parking lot, you say? In the daytime?"

"Well, they were inside a car, but that's not the worst," he gushed. "They did it in a library once and . . ."

"Randall, please," said Byron. "Don't you think you're talking out of school? There are such things as confidences among friends." He spoke to Harriet. "I think your friend Veronica is sensible to be skeptical and cautious. She's certainly being much wiser than our Eleanor. Perhaps Randall is right and I'm just jealous and disappointed at the loss of a good friend, but I simply don't believe in ideal men. Do you, Harriet?"

CHAPTER FOURTEEN

What if, Taylor thought, distributing three drops of aftershave lotion over his face, shoulders, and chest and, slipping his hand beneath the towel draped around his hips, into his pubic hair just in case Erin might finally, by mistake or in some sort of delirium, put her face down there—what if he had met Erin before the bet? It was unlikely he would have courted her because he would have judged her ingenuousness as intellectual laziness and her innocence as dangerous gullibility, and disqualified her peremptorily. If, however, he had kept his mind open and his mouth shut for a change, as he was required to in the bet, and discovered, as he had in Erin, charm where he expected haughtiness and honesty where he expected conceit, how would he have reacted to her?

He spoke to his image in the mirror: "You would have tried to fuck her and if she consented, you would have despised her for being an easy trick, and if she declined you would have despised her for being a tease. Either way you would have ended up complaining to

Ned about beautiful women and their congenital fluffy-headedness."

Taylor frowned at himself and wondered if everybody had rude voices in their heads. Everybody allegedly had a conscience, but he had a deliberative assembly the size of the U.S. Congress, representing about the same diversity of philosophical viewpoints. He had inquisitors in there and prosecutors, sycophants, bleeding-heart liberals, greedy moneygrabbers, idealists, reactionaries, pessimists, apologists, layabouts, workaholics, and one positively virulent critic, and every one of them at one time or another had the floor. Before the bet, despite this mental gallery of kibitzers, he had possessed a single, recognizable personality to which he could confidently refer as "I," but recently his "self" had become as substantial as puff pastry. Maybe he was simply getting tired. The demands of three women weren't exactly insignificant. "Or," he said aloud, searching his reflection for clues, "maybe it's love."

If Erin lacked a fabulous I.Q, or any special talent except what Truck defined as the ability to keep a professional football organization at bay by force of will, she also lacked some other features Taylor thought came as standard equipment on magnificent female bodies—arrogance, insolence, and impudence. She may not have worked her way through her egotism to altruism, but neither had she exploited her advantages. With her looks, she could have been a consummate bitch—like Eleanor, who managed with only a good pair of legs and a fashionable figure—but she wasn't. She was pleasant, cheerful, trusting, and fond of and faithful to solid traditional values, traits that someday would make her a fine wife to somebody. Taylor squeezed the surplus inch or so of flesh at his sides and frowned.

Lately, he'd been wondering whether that somebody should be he.

He knew, of course, marriage was a bad risk. If it were a mutual fund with a similar performance record, he wouldn't consider investing in it. According to the latest figures, about half of all marriages end in divorce. He could get better odds for success dealing drugs. Plus, divorce is harder on men than women, and not only financially. The divorced male's death and disease rate is five times the female's. Only a few men, like Ned, had anything good to say about marriage, and Taylor suspected most of them either of being cowards—of refusing to accept, in Kris Kristofferson's words, the "burden of freedom"—or tyrants—some men he knew ran their households like little fiefdoms. Still, Taylor had met a few who enjoyed mutually honorable relationships with their wives, and in every case they exhibited the rare quality of completeness. To Taylor, a happy, successful pairing was one based on respect and admiration, on active, spontaneously regenerating love. "Can you hear the strains of 'Camelot' in the background?" he asked himself. "Can you see the petal-strewn primrose path? Have you ever heard of fat chance?"

Taylor picked through his mat of chest hair like a monkey grooming itself, found an off-color strand, and plucked it. It was as white as Moses' beard. He searched his eyes in the mirror. "Do you want to get married?" he asked himself. "What are your options?"

He could remain a bachelor and watch himself become slowly petrified by the zero-sum, I-win-you-lose, me-or-you-not-both cynicism he was already beginning to experience like neurological arthritis; or he could find a woman with whom to cohabit. This arrangement he'd tried before and failed at it because he withheld a portion of himself for the critical breaking-up moment, the moment all his cohab acquaintances anxiously or dreadfully anticipated, whether they admitted it or not. And what about children? He wanted offspring, but he never thought "child" unless concomitantly he thought "wife"; and since he never realistically considered marriage, children remained an abstraction.

He stepped out of the bathroom, into the bedroom to the closet to select a suit to wear to Erin's. She had invited him for dinner and, as she had never cooked for him before, this evening represented something of a landmark in their relationship. He perused his wardrobe. Casual elegance was called for, he thought, the Continental look, dashing but informal, something appropriate for leaning against the door jamb with drink in hand, watching a staggeringly beautiful woman, an apron over her simple cocktail dress, hair clipped off her forehead, scurrying around the kitchen, busily attending to final details. "Anything I can do, darling?" he would ask. "Not a thing," she would answer. "May I freshen your drink?," and he'd hand her his glass, fold his arms across his chest, and admire her fine legs, stunning ass, the magnificent swell of her tits, and the supple, dynamic, three-dimensional curvaceousness binding her separate elements together as gracefully, as magically as the fabric of space maintains order among the planets. What a prize she was, this Miss Erin Dolan, what a precious symbol of success, like unlimited cocaine or a Super Bowl ring.

But marry her? Earlier in his career he wouldn't have considered accepting any woman who possessed less than a preset minimum of beauty, sexiness, intelligence, and humor, but now he wondered whether the qualities should be weighted. Perhaps beauty off the scale should lower the requirements in other categories. Erin, because of her looks, had rarely faced challenges, had never been forced to take risks or asked to make sacrifices. Could Taylor legitimately indict her for something she had not done?

He selected a suit and took his time getting ready. He sat around in his underwear while his deodorant dried. He tried on several different shirts, matching them with different ties. He had a cocktail. It was wonderful not to have to think about dinner reservations, and money, and where to go afterward. He was allowed—what a sweet word—to relax and enjoy the evening, mindless, absolved of responsibility. It was a glorious, foreign feeling, satisfying, self-indulgent, in short, feminine, and Taylor loved it. Tonight, Erin Dolan, one of the world's most pampered, desired women, had volunteered, without prompting, spontaneously, to make dinner for him. He didn't even have to bring wine. "All you have to do is be there," she'd said. "I'll take care of everything." Glory, glory, hallelujah. Perhaps the world was in fact evolving. Perhaps there was reason for hope.

Forty-five minutes later, Taylor parked his car in the lot near Erin's apartment. His stomach growled with hunger. Intentionally, he hadn't eaten lunch in order to be free to gorge himself on Erin's hospitality. His mouth watered and not merely at the prospect of food. He wondered what she would be wearing. Unlike Veronica, who tended to wear subdued colors and utilitarian though fashionable clothes, and Eleanor, whose every outfit was selected to complement her long, lean body style, Erin could wear anything—sports clothes, sleazy clothes, bulky clothes, punk costumes, elegant dresses, ruffled confections, or severe sheaths—and look positively delectable. He waited in delicious anticipation for her to open the door, to present herself, a divine vision brought forth for his pleasure, her lips red and parted, her eyes blue and inviting, her body voluptuous and alluring. She would take his hand, press her breasts against him, and her aura would envelop him, enfold him in love.

"Is that you, Taylor?"

"Your one and only."

"I'm going to unlock the door but you have to promise not to come in until you count to ten.

Aha. His imagination conjured sexy scenarios. He envisioned elaborate seduction schemes, with gorgeous Erin as the director and himself the object of her plans.

"I'm counting, love."

"Good, 'cause I'm not ready and I don't want you to see me yet.

"Oh," he said. Damn, he thought.

Of the various personae in his head, the one of which Taylor was most wary, not for what it represented but for the effect it had on his life, was The Critic because The Critic, uniquely capable of perceiving perfection, continually analyzed the separate elements of Taylor's flawed existence and compared them with ideals. The Critic was useful, urging Taylor to strive for improvement as well as cautioning him against false pride, but with respect to Taylor's women, this source of eternal dissatisfaction had been a major pain in the ass, eventually disqualifying every woman Taylor considered he might be able to love for her failure to meet enough of the requirements of the perfect female.

Inside Erin's apartment, holding a drink he'd mixed for himself, Taylor faced the glass doors leading onto Erin's tiny balcony, and the unbidden litany in his

WORTH WINNING

mind began. The perfect female would not live in a mundane apartment in a mundane apartment complex, and if she did, her nest would be distinctive, reflecting her creativity and individuality. The perfect female would not be a slave to fashion and would be contemptuous of fads. The perfect female would be artistic and the accoutrements of her life would reflect her originality.

Taylor glanced around Erin's living room. It was clean and neat but unremarkable. The furniture wasn't cheap, but it was in no way extraordinary, either. The prints on the wall had obviously been chosen to match the carpet color, and Taylor searched in vain for a stylistic touch that would reveal the personality of the woman who lived there, but he could have been standing in the middle of a jobber's display at a home show. The fact that his own house was hardly more distinctive or that his own artistic ability was practically nil did not affect his analysis. Wasn't the purpose of one's ideal mate to provide the qualities lacking in oneself?

He thought of Eleanor's house. Although she hadn't paid for as much as an ashtray, her place was functional, comfortable, even homey in a country-club-correct way. Except for her husband's favorite chair, which she despised but which he forbade her to have reupholstered, the decor suggested easy elegance. You wouldn't put your feet up on the coffee table, for instance, but you might flop your legs over the sides of a chair or sling a few pillows on the floor and relax, as he and Eleanor had done one afternoon, thrashing around on the plush carpet that must have set Howard back quite some.

And Veronica's place. Now, there was a piece of work. In accordance with her horror at the banality of middle-class American tastes, her apartment overflowed with eclectic charm. Her furniture, a curious mixture of periods and fabrics, invited you to come in and be at home. Her bedroom, with its cavelike intimacy and pervasive scent of incense, could have been in another house altogether and, indeed, often seemed to Taylor to be in another world.

He shut off one lamp, then another, but couldn't achieve the lighting effect he desired. He looked around for candles but found none. The magazine rack overflowed with copies of *Glamour*, *Vogue*, and *Harper's Bazaar*. The Critic started up again, this time on the subject of cosmetics. An hour previously, Taylor had been contemplating marriage. Now his mind was filling up with resentment, and the feeling was as old as dating itself. A woman could excuse herself to go to the bathroom, leaving a loving, attentive Taylor behind, and in her brief absence, without suspecting a thing, she could lose him to The Critic, an invisible, relentless adversary whose notepad was full of requirements she never knew she had to meet.

Taylor didn't want it to happen again. He was tired. Couldn't he, just this once, take a woman for what she was? "Please," he mumbled, pressing his eyes with his fingers.

"I beg your pardon?" Erin's voice was as soft as dusk.

Taylor turned to look at her and The Critic vanished. "Wow," was all he could say.

"Like it?" she asked and did a model's turn to give him an all-sides view.

She wore her hair up, elaborately curled and pinned. Her face could have come straight off the cover of one of the magazines in the rack at Taylor's feet. Pearls on small chains dangled from her ears. A matching string encircled her neck. Her sky-blue dress, a shimmery, gossamer affair, bared one shoulder completely. It was gathered at the waist and the skirt flared slightly in graceful folds to just below her knees, giving it a kicky, carefree look. When she spun, the skirt swirled upward, and Taylor caught his breath at the sight of her terrific legs in high-heeled blue pumps.

"You are so beautiful," he said reverently. "I wonder how many ugly girls God had to make to save up so much beauty for you." He kissed her, and she felt so good he gathered her to him and kissed her again, running his hands down the silky bareness of her back. He wanted to apologize to her, feeling he had wronged her. He wanted to thank her for coming back to him after all the terrible things he had thought about her.

"My goodness," she said, breaking the kiss, easing away from him, patting her hair. "We've got a dinner to eat and I'm not about to miss out on it. I've worked too hard putting it together."

Taylor was left panting as usual.

"Notice, please, how clean everything is," Erin announced proudly. "All dusted and swept and scrubbed and polished just for you." She gestured to the living room like a model in a TV commercial.

Taylor nodded and reached for her, for the reassuring feel of her, but she danced away. "I hope you're hungry. I'm starved." She led the way into the kitchen. "Will you open the wine?"

No leisurely cocktail? No quiet moment together holding hands? No hors d'oeuvres? No gastronomic foreplay? The litany resumed: The perfect female would be a capable hostess. The perfect female would not require constant reinforcement.

What was it? he wondered. And why? Why this unyielding vituperation? Was it the legitimate pursuit of excellence? Nonsense. He had run away from challenging women and stayed with losers. He had left women for spite and stayed with others for want of anything more interesting to do. He followed Erin's gently swaying skirt into the kitchen, and his heart ached. Most men would run naked through gunfire just to be this close to her. This girl could have the world without asking for it, and here she was, trying to please him, Taylor Worth, ordinary, hypercritical male. There was something wrong with him. Had to be.

"I put the kabobs in before I went in to change," she said. "They should be just about done by now." She held her skirt out of the way and opened the oven. "Hmm. I'll have to turn them."

Taylor pulled the cork from a bottle of Blue Nun. "Shrimp kabobs?" he asked.

"No. Beef," she said, poking inexpertly in the oven with a pair of tongs. "I know you're supposed to have red wine with meat, but you won't mind, will you? I don't like red wine and besides"—she shrugged—"there are so many different kinds, I wouldn't know what to pick."

She should have known what to pick. During every one of their restaurant dates, Taylor had told her at least one winelore anecdote—more cute stories; how many different stories had he told her over the past months? —partially to entertain her but also to educate her because he believed the perfect female would know something about wine. What had she been listening for? The tone of his voice? The moral of the fable? Or had she simply been patronizing him all this time, like the proper little date? Let the man talk. Men love to talk.

Erin closed the oven door and peeked under the lid

of a pot on the stove. "Everything's on schedule," she said. "Do you like the table settings? Did you notice the real linen napkins?"

She was trying so hard. Taylor felt ancient.

"What's the matter, hon?" she asked.

"Nothing," he said, giving her a smile in which his eyes did not participate. "Just hungry, I guess."

Erin invited Taylor to sit while she flashed between the kitchen and the dining nook, in and out of Taylor's vision, a veritable streak of blue and gold. A casserole dish overflowing with a gooey, bubbling marshmallow-and-sweet-potato mixture appeared on the table, followed by another casserole dish filled with green beans and almonds. A basket of steaming rolls materialized after another flash of blue skirt, and suddenly he found a huge bowl of green salad in front of him. Then there was the condiment tray and the butter dish. It looked like Thanksgiving dinner, and Erin showed no sign of slowing down. Taylor sipped his wine, convinced she had exhausted her culinary repertoire. Finally, with brand-new candles illuminating a repast fit for the crew of an aircraft carrier, she joined him, and when he offered a toast to the cook, she was almost too jittery to hold her glass.

Taylor filled his plate under Erin's anxious gaze. She's just a kid, he told himself, a full fourteen years his junior. Was he capable of staging a civilized dinner at age twenty-one? The potatoes had the texture of oatmeal. The kabobs were overdone. The green-bean casserole was the product of three cans. Erin was too nervous to eat. Taylor muttered his insincere compliments, while a full-scale debate raged in his mind.

Doesn't she deserve points for good intentions? The road to hell is paved with good intentions. Doesn't eagerness count for something? Eagerness and a half a buck will get you a cup of coffee anywhere in the city. So she has to be perfect, then. No, but she has to be somehow, in some way, complete, fully articulated. Her beauty is comprehensive. So is her immaturity.

He ate. She picked at her food. They spoke of insignificant things. She was gorgeous and looked at him adoringly. He smiled a lot and tried to silence The Critic, who grilled him, prosecutor fashion, about what it would be like to be married to Erin. They'd have a house; he'd have a job; she'd have kids. She'd have the security and stability she always wanted. He'd have the loveliest mate in the District. So, asked The Critic: What price beauty?

"And now for dessert," Erin said when Taylor pushed away his plate.

"How about a cup of coffee first?" he pleaded. "I couldn't . . ."

Erin frowned. "I pay attention to you," she said. "I know you never eat dessert. This is nothing to eat but it's sweet anyway. If you would take yourself into the living room, I'll join you in a jiffy."

"I'll help you with the dishes."

"You'll do as I tell you. Go."

Taylor burped his way into the living room, sour of stomach and temperament. The question Freud should have asked, he decided, was not "What do women want?" but "What are women for?"—besides having babies, of course, as consciously creative an act as growing fingernails. What was Erin for? If she were just for pretty, she could've been a flower. Given all the tools in the world and all of Time to play with them, what would she invent? Given all the world's libraries, could she synthesize a philosophy? And why Eleanor?

What contribution had she ever made to the planet? Half of Howard Junior? Some contribution. And to hear her complain about the kid was to believe she didn't have a thing to do with his development. Sanctified mothers had their little boy babies and nurtured them and cared for them lovingly. Then after time those babies miraculously became men: mean, awful, insensitive clones of their fathers. What exactly was the mother's responsibility here? Taylor made a mental note to ask Veronica. She'd definitely have an answer, or at least a theory, which was more than Erin or Eleanor could ever be expected to devise, but Veronica was a freak, an anomaly, a woman with a sense of humor—probably a mutant.

"Turn off that lamp, will you?" asked Erin as she switched off one on her side of the room and entered carrying lighted candles in a brass stand. She placed the candles on the coffee table, kissed Taylor on the cheek, and floated through the soft light to the stereo to put on some music. "Be right back," she said and left the room.

Simultaneously, and with equal fervor, he loved her and hated her. How could he blame his eyes for following her? How could he prevent his heart as well as much of his brain from melting in response to such a superbly graceful triumph of human genetics? How could he blame her for lacking anything? Some unconscious yet willful facet of the human race had striven for generations to build a specimen like her. Erin, walking toward him carrying a tray on which was balanced a coffee service and a package wrapped in gold paper, was spectacular. The knowledge that she was also astonishingly unpretentious caused his stomach to churn more violently.

She set the tray on the table and handed him the gift. "For you," she said, "the world's last true gentleman. The only man I ever met," she continued, as if reciting a prepared speech, "who's respectful enough to keep his hands to himself and courteous enough not to try to talk me into things I don't want to do."

The card on the package read "With all my love." Taylor opened the box and found a bottle of thirty-year-old Sandeman port flanked by a pair of exquisite crystal glasses. "Thank you," he said. The words barely shouldered past the lump in his throat.

Erin poured coffee. Taylor poured the tawny treasure. The coffee was rich and strong; the port as deep and sweet as fond memories. Taylor leaned back and savored.

"Now close your eyes," Erin said.

Taylor did so with pleasure. Much of the history of Western civilization resided in those flavors as well as a good bit of the story of his own maturity. It had been months since he'd simply sat and sipped, since long before the wager began. He inhaled the musky subtlety of the port, and it soothed his mind like balm. The coffee reminded him of the possibility, however remote, of peace.

"Keep your eyes closed but open your mouth," Erin said.

Taylor did as he was instructed and bit down on a cigar. "Erin," he exclaimed in disbelief.

"The man at the cigar store cut the little hole in the end for me." She snapped a lighter and held the flame steady.

Taylor didn't hesitate. He puffed appreciatively. Fine port, excellent coffee, a good cigar, and a beautiful woman who not only didn't mind all this masculine affectation but who had supplied the trove herself. The Critic was dead. Long live the five senses.

Erin put away the lighter and refilled cups and glasses. "Are you happy?"

Taylor exhaled cigar smoke, inhaled coffee vapor, and mingled those marvelously dark sensations with the flavor of the wine. The result was to his mouth what the sight of Erin was to his eyes. "Erin," he said and paused. Why not say it? he thought. The time was right, the emotion was right there, at hand. "I love you."

CHAPTER FIFTEEN

"It's a beautiful morning. These are beautiful bagels. This is beautiful champagne." Veronica's exuberance outshone the sunlight flooding through the bay windows of one of Taylor's favorite places for brunch. "*Garçon*, an extra plate of lox," she called to their waiter. "And alert the slaves to prepare my barge for sailing." The waiter came to the table, lifted the champagne from the ice bucket, expertly wrapped his linen towel around the bottle, and topped off Veronica's glass.

She leaned toward him, plucking at the daffodil in her hair. "Don't you just hate ostentation?" she asked.

"I like to see people enjoying themselves; makes it easier for me to be at work. What are you two celebrating by the way? Anniversary?"

With a toss of her head and a lilt in her voice, Veronica smiled and said, "My abortion."

The waiter's face fell. Taylor had to cover his mouth with a napkin to keep from spitting out his eggs Benedict.

Veronica winked at the waiter. "Little joke. Just teasing."

Taylor's eyes were watering. "You don't do straight material, do you?" he asked when he stopped coughing.

"In college, we called it guerrilla theater."

"Monkeying around, you mean."

"Isn't that what all kids do when they go out for rhesus?"

Taylor moaned. "Stop gibbon me a hard time."

Veronica laughed. "I like you, Taylor. You're smart, funny and you don't try to change me. Men always do that. You're very weird. Are you sure you're not married?"

"Positive."

"Never been married? No divorces? No dependent children?"

"Not a one."

"Amazing. And you've got your own teeth, too. So how come?"

"How come I have my own teeth?"

"How come you're not married?"

Taylor hesitated. Veronica had never been subtle, but she'd been extremely careful not to ask potentially embarrassing questions. He considered several clever answers before deciding on the truth. The truth worked well with Veronica, which surprised him because in his experience, honesty with women was about as effective as compassion in business. "I don't like women very much."

Veronica licked cream cheese off a finger. "Can't blame you for that."

"What's this?" Taylor exclaimed. "The feminist disparages her sisters?"

"Don't misunderstand me. I don't like men even more. My alias is Ann Thrope."

"Ann Thrope?"

"Miss Ann Thrope."

"Ah. Misanthrope. I get it," Taylor said. "That's cute."

"That's me all the way, Taylor. I live for cute."

WORTH WINNING

Images of Erin danced in Taylor's head: miniskirts and bobby socks; stuffed animals in her bedroom; her apoplectic adoration of puppies and babies.

"We're into a new era now," Veronica continued. "Postfeminism. It's what happens to the intelligent woman when she realizes her gender comprises fifty-one percent of the population, and almost fifty-three percent of the electorate. Post-feminism is a condition, a numbing comprehension that if women weren't willing to relinquish stewardship of the planet to men, we'd have control, not just equality."

Taylor collapsed in his chair. "Well, kiss my butt and call me Nancy," he said, astonished. "I never thought I'd hear a woman, especially a feminist, admit it. I could kiss you, Veronica."

"So what's stopping you?"

He leaned across the table and his lips met hers in lewd combat.

After brunch, the two of them wandered around Georgetown, hand in hand, window shopping, kibitzing, enjoying each other's company, the smell and feel of early spring, and the spectacle of Washington, D.C., on parade.

"I'd love to have the makeup concession for that bunch," Veronica said, noting a trio of girls dressed and coiffed to the teeth. "Are they in the theater or going to a masquerade? What do you think they look like when their faces are clean? Why do men find that attractive?"

Taylor watched the three girls walk away. They were young buds ready to burst. "Womancraft," he answered.

"I beg your pardon?"

"Womancraft," he said. "Women wear skirts in the winter. It must be cold. Womancraft. Why nylon stocking? I won't even mention high heels. It's what men don't do. *Vive la difference*, remember?" He mussed

Veronica's unruly auburn hair. "Those three are overdone, but then most women are. I guess they have to do something with their time."

Veronica snarled. "Uh-huh. Unlike men, who are about the important business of the world, you mean."

"Men don't spend ninety million dollars a year on paint and powder for their faces."

"You'd prefer they spent their money on guns like boys do? How much does a tank cost?"

Taylor stopped beside a shiny Porsche Cabriolet with its top down parked beside the curb. "OK, Veronica. Look at this machine. Do you agree it is a thing of some beauty or at least efficiency?"

Veronica frowned. "Yes, it's nice and yes, I agree if it weren't for men, we wouldn't have mechanical things like Porsches."

"Or airplanes," Taylor added.

"Or nuclear weapons."

"Or electric lights."

"Or acid rain."

"Or indoor plumbing."

"Or toxic wastes."

"Or cameras."

"Or an economy that tries to commit suicide every fifty years.

"Or musical instruments."

"Or racketeers or buccaneers or brigadiers."

Taylor grinned. "What would we have, Veronica?"

"A safer planet to live on, for one thing. Ever heard of an army of women marching off to war? Couldn't you just hear it? 'General Annette, the Third Division won't attack until after *The Young and the Restless.*' Who needs to kill people when you can ruin their reputations?"

Taylor laughed. "I like you. You're fair; you're funny;

you're not a wimp; and in your own short, round way, you're good-looking."

"Oh, thanks. Great compliment. On the order of 'You don't sweat much for a fat girl.'" She punched him.

Taylor put his arm around her and they continued along M Street. They joked. They poked their noses in the shops and poked fun at other people in the promenade.

"You think I'm fair, huh?" Veronica asked after a while.

"Amazingly. I didn't think women had the capacity until I met you."

"Another backhanded compliment, but I'll let it pass," Veronica replied. "So how about you? Are you fair?"

Taylor looked at her. It was her second serious question of the day.

Veronica continued. "I can't quite figure you. You're fair to me but, well, take that last crack for example. You never let up on women. We *are* all one species, you know. So in your mind, as in Christianity, are women the evil half and men the good half?"

"Man is the perfectly logical creature," Taylor said, baiting her.

"Spare me."

"Consider the beauty of this," Taylor said, stopping in the middle of the sidewalk, gesturing grandly. "Consider the male, peeping out at the octo-mega-quintillion parsecs of the universe from his infinitesimal mudball in an insignificant corner of an unremarkable galaxy and declaring, with a straight face, mind you, his intention to conquer space."

Relief flooded Veronica's aura.

"Consider the male," Taylor continued, holding forth theatrically, forcing passers-by to give him extra room, "surveying his own planet—water, vegetation, soil, the atmosphere of which he is an indivisible part, the utter absence of a truly threatening predator—and declaring, with a straight face, mind you, a war: man versus nature.

"What do I think of men, Veronica? They—we—are kookoo. Crazy as bedbugs."

"Hooray!" Veronica cheered. "Oh, hooray. I never thought I'd hear a man admit it. Taylor, I could kiss you."

"So what's stopping you?"

Veronica threw her arms around him and kissed him vigorously, repeatedly, enthusiastically.

Taylor at first shrank self-consciously from Veronica's deluge of affection. Erin waited for kissing like a flower waits for picking. Eleanor kissed, but hungrily, not affectionately. Veronica poured fondness over him like sunshine, and Taylor, tickled and flattered by her unabashed tribute, started to laugh. Veronica stuck her tongue in his ear, climbed up him like a monkey at play; and there in the middle of M Street, Taylor closed his eyes and absorbed the lovely sensation of being loved.

CHAPTER SIXTEEN

"I'm here, Taylor. I'm home!"

It was Eleanor. No mistaking those legs, long and thin, high-heeled, sticking out of a slender, slit skirt. Her upper body and face were hidden behind brown shopping bags from which spinach and celery appeared to grow. Taylor truly loved those legs, and for a minute he fantasized about attaching them to Erin's body, keeping Erin's face but draining out her brains and filling the cavity with Veronica's, and, just to make sure the transplant took, adding Veronica's amazing hair. There. The perfect woman. Not that Erin's legs were bad or Veronica's either for that matter, but Erin could go to fat if she weren't careful and Veronica, well, Veronica was short.

"Tell me again, my luscious man-hunk," Eleanor burbled. "Tell me out loud, again, that I can cook lunch and dinner for you and we'll be together all night in your bed, slithering and sliding over each other, melting into one another, skin to skin, sin to sin."

"All night," Taylor said obediently and added Eleanor's sexy vocabulary to his composite fantasy woman.

Eleanor could talk a man to erection. He slid his hand up her nylons to her crotch. To his surprise, he felt skin and hair. "Garter belt?" he asked.

"Crotchless pantyhose."

Taylor kneaded her cunt. "Sure, we can do all those things," he said. "Before lunch."

She sank her teeth into his neck; her twat, like some ravenous animal, gobbled at his hand; her feet were off the ground; she made muffled noises into his suitcoat; and he knew he needed only to speak a few magic words to trigger an orgasm. "I love your pussy," he whispered and her humping accelerated. "My cock needs your cunt." Key words, he thought, to open the door to frenzy. "Come, you harlot," he commanded. "Come right now, you sleazy bitch," and she did, right on cue, just before the strength gave out in Taylor's supporting arm.

With Eleanor, the orgasm marked no ending. She'd read enough about multiple-multiples in her innocuous homemaker magazines. A woman deserved multiples, needed them. Why have the equipment and let it atrophy? Taylor braced for Eleanor's onslaught and tried to recall, as he sank down under her insistent tugging, the last time he'd swept the kitchen floor. On their way down, she dutifully paused to suck him to full erection, but her intention unquestionably was to fuck. She craved fucking like a junkie. No other woman in Taylor's experience used him like Eleanor. Her cunt munched his cock, chewed him, savored him, nibbled him delicately, and tried to bite him off. Sometimes he felt like a cud, other times like a pacifier, and still other times like a hunk of meat in the jaws of a famished beast. Eleanor the gourmande, the epicurian fuck.

Subversive magazines, Taylor thought, as he drove into her and was devoured, ground into her and was gulped. Eleanor lying still, hips immobile, had more moves than most women in ecstasy. Even Veronica, as adept and as much fun as she was, could learn something about muscle control from this energetic mother and housewife. Sexercise, thought Taylor. Some self-improvement article in *Redbook* or *McCall's*. Innocent reading for the homebound woman. Are your menus boring? Here's how to make the perfect soufflé. Tired of your curtains? Sew your own with this unique pattern. Sex life stagnant? Try these exercises. Grow a pussy-tongue. Teach your twat to talk. Oh. Eleanor, how do you do that? Do it again. Do it some more.

Since their first time in the changing room at the department store, Taylor knew Eleanor was playing a game of catchup. She had years to catch up, thousands of orgasms to make up. No. For multiple-multiple Eleanor, make that hundreds of thousands. All those high-school-nice-girl years, when her long, skinny legs dangled out of legal-limit miniskirts. All that desperate inveigling followed by interminable teasing. Then her husband-hunting days and her obsessive protection of her precious reputation. Elegantly slender, then, and choosy. Then Howard, then Junior, then the country club, then the subversive magazines. Fifty percent of married women have affairs, according to the latest polls. Her closet was full of seductive clothes and her head was full of seduction scenes. Taylor wondered how much she'd caught up, whether this current orgasmic display had boomed and flashed for the high-school basketball team or for some later frustration, her tennis instructor perhaps or Howard Junior's scoutmaster.

They had squirmed beneath the table; her ankles rested on his shoulders; he sighted down a long, slick leg and felt his own orgasm rumbling within him. He closed his eyes and successive waves of heat rolled down his belly from his heart to his cock. Surf's up, he thought irrationally. Then the waves were beneath him, and he rose with them and rode them on a supple raft. All was liquid undulation; all was gooey sensation. Behind his eyes, red hair appeared, blond tits, legs going on forever. "Veroni . . ." he said involuntarily. No names! "Erin . . ." Shut up! The brain-maiming coming came, caution's bane, cause of all blame. He yelled a name, but it came out garbled, Erinor or Vereleanor, and he collapsed amid a hundred legs, chair legs, Eleanor's, and the table's.

Eleanor pulled herself along by her elbows until her back rested against the dishwasher and let her legs flop open. Jezebel, thought Taylor, a modern wanton who could straighten her skirt, tuck in her blouse, walk down the street, and nobody would notice. A few people might catch her scent, but the way Americans shut down their senses in public, they wouldn't give it a second thought. There's so much screwing going on, he mused. Everybody's screwing, everywhere, all the time. Whatever happened to modesty? To fidelity? She brushed back her hair with her hands. It looked fine, and L'Oréal or some such outfit guaranteed her makeup against the effects of a hurricane. Taylor noted he was more disheveled than she, and for the first time since the bet began, and for no particular reason he could isolate, he felt the control of his destiny slipping out of his fingers.

"Pox on diets and exercise," Eleanor announced. "Have you ever seen a woman look as good as when she's getting a good fucking regularly? The converse is also true: Have you ever seen a man look as bad as when he isn't? I know that for a fact. You should see Howard these days."

Taylor tried to gather himself together. He'd have to change his shirt at least, probably his entire suit. He brushed a popcorn kernel from his pantsleg and glanced at the clock. "It's late," he said. "I have to get back to work before Mac fires . . ." He stopped in midthought. "What did you say, Eleanor? What did you say about Howard?"

"I've made you miss your lunch, haven't I? Let me make you a sandwich. You can take it with you in the car."

"Sure. Fine. Great. But what did you say about Howard?"

Eleanor laughed. "Ever since I've cut him off, he's looked positively ill."

"You cut him off?" Taylor shrieked.

"Cold. I have you. I don't need him. I confronted him with all his past affairs and threw him out of the bedroom."

"Keep talking," Taylor said as he ran into the bedroom and started throwing clothes around in two distinctly different kinds of panic.

"I've wanted to for years," she called from the kitchen. "Besides, I can't come with him anymore, and I know it's because I want to be faithful to you."

Taylor tore off his tie and tossed it among his shoes at the bottom of the closet. His sticky underwear followed his tie. "I appreciate that, Eleanor, but do you think it's a good idea? Won't he start to get suspicious?"

"About us? He already knows."

Taylor, one leg into his pants, fell over sideways onto the bed. "Already knows!"

"Not about you. He doesn't know it's you. Do you take mustard or mayonnaise or both?"

Taylor rushed back into the kitchen, tightening his tie. "Eleanor, I'm not sure if it's right for you to, uh, I mean, Howard might, uh, it might be better if, uh, you do your wifely duty until, uh . . ."

Eleanor stretched her arms around his neck. "I don't want to talk about Howard. I'm with you now. I'll be here all night and I can pretend it's for forever."

Taylor wished blindness and paralysis on all purveyors of soap operas. "Got that sandwich ready?"

"I'm sorry, hon. You never answered me. Do you take mustard or mayonnaise?"

"I don't care." He stepped to the counter and saw arrayed there makings for a colossal Dagwood sandwich, none of it assembled. "Hey," he said, "this is sweet but I really don't have time, see? I'm supposed to be at a meeting in"—he glanced at the clock and groaned—"five minutes. Here." He grabbed a slice of bread. She put a tomato on it. He reached for the cheese. She tossed some shredded lettuce on it. He plastered a second slice of bread on top. "A pickle," she said. "Can't have a sandwich without a pickle." She followed him to the door with the kosher dill in her outstretched hand.

"Kiss?" she called and when he pecked her cheek, she slid the slimy pickle into his hand.

At the car, he threw the pickle away. He opened the sandwich to release the tomato and lettuce he knew would fall onto his shirt if he tried eating while driving and he lost the cheese as well. "Fuck," he said and threw everything to the ground. Taylor was losing it. Emotional disorientation was draining away his efficiency. Simple fatigue was affecting his judgment. Conditions were perfect for mistakes born of panic, but in classic masculine style, he ignored the warning signs.

Eleanor kicked off her shoes, peeled off her hose, and padded into the bathroom for a washcloth. She felt airy, light, and musical, like a wind chime in a Japanese garden. She held up her knee and curled her toes like a Kabuki dancer while she dabbed at her vagina. She never felt this way at home. At home she felt like a lavatory attendant.

Eleanor dried herself and headed directly for the kitchen to find a broom to sweep that gritty floor. To her, it was disgusting how some people lived. Once she finished the sweeping, she cleaned the silverware and utensil drawers, places which needed attention in every home except her own. Soon she had a long list of things to buy for the house, including a hanging notepad for the kitchen phone and a slotted spoon and a rubber spatula. Bachelors! How could anyone run a kitchen without a rubber spatula?

A half hour later, she moved her cleaning implements into the living room, which since her first visit had driven her crazy. She just knew Taylor never moved his sofa before vacuuming, and there were a couple of shelves above eye level that she was positive were coated with the dust of ages, like the very visible lower shelf of the coffee table, the screen of the television set, and the smoked-glass cover of the turntable. "Taylor, Taylor," she said aloud. "You certainly need a woman around here."

The bathroom was the worst, with mildew on the tiles and a disorderly mess beneath the sink, but she decided those items would have to wait for her next visit. Just now, she only had time to scrub the sink, the tub and the commode and sweep the floor because she still had the vacuuming to do and dinner to prepare and she wanted plenty of time to take a long, scented bath and make herself beautiful.

In the bedroom she dug out Taylor's socks from among his shoes in the closet, lined up the shoes two by two, hung the discarded tie on the rack, and deposited his hastily dropped underwear in the hamper. She hung up his suit and took a minute to rearrange the closet—

suits to the left, shirts to the right, outerwear and robes at either end. On the shelf above the suits was a disorderly pile of sweaters. "Men," she said, "are all alike."

She took a moment to stretch out on the bed and fantasize. It was difficult not to. Everything around her had the smell of Taylor; every accoutrement had the Taylor touch, from the selection of books on the headboard shelf to the—her fingers lifted a blond hair from the bedspread. Eleanor carefully held it up to the light. She felt the sting of jealousy and decided to try a little bit harder to render Taylor's wonderful cock useless after every fucking session.

She crawled off the bed and walked to his dresser, where she handled things—just to hold them, just to feel him through them: his hairbrush, his spare-change jar, his jewelry case. She hesitated a moment, then opened it. She found a couple of gold chains, a college ring, two watches, and probably twenty cufflinks, all unpaired—something else she'd take care of sometime. She continued to fish around in the disorderly case and found a small velvet box. She opened it. It contained a woman's engagement ring—one diamond, simple setting, perhaps a half carat in size. She slipped it on her finger.

Eleanor held up her hand and admired it, then she did a plié, using the dresser drawer as a barre. The drawer slid open. Eleanor hesitated. She glanced inside. She shut the drawer again, paused another moment, and reopened it. Very carefully, she began an inspection of Taylor's private things.

CHAPTER SEVENTEEN

When Taylor arrived at Veronica's, he could hear the party through the door. He knocked but no one answered. He would have needed a Klaxon horn to be heard above the shouting. Veronica had warned him. "Attend at your own risk. If you don't like basketball or if rabid sports madness offends you, then don't show up. Also, if you'd prefer not to see me loud, abusive, obnoxious, and probably drunk, then don't come, but if you want to experience me at my best, then by all means you're welcome." He shifted his twelve-pack of beer to his other hand and considered leaving. Taylor needed a party like the flu, but in true gentlemanly fashion he put duty above sanity. Strategically speaking, he could not have done otherwise because Sunday he was supposed to leave for a three-day beach trip with Erin, and Wednesday would be spent preparing for another three-day "intensive," this time with Eleanor, thanks to a Howard-Howard Junior father-son outing; therefore, except for Thursday, two days from now, when Taylor would probably work late to prepare his office for his weeklong "vacation," this was his only opportunity to be with Veronica. It gave him a headache. Was it actually necessary, he wondered, to expose his bruised and weary brain to a blathering gaggle of lapsed undergraduates? He decided it wasn't. Once Erin and Eleanor were in the bag, Veronica could have him to herself; he'd move in with her if that's what she wanted, but at the moment, quiet privacy was in order.

He was about to turn away from the door when a voice behind him said, "Her name is Veronica. She's the short, dark one, remember?"

Eyes wild with panic, Taylor whirled around to face an abundant woman in a University of Something sweatshirt.

"You looked so confused," she said. "Confusion's inappropriate in someone with your reputation." She offered her hand. "You're Taylor Worth. I know all about you. I'm Harriet Ingram, Veronica's counselor."

He shook her hand and mumbled a greeting while his heart tried to beat down the walls of his chest. His sudden, uncontrolled agitation made it clear to him that he was unfit to attend a party. But Harriet, along with scaring him senseless, had unwittingly cut off his retreat.

"If you're waiting for someone to announce you, you'll stand out here forever. Come on in."

In the middle of the living room among about a dozen guests, dressed in bluejeans and a ratty, faded University of North Carolina T-shirt, Veronica, with a beer can in her hand, held forth about some basketball player from her alma mater who "had the prettiest jump shot" and about his superhuman performance against the University of the Other Guys in the NCAA finals some years ago. She spotted Taylor and waved without interrupting her paean. She had also warned him she might ignore him but advised him not to take it personally. Certain events transcended ordinary social intercourse and an NBA playoff game starring four of her all-time favorite players was one of them.

Harriet led him inside. "There's a cooler full of ice for your beer in the kitchen and help yourself to the goodie table. I need to deliver a long overdue hug. Talk to you later."

The TV roared, two men in blazers sang a college fight song, the high-pitched whine of feminine chatter mingled with the midrange drone of masculine imperatives, and Taylor felt like a bubble in a bathtub of noise.

"Hey, baby," said Veronica, kissing him on the cheek.

"Your southern drawl is showing," he said, forcing a grin.

"Y'ain't heard nothin' yet," she teased. "By half time you'll hear languid breezes through magnolia trees. Come meet my friends."

She introduced him around and his blank, genial smile was met by the standard inane greetings of happy-faced sports buffs. Fortunately, he wasn't required to converse very much because with each soft, sincere hand he shook, with each pair of intelligent, appraising eyes he looked into, with each witty remark he parried, he lost a small measure of his social graces. He knew these people were Veronica's friends, but he saw them merely as standard-issue, upwardly mobile young Washingtonians and prayed the game would keep them occupied. He didn't know what he'd do if they started dropping political celebrity names and talking real estate prices.

Having convinced Veronica to leave him to his own devices, he poured down two quick beers and retreated to the fringes of the crowd. The noise was awful and the artificial revelry grated on his skin like sandpaper, but he decided to stay until after the game for the sake of appearances and slide out as soon as politely possible thereafter.

A bald guy jumped up, shouting at the TV. What was his name? Haldane or Haldoon or something like that. Definitely one of Veronica's former lovers. Taylor speculated about the short guy with the walrus moustache, too. A nice little incestuous group. He finished his third beer, nipped a quick shot from somebody's unattended bottle of bourbon, and watched the bountiful Harriet smother one of the male guests with her considerable bosom. See the women nervously giggle. Watch the men guffaw. Hey gang, he thought. How about an orgy? We can spread Cream Havarti and marinated artichoke hearts on the girls' aerobically tuned bodies. Prizes for the boys with the biggest love handles. Prizes for the biggest mortgages. It'll be a hip super-aware group-grope conducted by dress-for-success refugees from the sixties. Power to the people, all you lawyers, accountants, and businesswomen. Come on, Republicans. Let it all hang out! Taylor steadied himself against a table. He was definitely losing control.

Veronica found him. "How're you doing, handsome?" She threw her arms around him and planted a wet kiss on his cheek. "None of these matrons has tried to pick you up, have they?"

"Great. No."

There was a time out and the crowd surged against the treat table. Taylor grabbed an especially enormous olive he'd had his eyes on for some time, but Harriet snatched it out of his hand just as he was going to pop it into his mouth. "Mine," she said.

One of the lawyers (or was he in insurance?) teased Veronica. "Hey, kid, all this *très chic* food is fine for

WORTH WINNING

chamber music recitals, but this is a round-ball game and I've got a hankerin' for a hamburg."

Harriet, who could outpun Veronica, snorted, "Lowlife. Be careful or you'll get our hostess Bern-ed up."

The lawyers got it if Taylor didn't. "Ukraine talk like that to me."

"Why not?" demanded Harriet with a grin. "Can't Gdansk?"

From there, the exchange moved quicker than a Laker fast break, but Taylor, caught in the middle, was left flatfooted and dumbstruck.

"Oslo down. I can't keep up."

"Norway, man."

"Don't be Bulgar."

"Paris the thought."

With exaggerated moans and excessive laughter, the gang surged back to the TV and left Taylor in an altered state of mind. Maybe they weren't so bad after all, he told himself, trying to suppress feelings of inferiority. Veronica, whose opinions he respected, was proud of them. "In a place as impersonal as the District," she'd said, "to keep friends is an accomplishment against odds."

Heedless of an expanding melancholy, Taylor popped another beer and thought of friends. Did he have any? Could he get on the phone, call around, and fill his house with people who'd be comfortable together? He thought hard. He had golf buddies and business acquaintances, but Ned was probably his only friend. He corresponded with a few folks from college but rarely saw them. His little black book contained the names of dozens of women but Taylor's women were hardly friends.

As a single organism, Veronica's crowd erupted in a cheer. There were hugs and back-slapping all around, and Taylor unaccountably found himself on his feet, cheering too, anxious to be included in the congenial display of asexual, uncritical love. Who cared about nukes? Who cared about toxic waste? Here were a dozen or so intelligent people willingly suspending reality to hoist a few beers and share a few laughs. Was there anything intrinsically wrong in that? Or was there something wrong with him? Where was the fellowship in his life? He recalled an old friend's wise, patient laughter and it echoed through his inebriated mind.

Half time created a mad dash for the bathroom and the buffet, and the game was ten minutes into the second half before the crowd settled down again. Veronica found him and crawled into his lap. "I'm a little drunk."

"At five foot three inches, what other kind of drunk could you be?"

She grabbed his ear in her mouth and slobbered in it.

"Ach," he protested. "Get back to your game."

"Seriously," she whispered, "are you OK over here by yourself? I can make room for you on the floor next to me."

"I'm fine," he lied.

"You don't hate me for ignoring you?"

"It's nice to be anonymous once in a while. I'm enjoying just watching the fellowship."

The bad guys rallied just then and Veronica leaped away, back to her front-row seat, leaving Taylor bereft. She was a girl, a woman, he thought, who had her own—her own life, her own friends, her own mind, her own expectations, her own ideas of fun and not-fun, of right and wrong, completely independently of him or his opinions. He could be present or not, and Veronica, the person, the feminist, the pharmaceutical salesperson, would be essentially unchanged. Without him she might not have a fellow with whom to play clever word games in bed, but the integrated, functioning personality known as Veronica Bristow would continue and prosper. The revelation unbalanced him further.

The game ended. The good guys won. When Harriet and the others left at last, Taylor and Veronica were alone.

He flopped on the sofa beside her and put his hand on her leg. He wanted what she had, therefore he wanted her. "Great party, Veronica."

"I'm really drunk," she said, holding her head. "Getting old, I guess."

Taylor nibbled her ear. He felt a compelling need to be close to her.

She pulled away.

He cupped her breast with his hand.

"Not now, Taylor. OK?" she said quietly.

"Mmmm." He nuzzled her neck.

"Whoa boy," she said. "Easy."

He moved his hand to the waistband of her pants. "Nice and easy," he murmured, popping the button, finding skin with his fingers.

She tugged at his hand but met resistance. "Taylor, I'm serious," she said, annoyed. "No." She squirmed away and buttoned her slacks. "I appreciate your passion, but I'm just not very interested right now."

"It doesn't matter if you're bleeding," he said and pursued her.

"I'm not bleeding," she said, escaping. "I'm just beat. Understand?"

"OK, OK," he said, trying to keep the hurt out of his voice. He stopped, but the room continued swaying.

"That's my boy," she said. "Look, I'd appreciate some help cleaning up and you could tell me what you think of my friends, but all I want to do tonight is take a long, hot bath, crawl in bed alone, and embrace nothing but sleep." She started gathering ashtrays. "How about tomorrow night? I'll meet you downtown after work. We can grab a pizza or something and I'll be glad to bring you home and take a nice long ride on you. Whattaya say?"

"No," Taylor answered, collecting beer cans. "Can't tomorrow." He couldn't tell her about his date with Erin. "How about Thursday? There's a great classic double feature at the Art House."

"Sounds like fun, Taylor, but I can't." She hated to turn him down, but she couldn't tell him she was meeting the last member of her stable, to inform him it was all over. She smiled at the irony. She had to turn down a date with Taylor because it was Taylor she wanted to date, but if she didn't end the other affair now, she feared she never would, and she prided herself on breaking clean. "How about Friday? Come over Friday night and I'll treat you to breakfast on Saturday."

Taylor was glad she was in the kitchen so he didn't have to look at her when he lied. He'd be with Erin Saturday. He squirmed, felt his stomach turn over. He faced the wall, shut his eyes, and spoke through clenched teeth. "I'd love to but I can't, Veronica." Why hadn't he planned for this eventuality? Where was his head? A little forethought and this could have been avoided. He made up a story. "I have to fly to Chicago Friday morning and I won't be back till, uh, Wednesday. I'm staying with some friends for the weekend and then business in Detroit and . . ."

"Uh-huh," said Veronica from the kitchen and Taylor felt as hollow as a balloon and just as light, but no thermal would carry him skyward. The temperature in the apartment had dropped suddenly and kept dropping.

"Well, well," Veronica mumbled, and a familiar but

despised physical sickness gripped her. She wanted to protest but of course she wouldn't, not her, not tough Veronica, battle-hardened veteran of the sexual revolution. She had no claim on his time, had made no promises and asked for none. So why did she hurt? She dumped the ashtrays into a garbage bag and held her breath against tears. Her accessible man, her liberated lover, her pleasant, fun-to-be-with, intellectually challenging companion—what did she expect? She commanded herself not to cry and drank a glass of water to suppress the urge. Where was that emotional armor she had begun to discard? She slipped back into it easily. It was a perfect fit but why wouldn't it be? She had only recently set it aside.

Taylor called from the other room, "How about dinner Wednesday? I could . . ."

"No," she said out of spite, but regretted it instantly. She summoned all her courage. "Thursday?" she asked and her voice cracked as she said it.

Taylor felt as if he'd been kicked in the groin. Thursday was Eleanor. Thursday to Saturday. He wanted to speak but couldn't. It was as if somebody had drilled a hole in the bottom of his vocabulary and all the words had drained out.

"No deal, eh?" said Veronica to fill the silence.

When she came out of the kitchen, Taylor saw a strange Veronica, stiff, tight-lipped, guarded.

"Listen," she said. "I'm real tired. I think I'm going to leave this mess till later and take my bath." She opened the front door.

He reached for her but the chill repelled him. She winked, tried a smile that didn't work. "So I'll see you next month sometime. Take care," she said without inflection. "Keep in touch."

The door closed solidly. A Kirlian photograph would

have revealed two auras—one on either side of the door—trying to penetrate the wood, trying to slide through the cracks near the hinges.

Taylor took two steps down the hall and stopped. She has another man, he thought. Maybe more than one. A stainless-steel pin pierced his stomach and ran all the way through to his backbone. She's tired tonight, can't go out Thursday, has her time planned all the way into next week. He wanted to howl and rage and wail. Taylor walked away, stiff-legged, sick at heart, overflowing with jealousy and rapidly souring beer.

CHAPTER EIGHTEEN

"Howard Larimore's a changed man these days," Ned said. "A more solicitous gentleman I've never seen. I'm telling you, Taylor, he positively fawns over her." Ned scratched at a tiny raw place on his wrist. It looked like eczema and the worse his cash flow became, the worse it itched. His gambling luck hadn't changed.

"Eleanor cut him off," Taylor mumbled, and the words sparked images in his brain of a butcher knife glinting in cold light, slicing down toward his exposed gonads, Eleanor above him sneering. He shook his head to chase away the pictures, knowing from recent experience that if he didn't stop it quickly, the mental fragmentation would escalate. Lately, an event as innocuous as the slamming of a door would send him into panic. More than once he'd come bolting out of sleep, leaping from dead slumber into wide-awake terror for no apparent reason. Business associates inquired after his health. According to office gossip, he was doing drugs. He wasn't doing drugs; he was doing worse. He'd been in and out of different beds so many different times in the past week he'd forgotten as he nuzzled a nipple, whose nipple it was. Finally, he'd come to rely on pubic-hair texture to tell his women apart in the dark. Erin's—whose precious privates he'd been granted permission to see and fondle, if not penetrate—was the silkiest, wispiest, least dense. Veronica's was coarser, long, and softly curled. Eleanor's was kinky, lots of tiny curls, springy to the touch. How's that for an identification system? Computer, whose twat is this?

"I didn't hear you," Ned said.

"Eleanor cut him off."

"Did she tell you that herself?" Ned asked. He was delighted. Through Taylor, he had exacted retribution for Howard Larimore's arrogant advances toward his wife and daughter.

Taylor nodded. "She decided to take a moral stand." The idea struck him as funny and he started to laugh. The more he laughed, the more hilarious it seemed until he realized he was laughing alone. He stopped abruptly and cleared his throat. "She decided to confront him with her knowledge of his past affairs."

Ned stopped scratching. This was great. "It's a wonder it's taken Eleanor this long to figure him out. Larimore wants whatever he can't have, automatically, whether the thing has any value to him or not."

"Eleanor hasn't figured out squat," Taylor snorted. "She's just using men like always, only now she has two to play with." Unbidden and inexplicably, his imagination conjured a picture of the last time he and Eleanor had lunch. At her insistence, he'd been finger-fucking her at the table, his hand obscured from the view of the other patrons by the tablecloth. His fingers, in Eleanor's talented twat, felt like victims of peristalsis. He felt himself being dragged, hand first, beneath the table. He envisioned Eleanor, oblivious, head against the back of the booth, mouth open, eyes closed, groaning happily while his hand slid deeper into her, propelled by the wave action of her uniquely evolved vagina. The waiter appears and Taylor's in up to his elbow. He pleads for release, but Eleanor is in ecstasy. The waiter lifts the tablecloth to determine the problem and faints dead away. The inexorable suction takes Taylor's shoulder, then his head. He wriggles his feet as a sign to potential rescuers, but nobody notices and he slides in and in and in.

"You didn't realize it would get this sticky, did you?" Ned said, enjoying his friend's discomfort. "Good. Maybe now you'll give women credit for being bona-fide people with emotions, expectations, and all those other messy human qualities. You think Eleanor's a bitch and you're right, but I have a hunch Ms. Bristow is the one who's giving you fits. Am I right?"

Blood spattered against the backs of Taylor's eyeballs. In his mind's eye, he saw her on the arm of her other lover, a distinguished, gray-flanneled denizen of the capital's halls of power. Veronica whispers in the man's ear while both of them watch Taylor silently, dispassionately. The image pained him more than the swipe of Eleanor's knife.

He decided not to answer Ned's question. "What's Clara had to say about Eleanor lately? What's the scuttlebutt on the cocktail circuit?" He remembered Ned's offer of a month ago to renegotiate the terms of the bet and was monumentally sorry he hadn't at least listened to a proposal.

"Clara and the girls are having a terrific time with it."

"Does that concern you?"

"No," Ned lied.

"What would Clara and the girls think if they found out about our bet?"

Ned refused to consider the possibility. "Is that a threat?"

"Don't be ridiculous. I just wondered how you're going to explain away the loss of Grandma's Mercedes."

Ned had entered into the wager with Taylor for the sake of his friend's well-being, as a magnanimous gesture from which he couldn't lose because, as Taylor's current mental state proved, Taylor simply had no chance of winning. Accordingly, Ned had never considered deducting the value of the Mercedes from his net worth, even as a contingency. Conversely, however, because he had no intention of depriving his friend of the use of the fishing cabin, he had never considered the value of the river property—or more reasonably the mortgage value of the river property—as a potential addition to his gambling account. Taylor's comment somehow sparked the idea, and as soon as it occurred to Ned, it appealed to him. He pulled down his cuff over his wrist, pleased at having found a hidden asset. "I have a further hunch, Taylor, old friend. I think you're falling for the blonde. How's it feel?"

In his mind's eye, Taylor saw Erin running toward him, stopping, pointing, aiming the entire football squad directly at him. Sessums, Truck, and Bohan lead the snarling charge of several tons of males in full game pads. He tries to flee, but the team thunders on, gains ground, surrounds him, engulfs him.

"Falling," Taylor mumbled and as he said it, he thought: Yeah. Falling apart.

CHAPTER NINETEEN

Taylor jogged down the beach, rejoicing in the salt smell, the sound of the ocean, and the burning sensation of the sun on his back. Oh, sweet springtime, he thought. No brats to bother you, no crowds to crowd you, just sea and sky and sand, exquisite freedom in pale blue and white. He wished he could draw every molecule of air into his lungs and take it back to civilization. The fast crowd could keep their poppers, the rich crowd could keep their cocaine. All he wanted was a sniff of this fragrance every now and then. Here, have a little snort of mine, and Taylor inhaled a cubic liter of pure elation.

He wondered how far he had come. A mile? Maybe less. Hard to tell, running in sand. He felt wonderful, like he could run forever. Between here and "home," the rented house where Erin waited in her bikini on the sun deck, he had seen exactly six people, including fishermen. Won't be like this in another month, when the vacation hordes will have arrived. Next month the river would be the place to be. He'd go in his Mercedes.

Taylor had considered taking Erin to Ned's mountain

cabin, but full springtime had not yet arrived in the higher elevations. He'd also thought of taking her to his fishing cabin on the Pamlico, but considered it too primitive for her. Not that she wouldn't adapt. Since they had declared their love for each other, the change in her had been unbelievable. Poof, just like that, Erin had metamorphosed. Suddenly, she couldn't do enough for him. Even her cooking had improved. Taylor had heard hundreds of boozy stories from guys who complained that as soon as they were married, their women went upstairs, changed into wives, and came down totally unrecognizable. Erin hadn't waited that long. Taylor had decided against taking her to the funky river cabin, not because she wouldn't adore it but precisely because she would adore it, and he wasn't ready to have her spread her cute all over it yet. Instead, he'd brought her to North Carolina's barrier islands, the Outer Banks, and now that he was here, loping down the beach, with the Atlantic Ocean washing his mind clean with each breaking wave, he knew he had made the right decision. He gradually slowed his pace until he came to a stop.

It seemed as if the bet had been going on for years. On the one hand, it had been a valuable experience, forcing him back into circulation, compelling him to tolerate women again after a long hiatus, which he might not have done without prompting but which, he understood now, was necessary as a kind of final exam. Now, nearing the end of the bet, having done all the things gentlemen are supposed to do, he believed he knew to a satisfactory degree what could be expected of women. Eleanor's type would do you a deal on businesslike terms. As in any good commercial arrangement, it would be understood that nothing is written in stone, that loyalty is a minor consideration, that if a better opportunity came along, well, business is business and no hard feelings. She was not strictly speaking a parasite. She gave what was necessary to give and lived up to her part of the bargain, but a girl has to look out for her own interests after all. Veronica's type would challenge you, introduce you to a new understanding of your own sexuality, and force you to communicate differently, but consumed with a historical perspective and reflexively suspicious of anything resembling traditional behavior, she would analyze you to death and run you through tests and experiments like a rat through a maze, which on second thought might not be so bad if you were the only rat.

And Erin. Erin could try your patience with her practiced naïveté, but whereas the others were adversaries or associates or, at best, partners, Erin—her gorgeousness, her glorious form—was reward, priceless and irreplaceable.

On the other hand, the problem with the bet was that it forced Taylor to make immediate judgments about his women without the benefit of hindsight or deliberation. For all of Eleanor's calculating and conniving, for example, he had to admire her style. Her life, while not perfect, was extremely comfortable. She didn't have to worry about a single material thing and she enjoyed quite a lot of freedom. Taylor had no respect for her aspirations, but she had set a goal for herself and accomplished it in full appreciation of her own talents and abilities. In the grand scheme of things, she hadn't done badly. Also, she was a terrific fuck. If only Erin had some of that same hunger. But Erin had never been hungry—for anything—and although Taylor didn't want to wish misfortune on anybody, in a way he was sorry she hadn't. Also, however, if it weren't for the bet, he wouldn't have been forced to compare Erin's saccharine banality with Veronica's intelligence. In the cold glare of simultaneous analysis, his beautiful blonde tragically revealed all the intellectual spontaneity of asparagus. Not only was Veronica smarter, funnier, and more talented, her life was fuller, richer, and more various than Erin's—hell, for that matter, than Taylor's. Veronica not only had her job, she had her photography, at least one good friend, and a stupendous appetite for books. Erin had only her looks.

Taylor picked up a rock, heaved it into the ocean, and wondered if he was being exactly fair. Erin certainly had more than her looks. She couldn't spout epigrams like Veronica, but so what? Veronica, it seemed, needed nobody, but Erin made him feel important, powerful, wise, and strong. Veronica would laugh at that, but Erin could be molded, directed. In time, with encouragement she might develop some of Veronica's better features. Who knew what talents lay beneath Erin's lip gloss and facial blusher? It was unfair to write her off before she was tested, and the bare facts were that while Erin might be able to learn to paint, or write, or play the piano, Veronica could never be as knock-'em-dead beautiful as Erin, not even with the help of all the cosmetic surgeons in California.

Just three months ago, Taylor hadn't known of the existence of Erin, Veronica, or Eleanor, and now he knew their favorite colors, their pet peeves, their idiosyncrasies, and the locations of their moles and beauty spots. Amazing, he realized, the information available to the man who pursued it. How many questions had he asked? How many hours had he spent listening? Ned wanted him to spell out his formula. It was almost too simple: Pay attention and keep paying. Don't try to change anything. Don't offer advice. Just listen and nod and your passive interest will be interpreted as caring.

There it was, the shortest how-to-pick-up-girls manual ever written.

Taylor turned, hands on hips, drops of sweat sparkling in his black hair and trickling down the valleys between the muscles in his arms, and started walking up the beach. He smiled grimly. In Ned's parlance he'd just made the clubhouse turn. Walking toward Erin, he was beginning the stretch run. So, let's set the field, he thought, hearing Ned's Damon Runyon imitation in his mind: Ahead were the blond beauty; the spindly, long-legged striver; and the long shot, the high-spirited, temperamental bay.

The blonde presented no problem. She could be overtaken easily. She'd become the perfect prenuptial ingenue, supersaturated with anticipation. Taylor had only to whisper her name, and her eyes would become so teary he swore they'd dissolve azurely down her cheeks. Eleanor wasn't as much of a sure thing. If he were offering odds, he'd give three to two in his favor. Taylor was reasonably sure he could take her, but her weirdness constituted an element of unpredictability. And then there was Veronica. Taylor sighed.

Every time he thought of her, he thought of her in bed with another guy and it galled him unreasonably. He knew he had no right to expect fidelity and why did he care anyway? She was just another woman, just another part of the bet, right? Sure. Just like Erin was your average cutie. Veronica was the only one of the three who listened to him. Erin knew essentially nothing about him. Eleanor asked questions but they were gossip questions. Veronica gave a damn about what he thought, or she seemed to. She didn't agree very often, but she paid attention to what he said and responded intelligently. So why was she fucking somebody else? It drove him crazy. He knew Ned would love the irony.

Taylor had encouraged Eleanor to screw somebody else, even if it was her husband, and he wished Erin had, or would, just to give him some evidence she was capable of it; and here was Veronica doing what any normal, full-blooded human would do, and it fried Taylor's brain.

He tried to shake her out of his mind. The issue at hand was Erin, his eager, cheerful, adoring fiancée-to-be. He stopped walking, picked up another handful of pebbles, and started tossing them, one by one, into the ocean. It was certain he would propose. It was certain she would accept. It was certain she would take it seriously. The question was: would he?

The litany in his mind began again, and although strictly speaking he wasn't required to settle the issue now—the wager would go on; he could break off the engagement later if he chose—his romantic self demanded a decision. If a possibility existed he and Erin would someday be man and wife, then he wanted the proposal to be sincere, for his own purposes, for his own sanity. The questions reverberated inside his head like jungle drums. What could possibly be wrong with a good, honest, faithful woman? An astonishingly beautiful, good, honest, faithful woman? An astonishingly beautiful, good, honest, faithful woman who had seen the big time and was not impressed, who had been offered glamour and rejected it? Huh? Hey, you, Taylor Worth, hotshot, debonair dude. How about an answer?

He ran out of pebbles.

He knew instinctively negative questions couldn't be trusted. No computer he knew of could deal with them without balking. They were common devices employed by common intellects to talk themselves into things they would otherwise refuse. "Why don't you like classical music?" is much more difficult to answer than "Why do you like rock-and-roll?," which can be answered completely with a grin and a shake of the ass. He had to do better than "Why not?," but he couldn't.

Taylor wanted to settle down. That much was plain to him. He loved the feel of a woman, he didn't want to live alone anymore, and he didn't want to undergo the rigors of courtship again. But did he want to settle down with Erin? No one could blame him for grabbing her while he had the chance. She was certainly a prize catch and she certainly wanted him. So what was the problem?

He could tolerate Erin's terminal cuteness, her lack of creativity, and her premature wifehood, but one problem was impossible to overlook: sex.

He began walking again. He and Erin had bathed together and slept together, but they had never made love. He'd fondled her and she'd manipulated him, but she hadn't allowed him between her legs with anything other than a finger, and the finger had almost always come back dry. She was not a virgin and she was not, Taylor believed, technically, consciously a tease, although Erin dressed in burlap would be provocative to most men. Taylor couldn't figure her out exactly. She was Catholic, but that by itself didn't account for her reservations because she wasn't otherwise religious. She was still very much a little girl, but he suspected it was a role she affected to enhance her chosen brand of sexiness. No woman as gorgeous as she could maintain a naïveté as comprehensive as hers without working at it unless she was totally stupid, and Erin, as Truck had pointed out, was anything but stupid.

And so the dilemma: Erin obviously meant to "save" herself for marriage or, he suspected, the promise of marriage, whereas Taylor wanted to know about the sex part of marriage before he promised marriage.

He headed for home. Erin put aside her magazine and stood to greet him as he slogged toward her through the heavy sand, and he wondered again if *any* objection to a person so utterly fabulous-looking could be justified: dainty feet, shapely legs, flared hips covered by the merest triangle of cloth, flat belly, luxurious breasts, impeccable complexion, eyes like blue starbursts, and profligate hair the color of champagne. Who cared what she thought or if she thought at all? Historically, men received their intellectual stimulation from other men. He had found a treasure—a beautiful woman unwilling to use her devastating power to crush men's balls. He wanted intellect. Couldn't he settle for not-dumb? He wanted spontaneity. She loved him, for God's sake! Couldn't he settle for that?

"Take off the top of your bathing suit," he called from below.

Instinctively, Erin's hands flew to her chest.

"Come on," he urged. "No one but me will see. Strip for me. I want to see your incredible breasts in the sunlight."

She looked up and down the empty beach. The neighboring cottages were uninhabited. No telescope-wielding weirdo would spy on her. Tempted, she reached behind her but hesitated. "Come inside," she called. "I'll strip for you inside."

"Indulge me," he teased. "That tiny kerchief isn't covering anything but your nipples anyway. Take it off and throw it down to me. Show your tits to the sun." He thought of Eleanor, who would have peeled in a heartbeat and straddled the balcony railing; or Veronica, who would have been topless already, taking advantage of the privacy. "Disrobe, baby. Get nude."

Erin glanced around once more, hesitated, tugged the string, and the ounce of cloth dropped away.

"Yeeeehaah!" Taylor hollered. "Now put your hands on your head and stretch out for me. Get brazen, baby. Show off."

Tentatively she placed her hands on her head. The sun shining on her chest made her nipples harden. She leaned her breasts over the railing, blew Taylor a kiss, and ran inside the cottage.

Taylor took the weatherworn wooden steps two at a time. It must be the genetic memory of human beginnings, he thought, of concupiscent slithering in vernal pools, of a mindless urgency to procreate and guarantee the continuation of a species so recently sloshed up out of the eternal waves, that made folks horny near the ocean.

Inside, Erin stood with her hair undone and her hands lost within it. She stretched upward, as he had requested, until she stood on tiptoe and her nipples sought the ceiling. She turned then and showed him a whole-body profile. "Now I'll strip the rest of the way," she said and wriggled out of her bikini bottoms.

Nude and smiling, pale, pinkish, shimmery, round, and downy, Erin looked like the stuff halos were made of. The rare glory of her overwhelmed him. He could barely breathe and tears came to his eyes, but these were merely overt manifestations of a profound feeling of reverence and gratitude. He knew women didn't appreciate men this way. Most women weren't rendered weak-kneed and stupid by the naked masculine form, and although he knew strategically speaking they were better off in the eternal battle of the sexes, better able to outmaneuver a beauty-blind male—turn him, use him, take him—he also felt sorry for them. If they knew this feeling, so many mysteries would be dispelled and so many others revealed. Erin, as a female, might represent the divine, the ephemeral, but in Taylor's awe, the weakness in his brain, the power in his groin, he found humanity, life, a physicality Erin could never comprehend. He reached for her.

She came to him, leaned her nakedness against him. He held her for an eternity, mindlessly worshipful of proximate beauty.

A slanting column of sunlight cast a golden streak on the crisp bedsheets and Erin slid her blondness into it like a diamond into its setting. The air around her seemed to melt. Her aura, a halo of flowing pastels, had thickened, was indistinguishable from her flesh. Taylor peeled off his clothes. Dramatic shadows born of the interplay between himself and the afternoon sun streaked across the floor and up the walls. He caught a glimpse of his body in the mirror—fine, hairy, muscled, glowing with sexual fire and the kiss of the sun.

Erin spread her legs and Taylor dove into the pool of shimmering light. He entered her effortlessly and closed his eyes to allow his body to command his images. Gold and blue, he thought. Silver and ivory. Silky liquidity, viscid, lively, blood red, and milky. Flesh become fluid, reality gone askew, and, coming through the colors of his own coming, Erin's words, "I love you."

That evening at dinner, Taylor Worth, cerebellum and midsection still buoyant from his dazzling tryst with beauty, proposed marriage for the first time in his life. Although the tape recorder eavesdropped from the pocket of his coat and awareness of the wager remained, he spoke the words hopefully, anxious for Erin's response—not her decision, which was known, but her immediate, spontaneous reaction: the look in her eyes, the love in her aura. He wished for sincerity and tenderness, a dawning of understanding, a singular, original affection for him.

Effusively, breathlessly, Erin proclaimed her excitement, her pleasure, her joy, and waved her diamond-adorned hand around as if Taylor's proposal had come as the greatest surprise of her life. Erin wept. She laughed. She clutched the ring to her bosom and beamed her happiness to the universe exactly as romance-novel heroines and soap-opera actresses have since the genesis of melodrama.

Taylor looked away, disappointment and amazement vying for control of his consciousness. Erin played the scene the way she thought it was supposed to be played, and he knew at that moment he ranked third in importance behind the ring and the engagement, fourth if you counted the bride-to-be.

Over the past months, he had convinced himself that marriage per se was not objectionable. He had not, however, rid himself of his contempt for marriage as a production number in which every chorus of giggles from the bridesmaids, every garter-baring high kick of the bride, every pouty, petulant moment of girlish introspection, and every family argument over the guest list was prescribed by ritual. He yanked his gaze back to his fiancée, who continued to emote, using facial expressions worthy of the cover of *Mademoiselle* magazine, hair and makeup by Elizabeth Arden. Taylor blinked and saw her again, wearing a blue, off-the-shoulder dress. He blinked again and saw her in a short fur coat, designer jeans, and leg-warmers. He saw her in a leotard, an evening gown, a beautiful picture every time, a prefab fantasy presented in two dimensions.

That night, Taylor and Erin made love again, and in the darkness, unbedazzled by colors, he noted the minimal extent of her participation in the act.

In the morning they made love again. She accepted him passively but willingly.

In the shower, inflamed by the movement of water down her body, he pressed her against the tiles. "Not here, Taylor," she said with a giggle.

After lunch, his solar batteries charged, he cornered her in the kitchenette, with only the best culinary intentions. "Not now," she said, and the giggle was gone.

Before dinner, as they were dressing, Taylor suggested an appetizer, but Erin had already put on her face.

After dinner they walked along the beach. In the moonlight Erin looked like a scene from a movie: barefoot, shoes in hand, hair and skirt flying in the ocean breeze. Taylor nudged her toward a beached Hobie Cat sailboat. "We could use the trampoline," he said.

"It's too wet," she replied, "and I'm cold."

Back at the beach house, they cuddled. "Are you warming up?" he asked, groping under the blanket, but Erin was already, beautifully, asleep.

CHAPTER TWENTY

The name of the firm to which she had been dispatched by Mrs. Grabowski at the agency sounded familiar, but Harriet couldn't place it until she arrived and discovered the nature of the business. Computers. Of course. Taylor Worth, Veronica's boyfriend, worked there. At least, she thought as she pushed open the glass door, she wouldn't be completely friendless.

She was greeted not, as expected, by a standard-issue receptionist in a typical business office, but by a woman who appeared to be dressed for housecleaning. "Hi," the woman said from within a cloud of cigarette smoke. "You're, uh"—she flipped a few pages of a notepad—"Harriet. That right? Have a seat."

"Yes, ma'am." Harriet sat.

"I'm Georgia Watson, the office manager, and the reason I'm not in conventional work costume is the same reason you're here. Every year at this time, the office basically shuts down to compile a whole raft of special reports and such. The principals stay out and leave the place to the secretarial crew—eight of us plus an extra hand or two. The siege will continue for the next four days. Are you able to commit for that much time? It's hard work; what I mean is, continuous work, but you don't have to put up with any bullshit. Because the work is so tedious we take long lunches and long breaks, but when we work, we work. Are you game?"

"You mean I don't have to wear a skirt and hose?"

"You can come to work in your pajamas for all I care."

"Let's go."

Georgia stubbed out her cigarette and stood up. "I want to warn you that today will be a test day. If you're as good as Mrs. Grabowski says you are, you won't have any trouble, but I wanted to tell you so you'd understand if some of the girls are a little standoffish. We've had some real airheads in here."

Momentarily disappointed she wouldn't have Taylor to joke with, Harriet remembered his absence this week had caused Veronica some anxiety. At least Harriet could tell her friend he had a legitimate reason to be gone.

The "Hard Copy Center" of the spacious offices was a single large room equipped with as many computer terminals as NASA Launch Command. Harriet surveyed the ranks of plastic components and half-expected their hooded heads to turn toward her like those of their human attendants as she entered the room behind Georgia. Experiencing a nostalgia she never thought she'd feel, she pined for a good, old-fashioned, clackety-clack typewriter.

Georgia made some perfunctory introductions, sat Harriet down at a word processor, outlined her first task, and left. Harriet adjusted the height of her swivel chair, organized her work to her satisfaction, and glanced around her slick, white, frictionless environment. Welcome to the new age of information, she thought, and

WORTH WINNING

was visited by one of those irrational ideas that often invade the disoriented mind: You couldn't strike a match in here if your life depended on it. She shrugged involuntarily and flipped a switch, thereby initiating a dialogue with her machine.

Seven hours, two breaks, and a catered lunch later, Harriet was sipping an unexpected after-work gin and tonic in the plush conference room with the other secretaries. "Like the fancy food," Georgia told her, "the open bar is one of the perks we've negotiated over the years. Rather pleasant, isn't it?" she asked, leaning back in her armchair.

"Certainly is," Harriet replied, enjoying the rich feel of leather under her fingers. "But dangerous. I could see some of the women just camping out here." The open liquor cabinet sparkled like a jewelry case.

Georgia laughed. "Wait till Friday when the work's finished." She lit another cigarette and Harriet wondered what her lungs must look like. "Speaking of which," Georgia continued, "you've had a day of our company and we've decided you're good enough for us if we're good enough for you. Willing to stay?"

Harriet wondered whether it was feminine or simply human to respond so positively to stroking. She performed perfectly mechanical work for complete strangers and was absolutely thrilled at their approval. She smiled and said, "Certainly."

"One more G and T?" Georgia asked.

Harriet looked at her glass. "Sure, one more."

By the time she was halfway through her second drink, she'd been drawn into the friendly group of five women who had remained to fortify themselves with their boss's booze. They were a bawdy bunch, encouraged by their surroundings to let down their hair, and

Harriet was made privy to some of the more tawdry office gossip.

"Whatever you do while you're here," said the youngest, prettiest woman in the group, "don't fall in love with the local Lancelot."

"She won't even meet him, will she?"

"Probably not."

"He's a doll."

"You're married and all you can see is his manners."

"He's always been a gentleman to me."

"Me, too, that's what disappoints me."

Georgia laughed. "Every single girl—ha!—I meant to say unmarried, but I'll go with single—who's been through here has made a pass at Taylor Worth, but I've never seen him give any one of them a tumble. I asked him why one time and he apologized for his crassness, but he said, 'You don't get your meat the same place you get your bread.'"

"What did he mean by that?"

"Think, woman."

"Oh. I get it."

"He's scrupulous about not mixing business with sex."

"Seems like a sound policy to me," said Harriet. She had considered admitting she knew him, but couldn't resist the opportunity to gather juicy news. "I want to hear more."

The women described him physically and discussed his habits and idiosyncrasies in detail. According to consensus, Taylor was pleasant enough but enigmatic.

"He goes through phases," said Georgia, who'd been with the company longer than the others. "For three or four months at a time he'll have women, or a woman, hanging around all the time, calling the office, meeting him for lunch and after work. Then, just like that"—she snapped her fingers—"nothing. He'll withdraw, go into a hermit stage when you just know he's not seeing anybody."

"He gets surly."

"Yes. Gruff. Impatient. But that's when he looks his best, well pressed, manicured, gorgeous."

"Then one day he'll walk in with an armload of flowers, dump a bunch on everybody's desk, and apologize for being such a grump."

"I don't think he's in one of his hermit stages now."

Everybody but Harriet laughed. "I'd like to meet the babe who has her hooks into him this time."

More laughter. "I think it's more than one."

"I agree," said Georgia. "I've never seen him look quite as wasted. He's usually well dressed," she said to Harriet, "but I've seen him come in two days in a row in the same suit."

"And he's lost weight."

"And his car's dirty."

"And he forgets things."

"I've walked into his office and found him asleep with his head on his desk."

"No."

"I don't think he has a harem. I think one good woman is wearing him out."

"I don't know about that. Not many personal calls for him come through the switchboard."

"Well, if he had a number of women on the line he wouldn't want them calling work, would he? One of us might ask Suzy if we should tell Taylor Buffy called."

"I've done that kind of thing before. Believe me, it isn't funny."

"It's hilarious."

"Well, I think you're wrong about Taylor. I think he's dallying with a whole lot of women because I've heard rumors."

"Oh, boy. Tell us."

The group automatically closed ranks.

"Some of you know Joanne Minneman, my friend who works in Silver Springs? I know some of you have met her. She's been to lunch with us a couple of times."

"Uh-huh. Go ahead."

"Well, she knows who Taylor is because she saw him here once and wanted me to fix her up with him. I tried but he wouldn't go for it."

"Probably more of his famous scruples."

"More like Taylor's unwillingness to date the clerical help."

"Let her tell the story, will you, please?"

"Joanne works for this guy named Ned who's a friend of Taylor's and she told me she's overheard a lot of talk among the salesmen in her office lately that Taylor and Ned have made some kind of high-stakes bet. From what she's heard, Taylor and this Ned have bet a house or something that Taylor can get engaged to six women at the same time."

"My God!"

"That's ridiculous."

"Maybe so but that's what I've heard. Joanne says some of the other guys in her office have even placed side bets. She seems to think there's a lot of money riding on it."

"Who'd do a thing like that?"

"Men."

"Taylor wouldn't do anything like that."

"Wouldn't he?"

"Joanne says there's a time limit and everything."

"He certainly has looked beat lately."

Harriet felt her lungs constrict.

"He's been acting fishy about a lot of things lately."

"Like this vacation," said Georgia. "Why the big mystery about where he was going? He even refused to give me an emergency number."

Vacation! The word lit up Harriet's brain like a panic code. He'd told Veronica he was out of town on a work assignment. She ventured a question. "He couldn't be working on something, could he?"

"Not for this company," said Georgia.

"Maybe he's looking for another job?"

"Hey, there's an idea."

"Why should he want to leave? He's got it made here. He does what he wants, when he wants. And he's well paid."

"Maybe he figures he'll have to get out of town when this big bet is over."

More laughter.

Harriet, feeling slightly ill, decided it was time to excuse herself.

That night, Harriet held an intense debate with herself. Should she or should she not tell Veronica what she'd heard at the office gab session? The bet was rumor but the vacation was a sure thing. Should she increase Veronica's anxiety or should she keep silent? Perhaps he was out looking for a job. That would qualify as business, and Veronica at this point had no right to demand news of every aspect of his life. Also, perhaps he was moonlighting. Harriet had heard of the new breed of free-lance computer programmers. Perhaps he was hustling jobs he didn't want Georgia to know about. That would account for his refusal to provide an emergency phone number. She decided she had nothing but gossip to go on. Any news she'd give Veronica could only be destructive. She decided to keep it to herself. She was always too ready to believe the worst about men.

The phone rang.

"Harriet, darling." It was Randall.

"Well, hello, how are things at the bakery?"

"Hi, Harriet." It was Byron on another extension.

"Hi, there, you handsome brute."

"Stop that."

"What can I do for you?"

Both talked at once but Randall persisted. "We've called to ask a favor, dearie. You remember all our talk about our good friend Eleanor, the one who was running around with Don Juan?"

"The perfect man," said Harriet. "I remember."

"Well, she has agreed to go off with him for a three-day trip, just the two of them, for you can imagine what kind of salacious rendezvous."

"How awful."

Byron spoke. "And we decided it was our duty, as friends of course, to investigate this seducer."

"You've hired someone?"

"Oh no, dear, we've decided it was a chance for adventure. We've decided to play private detective and pry into this satyr's affairs."

"Please, Byron. Choose a better word."

"This I'd love to see," said Harriet. "So you two need a gun moll, a brassy, buxom babe to light your cigarettes? I think I still have a pair of platform shoes with ankle straps. I could buy a tight black skirt with a slit up the side and wave my hair like Veronica Lake."

"I'm sure you'd look devastating, Harriet love, but what we need is someone to keep an eye on the store while we're getting gum on our shoes."

"That doesn't sound right, Randall."

"When are you going to start this spy operation?" Harriet asked.

"Oh, we've already started. We've seen the Lothario

twice already, both times with a blonde who looks one size too large for her skin."

"Now there's an image," Harriet said. "Business or pleasure?"

"Well, we couldn't tell exactly. They kissed but in a kind of perfunctory way. We've decided to put full-time surveillance on him."

"We're going to homestake his apartment."

"Stake out, Randall."

"Oh yes. Sorry. Well, Harriet. Can you spare us a few days? We're not going through the agency this time because we'd rather pay you under the table."

"My, but we are becoming surreptitious these days," she said. "I can't, Randall, although I'd love to. I just this morning took a job for the rest of the week and I'd feel like a heel if I reneged. Why don't you put off your search for about a week? I can join you Monday . . . no, Tuesday. I have to get my passport Monday. I'm getting a little suspicious about these 'perfect' men myself and I'd adore getting the goods on one of them."

"We could do that, I suppose. What do you think, Byron?"

"Well, we know he'll be out of town from Thursday until Saturday with Eleanor, so I imagine it would be all right, although I'd like to get a photograph of him with that hussy before Thursday. I've purchased a fantastic new lens for my camera, Harriet."

"The dirty old lecher has been checking out crotch bulges from a block away."

"Randall!"

"But you should see the outfit I bought, Harriet. It took me two days but I finally found a genuine fedora. I look dashing in it. Tell her, Byron."

"But the best part was when we went into this men's store. You know the kind, with lots of dark wood and fake leather and awful stuff like corduroy shirts? Well, we waltzed in there and Randall, of course, was at his absolute best, bossing this ditsie salesman around . . ."

"I was looking for a trench coat and he was mortified. He looked like he wanted to spray us with disinfectant and . . ."

CHAPTER TWENTY-ONE

Taylor, looking tanned and splendid, acknowledged the waitress's flirtation with a wink. Do you like what you see, baby? he thought. Well, what are you going to do about it? Shake your ass at me? Bend over and let me see your tits? And when I walk out of here, are you going to regret a lost opportunity? Hell, no. I'll be just another male who missed his chance. Your memory of me will go into a drawer full of faded images of men who, failing to risk their egos for you, didn't live up to your standards. And what will you do? What will you end up doing? Falling for some bozo who knows the moves, whose only charm is his superficial understanding of what gets female motors running. He'll pay attention to you and make you feel special. Then he'll keep paying until he "wins" you, and later when he treats you like just another possession, because to him that's all you are, another thing he's had to pursue and purchase, you'll wonder what happened to the charming prince you met way back when.

"I guess you told her," said Ned over his drink.

Like a hooked fish, Taylor was snapped into reality. "Huh?"

"The waitress," Ned said with a jerk of his head. "Your thoughts are getting loud."

"What are you talking about?" Taylor asked, glancing around the room.

"Come on, partner. This is Ned, remember?"

"What are you trying to say?" asked Taylor with exaggerated innocence. He turned in his chair, looked behind him.

"I'm worried about you," Ned said. That he was also worried about himself enhanced his sincerity. "We both started this thing in a fit of pique but I hoped it would help you, get you back into the world of people, and out of that hatebox you'd made of your head. I thought you might learn something. Instead, you've turned mean."

Meanness was Taylor's only possible socially acceptable response. For him, the properly indoctrinated male, an expression of disappointment or sorrow equaled an admission of defeat. Time spent in self-pity was time wasted, and time, like money, is never static. Ten dollars uninvested is losing interest, therefore losing money. Also, according to the law of cause and effect, regret implied an *a priori* flaw. Taylor had made a mistake. Ignoring facts, he had hoped Erin would exhibit maturity. The misjudgment was his, so what was the good of self-pity? It would only encourage future errors. Anger, however, and bitterness, acrimony, rancor, all these were acceptable responses because they were well-known incentives to action.

"Nonsense," Taylor snarled. "On the contrary. The bet's been one of the more rewarding experiences of my life and I don't even have the car yet. By the way, did you bring the title and registration?" He craned his neck to see past Ned to the exit.

"Tall tales and fifty cents will get you a cup of coffee

anywhere in the city," said Ned. The suspense was killing him. He couldn't tell whether Taylor was angry because Erin turned him down or because he told her off. Ned prayed it was one or the other because he wanted to be done with the bet altogether. His luck had changed somewhat; his gambling account was holding steady at just above the critical level; and he wanted to end this ill-conceived business with Taylor. It had soiled their friendship to the extent that, as a result of his cash-flow troubles, he had for a time considered Taylor's value to him only in terms of the river property. This disgusted him. He wanted a clean break, especially since Taylor's attitude appeared to be swinging back toward misogyny. "Stop squirreling around," he said to his jittery friend. "Are you going to look under the table, too?"

Taylor tried to pass off his paranoia with a shrug. He reached into his pocket and produced a tape recorder about the size of a cigarette package. "You'll have to excuse the blurry sound. Her words are filtered by the linen of my dinner jacket." He pressed the "Play" button and Erin's voice joined them in the cocktail lounge. "Oh, Taylor. Oh yes. I'll marry you." A garbled noise followed.

"What was that?" Ned asked.

"A couple of plates hitting the floor. In her excitement to grab me she destroyed a table setting." Taylor snapped the microcassette out of the machine and flipped it to Ned. "One down," he said with a sneer, "and two to go."

Ned fingered the tiny cartridge. "You know, Taylor, back in February, this seemed like it would be great sport but I'll tell you the truth." He held up the tape. "This makes me feel dirty." It also made him feel a little nervous. Taylor, against long odds, had suppressed his own personality and overcome a gargantuan hatred of Erin's privileged naïveté. The idea scared him. "Erin's a sweet kid and you're going to feed her straight into an emotional meat grinder."

"Don't let it bother you," Taylor said bitterly. "She's sweet, no doubt. A more innocent creature never simpered her way through life. Don't worry too much about her, though. She sure as hell wouldn't bleed for you. If you set yourself afire, you'd be lucky if she noticed you."

Taylor tore at the paper label of the beer bottle in front of him. "Before this bet, despite centuries of literary tradition, some twenty-five years of personal experience, and the sage words of almost every man I'd ever spoken to on the subject, I still held some fuddlebrained notion that at least some women were multidimensional human beings. Thanks to you, though, and the wager, I'm disabused of those dangerous fantasies. I owe you."

Ned dropped the cassette into his pocket. "You're hysterical."

"You're wrong." The empty bottle slipped out of Taylor's fingers and banged on the table. "Never have I seen more clearly. Before, I had vague theories, shadowy ideas, but now all my thoughts on the subject have crystallized. I'v sailed through a storm of confusion into the calm, clear bay of knowledge." He gnawed at a fingernail.

"I can certainly see that," said Ned. "The word for you is placid. Ol' placid Taylor. Say, isn't that Veronica over there?"

"Where?" Taylor jumped but realized Ned was baiting him. "Not funny, Ned."

Ned sipped his drink. "I think I finally get it, Taylor. I understand this tantrum now, should have recognized it earlier. I've seen it in my kids often enough. You love Erin, don't you? You love her and you can't bring yourself to admit it yet."

Taylor's anger drained out of his face. "I can't help but think of Nazis, Ned. They were horrible bastards, but they couldn't have done what they did without malleable Fräuleins like Erin."

Ned was confused. "I thought she was Irish."

"What difference does it make? She thinks. I'm sure of that. I mean there's activity in her head, but it's as if no thought can get beyond her skin. She generates a thought and it expands outward, but as soon as it reaches the boundaries of her fabulous body, it's deflected back inside."

"What's any of this have to do with Nazis?"

Taylor responded as if he were speaking to an idiot. "Half the population of the world is male, historically predisposed toward torture and destruction and stuff like that. The other half of the population is female, predisposed toward itself. So what's to stop the destruction? Erin couldn't form a strong opinion if you threatened her. She doesn't provide any balance. She just isn't there. If I leaned on her, I'd hit the floor."

As Ned watched and listened to his friend, he realized he had badly underestimated Taylor's perseverance, and for the first time, he began to calculate the real—that is, monetary—effects of the bet if Taylor succeeded with Eleanor and Veronica as he had with Erin.

"Erin trusts me unreservedly," Taylor said. "All I had to do was ask and she put her life right here in my hand. Just like that."

Ned wondered who was more naïve, Erin or Taylor.

"I guess I should be flattered or charmed," Taylor continued, "that anybody would so willingly offer herself to me, but this girl doesn't know me. I suppose it's all part of her alleged innocence, but I'm not enchanted by innocence. Instead, I feel contempt. I've shown her one tiny facet of myself and that's enough for her. I ask her questions, listen to the answers, and ask more questions. That's why she loves me. I show an interest in her. I satisfy a deep need. Does it occur to her the need is universal?" He left the question unanswered.

Ned looked away. Erin would be slaughtered by this. Mutilated. The whole situation was out of control. It was never supposed to have reached this point.

"If I married Erin," Taylor continued, "in ten years I'd be just like Howard Larimore and Erin would be just like Eleanor, empty and unsatisfied even though the marriage would be everything she planned for it to be." He shook his head and tore away the last shred of the label from the beer bottle.

"Did I hear you say marriage?" Ned asked incredulously. He thought he saw a possible escape route for everybody. Everybody except Erin.

"Fuck off, Ned," Taylor said, expecting sarcasm.

"Let's cancel it, Taylor."

"What!"

"Let's call it off. The whole thing. This bet is wrong. The emotional price is too high. Have you thought about what it's going to do to Erin when you tell her it's over? Are you prepared for what it's going to do to you? You love her, Taylor. A little bit anyway. And you have to give these things time. I'm willing to cancel the bet right now. And no hard feelings. That way you can take some time with Erin and . . ."

"You gotta be outa your head!"

"This bet should never have come this far," Ned continued. "I intended it to get you out of your funk, but I never thought . . ."

"Listen to this shit," Taylor snapped. "You did this for my sake, right? For months I have chewed nails. I haven't had a peaceful night's rest since February. I have nearly killed Eleanor with my bare hands. And now you tell me it was all a little self-improvement exercise you cooked up for me! Well, you can kiss my . . ."

"Don't pass this up, Taylor. I won't make the offer again."

"Are you listening to yourself, Ned? As soon as you get the idea you might lose the bet, you fabricate this . . ."

"Be careful whom you're accusing of what," Ned said quietly. "I made a gentlemanly offer, no more, no less. Take it or leave it, but keep your accusations to yourself."

Ned's sudden coldness defused Taylor somewhat. "I'm going to leave it."

Ned shrugged. "Suit yourself, but I think you're asking for more grief than you can imagine."

"Let's quit the crap, OK? If you want to know what I've 'learned' over the past months, I'll tell you. I've learned that any woman who took a genuine interest in me, in what I am and what I'm not, in Taylor Worth, specifically and exclusively, could have me in a heartbeat."

Ned shook his head. "Poor Taylor. One woman makes him the center of her universe and he objects because her horizons are too narrow. Another one reveals that she might have another lover and it tears him in pieces. A third one treats him like the sex object he always wanted to be and he resents it. No, Taylor. I think you're kidding yourself. I don't think you could recognize genuine interest if it sat on your face."

Taylor, ready to leave, threw some money on the table.

"So who's next on your list?"

"Eleanor. She's coming over in the morning as soon as she sends the Howards off to the wilderness or some such goddam place."

"Where are you taking her?"

"New York. She wants to trip the light fantastic."

"Sounds exciting."

"Let the good times roll."

"And Veronica?"

"Since our little falling out, I've sent her a jungle's worth of flowers. She's agreed we had a harmless misunderstanding, and I talked her into going down to the river cabin with me."

"When?"

"Next week. We're leaving Tuesday."

"Aren't you going to be a bit worn out?"

"In the immortal words of Frank Zappa, 'My dick is a monster.'"

CHAPTER TWENTY-TWO

"I've been tanning these legs for you," Eleanor called from the bedroom. She had forbidden him to watch her dress. "Every sunny day, when the housework is finished, I go out on the patio and stretch my legs to the sun. I can't get naked out there—well, I guess I could but I'd be nervous about it—but I don't wear any underwear and as I sit down and start pulling my skirt up, I think of you. As I drag it above my knees, I think of that little black backless nothing you fucked me in the day I met you. Then as the sun starts to warm my thighs beneath the cloth of the dress, I hike it up further, to the legal limit, to just below my crotch, and I think of that long T-shirt I wore when we drove out to the country. Remember those men in that roadside bar? They'd never seen anything like it—a woman in their bar, on a Saturday afternoon, wearing nothing but a T-shirt that barely covered her ass and a pair of sassy high heels."

Taylor, leaning against the wall outside her door, sucking on a tall Scotch, remembered a hundred sexy moments with Eleanor and with Erin and with Veronica. Round robin. One woman after another. At first, it was incredibly exciting, different skin textures, different body types. He'd spent hours making the minutest comparisons, exploring each woman infinitesimally, but as the bet continued, he found it more and more difficult to get it up on contact, especially with Eleanor, whose demands were specific and nonnegotiable.

"I wanted to stand up on the table and peel that shirt off."

"Exhibitionist."

Eleanor purred. "Then, when I can feel the breeze tickle my cunt, I drag the skirt higher and let the sun feel me up. Oh, it's delicious. All that public warmth in that private place. One day last week it felt so good I must have had a dozen orgasms, all by myself. I had to hold on to things so I wouldn't float away. I wouldn't have done that a year ago. It's your influence, Taylor."

Oh, sure, he thought sarcastically. You needed a lot of prompting, months of training. There were times he had to bathe his poor aching cock in cool cloths. Sometimes Eleanor would keep him inside her even when she'd gone dry, bending him backward, rubbing him raw. She was the roughest, sleaziest woman he had ever courted. Under that handrubbed finish of hers, that studiously cool, Junior League aplomb, were the carnal instincts of an alley cat. She dressed for stripping, devoured pornography, and adored talking dirty, priding herself on her talent to "give good phone." OK, sleazebox, are you ready to take your strip show on the road? I'm betting you are, my little adulteress, my little wayward mother. "You're a depraved bitch, you know that? You're a sex glutton."

"Exactly," she said. "Now come in here."

There is pretty, then there is beautiful, then there is erotic. Eleanor wore a fawn-colored dress as substantial as an April evening. A light rain would have covered her more completely. The hemline, practically invisible, hung above her knees but Taylor could discern no cloth at her hips. Tendrils of fabric, only faintly darker than her skin, appeared to climb over her slenderness without support, revealing provocative patterns of flesh. Her left breast and nipple were clearly visible, and was that pubic hair? She turned and Taylor finally understood how the dress was made. It was a sheer body stocking decorated with swirls of light brown satin. If the dress had been an artist's canvas, the painting would have been completed with four, sweeping, curvilinear strokes, one of which disguised, but barely, the natural cleavage of Eleanor's ass.

"You'll be arrested," Taylor said.

"In the theater district? Who are you kidding?"

Taylor touched her. He slid his hand down her front and felt sparks of friction dance beneath his fingertips. "One for the road?" he teased, sliding his hand over the almost bare breast.

She smiled at him, but her eyes were stop signs. She avoided kissing him. "Thanks, but I think I'd like to tantalize you for a few hours."

Taylor's hand reached Eleanor's crotch. Sure enough. She wore nothing at all except this flimsy confection of nylon. His insistent fingers found her clitoris.

"If we do, darling, I'll have to re-do."

"Do-be-do-be-do."

"It'll take hours."

"How does this thing *un*-do?" He leaned down to kiss her, and she turned her head.

"Taylor." The word was halfway between a plea and a warning.

He reached for her hair, but she flinched away. "We would mess you up, wouldn't we?" he said. The makeup at the corners of Eleanor's eyes creased as she gave him her best Yes Dear smile, and Taylor watched a tiny edge of a carefully constructed plane of powder crumble and tumble into a shallow wrinkle, where it lodged like a cookie crumb in a kitchen crack. She blew him a kiss in order not to smear her lipstick.

All evening, like a good, self-effacing *porteur*, Taylor danced the male role, assisting Eleanor, attending her, escorting her through entrances and exits, from spotlight to spotlight. Was she noticed? She was ogled. If human stares were Star Trek "tractor beams," Eleanor would have been buffeted by rays of competing power. Every waiter at La Grenouille cruised their table; their cabbie nearly got them killed; two men at the theater, walking in opposite directions staring at her, collided comically; women clucked and sighed, and Eleanor soaked up the attention. The glory, the momentary notoriety, the lust, the envy, even the disapproval disappeared into her like rain into the ocean. At the beginning of the evening, her exhibitionism turned Taylor on, but his interest faded because Eleanor, busy displaying herself and watching for the reaction, practically ignored him. At dinner, between each course she sashayed through the dining room to the restroom. As they ate, Taylor could have recited baseball scores, and Eleanor would have awarded him with the same blank smiles and practiced expressions while she peered at the surrounding tables for another pair of male eyes to expose a tit to or for some matron to scandalize. Taylor didn't have the faintest chance of capturing her attention long enough to propose marriage. He would have liked to auction her off. Not only would she have brought a magnificent price, her fantasy-satisfaction quotient would have been off the scale.

They returned to the apartment at three A.M. Taylor's

fingers, slick with Eleanor's juices from the taxi ride, fumbled with the keys. Her aura, by now a roiling, fulminating purple, threatened to suffocate him as she plastered herself against him.

"Oh God, do I want to fuck you," she panted.

He wanted to brush his teeth.

"I want to drink your come."

He was thinking more of Alka-Seltzer.

"I want to smother you with my skin. I want to absorb you."

That would be fine. It was something she could do without his participation.

She flung herself on the bed. "Do it now, Taylor. Immediately."

Sit. Stay. Roll over. Buy me dinner. Get it up. Who was she kidding? Of course, he was supposed to be aroused. He was male, reputedly witless when it came to matters of the penis. See Taylor. See the horny woman. See Taylor's cock rise. The fact that he had been less important to her than her earrings for the past six hours meant nothing. Feelings? Don't be ridiculous. Men don't have feelings. Taylor needed time to drag his concentration into the present. "I've seen your exhibitionist persona all night," he said. "You're not going to stop now, are you?"

That's all Eleanor needed. She pointed one foot toward the ceiling and went into her most lewd and provocative act, usually guaranteed to bring Taylor's cock to rigid attention, but while she writhed and performed, and he undressed slowly, he waited in vain for the old, familiar neural connections to start firing.

Come on, he exhorted himself. There was Eleanor, spectacularly involved in her umpty-seventh multiple-multiple and his cock was dead. He enclosed it in his hand, tried to massage some life into it, but it felt like a three-inch brown trout. Rhythmically, he clenched abdominal muscles, trying to actuate the pumping action known and loved by every schoolboy but without luck. Next he closed his eyes and relaxed those same muscles lest he constrict critical arteries. He willed blood to his groin. Still no luck. Clench. Relax. Clench. Relax. No good. He opened his eyes. Eleanor, twitching, jerking, jackknifing, scissoring, looked like an animated folding carpenter's rule. That's supposed to be erotic, asshole, he told himself. If you saw that at a fuck show, you'd be climbing the wall; but his dick had all the rigidity of cooked pasta.

Taylor had always marveled at the apparent autonomy of the male member. It seemed to have a mind, if not a life, of its own and as such it was a fun, predictably wild, magnificently reliable partner—a witty sidekick, a roguish pal without whose waggish instincts and reckless attitude his life would have been incalculably duller—but now the playful scoundrel, the best rascal buddy a man ever had, had slipped away from the party and gone to sleep. Taylor looked down mournfully and thought, this is how Dan Aykroyd must have felt when John Belushi died.

Eleanor said his name, and he crawled onto the bed on his belly to keep his pathetic noodle out of sight, and began unbuckling the tiny gold clasp on one of her shoes. Judging from the aroma of the place, and the cool, blue aura of the now placid Eleanor, he decided he couldn't have picked a more opportune time to fail to get it up.

"I guess I got carried away," she said breathlessly, blinking her eyes as if she'd just awakened from a coma.

Taylor tossed the half-ounce of leather and glitter to the floor and went to work on the other shoe. "Just your industrial-grade sexual paroxysm, that's all." The second shoe hit the floor. The dress had been discarded much earlier.

"I wasn't oblivious, though," she said evenly. "I noticed you, uh, you, ah, weren't there and I couldn't stop. I would apologize but I'm not sorry. I was just so hot."

Taylor placed his nose in the hair between her legs and inhaled. 'Wow," he muttered reverently and flicked his tongue out for a taste, but Eleanor recoiled as if touched by fire.

"Please?" she said meekly. "I'm one big raw nerve down there."

Taylor nodded and rested his cheek on her belly. She stroked his hair. "Taylor." She cleared her throat. "Are you all right?"

He mumbled into her navel.

"I can't understand you, darling."

Like a shooting star, a flash of brilliance streaked across Taylor's consciousness. "I have to go to the bathroom," he announced and scrambled off the bed.

Staring into the mirror, the door firmly locked behind him, he whispered to his image, "You unspeakable louse. You're lower than a cesspool cockroach." He smiled. "Now is perfect." He brushed his teeth, splashed water on his face, ran a comb through his hair, and felt his penis twitch for the first time in hours.

Back in the dark bedroom, he made a great show of going through his clothing, ostensibly to locate a handkerchief. The tiny tape recorder was in the upper left inside pocket of his suitcoat. He felt along the row of controls and pressed what he knew was the "Record" button. Finally, he produced the handkerchief and crawled into bed beside Eleanor, who had covered herself with a sheet.

"Eleanor," he said tentatively. He couldn't use the

speech he had prepared to give at dinner, so he winged it. "What I have to say might surprise you, but I must say it."

Eleanor turned her head toward him.

He cleared his throat. "I know we've both acted supremely casual about this affair, very above it all and cavalier, but I'm afraid I can't maintain that sort of disinterested attitude." That wasn't all he couldn't maintain. "I can't continue making love to you like a thief, stealing moments, hours, an occasional night." He gestured to his flaccid penis. "You can see what it's doing to me."

Eleanor looked like he had kicked her in the stomach. Tears formed in her eyes. "You're not going to send me back to the Howards, are you?" she asked tremulously. "You're not going to tell me it's over? Oh, Taylor, please don't. I'm a new person now, a sexual person. I couldn't . . ." Her voice cracked.

"I want to marry you," Taylor said.

Eleanor's mouth fell open and hung there as if both jaw hinges had broken simultaneously. She couldn't have been more stunned if Howard Senior had walked in the door and jumped into bed with them.

The organization of Eleanor's mind resembled a neatly blocked grid, much like a patchwork quilt, in which the contents of any individual square seldom matched that of its neighbor, but Eleanor knew what belonged where and why it was where it was and what relationship it had with the whole. Each new experience constituted another discrete square, and so she had no difficulty reconciling her gay friends, say, with the disapproving, conservative members of her bridge club, and those rigid ladies with her alter ego as Taylor's mistress, and that image with her role as mother and wife. She saw her life as a single, continuous fabric, and she chose to regard its disharmonious aspects as signs of originality. Normally, Eleanor carefully selected each new experience before she sewed it in place. She had more or less chosen Howard Senior; decided, unilaterally, the best time to have Howard Junior; and had selected their neighborhood and house. She controlled her life. Taylor's sudden proposal bewildered her. "I need to make a list," she said.

Taylor's brow furrowed. "What a romantic thing to say."

Utterly disoriented, without so much as touching Taylor's hand, she crawled out of bed.

He grabbed her by the wrist as she floated by. "Hey," he said. "I didn't ask you if you wanted to go grocery shopping. I asked you to marry me." This was better anyway, nearer the tape recorder.

Eleanor flopped back onto the bed and threw her arms around his neck. "Of course I want to marry you." She kissed him. "It's so sudden, though. I'm confused. I can't . . . I just . . . I have to make a list. Where did I leave my purse?"

She left the room and Taylor turned off the tape recorder. It had been almost too easy. He wondered how much Eleanor's willingness to leave her husband and home was due to his own charm; how much was due to her new sexual identity; how much was due to the fact that he simply presented an alternative to a boring situation; and how much was due to the current fashionability of divorce. Erin's acceptance of his proposal had made Ned feel dirty. This one made Taylor feel dirty. It was too melodramatic, too soap operatic, too bloodlessly upper middle class. He offered if not a better deal, then at least an alternative deal to Eleanor, and she had jumped at it with the same lack of compunction with which professional athletes jumped leagues.

He pulled on a pair of pants and thought of a biblical phrase, "to cover his shame."

"Taylor, this is so exciting," Eleanor said, returning with notebook in hand. "I didn't think you would ever . . . but I'm so glad you did." She arranged pillows on the bed and crawled in beside him. "We have so much to plan, though. I think we should go slow. It would be worth more to us that way. Do you think I could get the house? Everybody knows about his affairs. I'll certainly keep my car and my jewelry. He owes me. A nice cash settlement would be excellent. I've always wanted to live in the country. Do you think we could afford it?"

Eleanor scribbled in her notebook and prattled on while Taylor lay beside her thinking how much he despised the first person plural as employed by women like Eleanor. All his life he'd heard it: "Shouldn't we be in the other lane, dear?" or "Could we turn up the heat?" Used this way, those polite phrases, those few efficient words organized just so, had no inclusive properties whatever; the sentence in which they appeared became a cleverly veiled imperative meaning "I want" and "You'd better" simultaneously. He knew what Veronica would say about it, that it was the woman's way to defer to the overactive male ego, to advance an idea without appearing to have had an original thought, but he considered it an ingenious blend of intellectual cowardice and overwhelming laziness, just one more way for women to coerce men into doing things for them while absolving themselves of responsibility for the acts and guaranteeing themselves a safe place on the sidelines in case something went wrong.

"Could we have a little Japanese garden, Taylor?" Eleanor asked. "Please? Just a little one. It wouldn't take much room and it'd be so pretty." She snuggled into him.

First "we'd" have to get a yard, he thought, and repressed an impulse to kick her across the room. He needed this bitch and her wish list like cholera, but he was too tired to pick a fight. "Let's talk about it tomorrow." He felt thoroughly debased.

"It's already tomorrow. There's daylight at the curtains."

"Let's talk about it when we wake up." He dreaded waking up. She'd be there, as welcome in his bed as a post-last-call pickup. A two-hour shower wouldn't help, wouldn't wash away her crudeness or the persistent aroma of his own corruption.

"I can't sleep now. How can you sleep now? How much is your town house worth? I'm not prying. I'm just trying to get an idea of our net worth. Net worth. That's funny." She jostled him. "Do you get it? Am I the woman to finally 'net' Taylor Worth?"

Taylor tuned her out, closed his eyes, and envisioned a Mercedes-Benz obliterating the memory of this night as if it were a beer can in the middle of the road.

CHAPTER TWENTY-THREE

On Monday night in Veronica's apartment, Harriet fondled the roses Taylor had sent and wondered where he was when he'd ordered them. Was he in Chicago, as he had told Veronica, or was he in some hotel lobby or at some beachside pay phone reciting the number of his credit card to an FTD operator while he glanced furtively around for the woman with whom he was sharing the holiday? Beyond casual hints that Taylor had a reputation as a bounder, Harriet hadn't said a word to Veronica about Taylor's alleged vacation, preferring to allow him the benefit of the doubt, at least for a little while longer. Also, she had no intention of interfering with Veronica's euphoria without solid evidence. It was ironic. Veronica had started out suspicious and had been won over by Taylor. Harriet had started out encouraging Veronica and now she was the one with suspicions. She hoped her misgivings were only misplaced envy. Veronica's apartment was abloom with plants and flowers he had sent, littered with cards and notes and gifts.

"Let me show you where it is," said Veronica excitedly, sprawled on the living room floor like a little kid, with an open atlas in front of her. "Pamlico Sound. Look, Harriet. It's sort of a bay."

"That's one of the definitions of 'sound,' " said Harriet. "I guess that's what makes you liberal arts graduates charming—your continual astonishment at discovering the real world."

"My, aren't we testy this evening."

Harriet flopped down onto the carpet. "Let me see," she said. "Mmm. Yup. Looks like good sailing country. Does he have a sailboat?"

"Hasn't mentioned one. He has a fishing boat, though."

"Do you fish?"

"I can clean a bass with the best of them."

"No kidding? That'll impress your date." Harriet participated in her friend's good humor as much as she was able. The invitation for the river trip, as it turned out, had been the straw that broke the back of Veronica's resistance. Taylor had spoken of his cabin so often and so reverentially it had come to represent the primal man Veronica wanted to know. Harriet admitted the trip sounded like fun, and she knew Veronica was especially pleased because the cabin was in North Carolina, her home state. Veronica's giddiness was infectious, and Harriet wished her friend the best but dammit, she couldn't shake her apprehension.

Nor were her misgivings assuaged when she saw Taylor and Veronica off the next morning. Despite his sexy Hawaiian shirt and the provocative bulge in his shorts, he looked terribly haggard, and when she told him where she had worked the previous week, he faltered visibly, as if struck from behind. Veronica said something then and he recovered nicely, making a wisecrack about potentially dangerous office gossip. Harriet saw

WORTH WINNING 257

obvious concern in his eyes but nothing approximating panic. As the car pulled away, with Veronica waving like an adolescent skipping school, Harriet decided the jury on the perfect man was still, unfortunately, out.

Randall opened the front door of the sprawling house before Harriet could ring the bell. "We almost called you last night. Come in. Come in." He held the skirt of his expansive robe off the floor with one hand and closed the door with the other. Harriet couldn't help but notice his satin slippers. "Byron is in the conservatory. Wait till you see. Absolutely conclusive evidence. Byron took the pictures Sunday. We followed the cad from the time he dropped Eleanor off at home until Monday morning. It was so exciting, but I'm certainly glad Byron has refused to trade that old gigantic Cadillac of his. It was so comfortable to sleep in. We were like two policemen in the movies. I slept while Byron kept watch and Byron slept while I stayed awake. Fortunately, I'd thought to make a pot of espresso and put it in the thermos before we left. Isn't that tacky? Espresso out of a thermos, but I had a nice lemon, so we had fresh peel all night. Here we are."

Byron stood to greet her. Too bad he was a dedicated homosexual, she thought again for the thousandth time. He was so dashingly European, elegantly genteel. "What a beautiful shirt," she said, caressing the bright yellow silk.

"Tut, tut," chirped Randall. "We must keep our hands to ourselves."

"Good morning, Harriet," Byron said, kissing her hand. "Won't you sit down?"

Of all the rooms of the house she'd seen, this was Harriet's favorite. Strikingly different from the Victorian clutter of the front rooms, the conservatory reflected Byron's taste in furnishings. One wall, built entirely of glass, gave onto a lush garden partially enclosed by a greenhouse. Plants hung and grew everywhere, but the central item was an enormous redwood hot tub which provided steam and a tropical atmosphere for a bewildering variety of broad-leafed greenery. The conservatory itself was practically bare. A predominantly blue Turkish carpet covered the center of the floor. Four rattan chairs and a matching low table comprised the sitting area, and a baby grand piano occupied the far corner like an honored guest.

Harriet sat and was served coffee from a magnificent porcelain pot. She sighed and wondered whether Randall and Byron had any use at all for a permanent female home furnishing. Didn't homosexuals prefer bawdy, buxom women with big butts? She could drape herself in a sheet and lounge bare-breasted among the statues in the foyer. She could pose within a frame and become kinetic Renaissance art. Their friends would love it. And she'd have the pleasure of life amid graciousness and lovely things.

"Show her the pictures, Byron. Show her the pictures," Randall insisted. "Byron took them with his wonderful new lens and paid a boy to develop them. They were delivered yesterday and we've been ruminating over what exactly to do with them. I believe we should take them to Eleanor immediately and let her deal with the scoundrel but . . ."

"But I haven't Randall's flair for the histrionic," Byron interrupted, taking a leather folder from the table in front of him and placing it carefully in his lap. "This fellow is indeed a scoundrel. He left Eleanor, went home only for an hour or so, and scurried off to meet his other girl friend—the blonde we mentioned earlier—and he stayed with her all night, after spending the previous two nights with Eleanor in New York!"

WORTH WINNING

Harriet agreed with Randall. She wanted to see the photographs, to get down in the dirt and muck around, but Byron continued to build suspense.

"This morning," Byron continued, "I called Eleanor to make an appointment to see her and I could hardly get a word in edgewise. She was so agitated I thought she might bubble up right through the phone. When I told her I had some important news for her, she said, 'It couldn't be anything like the news I have for you.' Then she said a shocking thing. 'My life is utterly changed.'" One of Byron's hands fluttered to his chest. "Well, I must tell you I was breathless. We agreed on a time to meet and I hung up without giving her a clue. I'm afraid our Eleanor is in grave trouble."

Harriet almost screamed at him to let her see the photographs, but instead sipped her coffee like a good guest. "Do you think Eleanor's thinking of leaving her husband?"

Randall piped in. "Well, we're not sure. Nor are we sure what this fellow's game is. He's apparently leading Eleanor to believe he cares for her while he's sleeping with this other floozy. I say he's a satyr."

Curiosity finally got the best of Harriet. She put her coffee cup on the table and gently lifted the folder from Byron's lap. "Well, I can't wait to see this bastard. He's handsome, you say?"

"Well, I wouldn't kick him out of bed," said Randall and Byron shot him a look of pure disgust.

Boys, boys, Harriet thought, then opened the folder and came as close to fainting as she ever had in her life. The breath rushed out of her; all the blood seemed to drain from her head; she collapsed against the cushion of her chair. The photographs scudded to the floor.

"My God, she's passed out."

"I'll fetch the smelling salts."

"We don't have any smelling salts, Randall. Get brandy."

"At this time of the morning?"

"Randall."

Too many thoughts, too much rage, too much sorrow, too much guilt tried to crowd into Harriet's brain all at once, and she began to cry. Huge sobs, great bubbles of grief formed in her chest and welled up and out of her uncontrollably. Poor Veronica. Poor trusting, exuberant Veronica.

"Harriet, what's wrong?" Byron came to her immediately, and his own tears, as if waiting for permission to fall, gathered in his eyes.

Harriet couldn't form words yet. She gave in to her sorrow and let it possess her.

Randall arrived with the brandy, found both of them bawling, and burst out crying immediately. He placed the glass of liquor on the table, sat down at Harriet's feet, put his head in her lap, and cried. For a solid five minutes the maudlin trio sniveled and wailed and wept.

CHAPTER TWENTY-FOUR

In the car Veronica sang a James Taylor song:

*In my mind I'm gone to Carolina
Can't you see the sunshine
Can't you just feel the moonshine
And ain't it like a friend of mine
To hit me from behind
And I'm gone to Carolina in my mind.*

She rolled her head toward the window and felt the breeze on her face. "I have a can opener in my purse," she said. "Next time we stop, do I have your permission to cut the top off the car?" She didn't wait for an answer. "Oh, how I love this. Here it is, the middle of the week, when I should be talking to an asshole doctor in some antiseptic, air-conditioned mausoleum and instead," she sighed grandly, "the sun's on my face and I'm flying free. My heart's so happy it wants to come out and smile at the sky."

Taylor laughed, similarly affected by the glorious morning despite his physical weariness and Harriet's bombshell. He wondered what she'd learned from the office snoops. He told himself to be calm. Whatever Harriet heard, if anything, it didn't matter. He was safe with Veronica, out of touch with civilization. The next four days would determine the outcome of the bet and not a minute too soon. Eleanor had worn him out in New York, and then Erin, whom he had to see before taking off with Veronica, had kept him awake most of Sunday night with an unending stream of drivel about silver patterns, honeymoon ideas, wedding plans, etc. Her apartment had become an enormous bin overflowing with four-color brochures. The evening hadn't been a total loss, though. On the pretense of having to examine her diamond for a suspected flaw, he managed to palm the original ring and replace it with a high-quality zircon replica. Taylor knew it wouldn't withstand expert inspection. It might not even withstand Erin's constant dewy-eyed admiration, but so what? If he could convince Veronica of his honorable intentions, the scam would be over in four days and Erin could keep the trinket as a souvenir and Taylor could breathe easily for the first time in months. The mere thought of peace and quiet, an orderly existence, and the absence of paranoia acted like a narcotic. His mind drifted to new possibilities, to leaving the city altogether, to joining the ranks of brave, new computer wizards who were carving out revolutionary, free-lance lifestyles based on the existence of vast technological networks. He was good enough to meet any challenge, to survive, no, to thrive by virtue of wits alone. His progress in the wager proved it.

"You know what always struck me as completely absurd?" he asked, apropos of nothing.

"Plastic ferns," Veronica suggested, as fast as the scenery flying past.

Taylor laughed again and reminded himself to change mental programs. Go to Veronica-mode, he instructed himself. Immediately.

"I'm sorry," she said automatically. "Actually," she continued, reconsidering, "I'm not sorry at all. But please go on. What do you consider completely absurd?"

He grinned. "How do you feel right now?"

"Splendid, superb, stupendous but otherwise OK. Why?"

"Because our society calls the kind of time we're spending, 'time off.' Isn't that ludicrous?"

"Never thought about it."

"It's as if we're machines. When we're working, we're 'on' but when we're not doing something for money, we're 'off.' Tell me, Ms. Bristow. Do you feel 'off'? Do you feel as if you are not functioning? Do you feel idle? Dormant? Disengaged?"

"I couldn't be in better sync," she said. "Do you want to know the expression that always bugs me?"

"What?"

" 'Doesn't matter.' That to me is absurd. What we intend to say—what we should say—is 'It's meaningless,' but no, good old material-minded westerners that we are, we say, 'Doesn't matter.' "

"Never thought about it."

Veronica leaned her head against the seat and said, "I feel wonderful, Taylor Worth. Wonderful."

"Good for you, but finish your thought."

"Doesn't matter," she recited as if she were sorry she'd brought it up. "It reveals our supreme faith in things tangible. If something can be apprehended by the sense, we trust it. Seeing is believing and all that. Our way of dismissing something, our way of relegating it to nothingness, is to repudiate its somethingness.

Forgive me. I tend to make up words in philosophical discussion."

"Sure. So?"

"So half of our existence is concerned with 'things' we can't see, hear, feel, taste, or smell . . ."

"Is that so?" asked Taylor skeptically.

"Certainly it's so," Veronica insisted, sitting up, facing him. "Would I make things up?"

"Name three."

"Originality, perfection, and difference."

"I'm not sure I'm ready for this kind of talk this early in the day, but what the hell?" He thought of Erin and all the stories he'd told her to fill their time together. He thought of Eleanor who could measure hope in terms of dollars and cents. "I can perceive originality," he said.

"Uh-uh," Veronica said, pulling up her hair, slipping an elastic band around it, creating an absurd little knot at the exact center of the top of her head. "You perceive the results of originality. Originality itself, the thing, is an ideal, purely conceptual, nonperceptual."

Taylor grinned. "I have to tell you something, Veronica. Usually I play verbal badminton with women. You know what I mean? You toss up a little birdie of a subject and tap it back and forth politely. You can bat it as hard as you please and the slightest breeze will stop it dead. But with you, conversation is a challenge and a pleasure. I appreciate that."

"Well, Taylor," Veronica responded, "it's rare to find a man who doesn't think with his dick all the time."

"What a charming thing to say. But we're off the subject. I'll concede your point about originality. What were the other two things?"

"Perfection and difference. No human being has ever seen perfection. It's a figment of the imagination."

Taylor thought about Erin's body and felt a pang of sorrow. "OK, but I don't know what you mean about difference."

"Show me one."

"There's a difference between this car and a Mercedes."

"Where?"

"Where what?"

"Where's the difference? You've shown me two perceptible objects, neither one of which is 'difference,' a thing we're certain exists but can't take a photograph of."

"Hmm," Taylor mused. The idea tried to wrinkle his brain. "Interesting. So where did this start? What were we talking about?"

"Absurd figures of speech."

"Right. 'It doesn't matter.' "

"Uh-huh. We say, 'It doesn't matter' or 'No matter,' and we dismiss a subject, render it insignificant."

Taylor nodded. "But non-matter is significant."

"At least half of life is non-matter."

Taylor glanced at her. With her clean, unpainted face and her chocolate-brown eyes and the wind doing pretty things with errant strands of hair, she looked . . . How did she look? The only satisfactory word was "alive." Unlike Erin or Eleanor, who needed a man for verification and definition, Veronica possessed a distinct, individual spirit. He thought about her latest idea, about real but invisible things. "Like love?" he asked.

An insuperable smile in full battle array claimed the territory of Veronica's face for the sovereign state of bliss. "Like happiness," she said. "Like freedom, the feeling of being right here, right now, and yes"—she wrinkled her nose at him—"like love."

Like most children of the sixties, for whom abstract principles for a brief moment became something more than dreams but less than ideals, simultaneously magical and accessible, both Veronica and Taylor shrank from the presence of the notion of love much as one would shrink in embarrassment at the sudden appearance of an old but long-neglected friend. For a few miles they rode in silence.

"Veronica," Taylor said when he turned off the Interstate onto a two-lane blacktop road that would carry them through the flat farmland of eastern North Carolina. "I have a confession to make." The Harriet connection had continued to bother him, and he decided to make a preemptive strike.

"You're married and have three kids," said Veronica, assuming the worst.

"No," laughed Taylor. Only two fiancées. "It's nothing like that, but it does involve deceit, something I'm ashamed of."

"Can you hold it till we're on our way home? I was hoping for a couple of carefree, barefoot days."

"Uh-h," he faltered.

"Go ahead," she said, touching his arm. "I was only teasing. You can tell me you've lied to me as long as the truth is you're secretly the crown prince of Liechtenstein and you must return to your country because your father, the king, is dying and you want me to be your queen. No, huh?" she said when she saw his frown. "OK. Hit me with your best shot. I can take it. You're very sorry but you've caught and are sure you've given me syphilis, right?"

"Veronica."

"I'll shut up now."

Taylor wondered if he should take up acting. With the number of half-truths and outright lies he'd told over the last few months, he figured he could blow Paul Newman off the screen. "It's about last week," he said solemnly, "when I told you I was away on a business trip."

Oh shit, thought Veronica, slipping off her shoes and putting her feet up on the dashboard.

"I know it was wrong to mislead you," he continued, "but it was a test for me. You see, you were turning my head, as they used to say in the old days. You wouldn't stay in that mental pigeonhole I wanted to keep you in. Instead, thoughts of you kept appearing when they weren't expected. At work. At home. Even when I was with other women."

Well, surprise, surprise, Veronica said to herself. Maybe she could shed some of her armor after all. It'd be awfully uncomfortable to sunbathe in anyway.

"So I decided to take some time away from you, to date some other women to find out if . . . uh, just to get a little perspective on things. I wasn't in Chicago or Detroit, Veronica, and I apologize for lying to you."

If Veronica had been male, she could have concentrated on the single, isolated point of his deceit and used it to advantage. Instead, she considered her stable of men and her own little deceptions. She hadn't lied but she hadn't told the truth, either. She cursed her carefully cultivated, feminine sense of fairness. He was admitting a sin and she felt guilty. Ridiculous. "Apology accepted," she said, deciding to play it cool. "So what did you find out?"

He guided the car through a tight curve. "First," he said, "let me say that I'm a reasonably aware person, that I understand we're living in a hands-off era, that lovers need to give each other space and all that California Mellowspeak stuff, and I don't want to appear pushy. OK?"

Push, Veronica thought. Harder. Give it a try. Veronica knew she had a formidable personality. She h* built it that way and fortified it against the onslaughts of jerks, but a strong-willed gentleman could walk in unannounced, so she thought, so she hoped, although in recent years when no such gentleman had appeared, she had begun to wonder. "OK," she said.

"I also know that by admitting these things to you, I'm putting a certain pressure on you anyway, but I'm afraid you'll have to take what I say for what it's worth."

So all right already, she thought. If you keep retreating from the subject, the car will start going backward.

"What I found out was what I thought I'd find out, Veronica. Nobody I know—or have ever known—has the combination of charm, intelligence, beauty, and sexiness that you do. There, I've said it. If you think I'm being too pushy, well, whatever."

"How romantic," she said drolly.

"Hey, I . . ."

"No, really," she said, placing her fingers on his lips. "That was very sweet, Taylor, and I appreciate it. A lot. A whole lot. In fact, feel my heart," she said, taking his hand to her chest.

He squeezed.

"My heart, you lecher," she laughed, flinging away his hand. She leaned across and kissed his cheek. "You don't have to couch your feelings in psychobabble with me, Taylor. Especially those kinds of feelings."

Again the idea of love, the long-neglected friend, returned. This time it settled comfortably into the seat between them and painted smiles on both their faces.

Veronica said, "I have some ideas about all this hands-off, ultracoolness myself, Taylor. I've been hearing it since college and I think it's simply an elaborate rationalization for cowardice. Remember that adage that was so popular for a while? They made samplers and hung them in every head shop. It went: 'I'm not here for your benefit and you're not here for mine but if our paths cross for a time it's groovy,' or something like that?"

Taylor laughed. "You've garbled it horribly, but I know the one you're talking about."

"Well, for my money, it's a load of pure bullshit."

"Do you know what I like about you? Your speech is so gracious. So ladylike."

"Lady is a four-letter word, buster."

"OK, OK," he said. "Go on."

"It's just another example of how our culture begins with a completely false proposition and then goes on to make logical deductions from it."

"Such as?"

"For example, I had a friend who fell in love with a doctor, an M.D. I work with doctors all the time. They're demagogues, tyrants. I warned her, told her he'd make her crazy, but she denied it. All she could see was the big house and sexy sportscar and the status of being Mrs. Doctor. 'He won't change me,' she said. Two years later she was a basket case. She believed there was something in her personality which could resist the most powerful influences. Nonsense. Change is constant and nothing changes a person like proximity to another person. I change—have changed—with respect to you, Taylor."

He threw her a glance. What was this? he wondered.

"I have a true confession of my own," she said and proceeded to tell him the details of her former life-style. She told him about her stable of lovers and the reason she couldn't go out with him when he asked her the previous week. "So I'm guilty of deception, too," she concluded.

"A Third Wave romance." He grinned, and Veronica sat up as if jolted by a cattle prod. "Can you pull over to the side?" she asked. Her head hung out the window as if she'd lost something and expected to find it beside the road.

"Well, sure, I guess," he said. "Anything wrong?" He steered onto the shoulder and stopped. The face she turned toward him could have belonged to a ten-year-old on her birthday.

"Come with me," she lilted, scrambling into her shoes. "Try not to concentrate on the empty beer cans and throwaway diapers in the ditch. The charm of the South is not to be found in the behavior of its benighted inhabitants but in the land, this most blessed, fertile earth. Look," she said, pointing, hugging his arm to her.

On the other side of the ditch, a tumbledown split-rail fence ran parallel with the road from the curve where they had slowed down to a stand of hardwoods perhaps a hundred yards away. On the other side of the fence, a meticulously cultivated field of short broad-leafed plants stretched into the distance toward another woods. The rows of plants undulated, snakelike, away from him, and he wasn't sure whether the sinuous curvings were the result of a tractor driver's unsteady hand or of the shimmering heat of early afternoon.

"Tobacco," said Veronica, biting off the word as if it were a plug of chew. She stepped into the ditch, over a discarded paint can to an oak tree that had been left, along with a few of its neighbors, on the edge of the field in apparent tribute more to sentimentality than to soil conservation. Veronica put her foot on a fence rail, reached into the branches of the tree, and plucked a blossom the color and shape of a bunch of grapes from an entangled vine. "Wisteria," she said proudly. "Isn't it beautiful? Smell it," she insisted, coming back to him. "That's the South, Yankee. Not the people, not the accent, but the land, the way it feels, the way it smells. The South is this: aromas of magnolia, gardenia, and honeysuckle hanging thick with scent and moisture on a sultry, airless summer afternoon." She sniffed the flower. "Mmmm. Smells like, like . . ."

"Smells like fucking to me, Scarlett."

"Well, I declare," Veronica drawled, enunciating carefully. "General Lee, I wouldn't allow such talk in my hearing, but I'll Grant you this is a special occasion."

Taylor groaned. He might be a Yankee, but he'd seen *Gone With the Wind* at least twice. "Don't turn Prissy on me," he grinned, "or I'll have to paddle your Ashley."

Veronica pinched both cheeks to bring out a blush, cocked her head to one side, batted her eyes, and simpered, "Oh, Mr. Worth. You do that and it'll Tara my little heart. Now that wouldn't be Rhett, would it? Not Rhett at all."

CHAPTER TWENTY-FIVE

They'd used so much Kleenex, the conservatory looked as if it had been hit by a freak snowstorm. "Do you know the bastard's phone number at that cabin?"

"No phone," answered Harriet. "I asked Veronica before she left."

"Do you know the address? The town?"

"The Pamlico River is all I know. I saw it on the map. Big river."

"We could call the Red Cross or the Highway Patrol."

"I don't think this qualifies as their type of emergency."

"I still think we should call Eleanor right away," Randall offered.

"I understand your feelings," Byron said, squeezing Randall's hand gently. "But I think Harriet is right. By proceeding slowly, we have a chance to make this vermin suffer." He practically drooled in anticipation. "But if we set off rapid alarms, he could slip away from us."

"But I'm afraid for Eleanor," Randall replied, again close to tears. "We don't know what happened in New York. Maybe this beast promised her something. Maybe she's already said something to Howard. She could be ruining her life while we sit around planning revenge."

"Good point," said Harriet, blowing her nose one more time. "I think you ought to call her but don't tell her what we know. Just ask her to delay doing anything drastic for, say, forty-eight hours. We know Taylor can't do any more damage to Eleanor while he's off savaging Veronica."

"I'll do that now," said Randall and left the room.

"I can't believe it," Byron said for the six-hundredth time. "A bet!"

"We don't know yet if the rumor's true," cautioned Harriet.

"What else could it be? Wanton cruelty?"

"Perhaps a personal challenge. I've heard of weirder things."

Randall returned. "She's not home."

"My turn," Harriet said and went for the phone. She talked to Georgia at Taylor's office, then to the girl who'd mentioned the rumor who gave Harriet the name and work number of the woman from whom she'd heard it in the first place. "The good-old-girl network," Harriet said acidly while she dialed. "The agents of the good-old-boy's destruction are already in place. Hello," she said into the designer instrument, "you don't know me but . . ."

"Don't bite your nails, Randall," Byron said while Harriet spoke the rudiments of their dilemma into the phone.

"I will if you'll stop snapping and unsnapping the clasp of your watchband," Randall replied, tearing at a thumbnail.

They stared sharpened icicles at each other. "I told you when this thing started, we should have hired a private detective right away."

"That's not true. You were the one who said it was a harmless fling. You even accused me of being jealous."

They aimed their stares toward the hot tub. The thermostatically controlled electric heater clicked on.

Randall's lower lip began to quiver. "Poor Eleanor. She'll be devastated."

"That cad. That wicked villain. I hope he gets herpes of the mouth. I hope he gets cancer of the scrotum and his penis becomes a scab."

"Poor Eleanor," Randall burbled. "How can we help her, Byron?"

"We can begin by not fighting each other."

"Oh, Byron. I'm sorry."

A new round of weeping commenced.

Harriet hung up the phone. "Dry your tears, boys, and you'd better change into something you can wear in public, Randall. We have a lunch date with Ms. Joanne Minneman at one o'clock."

While the proprietors of the Queen's Bakery left to primp, Harriet went into the greenhouse and wandered among the lush plants. Most of her grief had evaporated and she struggled to direct the rage which had replaced it. "Whatever your game is, Mr. Taylor Worth," she said aloud, dipping her hand into the overheated water of the redwood tub, "you'd better be awfully good, or else before this thing's over, I'm going to have your cock in my pocket."

"It's beautiful," said Veronica, standing on the end of the narrow dock, trying to look in every direction at once.

Taylor had as much luck controlling his grin as he would have had picking up the river with his fingers. "It sure is," he said, "but it's never been as beautiful as with you standing here."

"Oh, pshaw," Veronica said, blushing in spite of herself.

"Take that knot out of your hair," he said. "I want to see how the sun reacts to a glory rivaling its own."

"Taylor, you have to quit that," she said, not meaning it for a second.

"Have I ever told you what I've decided about your hair?"

"Decided about it?" she asked, slipping off the elastic band.

"Uh-huh," he said. "I think your hair is a training station for light."

"I can't wait to hear the rest of this."

"I'm convinced of it. I think your hair is where light goes to learn the color red, and believe me, not a single photon loafs the course." He stepped closer to her, put his face against her head, and rubbed back and forth. "Fire and fuchsia, carmine and crimson," he said. The river encouraged his best poetry. "Once caught within this wavy maze, light learns shades of meaning at a blazing pace. Maroon and magenta. Ruby and puce."

"Tell me more," she said.

"By the time it leaves this fabulous place," Taylor continued, his face radiant in the reflection of the rippling water, "it knows exactly what to do, precisely how to act in case it ever finds itself inside a mahogany finish or a glass of Burgundy."

"Taylor," she exclaimed. "Thank you."

"You only get what you deserve, you know," he said, hugging her, rejoicing in the freedom of the river and his pleasure in delivering the first compliment in two weeks that didn't get stuck in his throat.

"I shouldn't be talking out of school like this," said Joanne Minneman, spooning Kahlua parfait into the cupid's-bow between her heavily rouged cheeks, "but I think what these men are doing is abominable. I'm not surprised at Taylor Worth, though. Oh no. He's such a conceited person. Do you know he wouldn't even consider dating me? He wouldn't hear a word Karen had to say about me. Karen thinks it was because I'm just a secretary. Just a secretary! How does he think the work gets done in American business? Who does he think takes care of the details? And the way he struts around, pretending to be classy and debonair. He's just a cold fish, if you ask me. And if he's doing this to these women like you say, well . . ."

"Ms. Minneman," Byron interjected, all Continental polish and politeness, "it is you to whom we've come for verification. We can only prove he's been seeing three women at the same time, which is loathsome we all agree, but hardly, you will forgive me, unusual."

Joanne reached out to pat Byron's hand. "I could listen to you talk for hours. Were you educated in England?"

Randall looked as if he were being forced to take lunch beside a pile of dirty socks. Harriet squeezed his knee beneath the table and, giving him soulful, knowing looks, tried to defuse his increasing impatience.

"Thank you, I'm quite flattered, Ms. Minneman . . ."

"Call me Joanne."

". . . er, Joanne. I studied at . . ."

Randall interrupted. "Bryn Mawr," he said through pursed lips. "Class of thirty-six, wasn't it, Byron? He attended on a Tarnower-Harris fellowship."

Harriet took charge. "You've heard them talk about this bet in the office. Is that right?"

"Oh yes. Almost constantly. I wouldn't begin to guess how much money is floating on it. It's a big event, believe me."

"But who are the principals? It's not a lottery, is it?"

"Oh no. It started between my boss and Taylor. I'm sure of it. They're old friends. The other salesmen are only involved in it as side bettors."

"And how many women is he supposed to snare?"

"Well, I don't know exactly. I'm not included in their man-to-man conversations, you know." She stared down her nose at Randall, who retaliated with a feral sneer.

"Do you have any idea what the stakes of the main bet are?"

"Oh, there's lots of talk," she said, scraping the sides of the slender glass with her spoon. "I'm almost sure a car is involved. When I first heard of this thing, I thought I should really try to find out more about it, to warn the women, you know, because I think what's going on is so, so . . ."

"Reprehensible," Byron suggested.

"Oh, perfect. What a terrific vocabulary." She patted his hand again. Randall hissed. Harriet squeezed. Byron preened.

"But you haven't discovered any names or other details?" Harriet asked.

"That's right, but how was I to find out?" she snapped defensively. "I'm not my sister's keeper. It's not my job to police . . ."

This time Byron did the patting. "Of course not, Joanne," he crooned soothingly. "And you have your own position to consider as well. There is only a slim distinction between helping one's neighbor and prying. It was not your responsibility at all." As if to punctuate the sentence, he brushed a stray hair from Joanne's forehead.

Randall harrumphed and turned a huffy shoulder to Byron.

WORTH WINNING

Harriet toyed with her coffee cup while Joanne and Byron flirted. They weren't exactly at a dead end, but Joanne's information wasn't very enlightening, either. Harriet knew salesmen to be notorious blowhards and prevaricators. Perhaps they were simply admirers of a smooth operator. Maybe Taylor's adventures made good material for betting pools. Still, Taylor wouldn't run a major risk for a penny-ante betting pool. He's spending too much time and money of his own: Eleanor in New York, Veronica at the river, and who knows where he was last week with the blonde. No, she thought, this had all the markings of a bigger deal. An automobile sounded about right, something a man could gloat over, take title to, flaunt in front of the loser. She looked at Randall, who seemed determined to secure the world's frowning record. Deduce, she commanded herself. What would be some other characteristics of this kind of deal between businessmen? A single word lit up Harriet's brain like sunshine. "Of course," she said.

"I beg your pardon?" asked Byron.

Harriet smiled. "I have a question," she said confidently, and Randall's attention returned to the conversation. "If Joanne's boss and our Mr. Worth have a high-stakes bet going here, wouldn't one or the other or both of them, being smart businessmen, insist on writing up a legal contract in order to detail the exact provisions of the wager?"

"It would seem so," said Byron.

"Well, if they have a contract, I certainly didn't type it," Joanne offered.

"They wouldn't necessarily give it to you," Byron said. "It would make you a sort of accessory and they wouldn't want a woman to know their plans. It might excite sisterly loyalty."

Harriet felt like Harriet Vane. "OK. Let's assume these papers exist. Now, where are they likely to be kept?"

Randall enjoyed the game. "Mr. Worth wouldn't keep them at home unless he has a safe somewhere. He wouldn't want any of his many lovers to chance upon them."

"He wouldn't stash them at his office, either," said Harriet. "I've worked there and he's famous for keeping his private and work lives separate. So they are most likely to be kept by the other principal in the bet." She pointed at Joanne. "Your boss."

"I'm sorry to put a damper on this great idea of yours, Harriet," said Byron, "but there are plenty of other places. A lawyer might have them. They might be in a safety deposit box. Who knows?"

Harriet's face fell but only momentarily. "You're right, of course, but there is a chance they're where we can get our hands on them. Taylor's friend might have them in his office. It's logical. And they'd be safe there."

"It's plausible."

"If there are any papers like that, I've never seen them and I do all the filing," Joanne said.

"All the filing?" three voices chimed in unison.

Joanne smiled. "Well, Ned does have a personal file in his desk drawer."

"Does he keep it locked?"

"I have keys to everything in the office."

Byron took Joanne's hand and kissed it.

"How often do you get an opportunity to strike a blow for justice?" Harriet asked.

"Perhaps I should order a dessert wine," Randall cooed. "I believe I saw a Beerenauslese on the wine list. Waiter . . ."

CHAPTER TWENTY-SIX

All day long a song played in Taylor's mind, a bright, pop tune of not-so-recent vintage. The trouble was, he couldn't remember the words except for the tag end of one line: ". . . a woman who can be a friend of mine." He steered his skiff into a favorite fishing cove, cut the engine, and let the boat drift. If luck was with him, he and Veronica would have fresh bass for dinner. He could almost hear the frying pan sizzling, almost smell the clean-water aroma as the firm, white fillet slid into buttery oil, almost see the look of astonishment on Veronica's face. "Here, fishy," he whispered as, with a side-arm flick of the wrist, he flipped his lure into the shallows near a fallen tree.

Aha, he thought, and the sudden recollection satisfied him more than a tug at his fishing line. He'd remembered another line of the song. "Won't you meet me in the middle?" Taylor turned his face to the sun. Another line came. "Won't you love me just a little?"

The song was popular when Taylor was in college. He remembered his roommate's scorn when he expressed a fondness for its sentiment. "You want a woman for a friend? Find an ugly dyke who likes football, then restrict your conversation to tight ends. Sex is war," his roommate had said. "If you find a woman who wants the same things you do, you'll fight over how to get them. You're looking for bones in a potato, Taylor, drilling for water on the moon."

Was he right? Everybody seemed to think so, and so everybody waded into love as into battle, expecting casualties. There's a fine scenario for you, young lovers. Not quite what the songs tell you to expect, is it? Taylor slowly reeled in his lure and flicked it out again. His objections, of course, were the same as those he'd use against opponents of gun control or nuclear disarmament: If you go in looking for a fight, you're likely to find one; or, actuality tends to reflect expectations. So which comes first to the young lover, the fight or its prospect? Was there a clear difference between anticipation and intention? Which came first, the caviar or the sturgeon? The caviar, of course, silly. The appetizer always precedes the fish course.

Taylor slipped off his shoes and leaned his head against the gunwale. Ah yes, he ruminated, the classic inconclusive argument, one of the myriad, annoying split ends in the grand coiffure of life. Somehow, the river always did this to him. In the time it took sunlight to glint off the tip of a wavelet, the most profound notion metamorphosed into cliché, the least ambiguous fact became pregnant with implications. Well, if it doesn't matter anyway . . . oops . . . if it doesn't make any difference . . . oops again . . . if it's all meaningless, then why not speculate a bit?

What is a man who, in the face of evidence and advice, goes forth consciously intending to find a woman to be both his friend and lover? Is he a visionary, a bold, brave seer, the purest sort of scientist dedicated to the discovery of a truth he knows but as yet has no evidence to support; or is he quixotic, a demented idealist, a charming romancer, quaint but misguided; or is he hopelessly deficient in the ordinary mental powers, an idiot, an imbecile? Taylor pulled his hat lower on his head to shield his eyes against the lengthening rays of the sun. The man is any of the above, all of the above. He may be flesh and blood, but with respect to this problematical situation, he's also pure potential. Until he is placed in time, actualized, until the story ends, he's like an unobserved electron, a wave motion, potentially anything and anywhere. Taylor recalled what little he knew about quantum mechanics' and modern physics' dazzling new definition of reality, according to which a thing does not "exist" until it is observed. The implication is that the human mind shapes not only destiny but also physical reality by its ability to observe, to make a judgment. The magical electron, once observed, becomes a point. The wave motion "collapses" and the electron is "seen" to exist. Could people then will things into existence? Could Taylor Worth, Zen fisherman, will a bass onto his hook? Could Veronica Bristow, another wave motion, another unactualized phenomenon, if perceived as such, become his partner?

Taylor felt the tiniest increase in tension on his fishing line and inadvertently jerked his hand upward. Relax, he told himself. He closed his eyes. Become the bass. His lips parted, puckered, mimicking his unseen prey. Veronica, had she seen him, would have laughed. Taylor's senses flowed through the rod, down the line, to the lure. Steady, he cautioned himself. Wait. Don't shake. Don't move. Now. He jerked the line but missed the fish. So much for quantum theory, he thought, settling back again but not quite as nonchalantly. Time for some plain, old, down-home fishing now that he knew at least one critter was interested.

He also settled back into his speculative ruminations. Living with Veronica for the past few days had been great fun and miraculously, blessedly easy. She helped with the chores, but she wasn't martyrish about it like Eleanor would have been. Unlike Erin, she didn't require constant attention and reassurance. He felt comfortable with Veronica, not oldshoe, kick-it-in-the-corner-and-forget-about-it comfortable, but contented comfortable, warm, happy to have her around, anxious to hear her next remark, pleased to see her asleep in a chair by the fire or topless on the dock, amusing herself with a book or just soaking up the heat, processing it into serenity. Like most folks who based their ideas of love on what they'd seen in movies, Taylor associated feelings of love with obvious moments—when champagne glasses clinked together, when passion reached its peak—but with Veronica, he experienced powerful surges of affection at the oddest moments, when he watched her exercise, when he listened as she spoke *ex cathedra* on subjects as far from love as she was from Washington, D.C., when he sensed her bending her formidable intelligence to the jigsaw puzzle they worked on at night, TV-less, amid the incessant serenade of crickets chirruping and frogs croaking.

Taylor sensed the presence of a fish, and he drew a mental image of the crafty silver beast undulating through the brackish water, focusing on the lure, first with this eye, then, turning and swimming in the opposite direction, with the other, gills opening and closing, dull brain making slimy fish calculations regarding the savoriness of its potential dinner. Taylor gently reeled in, waited a moment, and aimed his next cast closer to the partially submerged tree.

WORTH WINNING

But back to Veronica. Perhaps the single most attractive aspect of her, beyond her hair, beyond her wit—and he knew this to be wickedly selfish—was her interest in him. She asked intelligent questions, not polite, obligatory queries intended to satisfy some requirement of the mating ritual. She listened attentively to his answers, then miraculously asked more questions based on his earlier answers. So extraordinary was this phenomenon, he at first mistrusted it, suspecting Veronica of an Eleanor-like meddlesomeness, but gradually he recognized it as sincere curiosity. For example, Taylor believed his work provided him with an unusual vision of the future and that anyone ignorant of the functioning of computers was a candidate for the Flat Earth Society. He also understood, however, how traditionally masculine a work obsession was and how boring he could seem to an indifferent listener. Erin couldn't have cared less about his job; Eleanor, when he felt compelled to hold forth about some aspect of it, placated him with pasty smiles and a brace of yes, dears; but Veronica, as much a fan of learning as of basketball, paid attention, enjoyed herself, and seemed to recognize his enthusiasm as an important element of his personality. Here, too, Taylor knew the dangers. He disliked pedantic men and despised obsequious women, but whereas he taught her about computers, she taught him about chemistry and modern medicine, aspects of her own work, as well as about photography and the properties of light. She was fun, smart, and sexy, a bone in a potato.

A few years previously, listening to the futurist R. Buckminster Fuller, Taylor had learned about the principle of synergism—the behavior of a whole system that is greater than and unpredicted by the sum of its parts. Steel is an example of the synergetic process, as is fermentation and so forth. Fuller presented the idea as a new way of looking at the world. Instead of an I win-you lose competitive model of the universe, Fuller suggested a complementary model emphasizing the occurrence of unaccountable cooperation in nature. Taylor embraced the idea like a new religion. It felt right to him, not only because it offered the possibility of hope, but because it represented the world as he saw it. The computer operated according to synergetic principles. The creation of one new function doesn't necessarily mean the destruction of one old one. More often it increases possibilities, generates new ideas, some of which are neither planned nor even suspected. Miraculous? Something from nothing? No. Synergetic. Happens all the time. Taylor became an advocate, a proselytizer on behalf of synergism until his associates began rolling their eyeballs and eventually his evangelism subsided. A single idea from that rare adult bout with optimism, however, remained: What if a man and a woman were to their marriage what carbon and iron were to steel?

He felt another nibble.

His old roommate after all might be right, he thought. Marriage might indeed be war, but the very existence of synergism suggested it didn't have to be, that no evolutionary mandate prevented it from being something else . . .

Taylor readied himself for the fish, felt its presence, sensed its being. He remained motionless, poised. The bass struck, and with a smooth, crisp motion, he set the hook. Dinner!

. . . and as long as there was a chance, as long as nature allowed the slimmest possibility, then that, in Taylor's sentimental state of mind, was enough.

CHAPTER TWENTY-SEVEN

Harriet checked the dashboard clock as she slid out of the car into the cool dawn. Six-twelve. The parking lot contained only four other cars, one of which was Joanne's. Only a few lights burned in the windows of the squat, square, six-story suburban office building. Randall lit a cigarette.

"You don't smoke, Randall," she said.

"It goes with the outfit." He wore his trench coat and fedora.

"A pastel cigarette?"

"Nuevo Wavo."

"Why are you two whispering?" asked Byron.

"Let's go," said Joanne, dangling a key ring that must have weighed three pounds.

Byron remained at the door of the building, Randall at the door of the suite, and Harriet at the door of Ned's office while Joanne did the dirty work. With a nod, Byron acknowledged the quizzical glance of a maintenance man. Randall stubbed out the yellow cigarette and selected a gold-filtered pink one from a slim, black box. Harriet fidgeted. Joanne carefully sifted through the file folders for any new or suspicious correspondence. Byron watched daylight wash across the indigo sky. Randall coughed and found a chair to sit on. Harriet inquired as to Joanne's progress. Joanne continued her search.

At six thirty-three, Harriet heard Joanne exclaim. She'd found a written, signed, and notarized contract. More incriminating than the neatly typed papers, however, more disturbing to the thieves poring through the file were the Polaroid photographs.

"That's Eleanor," gasped Randall. "And that's the blonde Byron took pictures of."

"Erin Dolan," Harriet said.

"What?"

"That's her name. It's right here in the agreement, along with your friend's name and Veronica's. The bastards."

"Quick, now," whispered Joanne, snatching the folder from Harriet. "I'll copy it."

"What are these?" Randall asked, holding two tiny cassettes.

"More evidence," said Harriet, taking them from him, leaving the room to find Joanne.

"Do you have a recorder small enough to play these?" she asked as Joanne adjusted the copier, trying to get a legible reproduction of the photographs.

"In my desk. Second drawer on the left. In the back."

"Looking for worms?" asked Veronica, trundling down barefoot from the cabin to the dock, where Taylor sat soaking up the morning. Her eyes were puffy, her hair was a mess, she was still in her nightie, and she clutched a coffee mug as if it held life itself.

"Good morning," he called. "You look great."

She grunted. "What's with the dawn patrol? I thought you liked to sleep late."

"In a couple days, I'll wake up in the city again." It was an adequate explanation.

They sat together, thigh to thigh, silently, watching the water make diamonds out of wind and sunlight for perhaps five minutes before Veronica said, "I'll have to take a swim today."

"Brave girl."

"Without any clothes on."

"I'll take pictures."

Veronica hugged her knees. "Do you want to know what I like about you, Taylor Worth?"

Taylor kissed her cheek.

"Besides your broad shoulders and hairy chest and gray eyes and big dick and your river cabin, I mean."

"What else is there?"

"You don't try to fix me."

"I might consider brushing your hair this morning."

"Lord knows there's plenty to fix," she continued, ignoring his wisecrack. "And you've had plenty of occasions to comment on my sometimes perverse behavior, but you've been . . ."

"Don't say supportive."

"Never. I was thinking more of something like—fair. Take my swimming idea, for example. You didn't warn me about the cold water or suggest that I was being adolescent. You shrugged your shoulders and saw it from my side. I like that. I appreciate it."

"You're a big girl."

"Exactly. But do you know how many men treat women like children?"

Taylor opened his mouth but shut it again before unnecessary words fell out.

"I know what you were going to say," Veronica said,

smiling, "and you're right, but not all women are wimps and not every man realizes what he's doing when he acts overprotective, but you're different. You don't 'tolerate' me or give me any of that good-old-boy, 'I like high-spirited women,' bullshit which is usually accompanied by a patronizing pat on the ass." Veronica laughed. "I sound like a character out of a bodice-ripper, but I feel—I believe—that you respect me."

Taylor, slightly discomfited, said, "I remember seeing a cartoon. A man and a woman are in bed and she says, 'I was afraid I'd hate myself in the morning but instead I hate you.' "

Veronica smiled. "Don't change the subject. I want you to understand I wouldn't settle for anything less than respect, but I also want you to know it's nice to get it without begging. It's a pleasure to be with you, to be free to be myself with you. I always dreamed of finding a man who would not only take me for what I am but like me for what I am. I've spent a long time and a lot of thought becoming this person you see on the dock this morning and I'm proud of my efforts." She cleared her throat of its sudden lump. "So, thanks, Taylor. You're a special man." She sniffed and surreptitiously wiped away a tear.

"Well, I . . ." Taylor began haltingly, but Veronica put her fingers to his lips.

"Well, you need some coffee," she said, getting to her feet. "Sit still. I'll bring it down to you. Then I'm going to wash this buzzard's nest that used to be my hair."

Taylor brightened. "Hey, can I do it?"

"Do what?"

"Wash your hair."

"You're kidding."

"Don't you trust me?"

"I'd adore it if you washed my hair. It'd be a fantasy fulfilled."

"Well, let's do it," he said, scrambling up. "Let's shampoo the morning away."

They started up the slope hand in hand. Veronica giggled. "Is that like having your morning coif-ee?"

"Argh," Taylor complained. "That's grounds for homicide."

"You know what, Taylor?" said Veronica, poking him in the ribs. "I think I love you."

CHAPTER TWENTY-EIGHT

"Taylor," Veronica purred, "it's not lunchtime." She arched her hips and squinted into the beam of sunlight angling through the open window. The gingham curtains fluttered on the same clean breeze that carried the scent of the river and the lilting cries of cardinals. She closed her eyes and the sunlight burst into a billion bits of color, spewing from their blazing yellow source like droplets from a fountain of light. She groaned and ground her soft parts against his tongue.

Taylor rubbed his face against her like an infant rubbing its face in food. "Man does not live by bread alone." Her excretions had achieved a signal sweetness, a slickness specifically suited to inspire blind, blundering sperm. Taylor reveled in it, romped in it, slurped, and splashed around.

Veronica's body, a tingling, tintinnabulous festival of sensation and time suspension, quivered and bucked to the accompaniment of low moans and sighs. She captured her breath momentarily, held it long enough to form a sentence. "It's ex—mmm—ex—uh—exceptional, Taylor, any way you slice it."

Swimmingly distracted, it took Taylor two slurps to catch the pun. He laughed in spite of himself. "You never quit, do you?" he asked, rubbing his mouth against her thigh, sliding up onto her, placing his smile directly opposite hers, gazing into her brilliant brown eyes, where the greatest performing team in the history of emotion—love and good humor—displayed unforgettable virtuosity.

"Just trying to get a rise out of you," she said, enveloping him with arms and legs, molding him to herself.

"Getting to be a crusty broad, aren't you?"

"Simply making sure you don't loaf."

At any other moment of his life, with any other woman, Taylor would have proceeded directly and more or less rapidly to the culmination of the sex act, driven onward by lust and the safe knowledge that all was in preparedness for if not simultaneous, then at least fairly synchronous orgasms, the goal which theretofore was the most he could hope to accomplish. With Veronica, however, in the springtime sunlight, on a pallet of quilts on the floor of the cabin, with tears in his eyes and his heart trying to exceed physical limits, to expand to the size of joy itself, the next procedural move was unclear, out of his control, but it was not a problem, not the age-old dilemma of the premature spasm. The sensation, rather, as he slid into her, was one of physical and emotional buoyancy, of unmistakable spiritual amplification. He heard words no one had ever spoken to him.

"You are beautiful, Taylor," she said.

He stared incredulity at her.

She replied, silently, with hope.

He celebrated her.

She honored him.

They rocked, eyes locked, together.

Taylor felt encompassing and encompassed, vulnerable yet fortified. If before Veronica, sex had been the horizon, then today love was the sky.

Ten minutes later, after having settled slowly back to earth, Taylor, emotions still overflowing, recited some words written by Jackson Browne. " 'Now we're lying here,' " he quoted, " 'so safe in the ruins of our pleasures.' "

Unexpectedly, Veronica finished the couplet, " 'And laughter marks the place where we have fallen.' "

Taylor looked over at her. "I'm surprised to be saying it," he said, "but I love you, Veronica."

"It's about time you admitted it," she said, kissing him. "Stubborn man."

When their lips parted, perhaps a half hour later, Taylor asked, "How does the rest of that verse go?"

" 'And our lives are near,' " she quoted, " 'so it wouldn't occur to us to wonder, is it the past or the future that is calling.' "

Taylor shook his head. "That's where Mr. Browne and I part company. It's the future." He propped himself on one elbow and said, "Marry me, Veronica."

It was his emotional appeal and it failed.

Earlier, he'd tried the shock approach. She'd taken a swim and come out of the water all pale and goosebumpy into a huge towel and an embrace. "You're crazy," he'd said. "Uh-huh," she'd replied. "Crazy enough to marry me?" he'd asked.

That didn't work either.

CHAPTER TWENTY-NINE

"I just don't believe in marriage," Veronica said. They were sharing their last beer of the trip on the dock. The car was packed, the cabin locked, their vacation was almost over. "I'll go steady with you, pledge my fidelity to you, move in with you, and share the bathroom mirror, but I haven't seen three good marriages in my life and I'm not about to buck those odds. Uh-uh. Not this girl."

It was Taylor's final appeal, the logical approach. "I concede the odds are bad, but those marriages involve other people. We're not other people. We're not even most people."

She frowned. "Brilliant, Taylor. Positively brilliant. But I refuse to be put on the defensive. This is your bright idea. Why are you so in favor of marriage all of a sudden?"

"Not all of a sudden, Veronica. Not all of a sudden at all." He picked a pebble off the dock and threw it into the water.

"Why do boys have to do that?"

"Do what?"

"Throw things into the water. I've never been tempted to throw a rock in the water in my life, and I've never known a male who didn't do it every chance he got."

He ignored her question and launched into his prepared remarks. "I've been in the sexual revolution for the duration, Veronica. I'm a much wounded, much decorated veteran. I am aware of every permutation of involvement and commitment known to humankind and I know more about space than Halley's comet. Do you want to know what space is? All that space is? It's a vacuum, Veronica, cold and lifeless."

"Very glib," she said taking a swallow from the beer can.

"Freedom is fine if it doesn't become shiftlessness or worse, licentiousness. Veronica, I don't have any feeling for the future, any real dedication to anything."

"Except your work."

"I'd give it up tomorrow. It's a substitute, my surrogate lover. I want to be done with this cool aloofness, this impersonal detachment, this charade of self-sufficiency. I want to proclaim my love before God and the world. I want to point to you and say, 'Her. That's the one. That's the one I want to be with. That's the one I care for. That's my partner and I'm proud of her.' I'm so tired of feigning disinterest I could cry. Veronica, I want to know you. I want to share with you. I want to give myself to you and have you give yourself back, unreservedly. I don't want any more escape routes. I don't want any more excuses. I don't want to enter a sphere of love and look over and see a little EXIT sign glowing above a porthole. Do you understand?" Taylor stood up, spread his arms and shouted, "I love you! I love *you*, Veronica Bristow. Specifically. Particularly. For what you are and for what you're not. For what you do and for what you don't do. I love you and I will love

WORTH WINNING

you and I want you to marry me." He dropped to one knee, took the beer can away from her, and clutched her hand to his chest. "I beg you, Veronica. Please. Say you'll marry me."

She laughed. "I wish you'd just say what you want. I hate it when you beat around the bush like that."

She's blushing, he thought. There's that at least. And her eyes are softening. She's beginning to waver a little.

"Veronica," he said, releasing her hand, standing up, "I know everything I've said sounds selfish. 'I want this and I want that,' but I think we, you and I, can be a fabulous pair. We're smart. We appreciate each other's sense of humor. We learn from each other. The fucking is fabulous. Hand in hand, we could stroll through this world as if it were our personal playground. But we have to count on each other. I've never done that with a woman, Veronica, but I've always dreamed of having a woman to trust, to rely on, to be willing to help and accept help from. I want to let down those goddam barriers and discover the potential of cooperation, to have a loving friend, to have faith in someone. Haven't you ever wondered what it's like, Veronica, to live a life of love, not puppy love but adult, informed, intelligent love, embarked upon with eyes open and defenses down? Doesn't that type of freedom appeal to you?"

She was still smiling, but tears were collecting at the corners of her eyes. "I'm afraid, Taylor."

"So am I and if we weren't we'd be crazy, not to mention stupid, but wouldn't you like to try, even if it was just a game of 'Let's Pretend'? Let's pretend, you and me, to trust each other. Let's pretend to have faith. Let's proceed, you and me, just the two of us, in our own little complementary fantasy, on the basis that happiness is possible and accessible. Won't you try? You said you loved me. Then experiment with me.

Become adventurous with me. Let's try to be what we both think we can be, but which nobody else believes is possible. Take my hand, Veronica. Please."

"Damn you, Taylor Worth," Veronica said, grabbing his outstretched hand. A steady stream of tears ran down each cheek. "You're not playing fair. Those are my fantasies, my thoughts. You can't just toss them up in the air like that. They become possibilities then and . . ." She shook her head. "Not marriage, Taylor. I know what it does to people. I can't . . ."

There. She's willing. She's ready to chance it. Now make it irresistible. Remove her final objection. His tape recorder, recording every word, lay concealed at the end of the dock, and he spoke to himself like a sales manager but, although he hardly believed it himself, he meant every word he said.

"OK, Veronica, I'll make you a deal. This marriage pledge obviously is for my benefit alone because I know what will happen if I don't get it. I'll do the same as I've always done with women, and if there's any love between us, I'll eventually destroy it. I'll tell you what will happen. I'll compile a little mental list of your potential disqualifying factors and keep it close at hand to refer to in case I ever need a reason to escape. It'll be full of the wildest rationalizations and exaggerations, but I'll keep glancing at it, just to protect myself. It's insane but I'll do it. I always have. I'll know it's wrong but still I'll do it. My filing system is incredibly elaborate. Convoluted, you might say. So here's the deal. I promise not to keep that record book and instead, to dedicate myself to this ideal game of 'Let's Pretend,' to proceed into the future as if you loved me and wanted to remain my partner if you will just say you'll marry me."

"Taylor," she complained. "There's no difference between what you just said and what you said earlier."

He held up his hand. "Let me finish." If she didn't go for this, he didn't know what he would do. "All you have to do is *say* you'll marry me, but you don't have to mean it. I'll close my eyes and you can cross your fingers if you want. It won't even be a lie because I'll know you'll be fibbing for my benefit. All you'll be agreeing to is that you would, given the right timing and the right circumstances, someday, perhaps, marry me. You wouldn't be agreeing to take my name or set a date or sign anything. We can maintain separate everythings if you like, but just for me, for my own peace of mind, to neutralize some of my madness, to encourage me to stride forward, guilelessly and confidently in love with you, just say you will marry me. I repeat, you don't have to mean it. Just say it once, out loud." He dropped to his knee again and wrapped both arms around her legs.

"You're as crazy as a bedbug. Do you realize that?"

"C'mon, Veronica," he urged, his face in her skirt. "You can do it. Just compose a little silent preamble for yourself. List every one of your reservations and then, at the end, as if it was an afterthought, add 'but I'll marry you, Taylor.' Try it. You'll be amazed how easy it is. Make it the first 'Let's Pretend' of an enduring, happy partnership."

Veronica, reviewing the pleasure of the last few days, looked up at the cabin, down the river, and back at Taylor. What he'd just said was what she'd hoped for since she got over her crush on Paul McCartney: a partnership based on articulated hopes, on mutual respect, on a mature appreciation of possibilities. Imagine having a man to cherish, respect, trust, have fun with, and love. The idea made her dizzy. She'd never met anyone before who was willing even to try. So why not say it? What harm could it do? Men had asked her to do far more distasteful things than . . . What was it he'd said? "To stroll through this world as if it were our personal playground . . . to be what we both think we can be, but which nobody else believes is possible." It's just an experiment, right? A little joke. A little game. So what the hell? "OK, madman," she said. "Under those conditions, sure, I'll marry you."

"Pardon me. I don't think I heard you."

She grinned. "I'll marry you."

"I think I hear music," he said, "but I'm not quite sure. What did you say?"

"You clown," she said and shouted, "I said I'll marry you!"

"Yeeeehaah!" Taylor leaped to his feet and did a reverse flip off the dock, shoes and all, into his beloved river.

CHAPTER THIRTY

As Taylor drove home from Veronica's, the sky, a glorious shade of evening violet, wrapped itself around his happiness like a regal robe. The winds of early summer blew through the car, stung his sunburned face, and mussed his hair. He was free and in love. The wager was over and he had won. He steered his Monte Carlo onto the beltway and pressed the accelerator to the floor. The lumbering Chevy engine revved laboriously and after a characteristic lag, kicked into passing gear. You old pig, he thought. You ponderous piece of American inefficiency. How nice it will be to be rid of you, to drive an automobile of quality for a change, something with class. Won't Veronica look terrific in that Mercedes, big grin on her face, hair flying in the wind? Oh, sweet life, he thought. What else is there? What else could anyone possibly want?

Dear Eleanor, he began mentally to compose his "Dear Jane" letter. He had decided on a letter because he figured Eleanor would be less inclined to heartbreak than to outrage. She wouldn't be as sad over the loss of love as angered over being denied something she wanted.

Dear Eleanor, As you are the only woman in my adult life who managed to render me impotent, I have decided . . . No, no, he admonished himself. There is no need for rancor. The bad times are over. Prosperity is as inevitable as August heat. Relax. Go home, pour yourself a congratulatory drink, and put your feet up. All is well in the world. Play it with Eleanor as you would play a tennis game. Toss up the ball and knock it into her court. Keep it simple and straightforward. *Dear Eleanor, I have met someone else. I must end our affair and terminate our engagement. Sincerely yours, Taylor.* There. That sounds good. Short. Concise. Not acrimonious in the least.

Given Eleanor's temperament, he knew some sort of scene would be inevitable, but eventually she'd just fade away. You're disappearing already, Eleanor, he thought. Thanks for the erotic memories. There you go, off into the mists of memory. I can't see your face anymore. Your body's indistinct in the fog. All that remains is the image of your legs, long and skinny and spread wide. And now that's gone, too. A foot is all I see. A slender ankle. One high heel. A holographic remembrance to be hung in the gallery among the memorabilia of other women known and, euphemistically, loved.

And what about Erin? Some of Taylor's glow faded. Hurting her was as appealing as pulling up flowers for the hell of it. He liked her. In some ways, he loved her. He could not despise her for her simplicity any more than he could fault her for her lack of a sexual appetite. That was Erin and that was that. Her heart, he knew, would break.

To dispel his rising feelings of remorse, Taylor turned his attention to work for the first time in two weeks. Mount Everest would represent a less formidable challenge. Three months of diminished productivity had

WORTH WINNING

produced a monstrous backlog of things to do, but his time off, some of it unanticipated, had created a virtual crisis. Mac, his hyperactive boss, would demand a string of eighty-hour workweeks. Taylor grinned into the wind. Compared to his efforts with his women, work would be simplicity itself.

Taylor parked the car and trudged to the door of his town house under a load of baggage. Home again, he said to himself, and peace, not actual as yet but at least potential. He pushed open the door with his knee and stumbled inside, dropping his luggage immediately. "Hello, house," he said out loud. "Miss me?" He kicked a gym bag out of his way and saw on the floor a pink envelope that had apparently been slipped under his door. Erin, was his first thought, as he recognized the handwriting. And just like her. Always count on Erin for the cutesy touch. He sniffed the letter. Perfumed even. Veronica, he pleaded silently, please don't turn cute on me. Become a harder-nosed bitch. Become a Jezebel. I can handle anything, I swear, anything but cute. He tossed the letter on the coffee table and went back to the car to fetch the remainder of his gear.

Later, his clothes in the washer, the groceries put away, with a snifter of brandy at his side, his feet propped against the tile wall straddling the faucet, immersed in bath bubbles to his shoulders, Taylor ripped open the fragrant envelope to read the message of his betrothed. He inspected the stationery before he began reading. The words of greeting emerged as if from the mouth of a bunny that had stopped grazing in a field of daisies long enough to say:

Hi Taylor!
    Love and kisses. I know that's usually left for the closing of a letter but I had to say it right away. I miss

you *so* much! When I'm Mrs. Worth, I'll go with you on your trips out of town. I can't stand being away from you. Did you miss me? Did you think of me *every* minute the way I thought of you?

Taylor held the aromatic paper away from his face, stuck his nose in the snifter, and thought how much he hated italicized words and exclamation points, the unmistakable *Cosmo* magazine style, according to which even the English language had to wear cosmetics. He put the fragile glass down carefully and went back to the letter:

> I have some utterly tremendous news! I wanted to tell you in person but I'm in St. Louis with my mother. She *must* be in on the wedding plans from the very beginning, you know. But anyway, the news. Brace yourself, Taylor. It's wonderful but shocking. It may have been better if it had waited until after we were married but I'm *thrilled* anyway. Are you ready? Please be as pleased as I am. Hold your breath. I'm *pregnant!* Isn't that amazing?

The paper slipped out of Taylor's hand and he shuddered. A spasm ran through him from his shoulders to his toes, turned around and ran the other way, and met another coming down toward it, causing extreme neurological turbulence. He grabbed for the side of the tub and hit the snifter, knocking it flying, sending a glittering amber arc of brandy across the room. The snifter smashed to the floor and shattered, as only crystal can, into a zillion tiny fragments, but Taylor noticed neither the noise nor the pretty momentary flying necklace of liquor. He retched. His stomach lurched sideways and folded itself against his backbone. His brain flashed him an italicized word: *pregnant!* His dinner, a beer, and the brandy, like a gelatinous spaceship lifting off, began an ascent through his esophagus. He scrambled to his feet, doubled over. The contents of his stomach accelerated, his mouth flew open, and stepping out of the tub onto innumerable slivers of broken glass, he vomited violently in the general direction of the commode.

CHAPTER THIRTY-ONE

The color white, so the physicists tell us, contains all other colors and such was the shade of terror stalking Taylor Worth that night. Faceless, featureless, ubiquitous, it lived within him and without him, in his bowels and in his mirror. The air he breathed contained it; the liquor he drank tasted of it. His stomach felt captured by two equal and opposing forces, one at his heart, the other at his groin, two pairs of powerful hands twisting in opposite directions as two people might squeeze water from a towel. He felt his face lift away from his head and turn lazily upside down. His spine, prickly with uncontrollable neural activity, itched beneath his skin. Adolescent girls, counting days on their fingers, trying to will menstrual blood to flow, know how Taylor felt. Their sexy boyfriends, swaggering and impecunious, faced with an imminent end to their irresponsible youth, know how Taylor felt. Hot and shivering, frightened and pitiful, invisible slivers of glass beginning to fester in the soles of his feet, he drank himself to sleep, finally, at about five-thirty A.M.

Four hours later, he was blasted into consciousness

by a furious pounding at his front door. Instantly, the terror of the previous night reasserted itself, made only thicker and more sour by his hangover. He opened the door to a hysterical Eleanor Larimore.

"That's it," she insisted, blowing past him into the living room, flinging a suitcase onto the couch, speaking as if Taylor had been privy to a long conversation. "I'll never make his greasy fried eggs for him again, never turn his smelly socks right side out again, never hang his pee-stained underwear on the line again. Never! And I'll never hear his insults again. And never put up with the derision of an eleven-year-old again. Not *that* overweight, snide eleven-year-old anyway. Not Howard's precious, loathsome Junior. Never! Do you hear me? Never again. Not once." Her fists flailed the air. Her face looked as if blood might burst directly out of her pores. Her words began to run together; her mouth ceased to function properly. Eventually her fury gathered itself into a single, keening wail that pierced Taylor's sore brain like a thin wire.

He grabbed her, not to comfort her but to quiet her. She was hurting him physically and he wanted it to stop, but in his compulsion to quell the pain in his head, he hadn't listened to what she was saying. Only slowly, as her wailing subsided, as the tiny knives of noise one by one slid out of the folds of his brain, did her complaints make any sense to him.

"Eleanor," he said, and shock, horror, fear, blame dripped from the name like sweat. Taylor thought he would be sick again, swallowing bubble after bubble of acrid bile.

"I've left him, Taylor," Eleanor said, composing herself, pulling away from him, dabbing at her eyes with a handkerchief. "This morning was more than I could tolerate. They don't love me. They don't appreciate me. They don't even notice me. They just use me. I am there to clean their toilets, to . . ."

Taylor interrupted her, grabbed her by the shoulders, panic forcing its way through his sickness. "You haven't told him . . ."

"Taylor," Eleanor said, looking at him for the first time. "You look terrible. Really awful. Are you well?"

Without intending to, he shook her, sank his fingers into her flesh. "Did you tell him about us?"

Eleanor peeled his hands off her arms and gently pushed him away. "I'll make you some coffee," she said. "Maybe you need something to eat as well. You don't look like yourself at all."

She moved away from him, strategically placing the coffee table between them.

"No food. Tell me, Eleanor." He pursued her around the table.

She turned her back to him, looked at him over her shoulder. "I told him I wanted a divorce," she said.

"Oh shit. Oh God." Taylor collapsed on the sofa.

"I didn't mention you, but I told him our marriage was over."

Taylor buried his face in his hands. He scratched at his eyes, tore at his hair.

She sat down beside him, placed her hand on his shoulder. "I know this is sudden, Taylor. I know you didn't plan to have me here this soon, but it was your idea that we should marry. I had hoped for it, of course, but I had no idea you wanted . . ." Her voice trailed off as anger gradually replaced entreaty in her eyes. "But why am I consoling you?" she demanded. "I'm taking all the risk. It's my life that's coming apart." She drew away from him. "What is this, Taylor? Taylor?"

Only his fingers moved, trying to rip through his scalp.

"I'm talking to you, goddammit!" she hollered, grabbing his arm, hauling it away from his face. "You will not ignore me. I've been ignored by professionals. You will look at me, Taylor. Taylor!" The pitch of her voice rose dangerously.

He looked at her finally, haggard, embattled, fatigued. He judged that he had no choice. He had to tell her now. "You can't stay here, Eleanor," he said with surprising calm. "It's impossible. I'm sorry you've broken with your husband. It was never part of the plan."

"What plan?" she demanded immediately.

"No plan," he said, looking past her, adding the acids produced by lying to the already vile mixture in his gut. "I . . . I've . . . I met someone else, Eleanor." He remembered the sentences he composed a hundred years ago, in a time of happiness, yesterday afternoon in the car. "I have to end our affair, terminate our engagement." As an afterthought, he added in a whisper, "I'm sorry."

It was Eleanor's turn to tear at her hair as rage built up pressure inside her. Hate radiated from her. Flashes of pure anger shot away from her skin like thin death rays. Her aura, purple and crimson, fulminated and swelled, turned on itself and roiled like an animated bruise.

Taylor shrank away from her as he witnessed the initial volatility of the most sensational fury known to man.

She mocked him. " 'You can't stay here, Eleanor. I've met someone else, Eleanor. Terminate, Eleanor.' " Visible tremors shook her body. She grabbed an ashtray from the coffee table and flung it at the wall. It connected, dead center, with Taylor's only legitimate art object, the De Kooning print. Glass shattered. The painting leaped off the wall and crashed to the floor.

"I'll terminate, you fucking bastard," she growled. She tore a lamp away from the wall and assaulted Taylor's stereo system, pounding the fragile turntable with the lamp's heavy base. The plastic dust cover splintered with a horrifying shriek and Eleanor's next blow snapped the tone arm in half.

Taylor came to life, jumped at her. Eleanor swung the lamp at him but missed, spinning herself around. She hissed at him and backed away, holding the lamp high as if to strike him. "Eleanor, please," he whispered soothingly, advancing on her. "Give me the lamp. Take it easy. Maybe we can . . ."

But Eleanor had backed into the television set and had no place else to go. Fierce fires blazed in her eyes. "I'll give you the lamp, prick," she snarled. She lifted it above her head and Taylor flinched automatically, but she didn't aim at him. The lamp swung down through its full arc directly past her hip and smashed through the TV screen. The picture tube imploded with a shattering crash and the sound of a cannon.

Taylor, angry now, no longer on the defensive, no longer lethargic with self-pity, grabbed for her, but she danced away, snarling at him, spitting at him, unleashing a lurid stream of expletives made fouler by their origin in the mouth of a woman.

He stalked her and she broke for the kitchen door. He leaped for her and caught her shoulders, but his hands slipped down her arms. She spun away from him; he grabbed her legs and tackled her, bringing her to the carpet like a linebacker. She kicked at him, scratched at him, slapped him while vilifying him every second.

"Dirty bitch," he snarled, as he tried to pin her to the floor, but she slithered away and began screaming at the top of her voice, one piercing, eardrum-shattering howl after another. Would she holler rape? he wondered fleetingly. What then? His mind simply would not function. He appealed to her, but she continued to scream, awful, horrible, hysterical screams. Another, another. Again and again.

As he got to his feet, he grabbed her suitcase, flinching from the pain of the noise. "Here, Eleanor. You've made your scene. You've destroyed enough. Get out. Get out now."

Eleanor was simply crazy. Her hair looked like a whirlwind. Her face, crimson with fury, looked bruised although Taylor hadn't struck her.

"I'm going to tell the world about you, Taylor," she said between shrieks. "Everyone will know what a fucker you are, what a liar, what a bastard." She threw open the front door and screeched as loudly as her shredded vocal chords would allow. "Wake up, neighbors. For your Sunday morning entertainment, we have Taylor Worth, motherfucker and son of a bitch!"

Taylor saw his opportunity, flung her suitcase outside, gave her a shove, slammed the door, and locked it. Still she screamed. Still she accused him, in a rapidly dying voice, of transgressing every law of decency. Through the door, he heard one of his neighbors.

"Be quiet, lady, or I'll call the cops."

Another voice, female, said, "I won't have my children hear this sort of thing. I'm calling the police. Right now." A door slammed.

Eleanor stopped shouting, but she didn't leave. She remained outside, methodically, obsessively pressing the doorbell. Taylor sat inside on the floor with his back against the door, listening to her whispered curses, hearing the incessant, annoying bell, ringing, ringing, ringing, until he stood up wearily, maneuvered his infected feet through the dustlike glass remains of the

WORTH WINNING

TV screen, into the hall, where he located the electric chime and pulled the wires loose.

After a while, Eleanor went away and Taylor, aquiver with the spent-adrenaline shakes, crawled back into bed. He thought of calling Ned and, irrationally, Veronica. He curled himself into a tiny fetal ball and tried to dispel the noise in his head without much success. The television set kept exploding. His ears continued to hear Eleanor's appalling screams. He recalled what little he knew about meditation. The mind is a drunken monkey swinging from branch to branch in a forest of thoughts. Quiet the monkey. Seek the void. Think of nothing. His heartbeat slowed. His breathing became regular again. The bed felt warm and friendly and he embraced the silence.

Then the phone rang.

As if all the bedsprings had uncoiled at once, Taylor shot bodily into the air above the bed. Coming down, arms swinging, he knocked the phone off the nighttable to the floor. "Sorry," he said, locating the receiver, bringing it to his ear with a shaky hand.

"It's me. Veronica."

Taylor could only sigh.

"I can't talk. I've only got a minute. Will you have lunch with me tomorrow?"

"Veronica, I . . ."

"Tomorrow at one-thirty. Brian's. I'll meet you. Love ya." And she hung up.

Taylor blinked. "I've become a punching bag," he said to nobody, "a revolving door." He put the phone back together and had no sooner replaced it on the table when it rang again, scaring him again, but instead of picking it up, he watched it as it rang. He counted. Fifteen, sixteen, seventeen. Persistent bastards, he thought. At the twentieth ring, he answered.

"You asshole, you shithead, you slimy bastard, you . . ."

"Hi, Eleanor. 'Bye, Eleanor." Taylor dropped the phone on the carpet, covered it with a pillow, and shoved the whole mess under the bed.

CHAPTER THIRTY-TWO

Randall inspected his face in the rearview mirror of Byron's Cadillac, picked at an errant speck of mascara, smoothed an already perfectly arranged eyebrow. "Why do teeth always look so yellow surrounded by lipstick?" he complained.

"It has to do with contrast," Byron replied dryly. "A reflection of your sallow cheeks."

"Byron, how unkind!" Randall snapped, and folded his hands in his lap. "You've been exceptionally snippy lately. Are you tiring of me? Tell me truthfully. Would you prefer it if I faded away, out of your life?" His face began to rearrange itself.

"Don't cry, Randall," Harriet admonished. "You'll ruin your eyes."

Byron patted Randall's hands. "I'm sorry. Please forgive me. These last few days have been so, well, disquieting. And we've practically ignored the bakery."

"It's that football player, isn't it?" Randall's accusing tone was accompanied by a narrowing of eyes, a pursing of lips. "It's that strumpet's hunky bodyguard, isn't it, Erin's seven-foot sycophant? You look at that craggy face, those muscles like boulders, those mountainous shoulders, and you just want to climb him, don't you? Sling ropes around his arms and scale him, pull yourself up the slab of his chest, straddle those rock-hard arms and . . ."

Harriet interrupted. "Settle down, Randall, old boy. You don't want to get all into a lather before your big performance. What time do you have, Byron?"

Byron, shaking his head, gazing wisely, affectionately at his friend, didn't hear her.

"Byron?"

Randall's hands fluttered at each other like scuffling butterflies. Shyly, he glanced an apology at Byron, who accepted it with a nod.

"The time?" Harriet insisted. "We're on a schedule here."

"Oh yes. It's one-fifteen."

"He ought to be leaving soon," Harriet said, peering through the car window for a better view of the office building from which she expected Taylor to emerge. "Brian's is at least a fifteen-minute drive, maybe more. He's cutting it close."

"You said he'd be terribly busy this week," Randall said. "He's probably trying to fit in as much work as he can before lunch."

"I wonder how productive his day has been so far?" Byron mused. "I wonder how much sleep he got last night?"

Harriet's grin was feral. "For Veronica's sake, I hope he sweated till dawn."

Randall moved away from her slightly. He thought her resentment excessive. *Her* friend, at least, wasn't married. "Where is Veronica today? Did she go to work?"

"No. She's getting her passport."

"So she's decided to go with you on your trip to Europe?"

"Will she quit her job?"

"She's decided to request a leave of absence."

"I must admit, Harriet," said Randall, "that I was a little surprised when I met Veronica. As a friend of yours I thought she would be . . . well, what I mean to say is, she seems to be such a cold person. At our house, I would have sworn she was made of ice."

Harriet watched the door of the building with the patience of a cat at a mousehole. "Well, she isn't," Harriet said flatly. "It's just her reaction to *him*." She nodded toward the building. "You should have seen her Saturday night, after they returned from the river. I'd never seen her looking more beautiful. She was radiant, aglow with love, happy as a little girl, but when I showed her the contract, this ice curtain descended and the expression on her face hasn't changed since."

"No tears?"

"Not a one. And it scares me. She needs to cry. It isn't natural."

"Yes, she does," Byron said sagely. "You can feel it caged up inside her."

Bastard, Harriet thought, directing her animosity toward Taylor. You cunning, cold-hearted bastard. She wondered again for the thousandth time how anybody could be so calculating and, she admitted begrudgingly, so accomplished as to entrance three women as different as Eleanor, Erin and Veronica because certainly at least Erin and Veronica were in love with him. Nothing but love, not even straightforward treachery, could have affected Veronica so deeply.

Harriet glared enmity at the building. Veronica's belief in Taylor, her affection for him, her trust in him had coaxed her out of suspicion and fear into the warmth of love for the first time since . . . since when? . . . since her adolescence? God damn your eyes, Taylor Worth, Harriet thought. You don't have the right to hurt people that way. Would Veronica ever let her spontaneity out again? Would her smile ever be as guileless and charming as it was last Saturday night? Harriet hoped revenge would bring her back to life but she doubted it. You bastard, she said to herself, watching Taylor's car. You odious, detestable creep.

"Well, I won't have any trouble carrying out my part of the plan," Randall chirped. "In fact, I'm looking forward to it. It'll be great fun. But you'd better rehearse me one more time, Harriet. Taylor's boss's name is Mac. Is that right?"

"Correct. And Mac's former lover is who?"

"Marylou. She's a blonde with a big bust like yours."

Harriet scowled. "And the office manager is?"

"Georgia, but I'm not supposed to go rough on her. The head bitch, the one I'm supposed to go after, is Jackie. How am I doing so far?"

"Perfectly."

Byron, who would have preferred not to be involved at all, held up a box of designer tissues. "My job will be simple."

"You just keep an eye out for danger," Randall instructed. "I plan to be devastatingly catty. I won't be worrying about bystanders."

Byron interrupted. "There he is. Keep your head down, Harriet."

"What's the time exactly?" she asked, ducking down.

"One twenty-seven."

"OK," she said. "Ready, Randall?"

"Certainly."

"Give him five minutes and go, but be out of there by two o'clock. Under no circumstances remain inside for one second after two o'clock. He'll be late for lunch with Veronica as it is, and when he gets her message that she couldn't make it, he might just turn right around and come back without stopping to eat. Got it?"

"I don't foresee it taking more than fifteen minutes, love. I don't anticipate being invited to stay for coffee." He looked at Byron. "Well, Tonto, or is it Sancho, shall we go?"

They hit the door of Taylor's firm's suite of offices swishing and flourishing like a two-man Easter parade, as fragrant as gardenias and as brassy as a high-school band.

"Yoo-hoo!" Randall chirped. "Taylor! Taylor Worth. Show your face, you beast. We're not playing hide-and-seek with the mannequins today, darling." He flounced past the receptionist in the hall as if he knew the place like his own bedroom.

"Don't get up, dear," Byron soothed the astonished girl. "We know where to find him."

Randall sang like a diva in a death scene as he poked his head into every office he passed. "I warned you I'd drag you out of your closet if you ever played sly-guy with me. And here I am, you two-faced tease." Anacondas spoke with less sibilance than Randall. He blew his nose theatrically into a yellow Kleenex, tossed it over his shoulder, and took another from the box proffered by Byron. "You can't hide from me, Taylor Worth. You can't hide from anyone anymore. Your secret is out. I'm here to shout it. Taylor Worth is as gay as a Christmas cookie," he sang. "There! What do you think about that? Come out here this instant, you coward. Come out and face the queen you cuckolded."

Not a single employee in the suite remained at work. Both long hallways filled up with people with pens and papers in hand. Every doorway contained at least one gawker. Already giggles and titters and gasps were slithering through the ranks.

"Well, what have we here?" Randall cried, sweeping past a knot of women gathered at a double door. "Of course. This is what Taylor lovingly refers to as the secretarial cesspool."

Georgia, whose desk was at the far end of the room, made her way forward toward the garish spectacle whose surprise arrival had disrupted productivity.

"Let's see," Randall went on, dropping a tissue, reaching blindly for another. Obediently, Byron found the seeking hand and placed the box beneath it. The hand flew about as if disembodied until it found what it wanted and, pinkie extended, snatched another Kleenex. "I know many of you by reputation." He saw Georgia steaming toward him and accelerated his delivery, realizing he would soon lose the spotlight. He scanned the room quickly and spotted his target. "You must be Jackie. I couldn't possibly mistake you. You're exactly as Taylor described you—porcine face and elephantine legs. And which one is Marylou?"

Heads turned. Marylou blushed.

Randall's voice took on a conspiratorial shading. He winked knowingly. "Taylor told me Mac was a tit man," he said, acknowledging Marylou's cantilevered bosom.

"That will be just about enough," Georgia shouted and her voice shattered the mood as surely as a lamp will shatter a TV screen. The women suddenly came to life, outrage replacing curiosity in some faces.

Byron began edging toward the door, but Randall turned on his heel and strode out like a queen of England, jabbering all the way. "Taylor's not here, eh?" he said, ignoring Georgia's commands to stop. "Conveniently out, eh?" They reached the reception room, which contained a couple of official-looking men in gray suits. Byron sneaked past them to the door.

Randall strode up to the tallest one. "You must be Mac," he said, voice suddenly masculine and gruff.

Georgia stopped in her tracks.

"No. He is," said the man, pointing.

"Ah." Randall thrust out his hand. He felt in control again as the hubbub subsided in deference to the boss. Time, he thought, for one more zinger. "How do you do?" he said, letting his hand melt in Mac's. "Taylor Worth did me dirt and I'm going to return the favor. Your whiz kid wants to steal the Allied account and go free-lance, so don't turn your back." Randall let his eyes roam down and up Mac's slender form, then he pursed his lips slightly and purred, "For more reasons than one." And with a wink and a wave, he vanished.

CHAPTER THIRTY-THREE

"What the hell happened to you?" Ned asked when Taylor opened the door. "Have you been in a fight?"

The ice in Taylor's glass rattled in reply.

"You're drunk," Ned said and leaped to the conclusion he'd prayed for. Since Eleanor's capitulation he'd worn the keys off his calculator by day and lain awake every night trying in vain to concoct a plausible explanation for Clara. "Veronica turned you down, eh? Well, Taylor old friend, I guess . . . Good grief, man, there's a lamp in your television set!"

Taylor closed the door. "Don't you have one in yours?" he asked in a soft voice entirely out of character with his dissipated appearance. "It's all the rage in New York. To be absolutely chic, though, you're supposed to leave the Bloomingdale's tag on the part of the lamp that's sticking out." He took Ned by the arm. "Don't walk over there. The rug's soaked with glass."

"What the hell!" Ned saw the shattered turntable and the ruined print. "Taylor!" He pointed.

Taylor guided the shorter man into the kitchen. "Want

a snack?" Taylor's words had a furry quality. "Help yourself." He gestured to the drainboard, where several liquor bottles, tops off, surrounded by melting ice, stood like alcoholics' gravestones. "I'm on the Dangerfield Diet. Fermented foods only."

"I think I need one." Ned poured with a shaky hand, unutterably thankful for his gallows reprieve. If he had lost the bet and if Clara had insisted he replace the car, his gambling account would have gone belly up, which was unthinkable. Ned was intelligent enough to recognize the evidence of aberrant behavior in his gambling, but like the alcoholic who contends as long as the compulsion produces only private anguish it's under control, Ned believed as long as his gambling account was solvent, as long as his compulsion did not materially harm his family, it was his own personal vice, an acceptable imperfection. "Never again," he muttered and threw a quick shot down his throat. "What's all this shit on the floor?" he asked as he poured himself another.

"Wedding shit mostly," Taylor answered. "Bring that Jack Daniels over here when you come. Silver patterns, honeymoon brochures, information about crystal, china, etiquette, invitations, announcements. You know the drill. If you don't, then take it all home with you. You have two girls. You'll need the practice."

Ned put the bottle on the table and bent over to pick a sheet of paper off the floor. He read the headline and turned a quizzical face to his friend.

"Oh yeah," said Taylor, looking tragic. "And baby stuff, too. The latest word on the Lamaze method. Somewhere in all that is a monograph on the ancient art of midwifery, too." Slowly, inexorably, like a stone fence crumbling in an earthquake, Taylor's hard expression began to disintegrate. His eyelids drooped, the firm lines of his jaw sagged. "Aw, Ned," he said. "Ned, it's all gone to hell." He ran his hand through his disheveled hair. "Erin's pregnant."

"Oh no," Ned said, and Erin's misfortune registered on his brain but barely. He was otherwise occupied in silent celebration over the fortuitous outcome of the wager. "How did she get pregnant?"

Taylor looked at him as if he'd just crawled out from under a rock. "The usual way. She caught it from a toilet seat. What the hell do you mean, 'How did she get pregnant,' asshole?"

"Sorry."

"Plus," Taylor continued, "your lean, spitfire friend broke up with her husband before I had a chance to cancel my proposal and when I told her, she trashed my house."

Ned's mouth fell open. "I'll be damned." He nearly giggled, proud of his behind-the-scenes devastation of Howard Larimore. His revenge was complete. "So they'll be getting a divorce."

"Which makes me a corespondent."

"If you're smart, you'll become a foreign correspondent. Aruba, I hear, is nice and private." But Ned's attempt at levity was lost on Taylor. He tried to repress his good humor. "What have you told Erin?"

"Nothing. Not a word. Haven't seen her. She left me a note and sent me about four reams of this garbage." He indicated the printed material scattered around the kitchen.

"I don't follow."

"She's visiting her mother in St. Louis. She'll be back tomorrow."

"She hasn't called?"

"No."

"Odd."

"You want to hear odd? I'll tell you odd. I left work

to go to lunch today and when I got back, the office was in a total panic. I'm talking hysteria, Ned. Pande-fucking-monium. Apparently, some flaming faggots came flouncing into the office when I was out and proclaimed my homosexuality to God, the world, and everybody I work with."

"What?"

Taylor nodded. "Weirdest thing I've ever heard of. This queer went through the place like he owned it, naming names, making accusations. He knew all kinds of inside gossip, just as if he were exactly who he claimed to be—my jilted lover."

Ned sat back in his chair. His voice revealed something like awe. "Taylor," he began tentatively.

Taylor recognized the tone. "Not you, too," he said exasperated. "You know better than that and even if you didn't, when in the last three months would I have had time?"

Ned nodded apologetically. "Yeah. You've been pretty heavy-duty hetero lately." He chuckled and covered his joviality with a fake cough. "You've gotta give Eleanor points for ingenious retaliation, though."

Taylor brightened. "Hey, that makes sense."

"What makes sense?"

"That it was Eleanor's doing." He sighed. "That's the first pleasant thought I've had in two days. I was afraid it might have been Harriet's doing."

"Got a girl friend on the side?" Ned asked incredulously.

"Don't be a jerk. She's a friend of Veronica's who was a temporary at my office. I was afraid she'd picked up some gossip or something."

Ned felt guilty about feeling so good, but each increment of Taylor's misery made his own safe escape that much more satisfying. "Speaking of Veronica," he said, "how'd she handle your proposal?"

Taylor, having held the bowstring until his hand shook, let his arrow fly. "She accepted it."

Ned's heart fell through his stomach. "Oh no." His world froze solid. For the first time in twenty years, he had gambled to excess. By his own definition, he was an addict. Then the world began to speed up again and didn't level off at a normal tempo, but kept speeding up, faster and faster, until everything tried to happen at once. "Taylor, I can't . . ." Ned babbled. "You have to give me time, a couple of days. I've gotta tell Clara something . . . I don't . . ."

Taylor poured him another drink.

Ned had gone slightly mad. He stood up, leaned across the table. "Swear, Taylor. Swear you'll never tell Clara under any circumstances. Even after I'm dead. Never. Swear, Taylor. She wouldn't . . . I couldn't . . ."

"You have my word, Ned, and a couple of days with the car. Just tell me what story you've decided on so I don't ruin it for you."

The phone rang.

Taylor ignored it.

It continued to ring.

Ned pounded the table.

The ringing continued.

"Answer that fucking phone."

Taylor picked it up.

"Taylor Worth?"

"Yeah."

"My name is Howard Larimore," said the voice and Taylor almost collapsed. "You've been sleeping with my wife for months. I have indisputable proof." The voice was level, emotionless. "I didn't know what I was going to do about it before tonight, but now that the worst has happened, my mind is made up."

"The worst?" Taylor stammered. "What do you mean, 'the worst'?"

"I mean Eleanor, your lover, my wife. She committed suicide tonight."

CHAPTER THIRTY-FOUR

That's all the man had said, not a word of remorse or a whisper about what he had decided with certainty to do. Taylor had yelled into the phone, but the sole answer was the sound of disconnection.

That night was worse than the previous one. Taylor's only sleep was liquor induced and interrupted continually by vivid nightmares containing dying women, pregnant women, angry women, flaming homosexuals, and people trying to kill him.

In the morning the phone again awakened him. "Yes," he said tentatively.

"Hello, Taylor. It's Veronica."

"Thank God you called. I've been trying to reach you since . . ."

"I've been with a sick friend. I have to talk to you."

"You wouldn't believe what's been happening to me, Veronica. I . . ."

"I'm sorry I missed you at lunch. I had to see a doctor."

Taylor finally heeded the tone of her voice. "Are you OK? Nothing's wrong, is it?"

"That's what I have to talk to you about. Take down this number." She gave him directions. "See you at noon."

At lunchtime, after a horrendous morning at work of apologies, disclaimers, denials, bad jokes, assurances, and promises, Taylor guided his car along the winding streets of an exclusive suburban Virginia neighborhood? Alternately somnolent and manic, his mind was in disarray, a brain after the bomb. Reality kept crashing down on him, obliterating any opportunity for calmness or clear thinking. Eleanor was dead. Dead. Because of a bet! Erin was pregnant. A child of his was growing inside her. A child of potentially incredible beauty. And what could he do? What did he want to do? He ached for Veronica, for her love, her strength, to give some stability to his disintegrating world. Taylor steered his car through an open gateway marked with the number she had given him, around a white stone circular driveway, past an obscene fountain, to the entranceway of a house that looked like a Miami restaurant. Veronica opened the door.

"Veronica!" She looked like a cancer victim, drawn, frail, and small, with bloodshot eyes sunk deep into darkened sockets. She looked nothing like the woman he'd loved four days earlier at the river. He reached for her, but she shrank away and panic started seeping in at the edges of his rapidly disassociating mind. "You're sick. You look . . ." He couldn't finish the sentence.

Veronica pulled her sweater closer over her slumped shoulders. "You don't look so hot yourself," she said without a trace of a smile.

He followed her through the ribald foyer, past the red-carpeted staircase and gilt-framed portraits, down the long hallway to the conservatory. "Whose place is this? What's going on?" he asked, but he didn't want to know. He didn't want to know anything else anymore. He just wanted to cry. Here, in this bizarre place, following an old sickly woman who until a minute ago had been his hope, he simply wanted to find a quiet, private corner and cry himself to sleep.

The sunny room dispelled some of his gloom and he decided on the spot, after having vacillated for two nights, to tell Veronica the truth—about the bet, about everything. When they sat down, he took one of her pale hands in his. "Veronica," he began and she looked at him. "I . . ." He faltered. "There's been . . ." He could not get started. "Veronica, I . . . I love you."

"Is that what you wanted to tell me?" she asked in a tiny, faraway voice.

Taylor shut his eyes and saw apocalyptic visions. "Yes, I, Veronica." He couldn't go through with it. "Tell me what's wrong. You're ill?"

Veronica appeared to shrink even further. She held her eyes closed for a full minute before a single tear slipped out. She wiped it away quickly and took a deep breath before saying, "Taylor, I have some dreadful news. Some horrible, horrible news."

Irrationally, Taylor almost laughed. What news could she have that could worsen the present calamities?

Tears fell freely from Veronica's eyes. "I'm dying, Taylor," she sobbed. "I'm dying. I have AIDS."

"What?" he said and nothing registered in his brain. She might have said, "I have dandelions" for all the sense the word made to him. He slid off his chair, knelt in front of her, and took her face between his hands. "Veronica, I don't understand. Veronica. Talk to me."

"I have AIDS," she cried. "I'm wasting away. It's not fair. I just found you." Her sobs came from the center of her self. "Can we still pretend?" Veronica pleaded. "Can we still pretend we're in love? Taylor . . ."

Taylor struggled to control his own tears while Veronica wept. AIDS. The word sparked some recognition, but he could only think of death. His mind was filling up with death. Death by suicide. Death by abortion. And now Veronica's death by something that made no sense to him, by a word that rattled through his head like gibberish.

Taylor felt a hand on his shoulder, heard a male voice above him. "Veronica refers to Acquired Immune Deficiency Syndrome. The body's immune systems degenerate. The victim eventually succumbs to infections and maladies he, or in this case she, could normally overcome. Hush now, Veronica. Shh."

Taylor looked up into the face of a balding, effeminate man who said, "I'm Dr. Randall. I'm sorry to have to be the one to tell you these things, Mr. Worth."

The story tumbled out: One of Veronica's former lovers had died recently of AIDS and she had been notified; nobody knew how the disease developed, inconclusive symptoms included fatigue, general malaise, sometimes a system of bruises called Kaposi's sarcoma, sometimes minor pneumonia; the disease exhibited no specific latency period; it was generally found in homosexuals but was proven to be transferable; more and more cases had developed outside the homosexual community; increasing evidence of spouses and children contracting the disease had been found; no intravenous-drug connection seemingly was required; it was reaching epidemic proportions; Veronica's was a particularly virulent strain.

Their words passed through Taylor like radiation, causing certain but undetectable damage. He had hoped to confide in Veronica, to beg for her understanding and her help, but he couldn't bring himself to do it when he had the opportunity and now he could not, ever.

Now she had no help to give. All she had was love and sorrow, and all Taylor had left was emptiness.

"And so, as you can understand, Mr. Worth," Randall concluded, "the public health department is acutely interested in the spread of this disease, and the public health department is notoriously indiscreet. The names of the afflicted in their hands are as good as in the hands of the media, and that's why I've taken time from my busy practice to meet with you and Veronica here today . . ."

He droned on, but Taylor stared into Veronica's mournful eyes. "Where am I going to find someone else like you?" he said. "There aren't any others like you. I know. I've looked." He started to cry.

". . . and if, as we suspect, you also have the disease, then . . ."

The words hit Taylor like a shotgun blast. For a time he was incoherent.

Was he fatigued?

He hadn't slept well but . . .

Did he have a cold?

He'd been sniffling but a lack of sleep will . . .

Bruises?

Only where he'd bumped his leg when they were at the river, and his arm on the side of the tub when he'd read Erin's letter. Oh God.

"How communicable is this stuff?"

"This particular 'stuff' is extremely communicable and so if you have had other, forgive me Veronica, lovers over the past few months . . ."

Taylor returned to his office physically sick and practically catatonic. The instant he walked in the door, the receptionist motioned to him.

"Can you hold, please?" she said into the phone and

pressed a button. "Mr. Worth, Erin Dolan calling long distance. And as soon as you get off the line, Mr. McElroy wants to see you."

At his desk, Taylor stared at the phone for a long time. Beside it lay the sheet of paper on which he had written the address of the clinic to which he was to report Thursday along with "anyone—and I can't overemphasize the importance of this, Mr. Worth—anyone with whom you have had intimate contact since you met Ms. Bristow."

He picked up the phone. "Hello, Erin." Words came harder than million-dollar checks.

"I love you, Taylor," were her first words. He sank deeper into the empty place death had begun to dig in his stomach.

"Me, too," he mumbled. "Are you . . ." he said and stopped. He'd almost said, Are you still pregnant? "Are you home?"

"No, I'm still at my mother's. I got sick, Taylor. Isn't that ridiculous? Mother says it's the excitement, but the doctor says I have a touch of pneumonia. I can't believe it, but I feel really tired all the time. I think it's the baby, but neither my mother nor the doctor know about that yet. And I've got these little bruises all over my arms and legs. Really weird. Babies do strange things to girls' bodies. Must be some kind of anemia." She paused. "Are you excited for us, Taylor?"

"I, uh—" He swallowed a lump of grief the size and density of a baseball. "I need to see you. When will you be home?"

"Tomorrow, no matter what the doctor says. I belong there, with you. It seems like I haven't seen you in a year."

"I'll pick you up at the airport," he said.

Erin hesitated. "That's not necessary." She hesitated.

"I'm flying home with my boss. His plane is here in St. Louis and I'm not sure exactly what time we'll arrive. Why don't I meet you someplace for lunch?"

"Sure," said Taylor and he gave her the address on the sheet of paper next to the phone, the one he'd received from Veronica's doctor.

"OK. 'Bye." Erin coughed weakly. "I love you."

The silence was like a great, dark, unfathomable cavern. "I love you, too," he said finally, and within the ringing, clanging echoes in his head, he thought he heard the devil's laughter.

The moment he hung up, his intercom line buzzed.

"Taylor? Mac. Come in here right away."

When Taylor presented himself, Mac was at the window, looking out. "Taylor," he began, "you're a good man. You do good business. You know your work as well as anybody but—" He turned and looked at Taylor. "My word, son, you look terrible."

"That bad, eh?"

"You look like the plague."

Taylor shook his head, looked at the floor.

Mac sat down at his desk. "Taylor, I don't know what you've been doing. I don't know anything about your personal life. And I don't want to know. Do you understand? I'm not trying to play hardball here. And if you have a problem, well, we'll try to work something out, but we just can't have this kind of thing."

"What kind of thing exactly?" asked Taylor. He had never in his life felt more exhausted.

"Your . . . your . . . boyfriend, or whatever he is, has been calling everybody in the office, and some people around here don't have the sense to hang up. Dammit, Worth, we must have lost a hundred man-hours because of you in the last two days. We can't have that. I *won't* have that. I can't afford it. Am I making myself clear?"

Taylor held his head in his hands. "Yeah."

"You haven't been here, Worth. You haven't performed up to par in, I don't know, over a month. I don't see you. You've missed meetings, deadlines. Two weeks ago, before you took off, you told me everything would be back to normal as soon as you returned and look what happens. My business has become a fucking soap opera!"

Mac paused, but Taylor had nothing to say. Death had finished excavating his stomach and had begun on his bowels.

"I don't want to lose you," Mac continued, "but unless things change, I won't be able to afford to keep you. Not only are you not earning your pay . . ." He let the sentence die. "Look," he said, coming around his desk after another pause Taylor made no attempt to fill, "I need you today, but you don't look like you're in any shape to accomplish anything. Why don't you go home and think about, well, everything? When you come in tomorrow, though, I expect you to talk to me, man to man. Fair enough?"

"Yeah." Taylor stood up.

Mac put his hand on Taylor's shoulder, but abruptly yanked it away. "Whatever it is, Taylor, if there's anything I can do, the door's always open."

Taylor thanked him and left, gathered a few of his things, walked outside, and piled into his car like a load of cement. He started the engine, put the car in gear, and stepped on the gas. The Monte Carlo moved but sluggishly. Taylor got out of the car to check for a flat tire. He had four flat tires. All four valve stems had been cut.

* * *

Two hours later, just about the time Taylor left the service station with four new valve stems and reinflated tires, a call was put through to Ned from a woman who identified herself as "Harriet Vane."

As soon as Taylor opened the door of his town house, the telephone rang. He had come to loathe the thing. Reluctantly, he answered.

"Enjoy your ride home, Worth?" said a male voice.

"Who is this?"

"Do you know how cheap it is to hire a kid to slash tires? At these prices, I can harass you forever. Think about it, Worth—a lifetime of minor annoyances, with a major one thrown in every now and then to keep things interesting."

"I'm sorry about your wife, Larimore, but this is blackmail and . . ."

"Do call the police, Worth. Call them immediately and tell them about the tire caper. They'll laugh you off the phone. Blackmail implies ransom and I don't want a thing from you. I prefer to think of this as terrorism. Good night, Worth. Sleep well. I'm certain tomorrow will be at least as interesting as today."

CHAPTER THIRTY-FIVE

Taylor supposed he slept that night, or at least dozed, but he wouldn't have sworn to it because he saw the clock's face once every hour and between those moments of lucidity, the horrific repertory that played in his mind was composed not of nightmares but of real, recognizable people and circumstances. The macabre quality of his night visions notwithstanding, or perhaps in spite of them, a persistent giddiness seemed intent on replacing his encompassing melancholia. The chaos of discarded clothes, empty glasses and bottles, and half-eaten snacks in his bedroom seemed funny to him. Compared with dying, the insignificance of everything—his job, the bet—made him laugh.

He switched off the alarm before it rang and stood in the shower for an aeon, trying to wash away some of his madness and confirm for himself the only decision he had made since yesterday: Under no circumstances could he continue to work for Mac, first because he was utterly incapable of thinking straight; second because he was determined not to lose Veronica or abandon Erin, both of whom would require more personal time than his fifty-hour-per-week job would allow him to devote; and third—he checked himself for bruises—because he might not be physically able to hold a job much longer.

Taylor left his town house and stepped into a splendid April morning. The dogwood trees lining the parking lot, blossoming brilliant white, framed by flawless blue sky behind and above and surrounded below by a riot of pink and magenta azaleas, seemed cruelly, mockingly festive. He inhaled the warm, fragrant air and had a crazy notion to take Veronica and Erin on a cross-country tour in the Mercedes, following springtime all the way to Alaska; but again he found himself laughing as he envisioned them, three, infirm, shriveled fogies-before-their-time, tooling over the road, scowling at the scenery.

Taylor checked the Monte Carlo for spikes under the tires and missing spark-plug wires, found none, gingerly started the engine, and listened for the grotesque crunch of nuts and bolts in the cylinders, heard none, and drove away to resign his job.

Four hours later, he was on his way to the showdown. Veronica said she'd be there. As if it were his mantra, Taylor repeated the phrase to himself: "Veronica said she'd be there"—to help, to hold his hand, to help hold together what little remained of him. He had no idea how he would handle the situation. "Veronica, I'd like you to meet Erin, my fiancée. Erin, this is Veronica, my betrothed. We're all dying. There was a third one, too, but she's already dead." Hysteria stalked him.

He drove past the address Dr. Randall had given him, turned around, drove by it again, and finally stopped on his third pass. He hadn't recognized the street number because he knew the place as the Jerome Building, where Ned worked. As he sat in the car ostensibly wondering why he hadn't been given a suite number but actually delaying the moment of the descent into his future, Erin scared him witless by rapping on the window.

"Hi," she said, waving.

Erin looked awful. Taylor stared, unbelieving. Her eyes had receded deep into their sockets and her high cheekbones, once essential marks of her classic beauty, now served only to emphasize the thinness of the skin over her skull. She pushed limp, greasy hair behind her ear with a bruised hand, and her pale lips tried to smile. "I've been waiting for you."

He climbed out of the car and held her. She began to cry.

"Why, Taylor?" she asked. Her sobs wracked her like blows.

He hugged her and it felt like the first time, when she was golden and blue and new.

"I'm not supposed to be doing this," Erin recited, not to him. "I'm not supposed to . . ."

Taylor saw her choke off a rising sob and try to compose herself. She wore drab clothes and looked already dead. His Erin. His incomparably gorgeous Erin.

"Well, here you are, Mr. Worth."

Taylor saw Veronica's Doctor Randall, who took Erin by the arm. "Come. I'll take you up."

Occupied with Erin, Taylor didn't notice the floor number when they exited the elevator, but recognized Ned's office just as Veronica opened the door to greet them.

"You're in the right place," she assured him. "Go right into the conference room."

Erin left his side and stood apart from him, trembling. Nobody spoke.

"Some clinic," Taylor said weakly after an uncomfortable minute. Veronica looked healthy.

"Who's your friend?" Veronica asked icily.

All of Taylor's neurons fired and every one fired incorrectly. He couldn't distinguish his hands from his feet. He felt his head being sucked into his torso. He felt inside out and upside down. No one helped him. "Erin Dolan," he squeaked, "Veronica Bristow."

Veronica, at her professional coolest, said to Erin, "Are you his lover?"

Tears poured down Erin's face. "I'm his fiancée."

Veronica turned her killing stare on Taylor. "How odd," she said. "So am I."

Taylor slipped his moorings. Hollow of heart and guts, he floated free from his body, watched his miserable self balance unsteadily on hollow legs.

"How can this be, Taylor?" Veronica asked and her icy demeanor began to melt. "Is this true?"

Erin, shoulders heaving, turned to the wall.

"I . . ." Taylor stammered. "I luh . . . luh . . . I luh . . ." The word refused to form. "I love . . ."

"Love? Yes. Tell us about love, Taylor," Veronica said and her voice cracked completely.

Taylor summoned more courage than he knew he had. "Truth, Veronica," he said and his eyes pleaded with hers. "I love you."

"And her?" Veronica cried, all her studied coolness gone. She trembled as violently as Erin. "What about her?"

"What *about* 'her'?" Erin shouted tearfully, turning on him. "What about ' *her*'?" Anger and outrage ignited her, filled her with color. She strode toward him.

Taylor looked at the floor. "Erin, I . . ."

She waited.

"Erin, it was a . . . I . . . I lied to you."

Erin swung with everything she had and the slap knocked Taylor sideways. The force of the blow even scared her. She was as surprised as Taylor when he hit the wall.

"Atta girl," said a voice behind him. It was a voice from the grave. "All this mewling and whimpering was about to make me throw up."

Taylor clung to the wall for support. He looked toward the voice and saw a ghost.

"I wanted to cut your balls off," Eleanor snarled. "I wanted to put your penis in a food processor, but these two . . ." She let the sentence float. "We know all about your bet. We know all about all of it. I hope she broke your jaw."

Taylor slid down the wall, sat on the floor, and tried to figure out the truth. His eyes sought Veronica's. Hers brimmed with tears. "Please believe me," he said, but she looked away.

"Come on in, Ned," Eleanor shouted, and Ned entered, carrying a piece of yellow paper. Harriet was with him.

"I don't know how they found out," Ned said to Taylor. "I swear I never said anything to anybody. They said they'd tell Clara if I didn't play along."

Veronica cleared her throat. "It's time to settle the wager. Mr. Brody, please sign that car title you have in your hand."

Ned signed. Harriet affixed a notary seal. Eleanor handed Erin a pen.

If Taylor's pleas had rekindled any affection in Veronica, it vanished when Ned entered the room in his three-piece suit. She turned to Taylor with loathing in her eyes. "Any objection to this transaction, Mr. Worth?"

Taylor looked at the floor and shook his head. "No objections."

Erin signed and Eleanor applauded. Ned tossed the keys on the table. "C'mon, Erin, honey. Let's go sell it," Eleanor said. "You'll feel better when you have some cash in your hand. Believe me."

Erin held the car title between her thumb and forefinger as if it were dirty underwear. "This is it, Taylor? You did it all for this?"

When Taylor didn't look up, Erin said, "It's a paltry price for heartache. Do you think it was worth winning?"

Taylor remained silent as Eleanor, Erin, and Randall left.

Harriet took up her notary seal. "Let's go, Veronica," she said. "It's over now."

Taylor stood. "Veronica, I . . ."

"Don't say a word," she commanded. She grabbed her purse and slung it over her shoulder, took a step toward the door, and stopped. "I never thought I'd hate anyone as much as I hated Richard Nixon," she said to Taylor. "But he's not even in your league. He was only elected. You were loved."

EPILOGUE

The Mercedes was sold. Harriet received ten percent for her detective work, Randall and Byron declined a share, and the balance was divided equally among Eleanor, Erin, and Veronica. None of the money went for abortions or other medical bills because Veronica's AIDS, like Erin's pregnancy and Eleanor's suicide, was invented for Taylor's edification.

Eleanor, of course, had never mentioned a word to her husband about her affair with Taylor, and after hiding her money in her underwear drawer because she didn't want to share it, she forgave Howard his past indiscretions, welcomed him back to her bed, and dazzled him with sexy new tricks and talents.

Erin returned Taylor's ring in a plain, white, unscented envelope. She did not include a note. Unsure of what to do with her share of the money, she solicited investment counseling from one of the team's accountants. He offered not only excellent advice but also, after a time, a proposal of marriage. Erin accepted both.

Veronica took a leave of absence from her job and a

month later left with Harriet for the Continent, traveling first class.

The bankruptcy of his gambling account and the astonishingly efficient physical and emotional devastation of his friend by wronged women stunned Ned into realizing the gravity of his betrayal of Clara's trust. Honestly contrite, he sought her help and vowed reform.

Once Taylor confirmed, after much unnecessary expense and embarrassment, that he did not have Acquired Immune Deficiency Syndrome, he went into seclusion for several weeks. When he emerged, he did not try to get his job back or establish a free-lance business. He refinanced his town house, took the money, and left for Europe, armed with a copy of Veronica's itinerary he inveigled from a female travel agent charmed into aiding a heartsick man on a romantic adventure.

He was too late to catch Veronica in London, and he missed her again in Paris, but he found her in Rome, sitting alone at a table at a streetside café. He offered to buy her a glass of wine.

She hesitated, but she accepted.

ⓈSIGNET (0451)

VINTAGE CAPOTE

- ☐ **OTHER VOICES, OTHER ROOMS.** An extraordinary novel of the modern South, it is the story of a sensitive boy who bridges the fears and loneliness of adolescence under the opposing influences of two people: his uncle—a cynical, too worldly-wise man... and his friend—a sassy, naive tomboy. (161890—$4.95)
- ☐ **BREAKFAST AT TIFFANY'S.** This world-famous novel reveals the life of a bad little good girl called Holly Golightly. "She's the hottest kitten ever to hit the keys of Truman Capote. She's a cross between a grown-up Lolita and a teen-age Auntie Mame... alone and a little afraid in a lot of beds she never made."—*Time Magazine* (161904—$3.95)
- ☐ **IN COLD BLOOD.** Capote's riveting re-creation of the brutal slaying of the Clutter family of Holcomb, Kansas—the police investigation that followed—and the capture, trial and execution of the two young murders Richard Hickock and Perry Smith. "A classic"—*Chicago Tribune* (154460—$4.95)
- ☐ **MUSIC FOR CHAMELEONS.** Includes *Handcarved Coffins*, a nonfiction novel about an American prairie town reeling from the onslaught of a killer... thirteen short stories... a gossip session with Marilyn Monroe... and a revealing self-interview in which Capote passes along bits of wisdom he has gleaned from an unorthodox life and a merciless self-examination of it. (161807—$4.95)
- ☐ **THE GRASS HARP & A TREE OF NIGHT.** *The Grass Harp* is a novel about people in search of love, defying the narrow conventions of a small town. In *A Tree of Night* and other stories, Capote explores the misery, horror and loneliness of modern life. Two of these tales, "Miriam," and "Shut A Final Door," have won O'Henry awards. (161777—$4.50)

Prices slightly higher in Canada.

Buy them at your local bookstore or use this convenient coupon for ordering.

NEW AMERICAN LIBRARY
P.O. Box 999, Bergenfield, New Jersey 07621

Please send me the books I have checked above. I am enclosing $_____
(please add $1.00 to this order to cover postage and handling). Send check or money order—no cash or C.O.D.'s. Prices and numbers are subject to change without notice.

Name_____

Address_____

City _____ State _____ Zip Code _____

Allow 4-6 weeks for delivery.
This offer is subject to withdrawal without notice.

① SIGNET (0451)

THE BEST IN MODERN FICTION

- [ ] **LULLABYE AND GOODNIGHT by Vincent T. Bugliosi.** Sex, murder—and New York in the Roaring Twenties... Emily Stanton came to this city of bright lights with a dream of Broadway stardom but instead found fame in the dazzling but dangerous underworld of speakeasies and mobsters. Inspired by a true sex scandal that rocked New York, this is the sizzling novel of crime and passion by the best-selling author of *Helter Skelter*.
(157087—$4.95)

- [ ] **IN COLD BLOOD by Truman Capote.** A riveting re-creation of the brutal slaying of the Clutter family of Holcomb, Kansas, the police investigation that followed, and the capture, trial and execution of the two young murderers. "A masterpiece... a spellbinding work."—*Life*
(154460—$4.95)

- [ ] **MUSIC FOR CHAMELEONS by Truman Capote.** This bestselling collection of writing includes thirteen short stories and a nonfiction novel. "A knockout... the most enjoyable book I've read this year!"—*Newsweek*
(161807—$4.95)

- [ ] **FEAR OF FLYING by Erica Jong.** A dazzling uninhibited novel that exposes a woman's most intimate sexual feelings. "A sexual frankness that belongs to, and hilariously extends the tradition of *The Catcher in the Rye* and *Portnoy's Complaint*... it has class and sass, brightness and bite."—John Updike, *The New Yorker* (158512—$4.95)

- [ ] **SONG OF SOLOMON by Toni Morrison.** A novel of beauty and power, creating a magical world out of four generations of black life in America. "*Song of Solomon* belongs in the small company of special books that are a privilege to review. Wonderful... a triumph."—*The New York Times*
(158288—$4.95)

Prices slightly higher in Canada

Buy them at your local

bookstore or use coupon

on next page for ordering.

○ **SIGNET** (0451)

LITERARY ORIGINALS

☐ **ON THE ROAD by Jack Kerouac.** The novel that turned on a whole generation to the youthful subculture that was about to crack the gray facade of the fifties wide open and begin the greening of America. It is, quite simply, one of the great novels and major milestones of our time.
(165624—$4.95)

☐ **THE DHARMA BUMS by Jack Kerouac.** Here is the book that turned on the psychedelic generation, a barrier-smashing novel about two rebels on a wild march for Experience from Frisco's swinging bars to the top of the snow-capped Sierras. (152751—$3.95)

☐ **GOD'S LITTLE ACRE by Erskine Caldwell.** The extraordinary novel that changed the definitions of decency in literature. When first published in 1933, it stunned the world and raised a storm of controversy. Rarely had literary language been so frank, rarely had literary situations been so boldly graphic. After fifty years and 8,000,000 paperback copies, it is recognized as an American classic. (519965—$3.50)

☐ **THE ARMIES OF THE NIGHT by Norman Mailer.** Mailer explores the novel as history and history as a novel in this brilliant work that won both the Pulitzer Prize and the National Book Award. "A fantastic document, rousing journalism, funny, outrageous, perceptive... A phenomenal piece of work."—*San Francisco Examiner-Chronicle* (140702—$4.95)

☐ **THE SILENT SNOW by Oliver Patton.** December, 1944. The U.S. Army thought the enemy was finished, but then came the Battle of the Bulge. And trapped behind the advancing German lines, a green infantry second lieutenant, a battle-wise black sergeant, and a terrified Belgian girl with only her body to trade for protection wage their private war in a bloodstained, freezing hell. (152832—$3.95)

Prices slightly higher in Canada

Buy them at your local bookstore or use this convenient coupon for ordering.
NEW AMERICAN LIBRARY
P.O. Box 999, Bergenfield, New Jersey 07621
Please send me the books I have checked above. I am enclosing $_____
(please add $1.00 to this order to cover postage and handling). Send check or money order—no cash or C.O.D.'s. Prices and numbers are subject to change without notice.

Name_____

Address_____

City _____ State _____ Zip Code _____

Allow 4-6 weeks for delivery.
This offer, prices and numbers are subject to change without notice.

27 million Americans can't read a bedtime story to a child.

It's because 27 million adults in this country simply can't read.

Functional illiteracy has reached one out of five Americans. It robs them of even the simplest of human pleasures, like reading a fairy tale to a child.

You can change all this by joining the fight against illiteracy.

Call the Coalition for Literacy at toll-free **1-800-228-8813** and volunteer.

Volunteer Against Illiteracy.
The only degree you need is a degree of caring.

THIS AD PRODUCED BY MARTIN LITHOGRAPHERS
A MARTIN COMMUNICATIONS COMPANY